THE MATCHMAKER

A BILLIONAIRE AGE GAP ROMANCE

BEAUFORT BILLIONAIRES
BOOK 1

ELLE NICOLL

Copyright © 2024 by Elle Nicoll

Rose Hope Publishing Ltd.
Lytchett House, 13 Freeland Park, Wareham Road,
Poole, Dorset, BH16 6FA

Visit
www.ellenicollauthor.com
for updates on new releases, exclusive content, and newsletter sign up.

Cover Photography by Michelle Lancaster
Model - David
Cover Design by Sara's Design Services
Editing by The Blue Couch Edits

All rights reserved. This book is protected under international and domestic copyright laws. No part of this publication may be reproduced, distributed, or transmitted in any form or by any means, electronically or mechanically, including photocopying, recording, or by any information storage and retrieval system, without the prior written permission of the author, except for the use of brief quotations in a book review.

This book is a work of fiction. Names, characters, places, and incidents are either products of the author's imagination or are used fictitiously. Any resemblance to actual persons, living or dead, events, or locales is entirely coincidental.

No AI was used in the writing or creation of this book. Without in any way limiting the author's exclusive rights under copyright, any use of this publication to "train" generative artificial intelligence (AI) technologies to generate text is expressly prohibited. This prohibition applies worldwide. The author reserves all rights to license uses of this work for generative AI training and development of machine learning language models.

For everyone who's been waiting for our filthy silver fox gentleman since we met him in The Men Series...

Enjoy Sterling ;)

STERLING
22 MONTHS EARLIER

A FAT RAINDROP LANDS ON MY COLORLESS DIAMOND cufflink as I step forward. I close my fist around dirt, scooping it up, before hovering my hand over the open hole in the ground. The earth around it is unmoving. Too hard to drive a shovel through. They would have needed to use a machine to dig.

It's all wrong.

The casket lies six feet beneath the sodden grass of the depressing graveyard. A place devoid of laughter. *Of life.*

He'd have damn well hated it here.

So would *she*.

I stare into the hole, the bleak, gray sky, and biting winter air barely registering. The last time I felt anything was weeks ago.

Rain hammers down onto the brass plaque mounted in the center of the lid. A lid that remained closed throughout the ceremony.

"Too badly burned... I'm sorry."

I uncurl my fingers and the dark earth falls, splattering

over the shining wood with an ominous staccato, like tiny bullets penetrating flesh.

"I love you, Son," I whisper.

A sob.

My daughter, Sinclair, is being held up next to me on trembling legs. Her knuckles are white where she's gripping my eldest son's jacket for support. *My only son now.*

He gives me a terse nod, his eyes shining, as he wraps an arm around his sister and whispers into her hair. She nods in response, before a fresh wave of tears wrack her thin frame. She's not old enough to legally drink, yet she's burying her mother and brother today. It breaks what's left of my shattered heart to see my little girl so overcome with grief that she can't bring herself to eat.

The priest stands between the freshly dug side-by-side graves. "Take all the time you need, Mr. Beaufort."

"Thank you."

I signal to Denver, my head of security, and he subtly alerts his team to begin steering the mourners toward the line of black cars waiting to take them to the hotel where the after service is being held.

Women huddle beneath umbrellas, pressing handkerchiefs to their eyes while they talk in hushed tones about how much they loved my wife, Elaina. About how beautiful she was. How kind. What an amazing mother she was.

I recognize many of them. But their black coats and heels all start to blur into one, swallowed up by a sea of young men in suits. All fit and muscular. All adrenaline junkies, living life on the edge. Just like my youngest son did. Before death stole him from us.

Stole them both in the cruelest way.

They say death by fire is one of the most painful ways to die. That a person can still be alive for ninety seconds while their flesh is melted from their bones.

"I'm sorry you can't see him... There isn't..."

The coroner didn't have to say the words. I knew what he meant. There wasn't enough left of my son to see.

"Sterling?"

A strong hand rests between my shoulder blades. So much emotion conveyed through the weight of his heavy palm.

"It's not goddamn fair, Mal."

"Life isn't. God's a fucking piece of shit."

It's said low enough that Sinclair doesn't hear her uncle's admission above her muffled sobs. But Sullivan's eyes meet mine over the top of her head.

"I'm going to take her to wait in the car, Dad."

"All right, Son. I'll come soon."

He leads her away, the sounds of her heartbroken crying tearing at my soul and leaving behind a stain like a rusty hook.

"She's strong," Mal adds.

"She is. But I wish she didn't have to be. This is all my fault."

"That's not true, so cut that shit out now, you hear me? It was an accident. A fucking awful accident. You couldn't have done anything differently. No one could." He runs a hand around his jaw, tears welling in his deep brown eyes. Eyes I've looked into countless times working together over the years.

Eyes so much like his sister's. Eyes that gave me three beautiful children and thirty years of marriage.

I swallow down the bile burning its way up my throat.

Mal stares into the first grave.

Hers.

"It should have been me. Not them. It should have damn well been me," I murmur.

As if to prove my point, my arm throbs beneath my jacket sleeve, the heat blazing a trail up the left side of my torso, culminating at my collarbone. I hiss out a rough curse, relishing the pain.

I deserve it. I didn't save them.

Mal dips his head in respect at the graves, then squeezes my shoulder. "You want more time?"

I nod, unable to form words as emotion clogs up my throat.

He steps away, leaving me staring at two holes in the ground where what's left of my wife and son are. The two mounds of earth piled either side sit ready, waiting to fill the holes. Allow them to be broken down and sucked back into the earth. Feed the flowers I know Sinclair will come and plant here in spring.

The circle of life.

What a goddamn joke.

Denver approaches, keeping a respectable distance so I can mourn in private.

After a few minutes, I turn and meet his eyes.

"Everyone's gone, Boss. I sent the rest of the team to the hotel with the guests."

I nod.

Like me, Denver's chosen to go without an umbrella. The rain falls over his dark brown hair, dropping from his chin onto his black wool coat.

"Just family left, huh?" I ask, looking past him to the two remaining cars. Mal's waiting by the side of one, and I can make out a hazy blur of blonde hair through the rain coated back window of the other, where Sinclair's sitting with Sullivan.

Denver clears his throat. "What can I do?"

I stare into his eyes. "Help me find out who's responsible. The yacht manufacturer, the crew onboard... I need to know what happened."

"Yes, Boss."

I turn back to my family's graves, pulling their faces from my memories.

Smiling. Laughing. Alive.

I ease my diamond signet ring over my knuckle, studying the intricate 'B' logo on it.

Beaufort Diamonds. Our family's empire.

What would have been our legacy to leave behind for our children.

I look at my wife's grave.

Then I kiss the ring and drop it.

It clatters, landing on top of my son's casket.

"I love you."

I nod at Denver, and he turns and walks through the rain with me, the ominous gray clouds mirroring the storm inside my soul.

1

HALLIDAY

PRESENT DAY

"It's a shame I won't be here for long. I could get used to living in New York." Excitement bubbles in my stomach as I walk through JFK airport alongside the other passengers who landed on the flight from London.

"You think he's going to be easy to match?" my friend, Sophie, asks.

I readjust my bag on my shoulder and pull my suitcase, keeping the phone glued to my ear with my other hand.

"Totally. I've already been through his social media. He knows a lot of women. I might even find a good energy match with someone who's already in his life." I smile at a lady holding up a homemade 'Welcome back' sign as I walk past. "I'm telling you, one month and I'll have found someone with a vibration that compliments his. In fact, make it three weeks. I'll be home before you know it."

"You're—"

"Gifted?"

Sophie chuckles. "Sure. Gifted. Because whatever magic it is you possess, you know how to make people fall madly in love with one another. I'm sure Sterling Beaufort will be no different."

My fingertips tingle with energy. "He won't. Love's coming his way, I can feel it."

Sophie hums her agreement. We've been friends for years and couldn't be more different. She's a lawyer for the Crown Prosecution Service in London and deals with facts and evidence all day long. And I've built a successful business, matching people on their vibrations and energies, finding them their spiritually aligned partners with whom love can flourish. I have a waiting list to work with me, and I love my job.

Adore it.

"I guess being a billionaire makes dating harder. Maybe he only meets women who are after his money."

I snort. "If you're a successful man, women line up to date you. If you're a successful woman—"

"Men are intimidated," Sophie finishes.

"Exactly," I huff.

I'm a shining contradiction of my recently exploding success. I find people love. Yet I've been single for years. And it's gotten worse as my business has grown. On the measly dates I have been on, the men's unease over my success vibrates off them with more buzz than a fully charged sex toy. I've given up waiting for that burst of energy when I meet someone. That bolt of divine intervention from the universe, telling me there's something there. Something special. *Something magical.*

Voices echo on the other end of the line as someone speaks to Sophie.

"I'm sorry, I've got to go, my meeting's about to start. Will you call me when you get to your apartment?"

"Sure will," I promise before ending our call.

I toss my phone into my purse and walk outside.

The Matchmaker

"Hello New York," I sing happily.

Autumnal coolness greets me as I scan the line of vehicles. Sterling's daughter, Sinclair Beaufort, whom I've been liaising with, said she'd arrange a car to collect me, but I have no idea what to look for.

I study the line of waiting traffic before a horn honks, a hand extending from a car window in a wave. I head in its direction, pulling my suitcase along.

The door of the sparkly white sports car flies open, and a blonde woman jumps out in sky high heels and white jeans hugging her long legs. Sinclair Beaufort, twenty-three-year-old supermodel daughter of Sterling. Face of the family empire, Beaufort Diamonds, and model for numerous luxury brands.

The woman who hired me to find her father love.

She sees me staring at her car and giggles.

"They're Swarovski crystals. Dad joked they should be diamonds because of the business. But I told him that would be impractical. I mean, can you imagine?"

I step closer to the gleaming vehicle. It's covered in tiny crystals. I run a hand lovingly over it, caressing the texture the crystals create. Personally, I'd go for rose quartz if I had to choose. The crystal for love. Although, for a vehicle, maybe black tourmaline would be a better choice due to its protective properties.

"People would try to prise diamonds off to steal though," I muse.

"Exactly!" Sinclair bobs her head enthusiastically. "Plus, every time I scrape it and lose some, the repair bill would be insane." She flicks a hand in the air before holding it out to me in a flourish. "Anyway." She flashes a mega-watt smile. "I know we've spoken on the phone, but it's great to finally meet you in person, Halliday. I've been counting down the days."

I take her hand, and she pulls me into a hug, my face landing in her long hair.

"It's good to meet you too, Sinclair... You smell incredible."

She laughs as I let her go. "A brand sent it to me as a gift. I forgot the name. Hang on." She turns and grabs a nude Birkin bag from the front seat of the car. She rummages around inside and then pulls out a frosted perfume bottle shaped like a moon. "Here." She reaches forward and pulls open the top of my purse, depositing it inside. "It's yours now. First new thing you've got in New York."

I gush out a surprised thanks, and she waves a hand at me. "Don't mention it. You ready to go?" She pops the trunk and then lifts my giant suitcase into it with surprising ease for someone who can't weigh more than 120lbs.

"Sure."

I climb into the passenger seat, and she sinks into the driver's side.

"Is the temperature okay? I can adjust it. What about the radio? What music do you like?" She looks at me eagerly, toying with her necklace with one hand.

"Put on anything you like."

"Okay." She chews her bottom lip and then her brows shoot up. "Ooh, how about this one? I set the station when I knew you were coming. It's got relaxing music on it. I thought you might like it. It sounded meditation-y."

Guilt niggles inside my gut that I dubbed Sinclair 'Park Avenue Princess' when I was telling Sophie about her. The press makes out she's a bratty, party girl. But meeting her face-to-face, I can tell she's really sweet and just excited that I'm finally here after all of our chats.

A yip from the back seat makes me jump.

"Monty!" Sinclair tuts. "Sorry if he scared you." She reaches into the back, sitting forward with a bundle of gray and white in her arms. Two shiny black eyes blink and a tiny nose sniffs the air in my direction.

"Oh my Goodness, he's so cute."

I've always fancied having my own dog, but work takes me all over the place. It wouldn't be fair to have a pet that I'd keep leaving behind.

"He really is." Sinclair kisses him on the nose. "You want to hold him?"

"Yes, please." I hold my arms out.

She deposits him into them, where he wags a tufted tail and sniffs happily at my face.

"He's a Chinese Crested. You're such a handsome boy, aren't you?" she coos.

Monty pants happily from his position in my lap as I stroke the white hair on his ears.

"I like your sweater," I tell him, earning myself a flurry of licks over my hand.

"Oh, Prada sent him that one. He gets cold being mostly hairless. We need to post a picture of you wearing it, don't we, Monty? We can't forget." Sinclair winks at him. "He has his own following online," she explains.

I continue fussing him. "That's great. Well done, Monty."

Sinclair's lips twist into a thoughtful smile, watching him lap up my attention. "You know, he isn't normally good with new people. But he loves you. I think dogs are the best judges of characters. They can sense things. You've passed the Monty test."

I smile. "Maybe I could employ him as my assistant. He can help with the matchmaking."

"Oh my god. I cannot wait to see you in action." Sinclair revs the engine and then swerves out into the traffic, earning an angry blare of a horn. She blows a kiss and an apologetic wave in her wingmirror to the car behind.

"Why don't you get me started?" I reach past Monty to grab my notebook and pen from my purse. I always start with handwritten notes. They resonate more and stay in my memory better than typed ones.

"Put him in the backseat if he's in your way."

"No, he's good." I straighten up and open my notebook as Monty settles in my lap, curling himself up so he can fit without falling off.

I've learned to go with the flow in my job as a divine power facilitator. Some people would call me a matchmaker or dating coach. But my title is more accurate. I truly believe the divine power of the universe sends love our way. I help people to recognize the signs, that's all. And signs are around us all the time. Like Monty accepting me. He's reinforcing Sinclair's belief in me. A belief which will help create positive energy around us as I work. And the more positivity, the faster love manifests.

Forget three weeks, I should have told Sophie to expect me home in two.

"So, Mr. Beaufort, he's been single for almost two years?"

"Yep, since my mother died."

"I'm sorry," I say, recognizing the lines caused by grief pinching the corners of her eyes. "What made him decide he was ready to open himself up to love again?"

I'll ask Sterling these same questions when I meet him. But getting a picture from loved ones first can be immensely helpful.

"He's ready," Sinclair says decidedly. "He's been dating a little, but it never develops into anything meaningful. He's lonely and he doesn't deserve to be."

"He's told you he feels lonely?"

"He doesn't have to." She sighs. "It's in his eyes. You'll see. He'll realize you're exactly what he needs."

I place the cap on my pen and close my notebook, careful not to disturb Monty.

"You have told your father that you hired me, right?"

She waves a hand in the air with a dismissive hum. "It's what he needs. He'll see that the minute he meets you."

I take a deep breath, looking out of the window at Manhattan's skyline looming on the horizon. I suspected this could be the case when Sinclair avoided questions surrounding Sterling's knowledge on our calls, and I've never actually spoken to him directly.

"Did I do something wrong? You can help him, can't you?"

I turn and the pure anguish in her eyes makes my heart sink. She cares a lot about her father's happiness, but it's important I'm honest with her.

"Your love for him radiates from you like warm waves. It's beautiful." I smile reassuringly. "And no, you didn't do anything wrong. I'm often hired by loved ones rather than the client themselves. But they are made aware of it before I arrive. You should understand, if the person isn't open to love, the chances are—"

"You've never failed though, right? You find everyone happiness."

I press my lips together before I speak, careful not to snuff out the hope glimmering in her eyes. "Y-yes, but it's not always straightforward. When I was asked to match the Prince of—"

"Oh, please." Sinclair wrinkles her nose. "I follow him online. Complete arrogant jerk. If you managed to find him love, then you'll have no problem finding it for my father. You're going to adore him. Everyone does. He puts everyone else before himself. He's a gentleman."

She turns toward me with renewed energy, causing another outraged horn to blare next to us as our car drifts out of the lane. The other driver shakes his head, but as he looks into the car and sees Sinclair blow him an apologetic kiss, his mouth curls into a smile.

I get it, Buddy. She's gorgeous. I want to stare at her too.

She sighs and refocuses on the road. "Trust me, finding love for my father will be easy. I have complete faith in you. We'll go to the apartment I set up for your stay, then I'll take you to meet him. Sound good?"

"Sounds great."

Excitement thrums in my veins. I don't need to worry. I can feel in my gut that I'm supposed to be here. Sinclair has faith in me. I have faith in myself. My instincts have always served me well. I've made love matches for even the most difficult clients. Including those who had completely given up on love.

This time will be no different than any other client I've been hired to work with.

I'll find the woman who will steal Sterling Beaufort's heart.

I have no doubt.

2

STERLING

"This isn't a fucking charity. What the hell do they expect?"

I lean back in my seat and smile at Sullivan's outburst.

He casts his gaze across the low-lit room to where the pianist, Vincent, is practicing on the stage. He takes in measured breaths, flexing his fingers against the velvet armrests of his chair.

The staff hustle around us. This evening, my club, Seasons, will be crammed like a subway in rush hour with New York's top everything—lawyers, politicians, doctors, CEOs—all seeking escape.

Fridays are always busy. People work and work, then look back at their week, wondering how they forgot to live, how they forgot to breathe. Then they come here and leave their worries at the door. No one cares who you are or how much money you make here. What mistakes you've made. What regrets you have.

Seasons doesn't ask questions.

"They'll not expect to continue doing business with you on their proposed new terms, that's for sure." I chuckle as I steeple my hands beneath my chin, my attention fixed on my eldest son.

Mal looks between the two of us, his face clouded in concern. Sullivan's been running Beaufort Diamonds for two years now. He knows exactly what he's doing. My son doesn't agree to anything unless he's certain it's the best for the business. Mal knows this.

"Go back and tell them my original offer stands. If they even attempt to ask me to increase it again, they can kiss goodbye to their contract. We'll source someone else."

Mal's face turns gray, his eyes meeting mine with uncertainty. He got the same response last time. Why he thought Sullivan might yield if he broached the subject again is beyond me.

But hey, at least it's amusing watching my son and his uncle butt heads.

I shake my head with a smile.

"Sullivan's right. I'd do the same thing. You let them think they can negotiate terms with us when there's a line of people who'll happily take their place, and before you know it, they'll be demanding something else. We pay them well for their services, more than they'd get elsewhere. Don't let them mistake our generosity for weakness. If they want to find a contract with another firm, let them be our guest. They'll realize what they lost when it's too late."

"Fine," Mal huffs.

He's been overseeing Africa for us for years, liaising with the company who arrange the diamonds from our mines in Botswana to be certified and shipped to the US. But from time to time, they get greedy.

Mal's made the mistake of befriending the owner, a guy called Ade, and holidaying at their lodge with his wife, Trudy, and Ade's wife, Sammy.

Number one rule in business—no one is your friend.

"You're a couple of assholes," Mal mutters.

Sullivan's demeanor softens, and he shoves his uncle playfully in the shoulder.

"Nah, *we're* a trio of assholes. But that's why we're the most globally recognized jewelry brand who get commissioned to make royalty's crown jewels. Maybe remind that fucker of that next time you're snuggled up beside him in the back of his jeep trying to spot warthogs." Sullivan's eyes gleam with mirth as Mal shakes his head with a muttered curse.

"He's got you there." I smirk.

Mal flips me off.

"We done?" My son's eyes meet mine.

I nod.

He checks his watch as he stands, buttoning up his suit jacket. "Good. I need to make some calls and pick up Molly. Catch you later, Dad. Always a pleasure, Uncle." He squeezes Mal's shoulder, making him chuckle in defeat.

"Likewise."

"Son?" I call before he gets to the door. "You heard from Sinclair today?"

My daughter calls me every day. But it's mid-afternoon and I haven't heard from her yet.

My phone rings, her smiling face lighting up the screen with her picture. "Never mind." I wave him off as I hit accept.

"You okay, Sweetheart?"

"Dad!"

Her voice brims with excitement, making my chest swell. Twenty-three years old and she's still my little girl, no matter how much she tries to tell me otherwise.

"What are you doing?" I ask, nodding at the bartender as he comes to refill our glasses with brandy.

"I'm on Fifth picking up something. I have a surprise for you!"

I chuckle. "Did Monty get hired to do his own calendar again?"

"No, this is even better." She sounds breathless as if she's rushing. "We'll be at your place in half an hour? You'll be home?"

I look at Mal, sipping on his brandy as he watches Vincent rehearse on the stage.

"If you need me there, then that's where I'll be."

"Thank you," she squeals. "You're going to love it."

"Mm-hm."

I hang up with a smile. Whatever makes my daughter sound happy and carefree gets my automatic approval. Diamond dog collars, crystal covered cars, her own penthouse on Park, even when I said she could live with me as long as she wanted to.

Anything that makes the nights I stayed up holding her as she fell apart with grief in my arms fade into a distant memory is fine with me.

"I've got to go," I announce, leaving my second brandy untouched. "Sinclair has something to show me at my house. See you tonight for dinner?"

"Sure." Mal lifts his drink. "Trudy and I will meet you at the restaurant."

I relay some quick plans with the club's manager on duty as I leave.

My driver's waiting for me as I exit. I look up at the green canopy over the doorway of the club as I slide into the cool leather interior of the car.

It's easy to lose track of time inside Seasons. Like an animal in hibernation, safely nestled inside its warm embrace. A place where the outside world doesn't exist if you don't want it to.

A place to forget what pain feels like.

It started as a small dream. A sanctuary. But two years ago, when things changed, I needed it more than ever. And so did others. What was once one private member's only club, has expanded into five exclusive, invitation-only places of solitude for those searching for peace inside its walls. New York, LA, Chicago, Hong Kong, and Sydney. And that's only the beginning. Plans are being drawn up for two new premises, with more to come.

Seasons kept me going. Loving me back when I needed it.

I pinch the bridge of my nose, urging the familiar gnawing pull in my gut away.

"Let's go," I signal my driver. "My daughter will be waiting."

3

HALLIDAY

I flit around my new apartment, humming as I unpack. Sinclair wasn't joking when she said she would set me up somewhere nice to stay while I'm here. I feel like I'm living someone else's life. *Their very glamorous life.*

I survey the open-plan loft style apartment complete with pink velvet couches. It's girly and gorgeous with polished wood floors and large windows that the afternoon sun is beaming through. And now that I've placed a few of my favorite crystals around, the energy it's giving off is zinging with possibility.

"This is exactly your kind of place, Jenny," I say softly as I unwrap the photo frame from my suitcase that I've carefully protected inside a folded sweater.

I walk to the window, tracing down the frame's cool glass with a fingertip. Over her cheek, along her smile. *She was always smiling.*

"Here you go. You can see it all from up here." I place the frame on the window ledge, spinning it around so it faces the view of Central Park edged by soaring skyscrapers.

I hum, lost in a moment as I remember her laugh.

Remember how she always picked out the purple skittles first, then gave me the rest. Except on my birthday.

"I saved these for you," she says, opening her palm. Her skin has turned purple where she's held them tightly for so long. She looks up into my eyes and we stare at one another. Then we start to laugh. We laugh so hard I have tears running down my cheeks.

A knock at the apartment door snaps me back to the present, and I blink, fanning my face with both hands as I move to answer it.

Sinclair greets me with Monty in her arms. "You ready?"

"Sure. Let me grab my purse."

After Sinclair dropped me off, I had time to shower, grab some food from the refrigerator she stocked up for me, call Sophie to tell her I'm living some cool Manhattanite's life, and unpack.

Now, I'm energized and itching to get started. I love the first meeting with a new client and getting that initial read of their energy. Seeing their aura for the first time. It's like peeling back the first layer of tissue paper on a beautiful gift. Infinite possibilities held inside. Waiting.

I step out into the hallway, grinning.

"Let's go."

"Your father's house is incredible."

I thought the apartment Sinclair set up for me was beautiful. But Sterling Beaufort's double-level penthouse is jaw-dropping. Polished marble floors, monochrome modern furniture, giant pieces of artwork hanging in the entryway. It's like something from a swanky *Billionaire's Homes* magazine.

"He likes it." Sinclair shrugs and places Monty onto the large sectional couch that has a backdrop of Manhattan's skyline. "He's here more now. He used to be on the yacht a lot, but..."

"I'm sorry."

My research told me that Sterling's wife and son died in some sort of accident on his yacht. It makes sense that he wouldn't want to be on it anymore.

My mind flits to the Google image Sophie pulled up before I left London. The one of Sterling on the water. All silver-flecked hair and handsome sun-kissed face. She couldn't believe he's fifty. I was more interested in the photos of him at various events. Always with a different woman on his arm.

Still, I don't mind a challenge. He'll only have eyes for one woman once I find him his perfect match.

"Yeah," Sinclair hums as she walks into the open kitchen area and opens the refrigerator. "At first, he was on the water a lot. But he doesn't do that now. It's rare for him to ever be at his house in LA or London anymore. And definitely not the one in Cape Town."

She takes out a plate of smoked salmon and places it on the marble counter. "Here you are, Monty. Grandad has leftovers. I'm sure he won't mind you having it."

Monty trots over, and Sinclair scoops him up, depositing him on the fancy bar stool where he can reach the plate. He starts to eat, and Sinclair fetches a crystal bowl from a cabinet and fills it with bottled water.

"Dad should be home soon. I told him we were on our way."

I nod as my gaze tracks back around the room. There was beautiful artwork in the entryway. But in here, the walls are mostly bare, apart from a few carefully hung framed photographs.

"Lovely photo," I say, taking in a framed image.

"That was taken in Cape Town a few days before the accident. It's the last picture we have of us all together," Sinclair says as she glances at the photograph, then looks away quickly.

Sterling is on one side of the group, his arm around a handsome man with dark hair and piercing blue eyes. Sinclair is in the middle, standing next to another younger man, so much like the first but with longer hair, wearing a giant grin. And next to him is a woman with long dark blonde hair that falls in waves to her shoulders.

"Your mother was beautiful."

"She was." Sinclair smiles sadly.

The click of the front door makes her eyes light up. She looks over my shoulder. "You're here!"

The hairs on the back of my neck prick up, like an electric current is passing through me. Energy thrums in my veins, heating my blood as I turn.

"Halliday. This is my brother, Sullivan. I called him too."

I lock eyes with the suited man in front of me, the air stalling inside my lungs with confusion. His piercing blue eyes penetrate mine as he holds out his hand.

"It's a pleasure to meet you, Halliday," he says in a polite, clipped tone as I shake it. "Sinclair told me why she hired you. I looked up your company and your reputation is quite something. I'm sorry my father will affect your otherwise immaculate success rate."

"The pleasure is all mine," I answer, ignoring his not-so-subtle negativity. I'm too distracted by the tingling racing up my arm from our joined hands. Gold dances in my vision from his aura. A sign of someone who is highly talented in their field. Disciplined.

"Don't worry. I'll take good care of your father. I find love for all my clients. It's out there for everyone. I'm sure he'll be no different," I say, fighting off the odd feeling his contact created.

"If you say so."

Sullivan's jaw locks as he assesses me. He has no faith in me yet. But he will.

He turns to Sinclair. "Where's Dad? I've got thirty minutes until I need to go."

"He's on his way," Sinclair answers, fussing with Monty as he does a meticulous job of licking his plate clean.

Tension radiates through Sullivan's designer suit, tinting the air around him. I felt a bolt of energy when he entered the room. One that made my body feel like it was about to burst. But it faded immediately. Now, it's like a current running underneath the surface of the ocean. There's something there, but I can't work out what. Something about him has the cells inside my body fizzing with anticipation.

"Hello?" a deep voice calls. "Sorry to keep you waiting, Sweetheart."

The bolt of energy returns like a flicked switch. It's sudden and all-consuming, like lightning in an otherwise pitch-black sky.

I take in the man entering the room, who Sinclair rushes to greet with a hug. He carries the same energy that I felt from Sullivan moments ago.

Only now, it's hitting me a billion times harder.

It wasn't his son my body was reacting to. It was the link he shares with his father.

Sterling Beaufort's eyes crinkle at the corners as he pats Sullivan on his upper arm.

Then his warm blue eyes find mine.

I swallow as a radiant glow blooms through my body like rays of sun bathing the forest floor through gaps in the trees.

"She's your gift!" Sinclair gushes as Sterling walks over, his eyes holding mine. "I mean... Dad, this is Halliday Burton. I hired her as a gift for you."

The warm blue twinkles in amusement, and he raises his brows at Sinclair's words.

"A gift for me?" The deep baritone of his voice is like a soothing caress over tired muscles. "I'm not sure I understand."

I reach out and take his offered hand, sliding my fingers into his large, strong palm. They're instantly hugged in a way that makes my breath hitch.

"I own Cosmic Connections. Your daughter hired me to bring love into your life," I say, gauging his reaction. Sinclair might insist her father is ready. But without a glimmer of belief from a client that they're open to love, my job is much, much harder.

His lips curl into a regretful smile, but he keeps my hand wrapped inside his. "Ah. In that case, I'm sorry, Miss Burton, but I can't accept you as my gift."

"I think you should." I frown, studying the sadness tinting his eyes and the way the laughter lines around them are tinged with pain.

I've seen more pain in eyes than I care to for a lifetime.

"I'm very good at what I do," I breathe, my pulse racing beneath his thumb that's gently resting against my wrist.

"She's right. Halliday is the best. She even found love for that awful Prince from wherever it was," Sinclair interjects.

"I'm sure you are exceptionally talented, Miss Burton, but—"

"Halliday."

His eyes soften at my correction. "Halliday... but that doesn't change the fact that I'm not looking for love."

I glance at our connected hands, and Sterling's eyes follow mine before he gives my palm a gentle squeeze and finally lets go.

"I've hired her for a month. She's got an apartment to stay in. You can't say no, Dad. Please."

He looks at Sinclair, then Monty. His brows pull together and heaviness seeps from him.

"You'll be wasting your time," he murmurs softly, turning to me. "I'm not looking for love. You could be helping someone who is."

"Friendship, then?" Sinclair pleads. "She's come all this way. You'll at least try, won't you? For me?"

His anguish wraps around my heart as it clouds his features. He's got his walls up like a shield. It's been almost two years since he lost his wife and son.

Maybe this is all too soon for him.

His attention flicks to Sullivan, and a look passes between them before he turns back to Sinclair.

"For you, Sweetheart?"

"Please." She stands rooted to the spot; eyes wide and hands clasped together in a prayer sign.

Sterling sighs. "One month. But don't be disappointed if—"

Sinclair vibrates on the spot with a squeal. "Thank you!"

The same burst of energy hits me in the chest as Sterling turns to me. I force it deep down, slamming a lid over it and locking it up. My body must be out of whack from the flight and time difference. I'm feeling energy that's similar to what I feel the first time I bring a client and their match together. But this is different. It's making my head light and my heart race in a way that's completely alien.

I actually feel a little nauseous.

It must be a strong sign of what's coming. Sterling's got an incredible connection to make with someone. I can sense it, feel it, taste it. I just need to find them.

"You're here for a month?" he asks, his voice making the tips of my fingers tingle.

I take a deep breath, composing myself as my excitement

builds. "Three weeks should be more than enough." I smile confidently.

With an energy this strong, something big is imminent.

Maybe I won't even need three.

"I've never not delivered for a client before. If you give me your trust, I'll give you my everything," I add.

Something flashes in his eyes, and he runs his hand over his jaw. He studies me for a beat, making my stomach flutter.

Say yes.

His pupils dilate as he looks into my eyes.

I hold my breath, waiting for him to let go. To give this a chance.

A charming smile settles on his face, and he holds out a hand, inviting us all to take a seat in the living area.

"Why don't we all have a drink? And you can tell me how this will work."

4

STERLING

I lean back in my armchair, one leg crossed over the other, arms draped over the sides as I watch my daughter's 'gift' to me take a seat opposite and retrieve a notebook from her purse.

Halliday Burton.

I've heard of her company. My brother, Clay, said she found a match for a business associate of his. The guy is expecting his second kid now. I don't buy into all the cosmic-universe-sends-you-gifts, though. If that were true, my son would still be alive, and Sinclair and Sullivan would still have their mother.

She tucks a strand of short ice-blonde hair behind her ear, her fingers catching a pink stone in her earring, which she rubs like it's a lucky talisman. She opens the notebook in her lap and smooths her hand over the pages.

"I have these questions in a digital file. So any you can't answer now, or want to take more time to think over, I can send you a copy, okay? At this stage though, I like to write your answers for my own reference. I get a stronger feel of the intention that way."

"Okay." I smile at her, watching the way her eyes fall closed for a moment and a peaceful expression overtakes her face as she takes a deep breath and picks up her pen.

"Right. Let's begin."

Sullivan crosses his arms from where he's chosen to stand, leaning against the kitchen counter, Monty on the stool beside him. Sinclair sits on the sofa, close to Halliday.

Everyone's eyes are on me.

"Do you see yourself with a woman, a man, both, or a multiple combination?"

Halliday blinks innocently as my brows shoot up. "That's…" I tilt my head, pursing my lips as I think. "… something I've never considered before."

"A woman," Sullivan clips. "*One* woman."

I chuckle and turn my palms upward. "One woman, like my son says."

"Mm-hm." Halliday writes something in her notebook. "And when was the last time you went on a date?"

"I don't recall."

"Two Saturdays ago, he took Lavinia to see a play," Sinclair offers.

"She's just a friend," I interject.

"Lavinia Weston? She runs the charity that raised five million for Morgan Stanley Children's Hospital, correct?" Halliday waits patiently for me to elaborate.

"You've done your research." I shift in my seat.

"I saw photographs of you at a fundraiser. Hmm, good." Halliday smiles. "I look forward to meeting her. Okay, next question."

"Go ahead."

"When was the last time you had sexual relations? That can include oral sex, manual stimulation from another… anything more than kissing."

Sullivan scoffs. "Fuck, I don't want to hear this."

"Shut up," Sinclair snaps at him, then looks at me expectantly. "It's fine, Dad. We're all adults here." Her eyes track to her brother's and narrow in warning. "Do you want Dad to be happy or not?"

"I am happy, Sweetheart. I've got Seasons, and you two and Molly keep me busy."

"I'll mark that one down as something you can let me know later," Halliday says as she writes in her notebook again.

Sullivan grunts, and Sinclair widens her eyes, shaking her head at him.

"I know we're getting straight to personal questions. But there's a reason they are structured this way. It really helps me get a read on your energy doing it like this," she explains patiently.

"Carry on." I roll my wrist, encouraging her. The sooner we're done, the sooner I can get something to drink that's stronger than the iced lemon spritzers Sinclair fixed for us.

"Thank you. Okay, what kind of kisser are you?"

"Jesus Christ, what did I do to deserve this today?" Sullivan grumbles under his breath, pinching the bridge of his nose.

Amusement rumbles in my chest. If nothing else, she's giving me some interesting topics to talk about with Mal later. Makes a change from diamond mines and club business.

"Do you require a demonstration?" I breathe out with a raspy chuckle.

Halliday fixes her gaze on mine, unblinking. "You're my client. That would be a gross breach of trust."

"Right." I clear my throat, my chuckle ceasing instantly. "Forgive me. That wasn't very gentlemanly of me."

Sullivan curses quietly before pushing off from the counter. "I need to go and pick up Molly. Halliday, it was nice to meet you. I'm sure I'll be seeing you again over the course of the month. Sinclair, Dad." He nods at us before striding from the room without looking back, his phone already up to his ear as he makes a call.

"My son runs our family business, Beaufort Diamonds," I explain. "He's got a new line about to launch. And he has a two-year-old daughter who still wakes in the night. He's busier than usual."

"I understand. He works hard. And he's a perfectionist. I could see it in his aura," Halliday says, unruffled by his swift departure.

"That he is." I run my pointer finger over my lips as she turns the page in her notebook before looking at me.

"Perhaps you can think on my last question and then give me your answer? It's important. Sex is great. But kissing and other intimate acts that are more subtle will strengthen bonds between partners and help align your frequencies." She twists her lips in thought. "For now, I'll put it requires work."

"Right." I frown.

"Okay, we're almost done with this section. Now, can you tell me the last time you saw a woman you were attracted to? How did you feel? How did your body react? What was it about her that drew you in?"

I take a deep breath as Sinclair nods at me encouragingly. She's glowing like a bright ball of sunshine. She honestly believes this is what I need.

"Well. I suppose it was..." I concentrate hard, trying to recall the last time I felt a deep pull of attraction, something deeper than mere surface lust for a physical itch that needed scratching.

I take in Halliday's feet clad in high heels, her fitted pencil skirt and pearly pink silk blouse with the top two buttons undone, all the way up to her neck, where her pulse flutters beneath her smooth skin.

The need to lick my lips is overwhelming.

"It was..."

Her eyes capture mine, and my heart thuds out a deep rhythm against my ribs. She's built a business from nothing and carries herself with the grace and elegance that I usually only see in women closer to my age. Women who've had longer to become confident in their unique strengths and beauty.

An allure that I very much admire.

She's not much older than my daughter.

I shake my head, holding her gaze.

"Like I said, I'm not looking for love."

5

HALLIDAY

"New York's great."

"Yeah? But I bet you miss home?"

I exhale steadily and count to five as I enter my apartment building and cross the lobby toward the concierge desk.

"Not really." I check my watch, holding my phone to my ear with my other hand. "Rory, I've got to go," I repeat for the third time.

He's been harping on for the last fifteen minutes, killing any peace I was hoping to have on my stroll back from Central Park. I went to sit there with a coffee while I worked on Sterling's match. I have a few females registered with Cosmic Connections already who could make a good connection with him. Although, until I get them in the same physical space, I won't be able to tell for sure.

"Maybe I could visit? It's always been on my bucket list."

I stiffen. "I've never heard you mention visiting New York before."

"Course I have. It'd be great. You and I could—"

"I'm sorry, I might lose you, I'm about to step into the elevator."

Rory continues talking, ignoring me.

"Rory? Can you hear me? Rory?"

I jab the end call button so hard that a sharp pain shoots up my finger.

"Ugh," I groan, throwing my phone into my purse. "Forgive me, Universe."

"Sounds like Rory had it coming."

I look at the woman leaning back against the concierge desk.

"In fact, I think the universe would be cheering you on in situations regarding guys who don't want to take the hint."

"That obvious?"

"Yep." She gives me a sympathetic smile. "What is he? An ex? Or a chancer?"

"He's something," I mutter.

"I'm Zoey. You're new here?"

"Halliday. I just moved in."

"From England?"

"The accent gives me away, huh? Yeah, from London. I'm here for work, though. It's not permanent."

Zoey straightens and beams at me. "You're who Sinclair hired for her dad."

"That's me. How did you—"

"I'm friends with her. I'm the one who told her an apartment was coming up in this building. They're like gold-fucking-dust. I swear someone has to die in order to get one. Although, that's not what happened in yours," she adds, looking at my shocked expression. "The woman who owns it took a job overseas for a year and decided to sublet it. Still, it's pretty sweet, isn't it? You're park-side, amazing views."

"They really are," I agree.

A door opens behind the desk as the concierge, Harry, returns from his office.

"Here you are, Miss Zoey. Guarded it myself."

She takes the luxurious shiny black box from his arms with a squeal. "You're the best."

"Just doing my job." His kind eyes travel to me. "Ah, Miss Halliday. You're here to see if your delivery arrived while you were working outside on this beautiful day, aren't you?"

I nod. There's something about Harry that I can't help but warm to. And judging by the way Zoey is smiling at him like he's Santa, I'd say it's a common feeling he evokes in people.

"Yes, please. It's for my client."

He holds up a finger, signaling for me to wait, and walks back into his office.

"It's nice to meet you," Zoey says. "I'm in 17B. Give me a knock if you need anything. Let's hang out one evening with Sinclair. We can introduce you to the best bars to go for a drink that won't be full of guys who keep calling when you don't want them to." She winks before her eyes return to the gleaming box in her hands and she beams at it.

I haven't seen anyone this excited since the Prince's dad when I successfully found his notoriously obnoxious son a match.

"Sure, sounds great."

"Great," she calls out before she spins, taking her box with her to the elevator bank.

"Here you are." Harry returns, passing a small brown parcel to me. "Bike courier came all the way from Soho with this. Good exercise if you're young enough."

"Thank you, Harry."

I already have these things at home, but I've learned after a memorable talk with airport customs that it's best to source them locally now, unless I like having my bags searched.

Harry waves me off as I head to the elevators, pulling out my phone and bringing up Sterling's number.

"Halliday?" His warm, slightly husky tone sends tingles up my spine as he answers on the first ring.

"Sterling," I return, his name rolling off my tongue with familiarity despite this being the first time we've spoken since meeting yesterday. "Is now a good time for me to come and spend some time with you?"

I've collated a couple of potential matches for him, and I want to get a read on his reaction when I broach the topic of his first date with one. He was guarded when we met, despite Sinclair's insistence that he's not as closed off to love as he'd like to have me believe.

"Now?" I can hear the frown in his voice. He's likely searching for a polite way to deter me.

I'll need a special approach if I want him to open up. His energy yesterday was confusing. Open and inquisitive at times, hopeful even. A contradiction to the answers he gave to my questions. The ones he did answer, that is. Most he avoided, albeit with charm.

"I won't take much of your time. In fact, just being with you while you work will be immensely helpful for me at this stage. You won't even know I'm there apart from one or two things I'd like us to discuss."

"Well—"

"Sinclair told me how busy you are. You'll barely notice me, I promise," I add.

Guilt I could feel at using his daughter's name to sway him never comes. He's a loving father who will do anything to make his children happy. I didn't need to read any auras to see that when we met.

And I agree with Sinclair. He seems lonely. I want to help him. I *can* help him.

If he'll let me.

"I doubt you'd ever go unnoticed, Miss Burton. I'll send a car for you."

I smile as he submits.

"No need. I'll enjoy the walk."

"I've booked a restaurant for you tomorrow night. She likes seafood but is gluten intolerant. I know it's a Sunday. Not the ideal night for a first date. Thursdays are my preference."

"Thursdays?" Sterling arches a brow at me as he places the profile photograph of his first date on his desk and runs a hand over the silver-flecked stubble dusting his jaw.

"Uh-huh," I confirm.

I'm glad I've managed to talk him into a date at all. He's shot down every potential match I've shown him since I arrived at his office. It's only when his defiance waved a little on one client's photograph before he excused himself to use the restroom that I made the call to secure the table for tomorrow evening.

I walk around his office, deciding where to place the crystals I've bought to maximize their effect.

"Thursdays are the perfect out. You can say you have work the next day if you don't feel a connection. But if you do, then you only have one more day until the weekend to get through on little to no sleep if you decide to make a whole night of it."

I spot the perfect place for the small heart-shaped rose quartz next to his desk phone and place it there.

"Although, you're here, working on a Saturday. So maybe that theory doesn't count." I offer him a friendly smile.

"As are you," he muses, watching me with interest as I rummage inside the brown parcel on his desk and take out what I'm looking for.

"Destiny doesn't take weekends off. So neither will I until

I align you with what's meant for you." I reach into my purse and take out my lighter, flicking it on.

Sterling stiffens in his seat as the flame bursts to life. "What are you doing with that?"

I pass the lighter beneath the end of the sage leaves until they catch fire, then blow the flame out until they settle into a smolder.

"It's called smudging. Sage is an excellent clearer of past negative energy."

I walk around the back of his desk behind him and then around the expanse of his office, slowly wafting the sage through the air.

He follows my every move with an interested, amused gaze.

"You really believe there's a destiny for everyone?"

"Yes." I answer simply.

"What about those of us who've lived through theirs already?" He spreads his hands, clearing his throat. "I'm fifty, Halliday. I've been married. You could be helping someone younger find love."

I stop, catching his gaze sliding up my body as I turn to face him.

"Love knows no age. Everyone deserves it in their life. Just because they've had it once, doesn't mean they don't deserve it again. I know you're only doing this for Sinclair. But can you please try and consider doing it for yourself, too? You might be surprised about what the universe has planned."

"Did it plan to send me you?" he rasps, his eyes penetrating mine.

I hold the sage further away, so it isn't near my face, even though I'm certain the smoldering leaves aren't what's causing my cheeks to heat.

"Yes."

His gaze heats, and electricity shoots up my spine.

"I can sense it." Energy radiates around my body, screaming at me that I'm in the right place, doing exactly what needs to be done. "You're not going to need me for long."

"Hmm." His attention drops back to the photograph on his desk.

I walk over and stop in front of him.

"Juliette runs her own PR company." I look at the beautiful platinum blonde in the image. Her hair is the same shade as mine. "And she lost her partner, too."

"She has my sympathies," Sterling says, moving her photo aside.

"I have a good feeling about her. When we spoke, she was very complimentary of Beaufort Diamonds. I believe she owns some pieces."

"I hope she enjoys them."

He picks up a folder on his desk and opens it, reading the paperwork inside.

"Almost as beautiful as the person wearing them," I say, repeating the company slogan.

He looks at me from beneath set brows.

"She is rather beautiful, wouldn't you agree? I don't match people based on their physical appearance. But a certain level of physical attraction can help to unlock other compatibilities faster."

I slide the photograph of her back in front of him. He glances at it, then flicks his eyes up, watching me as I tuck a lock of hair behind my ear.

"7 p.m., tomorrow night. I'll be there to make the introduction and absorb what I can from your initial contact. Then I'll leave you to enjoy your date and we'll have a breakfast meeting on Monday to discuss how it went. That is, unless you still have company. Then, we can do it over coffee."

"If I still have company?" The serious rumble in Sterling's

tone makes me lift my eyes from where they've fallen back to Juliette's picture.

"Yes."

"After a first dinner date?"

"A lot can manifest on a first date. After eating a five-course dinner, I'd rather be laid out in comfort and a stretchy waistband than being intimate with someone new and thinking about how I look naked. But not everyone shares that view."

Sterling barks out a rich chuckle. "You'd look beautiful, I have no doubt." His eyes roam over my fitted pant suit before he clears his throat.

My phone buzzes on his mahogany desk. He tilts his head to the side, reading the upside-down screen.

"Rory's calling you."

I reach forward and send the call to voicemail.

"I'll meet you in the restaurant bar half an hour before, and we can—"

My phone chimes with an incoming text.

> Call me.

I ignore the message lighting up the screen.

"We can have a drink and talk about—"

My phone chimes again.

> Atlantic Airways has an offer on. I could come next weekend.

Dread slithers up my spine.

"If you need to call Rory—"

"I don't need to call him." I place my phone on silent before tossing it into my purse.

Sterling's studying me as I look back up.

"Halliday," he says softly. "As you said yourself, I'm doing this for my daughter. So yes, I will meet you tomorrow night and go on the date you've arranged. But..." He spreads his palms out before clasping them back together and sighing. "...I'm making no promises."

It's already better than *"I'm not looking for love."*

"You don't have to promise anything. Just leave it all to me. I'll take care of you."

He holds my eyes, his words rolling over his tongue like velvet.

"In that case, tomorrow night, I'm all yours."

6

STERLING

"I thought when we dissolved the company, we might have gotten some answers." I clench my fist, cursing under my breath. "None of the employees had anything to say?"

Denver shakes his head.

"Nothing?" Mal scoffs. "You don't manufacture yachts for more than four decades and not amass some disgruntled employees who are happy to slate the company. Especially when it folds and leaves them unemployed."

"Boss, we've been back and forth since it happened." Denver meets my gaze.

He's right. I've been sending him and his security team on a wild chase around Cape Town for two years, refusing to allow myself to believe there isn't an explanation for what happened.

The report into the yacht fire was inconclusive. But I was convinced someone was to blame for losing my wife and son. Because if it wasn't someone else's fault they died, then that leaves me.

I didn't save them.

"The engine design?"

Denver shakes his head like it's the first time I've asked him. When in reality, it's the first thing he checked out years ago.

"Same one that's in thousands of others without issue. There hasn't been another fire in any of them since…"

I drag my hands down my face.

"So it wasn't the company who built the yacht or the one that designed it. We're back to square fucking one," Mal hisses, tension lining his forehead.

"I've got a contact," Denver says, leaning forward in his black suit, elbows resting on his knees. "He might be able to help. Someone he knows just started working at the marina. Those CCTV cameras they claimed were out of action?" He cracks his knuckles. "Yeah, turns out they might not have been completely honest with us."

"How long until you can get your hands on them?" Mal asks, a murderous glint shining in his eyes.

He's been as hell-bent as me on finding out what really happened that day. What stole his sister and nephew from him. She was the only family he had. Not counting myself and the kids. He and Elaina lost their parents long before mine passed. They were close. He's never given up hunting for answers, the same as me.

But I'm starting to believe we'll never get any answers.

"Shouldn't be long." Denver looks at Jenson and Killian, two of his team members, flanking one side of my desk.

Beaufort Diamonds has its own security team, as does Seasons. Jenson and Killian work for the family, doing whatever we need. And they're headed by Denver, an ex-special forces guy who's worked for me for years.

I trust him with my life.

"Whatever you need, the jet, the house in Cape Town, it's yours. Do whatever you have to."

"Thanks, Boss." He nods.

"That's not a damn toy," I snap at Jenson.

"Sorry, Boss." He catches the pink stone mid-air that he's been throwing up and down absentmindedly and places it back on my desk. I pin him with a glare until he twists the crystal heart back into the exact position he found it in.

Mal eyes me with interest. "Been accessorizing?"

"They're Halliday's."

"Ah. The love expert."

"The lady you've got us running a check on, Boss?"

I grimace at Killian's question, guilt swimming in my stomach. We check out everyone who comes into close contact with our family. It's the way it's always been. If someone new comes to work for us, we dig deep. We have to know everything. Being the largest diamond jewelry brand in the world comes at a cost. There are always people with ulterior motives.

But Halliday isn't working within Beaufort Diamonds or Seasons. She's working with me personally. The only sensitive information she'll have access to is what I choose to share with her.

"Just surface level. Criminal history, that's all. I don't want to know anything personal. She's not a threat."

"Maybe not, but she sure is pretty." Jenson whistles. "I would."

"You. Would. Not," I grit. "Halliday's too sophisticated for a kid like you."

Jenson scowls as Killian breaks out laughing.

"Maybe when your training wheels are off, eh?" Denver smirks.

"I'm twenty-fucking-one," Jenson grumbles.

"Yeah, and if it weren't for the fact you're built like a truck, you'd look about twelve," Killian jibes.

Jenson's got a baby face. But Denver trusts him, and his work is impeccable. He's smart with good instincts. The bravado and cockiness that rolls off him will lessen with age and experience.

I throw him a brief wink so he knows we're messing.

"All right. Keep me up to date and let me know if you need anything else."

"Boss." Denver nods, exiting my office with Jenson and Killian on his heels.

"So this date you're going on?" Mal arches a brow, his lips curling up.

"To appease Sinclair, that's all."

"Hey, we've known each other long enough now. I'm happy for you. I know you and Elaina were… I know things weren't good in those months before she died. You should think about what Sinclair wants for you. Maybe she's right. Maybe it's time."

I crack my knuckles, tension bunching up the muscles in my shoulders.

"Maybe it will never be time."

"Sinclair and Sullivan are adults now. They don't need you the same as they once did."

I wince at his words, and he sighs.

"Why not get some happiness for you?"

"I'm not lonely…"

"When was the last time you saw the same woman twice? Shared a bed with her for more than a night?"

I shake my head. "Don't."

"I'm just saying. You only live once. Make it count."

"Are you heading back to Africa before I go to LA to check on things there?"

Mal chuckles. "Trying to get rid of me, huh? How long will you be gone?"

"Only a day or two. I'll check on the club. Visit Clay."

Mal nods. "Give your brother my regards."

"I will."

The LA club is fine without me. Bradley has been doing a good job since he came onboard as a manager six months ago. But I still like to check in once a month. It's what I do.

Work.

Sinclair pursued modeling after what happened. And Sullivan told me he wanted to take over as CEO of Beaufort Diamonds earlier than we had planned. We all needed to keep busy, by any means possible.

Everything changed the day we lost them both.

"I'll head out in a week or so. Ade already knows how my chat with Sullivan went, but I'll visit him in person. Then I'll be back. Trudy's mother is coming to stay next month," Mal says, breaking the contemplative silence.

I chuckle at his grimace. "Ah, the mother-in-law."

"Yeah. Maybe I'll stay in Africa." He snorts. "At least my mother loved you."

"God rest her soul," I say.

Mal nods. "God rest all their souls."

♦

At 6:15, Halliday walks into the restaurant's bar in a fitted black dress and heels. I rise from my seat and signal to her.

She walks to me and kisses me on both cheeks. "You're early."

"So are you."

A smile curves her lips. "Can I take this as a sign of you being keen to meet Juliette?"

"You can take it as a sign that a gentleman should always be first, so he never keeps a lady waiting."

"Ah." She sits as I pull out a chair for her. "So in this

instance, it's me who was on the gentleman's mind?" she teases.

"Indeed," I murmur. "I believe you've been on it ever since you suggested my kissing needed work. A man doesn't easily forget a woman who suggests such things."

She laughs as I wink at her and take the seat beside her, signaling the bartender. He takes our order, then leaves.

"Don't take it personally. I ask everyone that question."

"And do they?"

"Do they what?" Halliday's eyes are bright as she looks into mine.

"All require work?"

She pokes her bottom lip out, and the urge to suck it past mine and see what it tastes like smacks me like a punch to the jaw. She's barely thirty. Not much older than my daughter. The daughter who hired her to find me love with a woman *my age*. I'm the proverbial dirty old man, having impure thoughts about my relationship coach.

My gift, as Sinclair reminded me when we spoke earlier.

"Almost always." Halliday holds my eyes, hers twinkling. "But they get to work on it once I match them, so..." She shrugs. "I don't think they mind putting in the work."

"I see." I chuckle as the bartender returns and places two glasses down.

"You didn't want something stronger?" I ask as she takes a sip of her orange juice.

"I don't drink." Her smile thins before she places her glass down.

I nod and lift my brandy to my lips.

Her phone chimes in her purse, and she pulls it out.

"Rory?" I enquire.

She's frowning as she looks at the screen, then her features soften into a beautiful smile. She turns the phone toward me.

"She spoils that dog," I say as I look at the photo of Monty wearing a sweater with a cupcake printed on it.

"She says it's his birthday soon?" Halliday types a reply to my daughter, then slides her phone into her purse.

"It is. I got him as a gift for her shortly after…" I swirl the amber liquid in my glass before lifting it to take a large gulp, savoring the burn that runs down my throat.

"I'm sorry."

Soft, warm fingers curl around mine on the tabletop. Pale pink nails glisten back at me.

"Thank you," I murmur, something shifting in my chest as I stare at her hand on mine. It should look wrong against mine. It should *feel* wrong.

I turn my wrist and entwine my fingers with hers until there's one beautiful, slender finger followed by a rougher, weathered one.

One, then the other, over, and over.

I take a deep breath, studying how they look side by side.

"That dog is about the only thing that makes her smile. I'd get her a whole pack if I thought they'd make it happen more often."

"Sterling." Halliday's voice comes out breathy.

"I love my family. They're everything to me. All I have."

She listens intently, and I can feel her gaze fixed on my face as I admire our entwined fingers. I stroke her thumb, desperately soaking in the way her small hand fits inside mine like I was always meant to keep it safe.

Treasure it.

I don't know what possesses me, but I bring our joined hands to my lips and press a soft kiss to the back of hers.

"Thank you," I murmur, placing them onto the table, running my thumb over her knuckles in a gentle sweep before letting go.

"Why are you thanking me? I haven't done anything yet." Frowning, she looks into my eyes like she's trying to figure out a puzzle that has no answer.

"You've given my daughter something to feel excited about. This quest of hers to find me someone—regardless of if it happens—it's made her happier. Given her something new to focus on."

"The only reason it won't happen is if you refuse to allow it to. If you choose not to be open to it. It's your choice, Sterling. And yours alone."

I look into her eyes, a confession from the past teetering on the tip of my tongue.

Choice.

So much in life boils down to it.

I take another sip of brandy to prevent myself from speaking. When I know I can trust my own voice, I speak again.

"Tell me about you. Your family. Life in London."

"Actually, I thought we could go over Juliette's—"

"I'd love for you to share it with me. You're getting to know me. I'd like to know more about you too."

She hesitates, and maybe she'll put my interest down to reluctance to my upcoming date. But it's not.

I just want to know more about her.

It's both as simple and as complicated as that.

Her lashes flutter, and she bites her lip.

"Please, Hallie," I breathe.

The name slips out so easily, as if it was always supposed to be what I call her.

Her brows shoot up before lines pinch the corners of her eyes as though she's in pain.

I've overstepped.

"Forgive me, I—"

"What do you want to know?" She captures me in her gaze, dark lashes fanning out over her cheeks with each blink.

And I'm damn mesmerized.

"Everything," I rasp, unable to tear my eyes from her as she blushes. "Every little detail."

7

HALLIDAY

I speed up, eager to get to the breakfast meeting with Sterling to talk about last night's date with Juliette.

She was early. I spotted her across the restaurant moments after Sterling asked me to tell him about my family. I never got to go over date preparation with him before she arrived. But I'm sure he coped fine.

Juliette seemed happy when I made the introductions. Her eyes lit up, and I didn't miss the way they roamed over Sterling's muscular frame in his suit after he kissed her hello on her cheeks and complimented her.

Sterling Beaufort is charming.

A gentleman.

A silver fox.

Of course she found him attractive. I just hope there was a deeper connection once they had dinner and got to know one another.

I thank the doorman of the hotel, The Songbird, as I walk inside and head to their ground floor restaurant. Sterling stands as I approach. He's wearing a deep blue suit today and silver tie that matches the flecks in his stubble.

His eyes drop over my workout tights and vest and unexpected heat fires low in my belly as I approach.

"Good morning." He kisses my cheeks, one hand wrapping around my upper arm as he holds me close.

"So? How was it?"

His hand lingers on my arm for a moment before he lets go. Energy zings around my system. It's Juliette. It must be. I could feel her attraction to him last night. I didn't get much of a read off Sterling. But I'm sure his attraction came later once he talked with her.

I knew he'd be quick to match the moment I met him. I could sense it. This is what the universe wants.

"Been working out?" Sterling eyes my rosy cheeks, and I wave a hand in the air, wanting to get straight to the point as he pulls my chair out for me.

"I went to a sunrise yoga class I found online. They do it in the park. Quite uplifting. Maybe you can come next time?"

His eyes dance with amusement. "Maybe."

"So?" I eye him across the table as he takes a seat opposite me, unable to hold back my beaming smile. "Last night?"

"Last night, you looked beautiful. Were you going somewhere special after I saw you?"

I laugh, recognizing his compliments as deflections. If he's feeling coy about talking about his date last night, perhaps it ended in more than just a goodbye.

"I went for drinks with Sinclair and Zoey."

"Ah." He leans back in his seat, his eyes roaming over my make-up free face and messy bun. His eyes soften but before he can say anything, the server comes to take our order, pouring us both a coffee.

"So last night? How was it?" I ask once again, lifting my cup to take a sip.

"A disaster."

I almost spit out my coffee.

"What? Why?"

Sterling sighs. "The restaurant screwed up and her entrée had gluten in. She felt sick even before the main course arrived. I dropped her home less than an hour after you left."

My mouth drops open. "Oh god. Poor Juliette."

"She's okay. I called her this morning and checked."

"Oh?" *Maybe all is not lost.* "You exchanged numbers? That's great."

"She had some interesting PR ideas I thought Sullivan might like to discuss with her for the new launch." Sterling lifts his mug and takes a slow mouthful, his eyes holding mine over the rim.

I watch his tongue dart out to lick his lips between his silver stubble as he lowers it.

The milk from my coffee curdles in my stomach. I don't get these things wrong. I can't afford to get them wrong. My business is new, but I've amassed a powerful reputation for success from the high-profile clients I have matched. A reputation I need to maintain at all costs.

"So there wasn't a spark? You didn't feel anything?"

"No." He places his cup down and watches me with interest.

My neck heats, and I run a hand over it as I glance around the restaurant at all the other diners enjoying their delicious breakfasts.

I might be sick.

I drag in a slow, deep breath. "It's fine, don't worry. You'd be surprised how many times the first match isn't the one. Sometimes it takes a few dates before we find that connection, no matter how good it seems in theory."

Juliette seemed perfect on paper. But I have to trust the

energies when people are brought together physically. Sometimes the link just isn't there.

It's fine. I'm not going to fail.

"Okay. So, the next date. I'll arrange it for tomorrow night. How's that sound?"

Sterling's expression stutters. "That soon?"

"Are you busy?"

"No. I can make it work. But Hallie—"

I stiffen and concern paints itself over his face.

"You don't like being called Hallie?"

"I..." I blink rapidly, my throat tightening. "My sister was the only one who ever called me it, that's all."

"Your sister?"

I nod, unable to answer as my throat burns.

He leans forward, resting his forearms on the white tablecloth. "I'm sorry. I didn't know. I should have realized last night when you looked... I don't even know why I did it. It just slipped out."

"I..." I search for the right words, but none come.

I know why.

"I'm the King." Jenny laughs. "And you're Queen Hallie. Now we get married." We hug each other, gripping on tight as the homemade crowns we spent the afternoon gluing and covering in glitter fall over our eyes. Jenny presses a sloppy kiss to my cheek. "Happily ever after for Queen Hallie." She kisses me again. The music she's put on changes to another song. "Now we dance." She beams as she begins to sway. I rest my head on top of hers as we move together, closing my eyes and getting lost in the music.

"When did you lose her?" Sterling asks softly.

Understanding fills his eyes. He knows what it's like for your family to shrink. And for you to be unable to do a thing about it.

"Five years ago. Jenny caught pneumonia and..." I inhale

shakily, my fingers trembling around my coffee mug. "She was only eighteen."

"I'm so sorry."

"She had so much love to give. The purest heart, honestly." I blink rapidly. "It's why I started Cosmic Connections. She would have loved to have heard about the matches I've made. All those love stories starting out. She believed in love more than anyone I've ever met. She *was* love. I miss her every day."

"It never gets easier. Time, I mean... you just get better at coping with it. But it never hurts less. Not really."

Sterling's warm voice wraps around my cracked heart, and I nod, fighting back tears.

"No, it doesn't."

"Forgive me, Halliday. I didn't mean to—"

"It's okay. I like talking about her. Don't apologize for making me think of her."

Or for calling me Hallie, like it's a sign from Jenny.

"She loved love stories. We would curl up and watch romance films together. She'd pick the most unlikely pairs, hoping they'd get together, even if she already knew they weren't the ones supposed to get the happy ending.

"Honestly, the whole of New York makes me think of her. She wanted to visit the Statue of Liberty. See her crown."

I look into Sterling's eyes. I'm the one who's supposed to be helping him. Not the other way around.

"So the next date?" I sniff, forcing my voice to brighten.

His gaze never falters. Almost like he sees the most broken parts of me, and they only make him want him to look more.

He nods, his tone soft. "The next date."

"It's trickier than I anticipated." I place my bottle of juice on the counter and wander toward the window.

"So you'll be there the whole month?"

"I... No, I don't think so. He's more closed off than I anticipated, but it'll be fine," I tell Sophie as I lift the frame.

Jenny's bright smile shines back at me.

"You don't need to worry. I'll be back in plenty of time to prepare for being the coolest Auntie that ever walked the earth."

"You better." Sophie sighs. "I miss you."

"I miss you too."

"I bet your parents are missing you as well."

"They are." I place the frame down, facing the window. "Mum calls at least once a day... So does Rory."

"Rory?"

"Yeah." I bite my lower lip at Sophie's exasperated huff.

"Halliday, you need to get it through to him that he needs to leave you alone. This is getting ridiculous. It's been years. I told you, just give me the word and I'll have a restraining order like that."

She snaps her fingers down the phone. She has no idea how tempting her suggestion would be if it weren't for my knowledge of what Rory might do in retaliation.

"Mm, remind me again.... This baby daddy of yours... Didn't you have one against him?"

Sophie curses good-naturedly as I steer our conversation away from Rory.

I knew Drew Harper, the man who chased her for years, was special. I could tell by the energy she gave off when she spoke about meeting him on a blind date. He wasn't even her date. But the universe didn't care. When it wants something, it wants something.

And it wanted Sophie to start a family with Drew.

It didn't matter that she'd jokingly threatened him with a restraining order when he was persistent.

They were inevitable.

"Just be careful," she warns. "I don't like how he's trying to weasel his way back into your life. You should have been able to escape him all the way over in New York."

"He suggested he visit me."

"Asshole."

"Well, he's not coming," I scoff.

I can't think of anything worse than having Rory here. It's bad enough that he happens to be visiting his parents, who live next door to my mum and dad, whenever I'm at their house, which usually results in us all having dinner together. If it weren't for the support from his family over the years, then it might be easier to get him out of my life.

Unfortunately, it's not.

"Sterling called me Hallie," I blurt.

"Sterling?" Sophie's usually calm voice hitches. "How did that make you feel?"

"Like she was right there in the room with us." I sniff as hot tears well in my eyes. "Like she was… It's too crazy to even say out loud."

"You thrive on crazy."

I laugh. "I know, right?"

She stays silent as I sniff a couple more times and swipe my palm over my hot cheeks. But I can hear her gentle breathing as she waits for me to be ready.

"He…"

I swallow as I recall the way my hand felt inside Sterling's. My fingers pulsed with energy long after he let it go.

"I feel things when I'm with him. All this wild energy. It's like a dam waiting to burst. He lost his wife and son. We must be connected through grief, it's the only thing that explains it. He's twenty years older than me."

"It's not the only thing that might explain it."

"No way." I shake my head.

Sophie's being ridiculous. Pregnancy hormones must be affecting her logic. She's always the logical one. I'm the one who is swept along by ideas that arrive on the wind.

"You always said love knows no age."

"I am not a match for Sterling."

I run my hand around the back of my neck. It's burning hotter than my cheeks did when he told me I looked beautiful.

"I'm not. He's fifty. He's my *client*. And he's also going on a date with an absolutely incredible woman who I'm sure is going to create a vibration strong enough to shake the whole of Manhattan when he meets her."

"Whatever happens, just know that I love you," she says. "Remember that."

I drop onto the couch and blow out a breath. "I love you too."

There's a hammering at the door, and the sound of giggles float through, accompanied by an excited yip.

"Just a second," I call out.

"I've got visitors," I say to Sophie as I walk to the door.

"I'll let you go. Have fun. I'll call you later."

"Look after that bump," I say, hanging up.

I peer through the spyhole. Zoey's brandishing a take-out bag, and Sinclair is standing next to her, waving Monty's paw in the air.

"Let us in! We brought food," Zoey shouts.

"And furry snuggles," Sinclair adds.

Smiling, I open the door and they barrel inside. It's not even been a week, but these girls are already friends. Zoey was true to her word last night, taking us to a beautiful lounge with the best mocktails I've ever had. One where we weren't bothered by anyone all evening.

Sinclair knew the owner and we were escorted straight to a

private area where they regaled me with gossip about a model who was caught sucking off a rival designer backstage at Sinclair's latest runway show. All the while wearing the show designer's key piece, which she then got his *excitement* all over. She then strutted down the runway in it before the designer ripped it from her as she came off stage, then threw her out by her hair. Turns out the rival designer was her ex-husband who always had an eye for the models, even during their marriage. Obviously struck a nerve.

The distraction was exactly what I needed after hearing Sterling call me Hallie.

"What's the occasion?" I ask as Zoey places the take-out bag on the kitchen counter and presents a hidden bottle from behind her back with a flourish.

"Oh? Just this!" Sinclair shifts Monty to one arm and grabs Zoey's left hand, thrusting it into my face.

"An iceberg that's about to sink the whole upper west side?" I squeal as I take in the huge diamond on her finger.

"And it's a Beaufort," Zoey trills.

"Please." Sinclair rolls her eyes. "Like Ashton would let you have anything else. We are the best." She bounces on her toes. "It's gorgeous, isn't it? It's a custom design, based on the new line. No one's even seen any of the new settings yet."

I learned all about Zoey's fiancé, Ashton, last night over drinks. He's an artist who fell in love with Zoey when she posed for him and became his muse. His most famous work is of her. But he'd never seen her face and didn't know it was her when they first met. They almost didn't end up together.

I tilt her hand so I can admire the intricate swirls of platinum that the diamond is mounted with. They make a B shape, with a smaller yellow diamond nestled inside.

"Hidden treasure," Sinclair muses. "Sullivan's idea. He has *some* good ones."

"Some?" I arch a brow as she deposits Monty into my

arms so she can help Zoey as she opens cabinets and takes out glasses and plates.

Monty licks at my chin happily, and I tickle behind his ears.

"Ignore her. She's feeling bitchy because she saw darling brother leaving The Lanceford last night," Zoey says as she forks noodles out of a container onto plates.

"That's a luxury hotel, right?" I ask, picturing the sleek black exterior that I walked past on my first day here when I was getting my bearings.

"Yep. Close to his office, and our store on Fifth." Sinclair snorts. "He's making it convenient for himself."

"I don't understand."

"He fucks the women he picks up there. Only my brother would permanently book a multi-million-dollar apartment he never intends to stay more than a few hours a week in." Sinclair screws up her face in disgust.

"It's true." Zoey lifts her brows as her eyes remain on the task of plating up the food. "He takes them there, then leaves a couple of hours later. Always a different woman... or two."

"It's gross. At least when he had his old place downtown, I didn't have to see it. I can't believe he's moved his man-whoring pad to my neighborhood." Sinclair grimaces as she pops the cork off the champagne, then takes a swig straight from the bottle. "Ugh, I forgot. It's alcohol free." She puts the bottle down with a heavy thud.

"You didn't have to get alcohol free just because of me," I say.

"We did. You inspired us to be healthier. Zoey and I decided we won't drink Monday through Thursday. Why couldn't I have seen Sullivan on a weekend? I need a drink after that." Sinclair snorts.

Zoey pushes three plates piled high with food across the

counter as Sinclair pours the champagne into three glasses. I slide into a seat, still cuddling Monty in one arm.

"Sullivan doesn't have a girlfriend, then?" I ask as I get comfy and try the champagne. The bubbles fizz on my tongue. They have all the flavor I like. But none of the problems that alcohol can create.

"Not for two years, since..." Sinclair shrugs, fiddling with her necklace instead of saying the words out loud.

"He regularly beds women in his little pad that he thinks is a secret, though," Zoey adds. "Just never anything serious. Same as Sterling."

The hairs on the back of my neck prickle at his name. Of course I know he's probably been intimate with other women since losing his wife. If he hadn't, then my job would be even harder. It would be a sign he might not be ready.

"Dad doesn't have a special apartment for it, though," Sinclair says. "And I really don't think there have been many, not like Sullivan."

The knots in my stomach ease enough that I'm able to eat the noodles I've twirled around my fork.

"You've got another date lined up for him, haven't you?" Sinclair asks.

"I have. She's really nice. I've met her in person before. She didn't match with a previous client, but she's keen to meet someone. And she loves animals." I stroke Monty with one hand where he's curled himself up on my thighs.

"She already sounds good." Sinclair beams. "Do you think Dad will like her?"

I lift my glass and swallow some champagne, but it does nothing to ease the sudden dryness in my throat. I can still feel the way his fingers threaded through mine. Feel the rough graze of his stubble and the soft contrast of his warm lips as he kissed my hand.

"I hope so," I answer truthfully because Sterling liking her would make sense.

Him and a beautiful, educated woman at a similar stage of life makes sense.

Him and I... do not.

United by the shared pain of grief. That's all.

My phone rings on the counter and my stomach clenches. It better not be Rory calling again. I've managed to send his last two calls to voicemail, but I know that won't deter him for long.

"Here you go." Sinclair hands it to me, and I read the name on the screen.

"Deborah?" I smile as I answer. "How are you? Did you want to discuss your date with—?"

I snap my mouth shut with a frown as Sterling's potential future tells me that her grandmother was taken ill, and she's flown home to Maine to care for her.

I end the call.

"She's not coming, is she?" Sinclair's disappointed eyes search mine.

I shake my head. "Family emergency."

She turns her attention to her plate and stares at it, pushing a piece of chicken around with her fork.

"But it's fine. Have faith." I reach over and squeeze her forearm.

"Your dad will probably be relieved." Zoey winces. "He doesn't sound like he's onboard with the whole idea."

"I guess I hoped he would come around when the time came. That he'd see..." Sinclair sighs and looks at me. "I hoped when you arrived that the rest would be easy. That it'd be this instant thing that would happen. Like magic. And that he'd know I was right to bring you to him."

"He's making progress," I say. "Last night's date didn't work out. But it wasn't his doing. It just wasn't meant to be.

He seemed happy about having another date when I met him this morning."

"Really?" She smiles hopefully, and guilt tugs at my stomach.

Sterling didn't exactly jump for joy. But he did listen intently as I told him about Deborah and how I'd planned tickets to a symphony show for them to enjoy, and suggested he send her chocolates on the morning of their date because she doesn't care much for flowers.

He was even smiling as he kissed me goodbye on both cheeks, his hand finding my lower back and creating a centering warmth as he pulled me closer to him with the perfect amount of pressure.

And he smelled incredible. Woody, warm, spicy. A scent that had me breathing in and being filled with a sense of hope. Like the sparkly glow of a flame illuminating the dark.

I should call him and tell him to make sure he wears that cologne on his dates.

Sinclair looks between me and Zoey. "I just want him to be happy. He deserves it after everything that's happened."

"He does," I agree. "And I will do whatever it takes to help bring it to him."

"Thank you, Halliday. I know you will."

"I have other potential matches to explore. And he has a lot of female acquaintances. I'd like to meet more of them and get a feel for things. Maybe he already has a friendship that he's held himself back from and needs a little encouragement to see what's in front of him."

"What about the fundraiser?" Zoey asks as she scoops up some rice from another container and puts it on her plate.

Sinclair gasps. "Yes!"

"The one for the children's charity? That's perfect."

I sit straighter in my seat, energy buzzing up my spine. I was going to ask Sterling about the fundraiser after seeing it mentioned on Lavinia's business website. She's one of his acquaintances that I'm eager to meet, but she's been out of town.

"Almost every woman Dad knows in New York will be there." Sinclair squeals as she jumps off her stool and grabs her phone from her purse. She places it on the counter, putting it on speaker as it rings.

"Dad?" she gushes the moment it connects.

"Hi, Sweetheart."

The deep rumble of his voice washes over me like a tropical wave. Monty lifts his head from my legs and tilts it to one side, looking at me with shiny black eyes.

"I've got a great idea about the fundraiser on Thursday."

"However much you need, just tell me, I'll add it to my contribution."

"No, not that. You've been generous enough already. This is about you."

"Mm-hm."

I shift in my seat, and Monty tilts his head to the other side.

I'm fine, I mouth.

"Halliday's going to accompany you. That way she can meet some of your friends."

There's a pause, and for an excruciating moment, I think I'm going to hear something I can't unhear. Like Sterling listing off excuses not to spend the evening with me.

"I'd be honored. I'll call her and suggest it."

My heart beats wildly in my chest at the lift in his voice as though he likes the idea.

"No need, Dad. She's sitting beside me." Sinclair grins at me.

"Ah, I see." He chuckles. "Hi Halliday."

"Hi..."

"Is my daughter taking you out for another night out?"

"We're having take-out," Zoey chirps.

"Hi, Zoey."

"Hi, Mr. Beaufort."

Sterling's chuckle deepens. "I'll leave you ladies to it. Have fun."

"We will." Sinclair makes a *mwah* sound.

"Halliday?" he adds before she can hang up.

"Yes?"

"Are you free in the morning? There's somewhere I want to take you."

I keep my attention fixed on the phone screen, unable to meet Sinclair's eyes as his voice makes me shiver.

"Sure. We can go over things for Thursday at the same time."

"Wonderful. I'll see you tomorrow."

8

HALLIDAY

My phone ringing wakes me.

I glance at the clock. 5:30. No one calls this early unless something's wrong. I lurch up into a sitting position, my breath catching as I swipe my phone up and hit answer.

"Hello?"

"Good Morning."

"Sterling?"

Goosebumps pepper along my arms at his deep voice.

"Can I still have your company this morning?"

I flick the bedside lamp on and run a hand back through my hair. "I, um... I'm still in bed."

"So am I."

The rough gravel of his sleepy voice has my stomach dancing as I picture him calling me from his bed. Is he sitting up like me? Or lying, with his head resting on the pillow? Was I his first thought as he woke up? Does he sleep naked?

"I... yes, absolutely," I croak.

I need to pull myself together. This weird pull toward him has to stop. I'm getting everything mixed up. I'm here to find him a match. So why do the flutters in my stomach feel more like they're trying to tell me something, and less like the usual buzz of energy I get while working with clients?

"Great. I'll be with you within thirty minutes."

"Okay. See you then."

I toss my phone down and launch the covers back from the bed, my heart racing. Thirty minutes to calm the hell down and get some sense into myself.

I spend the first ten minutes trying, and failing, to meditate, the way I usually start each day. But my mind keeps wandering, hearing his voice over and over as he called me from his bed.

The buzzer for the door goes moments after I step out of the shower. I walk to the security panel and peer at Sterling's suited form waiting outside on the street.

"You're early," I say, clutching my towel around my chest after I press the speaker button.

He looks up, straight into the camera, a warm smile on his face. "There's no rush. I'll wait down here."

"No, come on up." I press the button to unlock the main door. Maybe he brought a car he can wait in. But it's still dark outside. I can't leave him waiting there if he hasn't.

I don't even have time to get my underwear on before there's a soft knock at the door. I go to open it, holding my towel around myself.

"Hi."

"Good morning," he rasps. His eyes meet mine, and for a moment, we just stand and stare at each other.

"Um, come in." I stand back and am greeted by the aroma of his aftershave as he walks past me into the apartment.

"I'll just get dressed. I won't be a minute," I say, closing the door behind him.

He turns, and his eyes drop down my body, noting my towel for the first time. He clears his throat before looking away. "Right, yes. I'll wait here."

He strolls toward the living area window, pushing his hands into his pant pockets. I study his back. The way his broad shoulders fill out his dark gray suit. The way his suit pants fit him, hinting at the defined thighs beneath them... and a firm, muscular ass.

I hurry to my bedroom, pulling on my underwear and selecting a silk blouse and smart jeans to wear. I run my fingers through my hair, hoping it looks more 'cute waves' than tangled mess, slip on a pair of ballet pumps, and grab a black blazer. I don't have time for makeup, only a swipe of lip balm before I walk into the living area.

Sterling looks up as I enter, his gaze subtly dropping down my body and back up in a way that makes my thighs clench. "You look lovely."

"Thank you."

He tilts an object in his hand toward me. "Jenny?"

I walk over and look at the photograph he's holding. Jenny and I have our arms around one another. And there's a huge cake on the table in front of us. It's the last picture we took together before she got ill.

"Her eighteenth birthday." I smile sadly.

"Ah," Sterling murmurs softly, studying the image. "She has such a beautiful smile. And I take it she liked Taylor Swift?" He chuckles at the 'I'm Taylor's biggest fan' T-shirt Jenny's wearing.

"She really did. Knew every single word of every single song." I smile as I stand next to him, close enough that my arm brushes his jacket sleeve.

"As a biggest fan should," he muses, smile lines crinkling around his eyes as he admires the picture.

"Thank you," I whisper.

"What for?"

"Most people see the Down syndrome first. They don't see Jenny."

He holds my eyes for a moment, his brows creasing, before looking back at the image.

"Well, she deserves to be seen. Why don't you bring her with us?"

"What?" I frown as he holds the frame out to me.

"Give her a different view today."

I take the photo from him and look at it, my throat tightening. Instead of putting it back, I walk to my purse on the kitchen counter and slide it inside. "I'm ready when you are." I look back to find him watching me.

"Then shall we?" His soft smile has me looking away with a quick nod to hide the heat blooming in my cheeks.

◆

"Liberty enlightening the world," I murmur with a bittersweet smile as I stand looking out at New York's harbor lit up by the sunrise.

A new day. New possibilities.

"Indeed," Sterling rumbles as he comes to stand by my side.

"Thank you for bringing me here." Emotion bubbles in my throat as I slip Jenny's photo out of my purse and hold it in front of me, facing out, so she can see. "The view is stunning. She would have loved it."

After we left my apartment, he showed me to his car, where his driver was waiting. He drove us to a private boat that brought us to Liberty Island, where we climbed up inside Lady Liberty.

Right inside her crown.

No one else is here. It's just me, Sterling, Jenny's photo,

and a thousand memories. All witnessing the way the sky is turning every shade of orange over the glistening water.

"How did you even arrange this? I only told you yesterday how much she wanted to come here. I tried getting a ticket before I left England, but they were booked up for months."

I turn to look at him as he watches the sunrise, and he tips his head casually. "I made some calls, that's all."

A smile twists my lips. Some calls. It's easy to forget he's a billionaire with a wealth of connections at his fingertips. To me, he's a man with a hidden pain that I recognize in his eyes.

Pain that I'm determined to help lessen before my time with him is up.

"You know, the twenty-five windows of her crown each represent a different gemstone on Earth?" I say as I look out of the window in front of us.

I sneak a sideways glance at him. A knowing smile graces his lips, but he keeps his eyes forward.

"But of course, you know that. You've lived here your whole life, and your family's history is built around diamonds and jewels." I roll my eyes with a smile.

"It is. We've become known for our family-mined diamonds. But it wasn't always diamonds. It was all kinds of gemstones once."

"Before you met your wife?"

His smile vanishes, and he gives a tight nod.

It's something I came across in my research after Sinclair hired me. Sterling's family owned an established jewelry firm on the East Coast. But it's only been in the past thirty years that they've become famous for the diamonds they source from their own mines. Mines that were previously linked to his late wife's family.

"What was she like?" I ask, hugging Jenny's photo against my chest as the sun rises higher in the sky.

"She..." Sterling runs a hand around his jaw, exhaling

slowly. "She was a great mom. She loved the kids more than anything."

"And you," I add softly. "She loved you more than anything too."

A muscle clenches in his cheek, and he keeps his focus trained on something in the distance.

Guilt tugs at me for being the reason a heaviness has shrouded him all of a sudden. I know what it's like, remembering how much someone who's gone loved you. It makes you feel like your heart is being torn out, knowing you won't ever hear them say it again.

"It's okay to let yourself be loved again. You deserve it," I say gently.

"Thank you, Halliday." His voice is weighted with something I can't place.

The sun's rays flow over the two of us, warming my skin and making my fingertips tingle around Jenny's photograph like she's trying to tell me something.

"Hallie," I whisper.

It's barely more than a breath through my lips, but Sterling turns and looks at me with such an intensity that I know he heard.

"I..." I falter, avoiding his gaze, before allowing a small smile to lift my lips. "I liked the way hearing it again made me feel. How it made memories, happy ones, surface again."

I chance a look into his eyes and they're shining, studying me.

"I'd like it if you call me Hallie," I breathe.

His gaze softens, the heaviness that was in him moments ago, gone. "Of course. If that's what you want."

I nod, unable to add that I only want *him* to call me Hallie. No one else. That I loved the way his deep tone made goosebumps scatter up my spine when it rolled from his tongue like butter on hot toast.

Perhaps the universe put us together for this reason. Maybe while I find him love, he's supposed to help me remember it. Remember to focus on the things that made my heart lift in my chest and not on the gaping hole that's been left there in its place. Because any other explanation for the way my body lights up when he's around just doesn't make sense.

"You okay?"

"Yep," I reply too fast, my voice cracking. "Fine."

"Hallie?"

The sound of my name from his lips again makes me choke out a small, muffled squeak.

Everything rushes me at once. Jenny's smile. Her laugh. The way she felt in my arms when we hugged.

Memories of a love so pure.

One I'll miss every day for the rest of my life.

"I'm f-fine," I lie without conviction.

Strong arms surround me, gathering me up gently and drawing me in against his warm, solid chest. I rest my cheek over his heart and listen to the steady thud of life inside him.

"It's okay," he soothes as I clutch Jenny's photograph with one hand and slide my other hand beneath his jacket to cling on to a handful of his shirt at his back like it has the power to ground me.

A tear slips free, sinking into the cotton. I suck in a shaky breath, willing my throat to stop burning, scared I might burst into full-blown sobs at any moment.

Sterling strokes my hair from my face and dips his head, pressing his nose into the strands. He inhales slowly, making his chest expand against my cheek.

"You're not alone, I'm here," he says, pressing a kiss to the top of my head.

"I'm sorry. I just need a minute."

I fist his shirt harder and tilt my chin up, letting his eyes capture mine between my damp lashes.

He stares with a tenderness that makes my heart stall.

"Take all the time you need."

I nod, unable to respond with words.

He traces my jaw with his thumb, following its path with his eyes until he reaches my chin. His brows scrunch together, his attention falling to my mouth. He exhales, and his minty breath flows over my lips.

I part my own to breathe him in.

"I'll be here anytime you need me, Hallie."

He dusts his thumb over my cheek one final time.

Then it's gone.

I miss his touch immediately. But his eyes stay on mine, the same promise held in them; he'll be here anytime I need him.

Anytime I need him.

I gaze back up at him and he smiles at me softly, his blue eyes bringing with them a calm reassurance that I've never felt before.

Sterling Beaufort sees my broken parts.

And for the first time, I'm not overcome by the need to hide them.

9

STERLING

I read the texts from Hallie again.

> I'm sorry I couldn't make dinner. I've been meeting with potential matches. H.

> Thank you for the flowers. They've actually got me thinking. I have a lady who runs her own floral company. I'd like you to meet her. H.

> How is Saturday night for a date? H.

I almost type back to the last one telling her I'll look forward to it more than a kid looks forward to a vacation at Disney World.

Then I remember she doesn't mean a date with her.

"Jesus Christ," I groan, leaning back in my chair.

I'm attracted to her. More than attracted to her. I can't stop thinking about her. About the way her eyes light up when she talks about energy and vibrations. How her voice gets light and breathy when she's excited. The way her hair shines like an angel's. The way her cheeks flush and her lips part every time she's caught me staring at her.

The way her hips curve below her waist, creating the perfect ledge for my hand to rest on if I were to slide my arm around her like she was mine...

The perfect ledge to grip on to as I work her up and down my dick.

"Damn it." I clench my fist around the rose quartz heart.

I'm surprised I don't have an indent of the thing permanently pressed into my palm.

It's what I do now. Whenever I'm at work, one hand is wrapped around the thing, like it's my connection to her. I think about her constantly. Rushing to read texts she sends me. Snatching up my phone the second it rings in case it's her.

Because since I held her in my arms at the Statue of Liberty, she's been avoiding me. I've no doubt about it.

So now, I'm gripping this pink stone like it holds the answers to what I'm supposed to do. If I'm not, then it's my dick at home I'm gripping, imagining the way she'd sound crying out my name, her nails digging into my ass as I thrust inside her.

Does she blush when she comes?

Would she manage to keep her eyes open and on mine as I come inside her, spilling every hot drop from my aching balls until it was running down her thighs?

Or would she close them, too overwhelmed with how hard I'd make her come all over my cock?

"Pervert," I mutter with disgust as the crotch of my suit pants grows uncomfortably tight.

My phone rings, and I grab it, adjusting myself as I see her name on the screen.

Hallie.

I changed it the moment she asked me to call her that.

"Hello?" I answer, guilt making my mouth sour. I'm

sitting here with a dick that's painfully hard and leaking, knowing without a doubt it'll not go fully down until I relieve myself to thoughts of her.

"Are you ready for tonight?"

The excited breathiness of her words has me biting the inside of my cheek to stop my groan.

"I am. Are you?"

"Definitely. I've got a good feeling about it. I even got a new dress."

"You did?"

I relax in my seat as I listen to her chat easily. It's like a caress of calm to my soul. We have the charity gala this evening. So even though she's been avoiding seeing me in person, we're about to spend all evening in one another's company.

"I did. Sinclair took me shopping."

Those four words are a wrecking ball shattering the peace in my chest and replacing it with a cold, stark reality.

My daughter.

The daughter who hired Hallie to find me love. My daughter, who is much closer in age than I am to the woman starring in my depraved fantasies. Ones filled with desperate, hot, sticky sex and mind-altering synchronized orgasms.

She's twenty years younger than me.

She has her entire life ahead of her.

And it's not one that features a man old enough to be her father.

She'd be damn well ruined if I ever laid my hands on her.

"I can't wait to see it," I reply as smoothly as I can, while my pulse beats like a drum in my groin.

"Are you sure you don't want me to meet you there?"

"Of course not. I'll pick you up. Seven thirty?"

"That means seven-fifteen in Sterling time." She laughs.

I chuckle as I stroke the pink heart between my fingers, loving that she already knows me. "You're right."

"Okay. I'll see you tonight."

I can hear the smile in her voice before she rings off. It's been there every time we've spoken—which has been every day, usually two or three times.

But she's avoiding seeing me in person, which makes me wonder why.

Why would a beautiful, intelligent, thirty-year-old woman want to avoid being in physical proximity with me? Especially when she's been hired to work with me. Why would she suck in those small little gasps of air when my hand rests on her lower back? Why would her pulse flutter in her neck the way it does when I've kissed her hello on her cheek?

My dick throbs in my pants.

I close my fist around the crystal heart.

No. I can't allow myself to consider that she feels anything other than what is professionally appropriate toward me for a second.

Because if I do... Damn, if I do...

I readjust myself in my pants in the hope of relief.

But there's none.

I can't consider it. She's too young for me. That's all there is to it.

My hand lingers over my dick, before I cave and give it a firm squeeze.

The sound that seeps from my lips rivals one of a starving animal.

It pulses to life in my hand, pre-cum seeping from the end in desperation, eager to release to thoughts of her.

I could relieve the ache momentarily. But it will only return with a vengeance.

I can't escape it.

I can't fool my body into thinking some hastily jerked out orgasms will ever be a substitute for what it really craves.

Dropping my dick like it's a hot poker, I tighten my grip on the pink crystal heart and slam my other fist down against my desk.

"Goddamn it!"

Hallie thinks I'm a gentleman.

I can't do anything that will taint that.

Not a damn thing.

◆

"Wow. Lavinia has an incredible talent for style. This place looks amazing."

My eyes never stray from Hallie's face as she takes in the room, her gaze moving up the ballrooms giant stone pillars that are swathed in golden light.

"She does," I agree. "All the fundraising events she orchestrates are like this."

Hallie beams, her eyes twinkling as the string quartet on the far side of the ballroom seamlessly move into another song.

"So this is all for low-income city families?" Her eyes bounce around the room in wonder at all of the tuxedos and ballgowns as people move around and talk with champagne flutes in their hands. "Sinclair said over three million has been raised already."

"She's correct. And yes, it's for kids who don't get the opportunity to leave the city much and also for young caregivers. The charity arranges trips and vacations to the coast for them and their families."

I pluck two glasses of orange juice from a server's silver tray, thanking him before handing one to Hallie.

I slide my hand back to its position on her lower back the second she takes the glass from me. It's been there since the moment I helped her out of our limo, and I have no desire to move it unless she wants me to.

"Young caregivers." She shakes her head with a small, unbelieving smile. "It sounds like the charity that helped my family when Jenny and I were kids."

"It does?"

She tugs on her lower lip with her teeth before lifting her eyes to meet mine.

"My parents were there as much as possible for us. But Jenny's school wasn't cheap, and they both worked long hours to pay for it. I was the one taking her and picking her up from school and making us dinner each night. Doing the grocery shopping, getting the housework and laundry done. Just regular stuff, you know?"

"That's a lot of responsibility for a child."

She frowns. "I guess it is. I used to go to these activity summer camps for kids. My place was funded by a charity. It's where I met my best friend, Sophie. She's a lawyer in London now. And I..." She glances around the room again. "I get to come to places like this and help people find love. I'm blessed to be able to do something I care about."

She turns to me with a smile that doesn't quite reach her eyes.

I rub slow circles against the base of her spine with my thumb.

I lower my voice discreetly. "You had to grow up fast. It's okay to be conflicted in how you feel about that."

She blinks, her eyes shining as she leans into me. "I wouldn't change it. I loved every second I had with Jenny."

"And now you dedicate your life to finding love for other people. But who looks after you, Hallie?" I rasp.

Her lips part and her cheeks flush before she breaks our eye contact, dropping her gaze to her glass.

I wait for her to speak.

After a few seconds of silence, she lifts her glass. "Let's toast."

I mirror her movement, clinking my crystal flute against hers.

"To?"

"To love. And to dating."

She smiles as I chuckle.

"To love," I echo. "And to new friends."

My eyes fix on hers until she looks away, across the room, spotting something.

She rises on her toes to speak discreetly in my ear. "Is that Lavinia?"

Her fragrance surrounds me. Fresh, young, awakening. Like oranges and honey warmed by the sun. It's the same as in her hair when we were at Liberty Island. I inhale subtly as I continue tracing circles over her skin with my thumb.

I whisper in her ear, "It is."

"Wow. She's beautiful." Hallie places her free hand over my chest and rests it there. "Can we go and say hello?"

"In a moment."

I splay my fingers out against her lower back and pull her even closer. Her breath catches, and she blinks at me from beneath her lashes. I allow myself an indulgent sweep of her face, committing it to memory.

Fast beats of her pulse flutter beneath the surface of silky skin on her neck, the sight making my blood heat.

I'm playing a dangerous game here.

"Why not now?" she puffs out in a small whisper.

Her pupils dilate as she absentmindedly strokes my shirt with featherlight fingertips, right over my thundering heart.

"Sterling?" Her soft, full lips shine as her tongue darts out to wet them.

"Hallie?" I counter, relishing the way a tiny shiver runs through her as I say it.

The urge to keep her close, to pull her to me and not let go is overwhelming.

I flex my fingers against her back to prevent me from taking ahold of her chin and tilting it back so I can lower my mouth to hers.

I bet kissing her would be like kissing a ray of sun.

Warm. Inviting. Enlivening.

Her fingers trace figures of eight over my heart. I doubt she knows she's doing it.

She blinks up at me. "I'd like to donate tonight. Do I make out a cheque? Or transfer it to an account?"

"Any way you want to. The suggested donation is a minimum of two hundred thousand. It doesn't matter how it comes."

"Oh, okay."

She drops her hand from my chest and fiddles with her hair, tucking an invisible strand behind her ear.

She looks at her drink, lips pressed tightly together.

I study the lines creasing her forehead.

She's a wealthy woman. Wealthy enough to invest in the same project as me a few months ago. A bio-fuel rocket engine headed up by Logan Rich, a British engineer. It's one of the things that came up when Denver ran a security check on her. If I'd gone to the launch party in London, then I might have met her there. But I missed it because I was looking at potential premises to add to the Seasons portfolio.

"Hallie," I murmur. "Are you okay?"

"Huge turnout!" Sinclair gushes, appearing beside us, her head swiveling around the room as she waves to people she knows.

The Matchmaker

Hallie steps away from me, looking flustered. "It's incredible. The amount of people here, I can't quite believe it."

"I'm not surprised," Sullivan adds, sliding in beside Sinclair, his eyes calculating as he looks from Hallie and then to me.

I shake my head subtly, and he grunts into his champagne flute, taking a sip as he scans the room. His attention zeroes in on a woman in a skintight red dress who's looking over at him with hungry eyes.

"Who's that?" Sinclair sneers.

"No idea," he replies coolly, his eyes dropping to the woman's feet and back up, drinking her in.

"Bet you'll know later, though, right? When she's getting acquainted with your penthouse in The Lanceford." Sinclair knocks her champagne back and then switches it for another from a passing tray, knocking that one back too.

Sullivan's jaw clenches. "I don't know what you mean, Sis."

She snorts. "Like hell you don't."

She turns to Hallie with an apologetic smile, her eyes glassy, making me wonder how many of the free champagnes she's already taken advantage of.

"I'm sorry you have to hear about my brother's slutty behavior. It's the furthest thing from true love matches." She wobbles in her heels. "Kind of makes a sham of it all when he sticks his dick in a different woman every week."

"Sinclair," I warn. "That's enough."

My daughter's pained eyes meet mine and she fiddles with her diamond pendant. "I'm still holding out hope for you, Dad. Don't worry." She tips her empty glass toward the bar. "I'm going to get another drink."

"Is she okay?" Hallie looks after her with concern. "I should—"

"I'll go," Sullivan clips. "She had a run-in with another

model at her shoot earlier. Accused her of stealing one of her scarves. She's just letting off steam."

He squeezes my shoulder. "You look after Halliday. Introduce her to the... *appropriate* women she's going to set you up on dates with." His eyes darken before he strolls away in the direction of the bar.

My grip tightens around my glass.

I'm a fool.

I have no right to tangle Hallie up in any of my shit.

My other hand leaves her back for the first time since we arrived.

It happens at the exact same moment Lavinia breezes over, her arms outstretched.

"Sterling!" She beams, pulling me into a hug.

She rests her palm on my upper arm as she assesses me, her eyes twinkling.

"Lavinia." I smile. "I'd like you to meet Halliday Burton. She's my—"

"Divine power facilitator," Hallie interjects, smiling brightly at Lavinia and offering her hand.

Lavinia takes it, her brow scrunching in confusion. "Is that a... life coach?"

Hallie tilts her head, her lips pulling to one side as she thinks. "I suppose in a way. I help people to recognize signs from the universe. To unlock magic and love."

"She was my gift... From Sinclair," I add.

Hallie glances at me before turning her attention to Lavinia. "I'm here to meet Sterling's friends and get to know the people who are important to him. I can tell you more about my work when you have time tonight?"

Lavinia looks between the two of us as though she's about to ask more. But she promptly returns Hallie's beaming smile with a friendly one.

"How marvelous. I would love that. Why don't I introduce you to some people now? Sterling, you'll be okay?"

"Please, be my guest," I reply, holding up a hand in invitation.

Hallie throws me an encouraging smile before Lavinia leads her off into the crowd with their arms linked.

I let my eyes leave her for the first time all evening and turn, surveying the crowd of people congregated around the long bar.

I spot my friend, Lawson, and make my way to him. He's standing talking to Frankie Millington, a real estate agent with slicked back hair and receding morals. We've all known one another since college.

"Evening." I tip my chin at them.

"Sterling." Lawson's face lights up as he spots me. "You can settle this one for us. Frankie's got it in his head that Roman's missed out on tonight because Nina's got him on a tight leash."

I chuckle into my juice as I take a sip. Our friend, Roman, closed one of Manhattan's largest known deals on record for the sale of some commercial buildings. It's all just legal paperwork and negotiations to Roman, a lawyer who specializes in business and property litigation. But to Frankie, he might as well have hung the damn moon.

"I think you'll find he's at his cousin's wedding. And he asked Nina to go with him now that they've been dating awhile."

"Told you." Lawson raises his brows at Frankie, who shakes his head.

I exchange an amused look with Lawson. Frankie's first assumption is always that a woman is making demands. Possibly due to the messy divorce he's currently wrapped up in with his second wife.

"How's the gallery?" I ask.

Lawson adjusts his bowtie, tipping his head to one side. "It's good. But it would be even better if I could tie down another big name for a show. It's been months since we've generated enough buzz to get front page of *New York Magazine*. My contributors are getting impatient."

I slide one hand into my pant pocket. "How about Ashton Conti?"

"Keep talking." Lawson's lips curl into a smile.

"Sullivan helped him with his engagement ring. And Sinclair's friends with his fiancée."

"The mystery muse?" Lawson's smile transforms into a delighted laugh. "That was quite the story on the art circuit a couple of months back."

"I recall," I hum in amusement.

Maybe that's what prompted my daughter to contact Hallie. She saw her friend fall for an artist who fell in love with her without ever seeing her face. Sinclair probably thought it was a perfect example of the universe weaving its magic for love. She must have wondered what else it could do. Whether it could bring some light into her father's tormented existence.

"I'll swing by and see you at the club tomorrow. We can talk."

I nod. "You're buying lunch."

Frankie whistles.

"Is that the woman Sinclair hired for you? The matchmaker?"

My spine stiffens as I follow his beady eyes to Hallie, who's standing with Lavinia and chatting animatedly to a group of people.

"Halliday Burton," I confirm. "And she's a divine power facilitator."

"Divine... you can say that again," Frankie says.

He licks his lips, his eyes roaming over Hallie in her long silk dress that hugs her every curve. The back of it dips low. Far enough that I'm confident she isn't wearing a bra. But I've refrained from allowing my gaze to dip low enough over her front to check. My willpower can keep me from looking. But there's no telling how fast it could desert me if I were to glimpse her perfect tight nipples teasing beneath the silk of her dress.

I clear my throat. "She's not a damn steak, Frankie. Get your tongue back in your mouth."

"I'd rather get it in hers." He runs a hand around his jaw, eye-fucking Hallie without restraint.

My blood heats, rushing in my ears. "She's thirty," I snap.

Frankie chuckles, the sound making me want to rip his voice box out.

"Sounds like heaven. What I wouldn't give to have a younger woman bouncing on my balls. Bet she's got some energy."

He drinks her in until I adjust my position, blocking her from his eyeline. He leans to see around me, and I step to one side casually like I'm stretching my legs.

The glass in my hand threatens to shatter into pieces as I picture squeezing his neck.

"Isn't that what got you kicked out?" Lawson smirks.

"Thanks for the reminder," Frankie grunts, abandoning his attempts to watch Hallie. "Take it from me, gentlemen, if you're going to snort coke off a hooker's asshole and then fuck her there, don't record it for your personal use afterward. Wives find that shit like sniffer hounds."

Lawson snorts into his drink, and I muster every ounce of strength inside me not to drag Frankie outside right now and throw him under a cab.

"I'm going to go and introduce myself to the lovely Halliday," he purrs with a leery wink.

He takes a step, and I move forward so I'm toe to toe with him.

"No. You're not," I state flatly.

Something akin to understanding flashes in his eyes, and they spark with amusement as he opens his mouth.

But I'm not about to answer questions about my feelings toward Hallie to anyone. Especially Frankie.

A flash of red approaching catches the corner of my eye, and I take a calculated step at the perfect moment, causing the young woman to swerve to avoid me.

She crashes straight into Frankie's chest with a surprised gasp.

"My apologies," I say.

"Be more careful, Sterling," Frankie scolds as he steadies the blonde. "You almost knocked into this stunning woman."

"Katie," she pants, batting her eyelashes at Frankie.

"Katie," he repeats. "What a beautiful name." He feigns a look of concern that's as fake as a Canal street purse. "We should get you some water. You've had a shock. Allow me to help you. You don't feel lightheaded, do you?"

"No." She giggles, drinking up his attention.

"We need to make sure." He slides his hand around her wrist, cupping it with his fingers pressed against her skin. "Just as I thought. Your pulse is racing. You need to lie down. Come with me. I'll take you to the medical room."

He wraps his arm around her and throws a shit-eating grin over his shoulder at us as he leads her away.

"Bye, gentlemen," he calls.

Lawson chuckles. "That fucker."

"She didn't seem to mind," Sullivan clips as he joins us.

"Sorry, Son," I murmur.

He shrugs, not even glancing at the woman who had her eyes all over him earlier as she walks away with Frankie. He pulls out his phone and checks it.

"Don't be. Arabella's watching Molly. I want to get home."

"She still getting into bed with you?"

His face softens as he looks at the picture of Molly in a cat onesie that's his screensaver.

"We both get more sleep that way."

"Caving in to demands when she's not even three. Just wait until she's a teenager." I chuckle, tension leaving my body as a rare, genuine smile transforms my son's face.

"Like you didn't do it with the three of us." His smile falters as he realizes what he's just said.

"True." I clasp him on the shoulder. "I did. And I'd give anything to get to do it again. God knows I would."

"Yeah, wouldn't we all." He slides his phone into the inner pocket of his dinner jacket. "I have some people to speak to, then I'm heading out. I've already sent Sinclair home to sleep it off. I called Denver to collect her."

"Okay. Thanks, Son."

I don't push to talk about his comment. He won't thank me if I do. Sullivan rarely mentions what happened. It's the way he chooses to deal with it.

"No problem. It's not like she has a car to drive herself, even if she hadn't been drinking."

"True," I murmur.

Sinclair's car is in the workshop having another few hundred thousand crystals replaced after she banged it again. I wish she'd get herself something more practical. But if it makes her happy, then I don't have the heart to persuade her otherwise.

Happiness is worth grabbing on to however it comes to you.

"You don't need to keep checking on her. She's a big girl, she's doing fine without you over there."

I look away from Hallie across the room and meet Sullivan's eyes.

"I wasn't."

He shakes his head with a grunt.

"I was just thinking it's the first time I've seen her wear gray, that's all. It suits her."

"That's not gray, Dad."

"So it's silver. It looks good on her."

"Silver?" Sullivan arches a brow.

"That's what I said."

Lawson chuckles into his glass, his eyes scanning the room as he pretends he isn't listening to us.

"Sinclair told me it's a specific shade," Sullivan says, his voice low. "You know what it's called?"

My eyes slide over the curve of Hallie's hips from behind, and I swallow.

"Should I?"

My son leans closer, patting me on the back. "Apparently she's wearing *you*, Dad."

"Sterling silver," Lawson muses. "Well, you certainly do look good on her."

My eyes lock with Hallie's as she turns. She smiles, oblivious to the air that's been punched from my lungs.

She's thirty. She's not… She can never be… I can't allow myself to even consider it for a moment…

"Don't stay out too late, Dad," Sullivan warns before he walks away.

Lawson's eyes follow mine to Hallie, before he winks at me. "Or do."

10

HALLIDAY

The energy flowing from Lavinia is warm and inviting, and the way she talks about her fundraising is inspiring. She's a woman with a big heart and a lot to give. And I certainly didn't miss the way Sterling's hand left my back to embrace her the moment he saw her.

Energy tingled through my veins when Sterling picked me up this evening. It only intensified when we walked into the ballroom together. Could it be because Lavinia is here? It's the first time I've seen them together physically. I had a similar reaction when my last client met his date, who he's now engaged to. Similar, but not quite the same. But I can't read too much into that. Everyone's vibration is unique.

"You've known Sterling a long time. You must be close?"

Lavinia's light gray eyes sparkle as she reaches up to touch her earring. "Yes, Elaina and I were friends. I met him shortly after they got engaged."

"I'm so sorry you lost your friend."

She smiles sadly. "Thank you. Elaina was a wonderful person. A great mother."

"That's what Sterling says."

"I imagine it is. I'd expect nothing less than him to talk of her with fondness. He's a gentleman. Always has been." Her gaze flits across the room to where Sterling is watching us. He smiles at Lavinia and then carries on talking to Sullivan and the other man he's with. "I'm glad Sinclair hired you."

"You are?" Hope lifts my chest as she turns to me.

"He needs to see that he has options. And those include not being alone anymore. He has a lot to give and could make someone very happy. It would be a terrible waste for him not to realize that."

She blinks and looks away, fluffing her hair with one hand like she needs the distraction.

"Oh! There's Helen. You must meet her. She's one of the charity's board members."

◆

I fall into the backseat of the limo with a happy sigh as Sterling slides in beside me.

"Good night?"

His eyes sparkle as I turn to face him, resting my cheek against the cool leather headrest.

"Amazing." I beam. "Lavinia introduced me to so many people. A few asked about hiring me."

"Ah, but you'll need to have finished with me before that." Sterling smiles, soft lines creasing the corners of his eyes.

"I know." I roll my eyes dramatically. "Most difficult client ever."

He chuckles, resting his elbow on the door as he runs his hand around his silver-flecked jaw.

I met a lot of women tonight whose eyes lit up when Lavinia introduced me and explained to them that I'm helping

Sterling find love. A lot of women who were quick to slide their single status into conversation. I don't think he realizes how many admirers he had in that ballroom tonight. One of whom in particular, that had an insane amount of energy flowing from her whenever he looked in our direction.

"Lavinia was very complimentary about you."

I steal a sideways glance at Sterling when he doesn't respond. His eyes are narrowed as he gazes out of the limo's windows. His legs are spread wide, and he's reclined in his seat as if he's relaxed.

But I don't miss the way a muscle in his cheek flexes at her name.

"Especially when I told her I wished to donate, and she told me you'd already taken care of it... With three hundred thousand dollars," I add.

His brow scrunches. "Did I overstep?"

The deep rasp of his voice has delicious, tingling warmth wrapping around me like a cloak.

When I don't answer, he turns, pinning me with piercing blue eyes.

"Hallie? If I upset you, then I apologize. I could see the charity struck close to your heart, and I wanted to help."

"And... perhaps you could see the way I reacted when you told me what the minimum donation was?" I wince.

"Not at all." Sterling deflects smoothly, being the gentleman that Lavinia praises him to be.

"You're extremely generous." I stare out of the window, trying to form the words he needs to hear. "I should explain... I'm not as rich as the press articles make me out to be."

"Hallie, you don't need to—"

"I do." My apprehension melts away at the kindness waiting for me in his eyes. "The rumors went wild after I matched the Prince. And it's true that I have a long waiting list." I look at my dress and fiddle with the silk, twisting it between my fingers. "I've invested a lot of my fees, that's all. And the money isn't available to me—"

"Do you need help getting it back?"

Sterling's concerned tone makes me snap my eyes to his. He's sat forward in his seat, his full attention on me, like he's trying to gauge whether I'm in some sort of trouble.

"No. I don't want it back, I—"

He searches my eyes and exhales, sinking back in his seat, a soft smile lifting his lips.

"You gave it all to charity," he says.

I bite my lip as he watches me, something warm heating his gaze.

"Yes. I mean, most of it. Some I used to help Mum and Dad. And I invested a little in a rocket scheme. But that was in exchange for children from the charity that helped out family to be invited to see the engines being built. They'll love it," I gush.

"I'm sure." His eyes crinkle at the corners.

"I'm a terrible businesswoman. It's why I've only ever hired short-term help on occasion. I like to do everything myself because that means my overheads are lower and the charity can have more."

I press my fingertips to my lips and try not to laugh at the way Sterling's looking at me.

"What?"

He shakes his head and loosens his bow tie.

"You're perfect as you are."

Heat fizzes in my stomach at his words and I can tell he understands why I do it.

"Creating more love in the world is my legacy to Jenny. Doing it makes me happy. Makes me feel like I'm carrying a part of her with me."

His eyes soften. He has a way of looking at you and

making you feel like you're the most important person in the world.

That there's no place he'd rather be than in your company.

"Besides. What would I do with the money? Buy a mansion? Shoes?" I scoff. "I learned a long time ago that those things mean nothing on their own."

"You're wise beyond your years. Some people have their whole life to learn that lesson, and they still miss the class," he says with admiration.

"It's why I can never fail," I confess, my throat tightening. "I need to succeed, to maintain my reputation so I can keep donating. I can't let them down."

"You could never let anyone down, Hallie," Sterling says softly.

We hold each other's eyes, the air crackling between us, filling the interior of the limousine with something that's so electrically charged it could ignite at any moment, like a sky full of fireworks.

Our driver clears his throat. "There's an accident ahead, Mr. Beaufort. We could be here awhile."

Sterling surveys the gridlocked street ahead.

"I see."

He appears deep in thought as he checks his watch.

"My club is two blocks away."

"You're suggesting a nightcap on a Thursday?"

He chuckles at the teasing look I throw at him.

"Only a quick one. You can use your excruciatingly difficult client as an excuse to leave early."

I shrug. "Naturally. What's the alternative? Spending all night together?"

The second the words leave my mouth, I clamp it shut. He clears his throat, his eyes darkening.

It was a joke, of course. But one that's highly inappropriate of me to make. Not to mention, completely out of character.

He's my client.

"I, um..." I frown as my phone rings in my bag. I pull it out, the light of the screen bright inside the dim backseat.

Rory.

I grimace and send it to voicemail. It's already vibrating again in my hand as I flick the button to turn it onto silent.

"You know what? That sounds great." I shove my phone back inside my clutch. "Let's go and have that drink."

◆

I manage half a block before goosebumps win over, popping up over my arms and causing my teeth to chatter.

Sterling slides his tuxedo jacket off. He moves in front of me and wraps it around my shoulders, bringing the lapels together. The smooth lining of the jacket brushes over my puckered nipples which makes heat bloom in my cheeks.

"Thank you." I look at him, but his attention is fixed above my head like he doesn't want to look at me.

I breathe in his scent, already feeling my goosebumps disappearing. He glances at his jacket, his shoulders softening at the way it swamps me, keeping me warm.

"Of course. I should have offered the moment we stepped out of the car. I'm sorry."

"You don't need to apologize. It's not your fault I didn't plan ahead and bring a jacket."

"Ah, but you weren't expecting to be walking around Manhattan on a Thursday night to go for a drink with an old man."

"Fifty isn't old. I mean, look at you." I tip my head toward his broad chest in his crisp white shirt. The fabric is snug across his biceps, and I rip my eyes away from them before I lose myself to thoughts of how they'd look without the shirt. "You're a fox," I add.

He tucks both hands in his pant pockets, his lips twitching as he glances to his feet and then back up in a way that's full of a boyish charm that makes him look younger.

"A fox?" He arches a brow.

"You know? A silver fox. A hot and sexy older guy? One women would kill to be with. I met enough willing candidates this evening." I smirk and bump his shoulder with mine as we start to walk again.

"This is the part you tell me you're setting me up on another date, isn't it?" He sighs.

"You could try sounding even less thrilled about it?" I tease, but he remains silent.

"Sinclair got home okay. She texted me," I say, eager to break the sudden tension that's rolling off him.

He exhales, his jaw loosening. "She did. Denver came for her."

"Your head of security?"

"That, and a good friend. He's worked with our family for years now. Since before we lost..."

"I'm sorry," I whisper.

I pray he knows he isn't alone. That I'll walk beside him whenever he needs me to.

"Being a parent," he continues, "it makes you vulnerable. Opens you up to the possibility of the worst pain imaginable."

A lump thickens in my throat as my mind flits to Mum and Dad in those first months after we lost Jenny.

Before I can respond, we arrive at a large black door beneath a green awning. It's flanked by two doormen in black suits.

"Boss. Ma'am," they both acknowledge as one opens the door for us.

Sterling tips his chin in greeting and places his hand on my lower back as we walk inside. He leads me down a low-lit hallway. The sound of piano music, accompanied by sultry singing floats toward us.

He opens a large ornate door for me, and we walk into the main bar of Seasons.

My senses are immediately flooded.

The space is sumptuous. It smells of rich cognac and wood. Green velvet seats, candlelit booths and intimate tables are spread around the room, beneath crystal chandeliers. All of them face toward a small, raised stage where a grand piano sits, being played beautifully by a young man as an older woman in a glittery dress sits on a tall stool and sings.

Her voice is soothing, bringing a sense of peace and security with it.

"They're spectacular," I say to Sterling, unable to tear my eyes away from the lady with short white hair as she sings with grace and elegance.

"They are," he agrees. "Angela's retired from Broadway. She sings here Thursday through Saturday. And Vincent plays every night we open. He doesn't like anyone else touching his piano."

He leads me to a small table and pulls out the chair for me. I sit and smile as he takes the seat beside mine.

"This place is truly beautiful." I gaze around.

"I'm glad you like it."

A server appears and places two glasses down.

"Non-alcoholic," Sterling assures as I glance at the matching tumblers of deep amber liquid.

"Thank you," I breathe, shrugging his jacket from my shoulders. The fabric brushes my nipples, making them harden as I slide it off.

Sterling watches as my dress is uncovered and his eyes flash with something, before he pushes his thumb and finger into their sockets and rubs.

"Are you okay?" I ask in concern. "What you said before we came in, about parents and that pain, I... My mum and dad have said the same after losing Jenny. I can't... I mean..."

He removes his thumb and finger from his eyes, and the way he looks at me has me reaching into his lap and gathering his hand up in mine.

"You can talk to me, is what I'm trying to say. If you want to that is?" I offer.

His gaze drops to my hand wrapped around his with a frown, and a vein in his temple pulses.

"Or not," I offer with a small smile. "I'll be your silent companion if you like? And we can just enjoy this beautiful music together."

I squeeze his hand and let it go.

I look toward the stage and watch Angela and Vincent. The song they're performing together carries me away to a place where no pain exists. To where there is only peace and calm. I breathe out slowly, lost in every word about love and heartache that passes her scarlet lips.

One song flows into another, and as Vincent plays the opening chords, something warm and a little rough slides over the back of my hand.

Sterling dusts his thumb over my knuckles, back and forth, caressing my skin like the notes of the beautiful melody that surrounds us.

"She was in love with someone else."

The low confession is barely more than a hoarse exhale from his lips, like if he says it quietly enough, then it never really happened.

"Elaina?"

The depths of his pain swallows me whole as I turn to him, my breath suspended in my throat.

"Yes. My *wife*."

He exhales, and his entire body goes slack as he leans back in his chair.

My hand is now clasped inside his. I don't know when it happened. When he became the one doing the holding, the protecting. But the way he's keeping ahold of it is as if he needs it to tether himself to reality. As though holding me stops him from becoming lost to the anguish misting his eyes.

He looks toward the stage.

"I know she loved the kids. And she tried to love me. But it wasn't enough. I wasn't him."

My stomach knots.

"Who?"

His eyes are dull as he turns back to me, a heaviness weighing him down in a way he's never allowed me to witness before.

"Neil." He scrubs a hand down his face before reaching for his glass with his free hand and having a drink. "Elaina's first love. Her *only* one. He was always her first choice, even after all those years."

"I don't understand."

"We never chose each other, Hallie. It was decided for us. Elaina got pregnant when she was eighteen. Neil got out of here as fast as he could once she told him. Coward," he hisses. "Her parents went crazy because she wasn't married."

"Elaina was pregnant?"

Sterling sighs. "Was. She lost the baby not long after the wedding. Her parents saw a problem and mine saw an opportunity. Neil hadn't been gone a week before they got together and decided the two of us would marry. She wouldn't be a single mom, and I'd help grow the family business. Elaina's parents had links to mines in Africa. Our union made Beaufort Diamonds into what it is today. A globally acclaimed brand."

He places his glass on the table. "She didn't want it. I only went along with it because of my parents, and because what scared her more than marrying a man she didn't love, was to be alone with a baby she couldn't provide for. Her parents were going to disown her. And she and I were friends. It killed me to see her so terrified."

"God, Sterling, that's awful."

"I often wondered whether the stress of it all is what caused her to miscarry not long after. I'd never seen a woman grieve like that before. I didn't know how to help her. Then she came to me one night, needing comfort, begging me to give her a reason to carry on again. It was the one time. Two people lost together. We were only kids ourselves really. Then nine months later, Sullivan..."

His grip on my hand tightens, and I grab both of our hands.

"I had no idea," I whisper.

"Not many people know. Elaina's family kept her first pregnancy a secret. They thought it was a scandal. I'm not telling you so you'll give me sympathy. I've been blessed in my life. With my children. My business. Elaina and I might have been forced together, but we made it work. We had the kids. It wasn't the magic you talk about. I was never her first choice, but it was real until..."

His eyes cloud over.

"What changed?" I ask softly.

His gaze drops to our entwined hands, and he traces along my knuckles with his thumb. When he speaks again, I feel every sharp edge of his words, tearing at me.

"I found letters after she died. A whole box of them she'd hidden. Neil had gotten back in touch with her. For months she'd been meeting up with him... fucking him in hotels... and in our house. In our own damn bed. Telling him she'd never stopped loving him after all these years. There were photos of them together, arms around one another like they were on honeymoon without a care in the world. But do you know what hurt the most? More than the lies? The cheating?"

I shake my head, unable to speak as my eyes sting with tears.

"It's the way she looked at him. The fact that after years together, having our children, all that we'd been through, she never once looked at me like that."

"Like what?" I choke, my heart breaking for him as he looks at me with shining eyes.

He smiles sadly. "Like everything started and ended with me. Like I was at the center of every dream she'd ever had."

"Sterling..." I lean closer, wishing I could erase the pain from his eyes and make it go away forever.

"I shouldn't be angry about it. Or hurt. I loved her for being the mother of our children. And she was a damn good mother. And the truth is, I never looked at her like that, either."

He looks deep into my eyes, and his soften, as though sharing his deepest thoughts with me has brought him a sense of peace.

"I didn't love her the way she should have been loved. The way she must have felt when she was with him. I should have known as soon as the arguments increased that she was unhappy with me. But I thought it'd pass, the same way it always did whenever she would pick fights about nothing. I knew I wasn't enough and that she needed more. I should have told her it was okay if she wanted to leave. She'd have never left the kids, but I should have told her she had that option if it would have made her happy. It's as much my fault as it was hers."

"No." I shake my head. "She lied to you, she cheated on

you. She should have talked to you as soon as she heard from him. You... you..." I splutter, my voice cracking with emotion. "She hurt you even more than she needed to. And you never got the chance to hear it from her."

"Don't worry about me." His eyes roam over my face. "I'm a grown man. But now you know the truth. I'm a fifty-year-old who's never been in the kind of love that you work with every day. My chance has passed. You being here with me, it's holding you back. *I'm* holding you back."

"You're not."

"Hallie," he murmurs. "Listen to me. Sinclair knows everything. So does Sullivan. They were there with Uncle Mal when I found the letters. It's why Sinclair had this notion in her head about me dating again. She's like you. She believes in magic. And that's okay. In fact, it's beautiful, and I hope neither of you ever lose that. But she's wasting her time focusing on me. And so are you."

"No. You're wrong."

Sterling sighs, dropping his gaze to his drink.

"You're wrong," I repeat firmly. "Everyone should experience that magic. The soul-altering connection."

He lifts his tired eyes to mine, but there's a faint glimmer of hope in them, hiding deep down. He just needs help bringing it to the surface.

"You're going to say including me, aren't you?" he says.

"Especially you!"

I lift our joined hands and press them against the silk of my dress, over my heart.

"I'm so sorry," I say, my chest rising and falling with deep, emotional breaths. The warmth of his hand seeps through my dress and spreading over my skin. "I'm here now. And I promise you I'll help you find your soulmate. I'll do everything I can to bring you the love that you deserve."

Sterling's eyes drop to his hand against my chest, and he sucks in a breath.

"Hallie."

The hoarse rasp of my name from his lips has guilt filling my every pore. I've allowed myself to become distracted. Too dazzled by the new friendship and things I have in common with him to be focused on why I'm here.

To give him what he's never had. Someone who looks at him the way he described. The way he deserves.

To find him love.

"I'll find her. I won't leave you until I find her."

"What if that means you have to stay forever?" he says.

Tingles erupt over my skin. He must feel my shudder because his pupils dilate.

"I won't leave until you're happy. I promise you."

11

STERLING

"An extra three hundred thousand? Really, Dad?"

Sullivan grunts as I drive my fist into the pad he's holding.

"Sounds like an expensive date if you ask me," Mal quips from the workout bench, a towel slung around his shoulders, sweat dripping from his brow.

"I don't recall asking either of you. And it wasn't a date." I fire another jab toward my son.

He stands firm and catches it, his eyes glinting.

"What?" I huff.

"Nothing. Just got some extra power behind your hits today, that's all."

"He'll need it if he wants to keep up with her," Mal sniggers. "You remember Halliday's thirty?"

"You think I don't damn well know how old she is?"

I tear my boxing gloves off and drop them on the floor, slumping onto a bench and resting my elbows on my knees to get my breath back.

"You've got it wrong. I made an extra donation on her behalf, that's all. The charity needs it more than I do."

Sullivan grunts. "I thought she has her own money."

I roll out my tense shoulders. They're a pair of vultures. All Mal's talked about since we began our workout is Halliday accompanying me to the fundraiser. And Sullivan's been giving me knowing looks ever since he overheard Lavinia calling to thank me for the extra donation.

"She does," I clip.

My son hitches a brow but lets it drop. It's not his place to comment on how Hallie spends her money. If she chooses to donate most of it away that's her decision. I admire her for investing in something that means a lot to her. Yet, I can't shake the uneasiness in my gut when I think of her as a child, shouldering the responsibility of caring for her sister. Every cell in my body is urging me to find a way to support her so she never has to worry again. Spoil her. Give her everything she could ever need or want.

It's a living, breathing compulsion that I can't act upon. Because she isn't mine. And I'm selfish for even hoping there was a way she could be.

I'm shackling her to me. Stealing her future from her, one day at a time. As long as she's here, she's stuck. She won't leave until she completes her job to find me love.

But no matter how hard she looks she won't find what she's searching for.

There is no woman she will ever meet who can fill that void.

Because every inch of it is spilling over with thoughts of her.

I've fought against it, denied it, told myself it's ridiculous, that she's young enough to be my daughter, that I'm a creep for even looking at her.

But it's still there.

This unexplainable pull.

My pulse races and my blood heats the moment she walks

into a room. I want to invent reasons to touch her, to inhale her scent. To look into her eyes, admire their beauty, count the flutters in her neck her pulse makes when I say her name. Hear her talk about vibrations and energy. Watch her place crystals around with that serene smile of hers.

I want to watch everything she does, see every moment her face lights up the way it does when she's excited.

I want it *all*.

Everything pales into the background when she's near me. All I see is her.

I scrub my hands through my hair. Beads of sweat run down my naked torso, through my chest hair.

"Monty, watch your paws!"

I snap my head up.

Sinclair shrieks and swoops down, gathering the dog into her arms before he steps into a puddle of fresh sweat on the floor.

Hallie steps through the door behind her.

My mouth goes dry.

I jump to my feet, turning my back and grabbing my long-sleeved workout top, pulling it on as fast as I can.

Hallie's eyes bounce up from my naked back as I turn to face her.

"Sorry for showing up without calling. Sinclair said you'd be here," she says.

"No need to apologize."

I pick up my towel and rub it around my hairline.

She steps closer with a tray of fresh juices.

She watches me, her lips parting as I lift my chin and dry my neck, before slinging the towel over one shoulder.

"That for us?" Mal asks, tipping his head at the tray.

"Sure is." She holds it out so he can take one. She hands another to Sullivan, and then offers the final one to me.

"You didn't need to do that." I close my hand around the cup, my fingers brushing hers as I take it.

"It's called 'buttering you up' back home."

"Buttering me up?" I arch a brow, and her eyes sparkle as she grins.

"It means I'm trying to get you in a good mood so you'll say yes to what I'm going to ask you."

"Ah, I see." I lean closer, catching the scent of oranges and honey, and lower my voice. "Tell me what you need and it's yours."

Her eyes widen slightly as she blinks up at me. "Um... just your undivided attention?" She snags her lower lip between her teeth.

"You've always got that."

She lets out a cute little laugh, brushing off my comment.

"Tomorrow night, then? I can set it up?" She glances at Sinclair and then Sullivan and Mal. "Will you all be able to make it? I thought a big dinner with everyone would be perfect."

The excitement rolling off her makes me smile, but I hide it by taking a sip of juice when I catch Sullivan watching our interaction with growing interest.

"A big dinner?" Mal asks, slurping his drink and pulling an impressed face at the taste.

"Yes. With all of you, and your wife, Trudy, isn't it? And some of your work colleagues you're close to? Arabella?" She looks at Sullivan. "And Molly, of course. And Denver, and whoever else you want to invite."

"Sounds more like a wedding party. Do we need to send out invites?" Mal chuckles.

"It's going to be so much fun." Hallie beams, looking at me. "And I'm inviting someone special."

"A date for my father?" Sullivan says. "Why, it sounds perfect, doesn't it, Dad? Just what you wanted."

He throws me a dark look which Hallie doesn't see.

"So I can book us somewhere?" she asks me, her cheeks glowing.

I swallow down the acid rising up my windpipe. The thought of going on another date and not only having Hallie there watching us, but everyone else as well, makes me wish I could say no to her.

"Sterling?"

My name is a plea from her soft lips, disintegrating any excuses I could make.

I can't deny this woman anything. She could ask me for the moon and I'd find a way to get it for her.

"Why don't I get chefs in at Seasons? We can dine there before it opens," I suggest.

"Really? That would be incredible."

My reasons for suggesting my club are selfish. I can escape should I wish to. Say I'm going to get a bottle of wine and take my time. Pretend something came up in the kitchen with the chefs that I had to assist with.

I'd rather do anything than sit next to a woman all night who I don't know and have no interest in getting to know.

A woman who isn't Hallie.

"Just give me a time and I'll arrange the rest."

"You don't need to do that. It was my idea."

"I'll take care of it. I want to take care of it."

"In that case, thank you. Let's say seven. I'll meet you there early, although I don't think we'll need to go over much beforehand. She isn't a stranger."

"Who is she?" I ask, apprehension slithering up my spine.

Hallie gives me a coy smile and pats me on the chest. "You'll see."

12

HALLIDAY

"I really admire the charity work you do; it's inspiring," I say, smiling brightly at Lavinia seated next to me at the table.

"You're too kind, Halliday," she replies before her gaze tracks to Sterling sitting opposite her.

"It is inspiring." He nods his agreement, but it lacks any depth. I narrow my eyes at him in question, but he holds my gaze unperturbed.

He complimented Lavinia when she arrived and has made all the usual dinner conversation with everyone at the table, being his usual charming self. But he's wearing a practiced smile that doesn't reach his eyes.

He's got his defenses up, but why?

"Dad? Zoey said Ashton is doing a show next month at Lawson's gallery. Why don't you and Lavinia go? You bought one of his pieces, didn't you?" Sinclair says, her eyes brimming with hope as they volley between Lavinia and Sterling.

"Oh, I love his work," Lavinia chirps enthusiastically.

Hope swells my chest at the open energy flowing from her.

But Sterling's wearing an unreadable expression. His eyes pinch at the corners before he smiles politely at Lavinia.

"I'd be happy to escort you," he answers, but it lacks any real enthusiasm.

Sinclair smiles. "Perfect."

Sterling's eyes move to my face, and my cheeks heat.

He doesn't want to be here. He's managing to hide it well, but I've picked up on some of his quirks since we met. Like the way he takes a sip of his drink, letting the conversation move on before he has to respond to something he'd rather not discuss. And the way he leans back in his chair subtly, distancing himself whenever Lavinia leans forward to talk to him.

No one else seems to notice, but I do, and I can't understand why. The energy across the table is palpable. The air between Sterling's and Lavinia's seats is practically sizzling. Her aura, tinged with pink—symbolizes openness to love and romance. Sterling's, however, is conflicted. Blending red and indigo—indicating passion and connection—but also black, which means a blockage. More than one color at once can be a sign that someone is in the midst of a change or has a lot on their mind.

Around the table, Mal sits at one end with his wife, Trudy. Sullivan's PA, Arabella, a sweet-looking woman who must be in her late forties is opposite them. She's spent most of the evening talking and playing with Molly, who's sitting between her and Sullivan. Sinclair told me she used to be Sterling's PA, but when Sullivan took over the running of Beaufort Diamonds, she became his instead.

Sinclair is beside Sterling, opposite Denver. He's only spoken when he's been asked a direct question. Like when Sinclair asked him if he was jealous that Killian and Jenson are in Cape Town, and he was left behind in New York.

"And you get left here with us." She'd laughed. "Bummer.

You could have been letting loose with cocktails and all those hot girls at the beach like those two are."

"Killian and Jenson have a job to do, and they'll be doing it." Denver had all but growled.

"Yeah, I'm sure they are." She'd rolled her eyes. "Not switching out of work mode for a moment, just like their boss, huh?"

Denver ignored her jibe. She's annoyed that Sullivan called him to collect her from the fundraiser. She told me as such. She said it isn't the first time Denver's been called to take her home, and she hates feeling like he's been sent to babysit her.

We needed extra guests, like Denver and Arabella, who weren't partnered up. This needs to feel like a group of friends casually having dinner together, because Lavinia has no idea it's also serving as a date for her and Sterling.

But judging from the way her attention has been glued on him all night, I don't think she would have objected if I'd told her it was.

"You feed baby now?"

I turn toward Molly, who's toddled down the table and squeezed herself in between mine and Denver's chairs. She looks at me with wide, innocent eyes, a mop of adorable dark curls on her head as she presents her baby doll to me like it's the most precious thing in the world.

"Me?"

She nods, her little chubby cheeks rosy as she thrusts the doll into my arms.

"Oh, thank you." I take my time admiring the baby. "What's baby's name?"

"Baby," she says with all the cute seriousness that a two-year-old can muster.

"Baby," I repeat softly. "And I'm allowed to feed baby?"

Molly pushes the doll's head against my chest. "Feed baby," she repeats.

"Molly? Bring baby back here, Sweetheart," Sullivan calls.

"Baby needs feeding first," I reply, smiling at her.

She beams, her tiny white milk teeth on display. On her dress, there's a little round sticker featuring a picture of fruit, with the text, *Peach for the stars*.

I hold the doll against my breast, stroking its cheek gently as I pretend to nurse it. Molly watches with her bottom lip poking out before she declares baby has had enough. I carefully hand the doll back to her, and she goes to Sullivan and gives it to him. He places it up on his shoulder, patting its back as Molly climbs into his lap.

He wraps his arm around her, and she snuggles into his side, playing with his tie.

"Baby loves you, Daddy."

He continues to soothe the toy through an imaginary burp and kisses Molly's head. "And I love you and baby. I'm a very lucky daddy."

Molly giggles and pats the doll's back with him.

The usually stiff Sullivan doting on Molly with such adoration fills me with warmth. I turn to Sterling to see if he's noticed, but the moment I look across the table, his eyes meet mine, as if he's been watching me all along. They're darkened with a simmering heat that steals my breath.

"So sweet," Lavinia coos.

I swallow as Sterling holds my eyes over the rim of his glass and takes a sip. His eyes are burning like two blue flames. He places his glass on the table with a forceful thud, then he's on his feet.

"Excuse me." He clears his throat, buttons up his jacket, and slips out of the room.

I rise to my feet, my excuse about heading to the restroom unnecessary because the table has broken into smaller pockets of conversation, and no one notices as I leave.

I hurry down the corridor, bypassing the restrooms, and

head toward the strip of light glowing under Sterling's closed office door. The pleated skirt of my wrap dress settles against my thighs as I pause outside and take a deep breath.

I knock harder than I mean to.

"Come in."

I step inside, leaving the door partially open.

"Why are you fighting it? Do you think you don't deserve it, is that it?"

All thoughts of gently easing into this conversation evaporate at the sight of him sitting behind his desk, one hand running across his silver-flecked jawline.

"Hallie," he says wearily, like he knew I'd follow him and was hoping I wouldn't.

"I don't understand." I storm to his desk, planting both palms on the dark wood and leaning over it.

"What's there to understand?"

"Really?" I snap in exasperation. "Come on... I can feel the energy racing out of you, even now. It was practically clawing its way across the table back there." I shoot an arm out, pointing back through the open door. "But you're holding back, and I don't understand why."

"Clawing its way across the table?" He chuckles, but his eyes lack amusement.

"Yes! I felt it at the fundraiser too. And Lavinia's giving back just as much."

He hums, running his hand over his jaw again.

I want to smack it away and force him to listen to me. Really listen.

"Look, I've been doing this long enough to know energy like that when I feel it. She's attracted to you. And I think you're attracted to her. But something's stopping you."

"Lavinia is just a friend."

Irritation flares up my spine. I want to help him, but he needs to meet me halfway. Or a quarter. *Something.*

"She lost her partner too." I soften my voice and straighten from the desk, adopting a gentler approach. "You could open up to her. Maybe she can be more than a friend."

"I could."

I stare him down, refusing to break his gaze. But defeat weighs heavy on my shoulders, and I exhale wearily.

"But you won't."

His response is crystal clear from the unwavering return of his darkened gaze.

But I refuse to let him give up, to believe he's missed his chance or that he doesn't deserve another.

"Maybe another date? Some more time with her? I could arrange—"

"Stop."

"Let me help you," I plead. "She's a lovely woman, she's—"

"We slept together once, and I regretted it before it was even over!"

The air is sucked from the room as his sudden revelation bites through the gap between us.

He holds my eyes before cursing softly and shaking his head.

"I'm sorry if that's wrong of me to say, but it's the truth. I never looked at another woman after losing Elaina, despite what she did. Not until the anniversary of their deaths and I…"

He stands up and walks out from behind his desk. Slipping his hands into his pant pockets, he exhales. "Lavinia dropped by to check on me. I was still so angry about what Elaina did with Neil. I'd been drinking and I saw a way to get revenge with Elaina's friend, or at least feel something other than betrayed for a change."

"Sterling," I murmur, hating the way his face is screwed up like he detests himself.

"I faked my own damn orgasm." He grimaces. "Have you ever heard a man say that? Neither of us has ever mentioned it since. But it's why every time she asks me to take her to a play or be her plus one at an art show, I agree. Because I feel guilty for involving her in my selfish, stupid actions. So damn guilty."

"Why didn't you tell me?"

"Why didn't I tell you?" he repeats.

I nod, and he stiffens.

"I didn't tell you, Hallie, because talking to you about women I've had sex with feels more wrong than anything else I've ever done." He tips his head toward the ceiling with a curse. "... So damn wrong."

Realization over how wrong I've been settles like a lead weight in my gut.

"It's my fault. I swear I thought there was something there."

"There isn't."

I falter, wondering whether to reach out to him. To ease the turmoil creasing his brow. This is my doing.

"I'm so sorry. I thought with what I was feeling and picking up on.... I've never gotten it so wrong before."

No matter what I say, it won't change the fact I screwed up. I'm supposed to bring joy to my clients. But looking at Sterling's tightly clenched jaw, I can see how epically I've failed him.

"I'm sorry," I repeat weakly. "I can fix this, I can—"

"You can't, Hallie."

The finality of his words makes the air in my lungs burn. I always thought I couldn't fail, because if I did, then my large donations would cease. Jenny's charities would suffer. Other families like mine would pay the price. But now, it's something else that's making my mouth dry and my eyes sting.

It's the thought of Sterling feeling as alone as the defeat in his voice suggests.

"I promised you I'd help. Tell me what I can do." I take a tentative step toward him.

"You want to know what you can do?" He arches a thick brow, watching me move closer.

"Tell me what you need. What you want." I stand close enough that his breath falls against my face as I look into his eyes.

His gaze traces down my face, along my jaw, over my lips, until finally coming to rest on my eyes.

He's struggling to let me in. He must be wishing he never met me.

"Why don't you start by telling me what you don't want?" I suggest.

"What I don't want?" He places his hands on his hips like he needs to grip on to something.

I nod, desperate for a sparkle of light I can grab onto in the darkness. One I can use to pull him free.

"I don't want Lavinia," he grits.

"Okay." I nod, encouraging him to continue.

"I don't want to hear any more about a single other woman you've got lined up for me to meet."

I hold back my frown. "Okay."

"I don't want you to set me up on any more damn dates," he growls.

His eyes darken and drop to my mouth, cutting off my protest.

"No more, Hallie. It stops now. I'm not attracted to them. I will *never* want them."

"You're sure?"

A muscle ticks in his jaw, and he sucks in a breath.

"I'm damn sure. You know why?"

I shake my head, my voice stolen.

"Because none of them consume my every thought. None of them keep me awake at night because I can't stop thinking about them for even one goddamn minute. No one has ever done that to me before. Not Elaina. Not anyone." His eyes take on a wildness, like a hunter watching its prey. "Until now," he rasps.

My core clenches as he leans a fraction closer, and the heat of his body fills the small space between us.

He licks his lips before continuing, a gesture so natural yet it sends bursts of light racing through me as if I'm witnessing something extraordinary. "Now I wake every single night. It's like my blood has been lit by a fire she started with her smile, her laugh... her very essence."

"Who is she?" I whisper.

His lips thin into a grim smile.

"Who is she?" he repeats.

I gulp as he stares into my eyes.

"Hallie. If you honestly don't know the answer to that, then it's best we finish this conversation here. I'll settle whatever is outstanding, and we terminate your contract, and you board a flight to London."

My heart pounds so fiercely I'm scared it might burst out of my chest and fly into his perfectly tailored suit.

I sweep my gaze over his hair, more silver than dark now, then over his face, his silver brushed jawline, cut so sharply that if I were told touching it would result in my fingers coming away coated in blood, I'd believe it.

As handsome as he would have been aged twenty, thirty, forty, it's breathtakingly obvious that the wisdom, the confidence, the effortless gentlemanly charm he now possesses, have only made him more mesmerizing. Alluring.

Time has transformed him. Given him something else.

He is something else.

Tingles race down my arms, and I wiggle my fingers to

check they're still attached. The back of my neck grows hot, and the sound of my own breath echoes in my ears.

"Me?"

His eyes soften.

"You, Baby girl."

Those gently spoken words make me suck in a sharp breath.

He holds my eyes as I process them. *I knew.* Every cell in my body knew deep down. All the energy I've felt. The way I reacted to Sullivan when I met him, a tiny hint from their shared genes at what was to come when I met the man himself. Even the way I felt something flowing off him across the table tonight.

It wasn't because of Lavinia sitting next to me.

It was me. All because of me.

"I don't know what to say," I whisper.

"You don't know what to say?"

I shake my head, my lips parting with a splintered breath. "I…"

He slides his hands around my neck, cradling beneath my jaw and tilting my face up. His body presses against mine, bringing with it the scent of him I love so much. A grounding calm soothes my racing nerves, leaving behind a hunger… an insatiable one growing and reaching up from my core.

I slide my palms over his solid chest, feeling the heat seeping through from his skin.

He searches my eyes as I stare back, dumbstruck.

"Why don't you tell me if it still needs work?"

"What—?"

He slants his mouth over mine, stealing the words straight from them. A whimper climbs up my windpipe, escaping into his mouth as he kisses me with the skill of a man who knows exactly how to set energy racing through my veins. With soft lips, he commands all of my senses until I'm surrounded by him. Feeling his warmth, his solid strength, tasting him as he holds me to him.

"Oh my god," I moan when he lets me break for a breath, before sinking straight back into our kiss again.

A deep groan vibrates in his throat, and he slides his tongue into my mouth, making my legs weak. I wobble, and he grasps my hip, steadying me.

I let out a soft moan, opening myself fully to him, inviting him to give me everything. To show me everything.

His kiss deepens, each slip of his tongue against mine, every pass of our lips overwhelming my thoughts and my body, igniting explosions of pure bliss throughout me.

Dragging me toward a place of no return.

"Stop!" I pull away, panting.

My fingers fly to my tingling lips, expecting to feel stardust there.

"Hallie?" Sterling's voice is saturated with the same concern that's overtaken his eyes.

"I... I..." I move backward, creating space between us.

He steps toward me, and I step back.

We're in a dance, our eyes locked together.

We reach the doorway within seconds. Sterling's eyes dart toward it, and he swallows thickly as if he's considering the possibility I might bolt out of it.

My back hits the door and forces a breath from my lungs.

"Do you want to leave?"

"I... I..." My head and my heart and my body are all at war against one another.

"Hallie?" Sterling rasps. "Do you want to leave?"

I stare at his parted lips. Lips that were on mine mere moments ago. Lips that kissed me and made me feel what can only be described as something magical.

I shake my head, one word uttered out with blissful submission.

"No."

He exhales, and his breath fans over my lips.

"Good."

He places one palm against the wood above my head and slowly pushes. I move back with the door, jolting as it clicks closed.

He flicks the lock slowly.

The click echoes around the room and makes my nipples pucker into tight peaks through my dress.

Sterling's eyes drop to them, and I look at him through my lashes. He cups my chin, his thumb easing my teeth from my snagged lower lip as he holds my gaze.

"Baby girl," he breathes.

His broad chest expands, and I lift my hands to touch him, needing to feel the way his lungs fill with air, desperate for more oxygen after the soul-awakening kiss he gave me. His eyes are intent on mine as I relish feeling his life beneath my palms, the deep, steady beats of his heart.

"It needs more work," I whisper.

He arches a brow, his pupils blowing wide as I lose myself in his gaze.

"More?"

I nod. "More."

His eyes spark, and we crash together, a ball of bright buzzing energy. He lifts me into his arms, and I wrap my legs around his waist.

He moves away from the door and pins me roughly beneath his hard body and the wall.

The force of us crashing into it, hands and mouths devouring each other, sends his bookshelf shaking, and items topple off, crashing to the floor. Sterling ignores the chaos, groaning up a storm against my neck as he buries his face into it, kissing and sucking.

"So, so good," I whimper as he carries me to his desk,

blindly reaching out and swiping a stack of paperwork off it before he rests me on the edge.

He grips my outer thighs, bunching my dress around my hips. We kiss as if we're starved.

"Sterling," I gasp as a thick length presses against my inner thigh.

"Baby girl, this is so damn selfish of me. I'm twenty years older than you," he chokes at the same time I grab his belt with one hand and use it to yank him closer.

His cock is stuffed between the two of us, and I cry out as it rubs me through my panties.

My clit throbs painfully, and I wriggle against him.

"Hallie," he groans.

The sensation is so much better than anything I've ever felt before. His hot mouth, his deep, hoarse voice against my neck, breathing me in between fevered kisses he's pressing onto my blazing skin.

I stroke his jaw, skating along the rough stubble as I guide his mouth lower to where I ache to feel him.

"I want more. Please."

His gaze drops to the low neckline of my dress where I've forced his head. He drags his tongue over the swell of my breast above the fabric, leaving goosebumps behind.

"You want me to taste these delicious tits of yours, Baby girl?" He sucks on my skin with a deep moan as his eyes fall closed in ecstasy. He jerks back a fraction, letting out a rough curse. "Jesus, what am I saying?"

"Do it," I beg, arching my body back toward his mouth.

He groans like he's in physical pain before he yanks one side of my dress down. Cool air hits my nipple. He pauses for a beat, drinking me in.

The heat in his eyes as he glances at me has arousal soaking my panties.

Then he lowers his mouth and latches onto my nipple.

"God!" I arch into him, pleasure hurtling through me from where he's sucking and flicking his tongue over it. "Exactly like that," I cry.

It's like another force has taken over my body and the only thing that matters is having Sterling as close as I possibly can. I want to share every breath, feel every heartbeat, be warmed by every touch.

I reach for him, and my wrist grazes the head of his cock straining against his zipper.

He encircles my wrist, halting me before I can curl my hand around it to feel him pulsing in my palm.

"Baby girl, we've already crossed a line tonight."

My chest heaves with lust-fueled breaths as I lift my eyes to meet his.

Something seizes in my chest. Is he saying he doesn't want to? That he doesn't—

He groans, the sound laced with lust. "Believe me, I'll sprint over this one with you if that's what you want. But if we cross it, then you need to know that I'll fight so damn hard to keep you. No matter how selfish or wrong of me that is. I'll damn well worship you every day. I'll give you everything."

"Sterling..."

He holds my eyes, determination in his, backing up every word that he says next.

"If this is what you want, Hallie, then I'll take you home with me tonight. We'll call the whole damn matching thing off. It's your choice. One word and I'll make it all happen. One word."

My lips part but nothing comes out. I fight to make my tongue move. To form a syllable. To make a sound.

Silence.

Sterling strokes my wrist before he lets go. He gently straightens my dress, covering me up.

"You're my client," I choke out finally. "I..."

He cradles my face before pressing the softest of kisses to my forehead.

A kiss that makes my eyes sting with the threat of tears.

"It's okay. You don't need to explain. It's okay," he soothes.

He helps me down from his desk.

On shaky legs, I step around him, struggling to make sense of the emotions whirling around my head.

I've crossed a professional boundary. What the hell was I thinking?

I wasn't. I wasn't thinking. I let myself get carried away.

I almost ruined everything.

Clutching my hand to my mouth I walk to the door and unlock it, then glance back.

Sterling's gaze is cast downward to the pink rose quartz heart on his desk.

"I'm so sorry," I murmur and leave before his eyes have the chance to meet mine again.

13

HALLIDAY

Stupid, stupid, stupid.

It's repeating like a mantra in my head, re-playing last night's events over and over. I returned to the dinner table like nothing happened, followed by Sterling a few minutes later. I felt his gaze burning across the table for the rest of the evening, but I couldn't bring myself to look at him.

To face what I'd done.

He's my client.

I groan inwardly, pressing my fingertips to my aching temples and massaging them.

The coffee line grinds to a halt as a girl at the front reels off a long order. I don't mind the wait. Waiting in line is preferable to anything else I need to do today... like face Sterling.

My phone rings in my bag, and I pull it out.

"Dad?" I say as it connects.

"How are you, love? It's been a few days. Your mother and I were worried."

I almost smile for the first time since Sterling and I kissed.

Two days. It's been two days since I spoke to Mum and updated her on everything I've done here. All the sights I've seen, the shopping I've done with Sinclair, and the food we ate.

"I'm fine," I lie, failing to push past the tension that's fogged my head since I woke up. Even meditating hasn't taken the edge off.

"And work?"

"Great." Another lie.

"Oh well, that's good news. Your mother will be happy. She's missing you. She said you and her are going to watch that new movie when you come back. The one with that American fella in—what's his name?"

"Jay Anderson."

"That's him. Your mother's excited. We can get the guest room ready?"

The hope in his voice is like a barrel full of ants just tipped over in my stomach.

"Sure. Thanks."

Mum and Dad love when I visit home. I have my place in London that Sophie keeps an eye on for me when I'm away. Sometimes I let it out as an Airbnb if I think I'm going to be away for a while. Mum and Dad are always relieved when I take clients on closer to home. I know they worry with me being away.

And I know their house has felt too quiet and empty since we lost Jenny.

"Wonderful, wonderful." Dad's voice brims over with delight. "Thank you, love. You know how much this will mean to your mother."

"I can't wait to see you," I reply, moving along with the line as the girl with the big order gets served with two full take-out trays and leaves.

It's not a lie this time. I really can't wait to see them. I just didn't think I'd be going home having created such a huge mess here.

We chat a little more before I ring off and order a latte, standing at the counter to add sugar once I get it.

"Good night?"

I glance at the woman beside me and my spirits lift for the first time all morning.

"Zoey! Hey, how are you?"

"Good." Beaming, she takes her drink from the barista and thanks them.

"Sinclair told me last night was a success." She raises her brows at me in excitement, and the familiar guilt comes hurtling into my stomach.

"She did?"

"Uh-huh." Zoey holds the door for me as we both exit onto the street. "Is that why you're in the neighborhood? You going to do a de-brief with her dad?"

"Um." I bite my lower lip. "Something like that."

I've actually been walking the neighborhood where Seasons is for most of the morning trying to pluck up the courage to face him.

"I never really saw him with Lavinia." Zoey shrugs. "Although, I guess she's the only woman he's ever gone out with more than once. Usually he's a one and done guy."

I wince as I recall the photos I saw of Sterling with different women on his arm when I was researching ahead of my trip here. To the outside world, he looked like a man who was never short of female company. But photographs don't tell the whole story.

"I was never her first choice."

"I faked my own damn orgasm."

Sinclair hinted that she thought there had been other women since he lost their mother. Maybe after Lavinia, there were others?

I swallow down something that tastes like jealousy as it threatens to swirl from my gut.

"Sinclair's so excited. She said Sterling seemed different last night. Once you'd all left, she overheard Denver say something to him about lipstick on his jaw. Lavinia must have landed one on him when none of you were looking."

Something rises from my gut again, but this time it's not jealousy, it's bile.

"What's the matter? You look like you're about to barf."

"I…"

Zoey's dark brown eyes widen, the white of them bright against her rich skin as I struggle to answer.

"Halliday?" she coaxes.

I've always hated lying. I'm useless at it. I only allow myself the odd white lie, like to my father, to spare him and Mum from worrying about me. I'm sure people can see it written all over my face when I try.

I give her the briefest nod.

"Oh. My. God." She grabs my arm.

I glance at her giant twinkling engagement ring. Given to her by a man she's supposed to be with. Not one she was hired to help find love for, and then took a bite out of herself to quell her reckless desires. Not a man whose future happiness is in jeopardy from her actions.

"I didn't mean for this to happen. I wasn't supposed to match with him myself," I choke out.

"Fuck!" Zoey gasps.

She wraps an arm around me, steering me into a small park area and guiding me to a bench.

I slump into the seat gratefully as my legs wobble.

"Does he feel the same?"

"Yes."

She blows out a breath, leaning against the bench.

"Wow."

"You can say that again," I mutter.

She turns to me, her brow scrunching up in thought as she

meets my eyes, which I'm sure are filled with a mix of panic and guilt.

"Okay. Breathe. This isn't a bad thing."

"It isn't?" I stare at her, incredulous.

"No. Daddy Beaufort wants his English Queen. I mean, I can see why. You're driven and a little crazy, and so damn sweet. You're exactly the kind of person I would have put him with."

She holds my eyes with complete sincerity and despite the severity of the situation, I snort.

"The kind of person you'd put him with... except I'm twenty years younger? Oh, and he's my client." I screw my face up.

"Yeah." Her brow creases. "I get the client thing. But the age gap?" She shakes her head. "You're smart. You're a real bad-ass bitch building up your company the way you have. I mean, I imagine it's more like a meeting of minds, right? Do you notice his age when you're together?"

"No. He's just... Sterling."

I look down at my paper coffee cup and fiddle with the lid.

He's just Sterling. The man who told me to take my sister's photograph to a private viewing of the Statue of Liberty he arranged. The man who listens to me, who understands my past, my pain, my fears.

The man who understands *me*.

"And physically, Sterling's... Well, he's not like most guys his age, is he? Don't tell Sinclair I said this, but that man would blow guys half his age out of the water. And that whole suited gentleman vibe... Phew."

Zoey fans herself, and I'm grateful for her attempt to lighten the mood when all I see is darkness and uncertainty ahead.

"What am I supposed to tell Sinclair? She needs to know why I've failed her. Why I've failed him."

"Failed? No way." Zoey purses her lips. "Sinclair said the last couple of weeks are the happiest she's seen him in ages. Do you think she'll care that you're the one it's because of?"

"I—"

"Their family has been through so much. She wants him to be happy. It's all she's spoken about for months. It's like she refuses to get on with her own life until she knows he's okay. If you're worried about Sinclair's reaction, don't be. I mean that."

"God," I breathe, wrapping my hands around my coffee to keep them warm.

I want to believe her. I need there to be a way that I haven't screwed this all up.

"I don't know what to say. Thank you for making a hellish morning bearable."

Zoey returns my smile with one filled with hope. She's seen Sinclair go through the worst couple of years imaginable. I admire Zoey for wanting to latch on to the good in what's happened between Sterling and I. She wants there to be something to hold on to. Something that she thinks will bring not only Sterling, but her best friend, happiness.

But despite wishing I could share her optimism, I still can't.

Because that something isn't me.

It *cannot* be me.

He's my client. He lives in New York. A future with him would mean leaving my parents. Jeopardizing my reputation.

Jenny's charity will suffer.

I picture his face, recalling the way he called me *Baby girl* as he kissed me with a passion I only ever thought existed in the movies Jenny loved so much.

But none of that matters.

It cannot be me.

This time the universe has it wrong.

14

STERLING

"You've not put that thing down since we came back from lunch. What is it?"

I glance at Lawson, then loosen my grip on the rose quartz heart before sliding it into my pant pocket.

"A reminder of what I can't have," I murmur.

Lawson's brows rise but he doesn't push the subject.

"I need to head back. Ashton's coming in this afternoon to discuss the showing. Thank you for whatever you did there to get him to agree," he says.

I wave a hand in the air as we both rise from our seats. "It was nothing. Your gallery is the best in the city. He was going to call you anyway."

Lawson chuckles and claps a hand on my shoulder. "Right... Well, let me know if there's anything I can do for you. Anytime, okay?"

"Sure." I smile as I walk him out to the street entrance.

I've been back in my office a few minutes when a member of staff who has come in early to take care of the liquor delivery knocks at my door.

"Boss? Ms. Burton's here to see you."

"She is?"

I rise from my seat a little too fast and stride around my desk. I'm halfway to the door when he moves to one side and shows her in, closing the door behind her.

I halt.

We're standing a couple of feet apart, just looking at one another. Her eyes are filled with an uncertainty that hits me like a blow to the chest.

"Hallie?" I murmur, noting the way her pulse flutters in her neck at my voice.

I know what that neck tastes like now. The sounds she makes when she's writhing against me. The way her moans vibrate beneath my lips as I kiss her skin.

The feel of her nipple against my tongue as she shivers inside my arms.

"Sterling. I…" A beautiful blush stains her cheeks. "I came to apologize for last night. It was unprofessional of me. I should never have let my emotions take over like that. You gave me your trust and I abused it, and—"

I step forward, making her fall silent.

"Never apologize for anything you've done since you came into my life, you hear me? Not one damn thing."

Her eyes pinch at the corners as she blinks.

"I should be the one begging for your forgiveness," I rasp. "I wasn't a gentleman. I kissed you without asking first. Just because it felt like the best decision I've ever made doesn't mean I had the right to do it."

"You should always do what feels right, what your heart is telling you. And I'm just as guilty as you for what happened. But… it can't happen again."

I hang my head, running a hand over the tense lines marring my forehead. "I understand."

"You're my client. It's completely inappropriate. We got

carried away, that's all. We let our growing friendship cloud our judgment."

She looks at me with desperation, and I bite back the argument on my tongue. We both know it's a hell of a lot more than that. But she's here, asking me to pretend for her. What kind of man would I be if I were to deny her wishes? Force something that she clearly doesn't want?

"Of course," I reply smoothly.

I walk to the drinks cabinet, turning my back on her. I take my time pouring two glasses of iced water, willing the electricity in my veins to get back under control.

"Let me settle my daughter's account with you. And then—"

"And then?"

I turn and pass a glass to her, not missing the heaviness in her shoulders as she accepts it.

"And then you're free to do whatever you have planned next. I'll tell Sinclair I wasn't ready. You didn't fail, Hallie," I say softly. "I was just a bad client."

She sniffs, looking away from me. The urge to wrap her in my arms and tell her it'll all be okay is overwhelming. But I can't do anything more to contribute to the growing anxiety on her face. She's awoken something in me. A part of myself I gave up on ever seeing again a long time ago. But this is my fault. Maybe if I hadn't kissed her... If I hadn't devoured every inch of her skin I could get my hands on...

Maybe I wouldn't have frightened her into leaving.

She finally looks up, capturing me with her beautiful gaze, so vibrant, shining with unshed tears. It's like looking into a cave full of sapphires glinting beneath the surface of the ocean.

"I, um..." She attempts to compose herself, taking a slow, deliberate breath. "Sinclair told me a few days ago that tomorrow is the second anniversary of losing them."

"It is," I confirm, forcing some of the cool water down my

burning throat at the thought of my son being gone for seven hundred and thirty days.

"I remember how I felt on Jenny's. Is there anything I can do?"

It's completely selfish of me to ask, but I do it anyway.

"Stay."

"What?" she whispers.

"You've been my friend since you came here, Hallie, just like you said." My brow scrunches up as I get out the words I have no right to ask. "Don't leave until after. Save the goodbyes for another couple of days."

Her eyes soften and she nods.

Even though we both understand that we're delaying the inevitable.

That I have to let her go.

Just not yet.

15

STERLING

Hallie smiles as I look at her over the top of my book.

"You have a home cinema, and you'd rather read poetry?"

I lean back into the giant sofa of the cinema room as she leans her head against the cushion, her eyes on mine.

It's two years to the day since I lost my wife and son. A day that's so filled with hurt, anger, and pain. I don't even know how I functioned. We all went to their graves together just as we did the day we buried them after flying them home from Cape Town.

It rained. Like it did that day.

Sinclair broke down. Like she did that day.

Sullivan held her. Like he did that day. Only this time, he had Molly crushed to his chest in one arm too.

Mal came to stand by my side. Like he did that day.

And Denver stood to one side, along with Killian and Jenson who flew back yesterday, their hunt in Cape Town bringing up nothing to explain how the yacht exploded out of nowhere.

And I'm still left without answers.

Like I was that day.

But this year when we all came back to Seasons to have lunch together, a soft hand with caring fingers wrapped around mine tightly beneath the table and didn't let go.

I swear I almost kissed her again for being there waiting for us. Not the frantic kiss in my office where I barely controlled myself. A slow kiss. One conveying just how damn grateful I was for her being there.

For making me feel that little bit less alone.

"I happen to like poetry."

Her giggle makes my lips curl into a smile, and she darts her eyes around the rarely used room. She spotted it when I gave her a tour of my penthouse, doing everything I could to delay her from leaving. She'd walked inside in wonder, then made herself comfy on the couch, patting the cushion. Inviting me to sit beside her.

That was hours ago.

We started off talking about Jenny. About her funeral. All the love songs Hallie made her parents play because it's what Jenny would have wanted. How they all wore different colored socks in bright colors. How there were smiles as well as tears, and how Hallie felt love filling the church like Jenny was there with them.

Then I told her about my son. How he was an adrenaline junkie. How he loved to jump out of airplanes, white water raft, bungee jump. Anything that most sane people would balk at. How Sullivan called him a 'risk taker', the complete opposite of himself. I admitted that I worry for my remaining son. How losing them has hardened him. How if it weren't for Molly I don't know what kind of state he'd be in.

Hallie listened to every word, as they spilled from my lips like water from a faucet.

She shared her pain with me, and I shared mine with her.

And each extra word we shared was like a balm to my

cracked soul as I let myself remember him, and Hallie let herself remember her.

If Jenny was pure love like Hallie says, then my son was pure life. Living it on the edge every day.

Until he wasn't.

"Read me something," she murmurs, attempting to stifle a yawn.

It's late. Far too late for her to still be here. But I know she's reluctant to leave me today. If I ask her to stay all night, she probably will. But I can't ask that of her. I won't.

"Okay." I thumb through the worn book.

Hallie places a finger between the pages. "Let the universe pick."

"As you wish." I look at the page she stopped me on and read.

"When you're in love with a woman, you see the world in her eyes, and you see her eyes everywhere in the world."

She picks at some lint on her skirt, averting her eyes from my face. "So is this what you do when you invite women back to your place? Woo them with romantic poetry? Read to them in that voice?"

"What voice?"

She rolls her eyes, and a soft chuckle escapes me.

"There have been some women. But none have ever come here. And I've never read poetry to anyone in my life."

"Oh."

"I'll always be honest with you, Hallie," I promise, noting the way she's chewing her lower lip.

I place the book on the cushion beside me and lift her feet into my lap, my hand encasing one slender ankle.

"After what happened with Lavinia, I thought maybe I was broken. So I went out with other women. Took them to bed even. But I couldn't ever..." I run my free hand around my jaw with a quiet curse. "The thought of looking into their eyes and letting go just... I couldn't ever get that far."

"You don't have to explain."

I look into her open, trusting gaze. Admitting that I've had sex with beautiful women but been unable to finish isn't as hard to admit as I thought it would be. Maybe it's a deep-rooted issue from Elaina cheating on me. I have no problem getting hard. No problem fucking... just a problem getting over that finish line, unless I'm alone.

"In the end, I stopped trying to date altogether. Until Sinclair told me she bought me a gift."

"Me." Hallie smiles weakly as I skate my hand over her ankle, caressing her skin.

"You."

I press my thumb deeper, massaging the arch of her foot. Her lips part with a contented sigh and she shifts position, giving me easier access.

"I should go soon," she breathes.

I rub deeper, committing the way her lashes flutter with pleasure to my memory.

A deep chime over the built-in speaker system rings out, announcing a visitor. Whoever it is, the doorman must have recognized and let in, because the chime is the one for the penthouse door.

Hallie tugs her feet from my lap and straightens.

"Are you going to get that?"

"I'll be back in a minute."

I make my way down the hallway to the door. It's eleven o'clock. Not wildly late. But late enough that my heart races and my thoughts jump to Sinclair, Sullivan, and Molly.

Sullivan took Molly home after dinner. And Sinclair went to sleep over at Zoey's place. They both insisted that's what they wanted after we all finished dinner. Sullivan would have called if Molly was ill. And Denver took Sinclair to Zoey's. He would have told me if there was a problem.

I check the spyhole before opening the door.

"Lavinia?" I frown.

"Hi Sterling. I was just thinking about things, and I thought maybe you'd like someone to talk to tonight?" She holds up a bottle of wine.

I stare at her in her tightly wrapped coat, her nose pink on the end from the evening air.

"You thought I'd like company?"

She pouts, heat swimming in her gaze. "Mm-hm. Can I come in?"

My frown deepens. "I... was about to go to bed. It's late."

I realize my mistake the moment Lavinia's brows rise like I've issued an invitation.

"I knew you wanted more," she gushes, stepping forward and reaching for me.

She curls her hand around the back of my neck in an attempt to guide my mouth to hers.

"Lavinia," I snap with a little too much force, bracketing her upper arms and taking hold of her.

I ease her back, and her mouth falls open in shock.

"Lavinia, this isn't right. You and me... we're friends," I say, softening my voice.

She pats the back of her hair, flustered.

"I'm sorry, I don't know what came over me. I just thought you needed time. Last year, that incredible night together..."

She looks at me hopefully, but I can't hide the regret on my face. Regret at hurting her. Regret that that night even happened in the first place.

She takes a step back. "I should go. I've clearly remembered events differently than you have."

"I'm sorry. We should talk about this," I say, hating myself for the embarrassment taking over her face.

"Another time perhaps. Like you said, it's late." She pretends to check her watch and then spins away, striding to the elevators without looking back.

She gets straight inside a waiting one and the doors slide closed.

I contemplate going after her. But what would I say? And anyway, it's not a conversation for today of all days.

I close the door with a deep sigh.

"I can leave."

I turn.

Hallie stands behind me with her coat in her hand.

"Excuse me?"

"You can call Lavinia back if that's the company you need. The distraction. The—" She swallows, looking uneasy. "If that's what you need tonight."

"It isn't."

She nods but won't meet my eyes.

"Hallie?"

She still won't look at me, so I reach for her hand and pull her to my chest. Her coat slips through her fingers and drops to the floor, landing in a heap.

"You know damn well it isn't," I growl. "It will never be what I need. *She* will never be what I want."

We stare at each other, the air growing thick.

Hallie's eyes drop to my fingers, curled around hers. I loosen my grip but don't let go.

"Do you want to leave?"

"No," she whispers.

"Then why were you holding your coat like you want to walk out of here?" I say it like an accusation, unable to hide the undercurrent of hurt in my voice. "Why are you trying to walk out of the door when we both know that you're exactly where you belong? Here. With *me*."

I let her hand go with a muttered curse. I'm crossing the line between us that she's trying so hard to maintain.

And I don't just want to cross it. I want to scrub the damn thing away until no trace of it remains.

"Jesus, Hallie," I hiss, fisting my hands so I don't sink them into her hair and pull her lips to mine.

She bites her lip and places her palm on my chest, resting it over my thundering heart.

"I don't... I don't want to go anywhere."

My jaw clenches, but I say nothing.

"Sterling? Will you... will you kiss me again?" she breathes.

The air leaves my lungs.

"No."

Her eyes widen like I've slapped her before her expression closes off.

She tries to step away. But I wrap one arm around her waist and yank her to me, pinning her against my body.

I've waited. And I've hoped. And now she's on the verge of finally succumbing, admitting what I've known since I met her... I have to know she means it.

I dip my mouth to her ear, my lips tucking inside the silky blonde strands.

"Baby girl," I rasp.

My blood heats at her responding shiver.

"You want it? This time, you need to take it."

She snaps her eyes to mine.

"It's your choice," I say, remaining close, towering over her, but not quite sealing the gap between us.

"My choice?"

Seconds stretch between us as we stare at one another, both fighting our internal battles.

Her eyes drop to my mouth and back up again, and her

chest rises between us, her pebbled nipples screaming at me in invitation.

But I wait.

This is her choice.

"Sterling," she murmurs.

"Hall—"

She rises on her toes and crashes her lips against mine, cutting her name from my tongue, and sending heat ravaging through my veins like a fireball.

I lift her into my arms, turning and slamming us back against the closed front door.

"Oh god," she moans, sinking her fingers into my hair and tugging at the roots as she kisses me hard, inviting my tongue inside her mouth to meet hers.

I might explode at any moment. She's everywhere. Her breathy moans against my lips, her hands grabbing at me, her body, hot and needy in my arms.

My mouth slides all over her like it's got a mind of its own.

Nipping, kissing, tasting.

I plant my forearms against the wall on either side of her head and she crosses her ankles behind my back, clinging to me. She's suspended between me and the wall, pinned in place by my hips. I'm pressed so tightly against her that her writhing makes me choke out her name like a strained plea.

"Hallie."

I kiss her swollen lips, sliding my teeth over the lower one, making her tremble.

"Baby girl, I can feel your wetness soaking through my pants," I say with a tortured groan.

She gasps, but I swallow the sound with another searing kiss and take each of her hands from my hair, pinning them against the wall above her head.

"Take what you need," I coax as I slide my tongue inside her mouth again.

She doesn't hesitate, and the whimper from her throat as she rotates her hips is like a goddamn invitation for my dick to get as hard as steel.

"That's my good girl," I groan, pulling back to admire her flushed face. "Grind on it. Use it to make you feel good."

She wiggles, but I don't give her any more space. I hold her against the door as she squirms, dragging her damp panties in circles over the head of my aching dick.

"Sterling," she pleads.

"I love the way you moan my name. Like you're desperate for me to sink inside you and make you mine."

"Oh my god." She shudders in my arms.

I reposition myself before she allows doubt over what we're doing to creep in. When I move again, the length of my cock is forced against the hot apex of her thighs.

Her eyes pop wide.

"Now, make yourself come."

I capture her lips with a guttural growl.

"Make yourself come over my cock, Baby girl."

All civility leaves me when she pauses and stares at me like she's overthinking.

Now isn't the time for her to let her thoughts about us worry her.

I can't lose her again. Can't watch her walk away like she did in my office. Not until she sees how good we could be together.

I grind my rock-hard dick against her, making her eyes roll.

"I'm not getting any younger here, Hallie. Use my cock. And damn well show me what you look like when you come!" I bark.

She mewls, jumping back into life like my words have breathed life back into her, and gives over to her pleasure, digging her heels into my back, urging me to move with her.

"That's it, good girl."

I roll my hips in time with her a mere fraction, wanting her to do the work. To take what she wants. To accept that as much as she's going to wreck me if she leaves after this, that maybe a part of her will be broken too.

I place my forehead against hers, staring at her as her movements grow more urgent, more desperate.

"Please," she moans, moving as much as the position I have her in allows her to.

"Look at me."

Her eyelids shutter as she looks at me, teetering dangerously close to the edge.

My breath stalls in my throat as she whimpers out my name and rolls her hips, coating my pants in warm, slick heat. It seeps through the fabric, making every muscle in my body coil tight.

I let go of her wrists and grab two handfuls of her ass, unable to stop myself from thrusting my hips. It's like instinct has taken over, insisting that I do whatever it takes to show her she's supposed to be mine.

Like driving my aching cock over her in punishing strokes.

"Damn it, Baby girl," I choke, unable to rip my eyes from hers. "You've got me so damn hard. My cock's leaking at the thought of being buried inside you."

She grips my shoulders, sinking her nails into my skin.

"That what you want? For me to stretch you wide to take me? Have you filled with me so that when you come it's my cock your body squeezes?"

"Oh, fuck, Sterling. Fuck, fuck, fuck!"

I push my forehead harder against hers.

"You want to come with my cock inside you, don't you, Baby girl? You want to come for me. Again and again and again."

She whimpers. Her pupils dilate, and I witness the perfect moment she shatters, coming in a rush inside my arms.

I hold her eyes through all of it. My name on her lips. My eyes on her face.

Her cum soaking through onto my cock.

"Baby girl... Jesus..."

My hips speed up of their own accord, thrusting erratically. My breath comes out as gasps against her mouth as I kiss her fiercely.

All my blood rushes south.

Her beautiful eyes hold mine as she grabs my face and holds it against hers.

Every cell in my body is on fire.

I don't speak, I don't blink, *I don't breathe.*

A surge overtakes me, rushing all my senses at once.

And everything inside me comes back to life.

"Hallie!" I roar.

My legs buckle.

I struggle to keep standing.

But my eyes remain locked on hers, the one part of my body that remains strong.

The rest crumbles to ash and a choked groan leaves me.

"Hallie!"

I stiffen as my cock explodes and I finish inside my pants like a teenage boy.

"Jesus..." I screw my eyes shut, snapping them back open immediately so I don't lose her gaze. "Jesus..."

My head swims and bliss pumps through my veins as I keep grinding into the heat between her thighs.

I ride out every wave, every tremor... until the final drops leave my body.

Our hearts pound against one another's, our foreheads pressed together.

I flex my fingers, squeezing the handfuls of her ass that are filling my palms. The weight of her there feels so goddamn right. She clenches her thighs around my hips and the wet fabric drags over my spent cock making it twitch.

I pant. "That was—"

"It was," she breathes, running her fingertips along my jaw.

I incline my face to one side, catching her wrist in a kiss.

"You can't deny we have something." I kiss her skin over and over. "You can't, Hallie."

"I—"

"Stay."

The word doesn't slip free. It fires from me like a bullet from a gun. Straight to target. It's intent crystal clear.

I want her where she belongs.

"Stay?" she echoes.

"Yes. Stay. Not just for tonight. Don't go back to England. Live here. With me."

She laughs, then her eyes widen, as she sees I'm deadly serious.

"I... If people knew about us, it could ruin my business. The charity—"

"I'll cover that," I growl. "All of it. However much you want."

I let my pathetic heart lift at her intense gaze.

"I've never felt like this about anyone, Hallie. Never in my life. I gave up hoping for it a long time ago. Stay," I repeat softly, pressing a gentle kiss to her puffy lips.

She kisses me back, and my heart swells with hope.

The cell in my back pocket chooses now to ring out with piercing precision, slicing through the moment. It's the ring tone I set for Denver.

"Answer it. It might be important," Hallie says.

I take one hand from her ass. I have to push my hips forward to keep her held up. The small whimper that leaves her lips almost has me tossing my phone to the floor so I can get my hand back on her silky flesh again.

"Denver?" I answer, keeping my eyes on hers.

"Boss. I'm sorry to call. Especially tonight. But—"

"What is it?"

"The club in LA. There's been a fire."

Hallie's eyes widen as she listens.

"Was anyone hurt?"

"No. But there's been some damage."

I blow out a breath. Things can be replaced if they're burned. *People can't.*

"Get the jet ready. I'll call you when I'm in the car."

I end the call.

Hallie's worried eyes search mine. "You need to go."

"Come with me. We can talk on the flight." I press a kiss to her lips, my heart clenching when this time she doesn't return it.

"I can't."

"Can't come to LA with me, or can't be *with* me?"

Her eyes dart between mine like she's searching for reasons... for *excuses*.

"Say it," I utter, trying to rein in the devastation that's seeping through my body.

Her eyes drop from mine and they're shining when she lifts them.

It's the moment I realize I've lost her.

"My parents need me home. They've already lost one daughter. I can't move over here. It would destroy them. You're an amazing man." Her breathing quickens and for a goddamn awful minute I know she's about to cry. "If things were diff—"

"Ssh, it's okay." I can't stand a second of seeing her like this.

I lower her to the ground. I can fund her charity if she'd let me. But this is more. It's about her being her own person. Doing what speaks to her heart after losing her sister. It's about the people for Hallie. That much has been clear since the day I met her. She thinks of other people before herself, looks after their happiness before her own.

I wish she could see that I could take care of her without her giving any of that up. But she's convinced it could all be jeopardized.

The thought that there's more to it that she's not telling me makes my throat tighten.

"Give me one thing?" I tilt her chin up with my pointer finger.

She nods, tears pooling along her lower lashes. "Anything."

I stroke her cheek with the pad of my thumb. "A date."

"A date?"

I give her a bittersweet smile.

"With the only woman I've ever wanted since the day I met her. Give me one date, Hallie. Just one."

A lone tear slips free, and I brush it away.

"I'll be in LA a day, maybe two. When I come back—"

She dusts her fingertips over my lips.

"Okay," she whispers. "When you come back, we'll have our date."

16

STERLING

"Fuck," Denver grunts as he looks around the burned-out shell of Seasons, LA.

The stench of charred wood lances through my nostrils like acid, memories bubbling away just beneath the surface at the acrid aroma.

At least this time, it isn't tinted with melted flesh.

"All this from one flame," I mutter as I retrieve the remnants of a piano key from the floor.

"You want me to pay a visit to the guy, Boss?" Denver runs his tongue over his teeth and brings his thundered gaze to meet mine.

"No, that won't be necessary."

I drop the piano key into the ashes. A long-standing patron of ours, a judge, caused the fire when he got so pissed that he tried to light a cigar with a match and ended up dropping it into his drink. Rather than put it out calmly, he freaked and threw the glass away—straight into the top-shelf liquor behind the bar. The fire department said the place was an inferno by the time they got here.

"He just found out his wife has been having an affair with

his brother," I tell Denver. "He'll pay for the damage, with interest, just to keep this all quiet."

It'd be easy to go guns blazing for his blood at what he's caused. But something tells me he'll be shitting himself enough already. He's already lost his wife; he won't want to lose his career over this.

And I get it. The feeling of being betrayed.

"This is probably him," I say as my phone rings with an unknown number.

Denver's dark eyes sweep over the room again. "That's going to be one big bill."

I crack my neck as I survey what little is left one of my venues and hit answer. "Sure is."

◆

"If you want to move to the coast, live by the beach, you know you're always welcome here." My brother, Clay, steps out of the back door and onto the deck that runs along the rear of his house.

"I'll keep it in mind."

He's always talking about it, having us all live close to one another again. Me, him, and our brother, Jagger, who's in Boston.

Denver and I left the LA team in charge of the cleanup of the club. He said he wanted to visit some old buddies, so he dropped me at Clay's house and is coming back for me in the morning.

The sound of Clay's wife, Adaline, reading a story to their two young grandsons floats out before Clay slides the door closed.

"They'll want her to do the voices like you did," he says, handing me a glass of bourbon.

"I'm sure she does much better wizard impressions than me." I relax into my seat, looking out over the ocean.

Clay studies my face. "You worried about the club?"

"No. It's being handled. Renovations start tomorrow."

The judge was the one on the phone. He started spouting out figures, desperate to save his neck before I even greeted him.

He takes a sip of his drink. "And things back home? You filled me in on the kids and Mal and Trudy over dinner but missed out the dating stories. How's that going?"

I meet his eyes, noting the twinkle in his.

"About as well as you'd expect, Brother."

He chuckles. "Sinclair sure runs with an idea when she wants to."

"She does. But it's the happiest she's been since getting Monty."

He nods in understanding.

"She just keeps working, taking on more shoots, more shows. Same as Sullivan. If it weren't for Molly, he'd never stop. Sinclair's hit it off with Hallie, though. When I called earlier, she said they're going shopping tomorrow."

"Hallie? The dating coach?"

"That's her."

His eyes narrow and he studies me rolling my neck, attempting to ease the ache in it.

"What's she like?"

"She's..." My lips curl up. "... pretty damn incredible."

"I see." He lifts his glass with a knowing smirk. "Does she know?"

"She does." My mind flits back to the way she whimpered my name as she came.

And the way I blew in my pants when she did.

"What you going to do? She's from England, right?"

I tighten my grip around the glass.

"She's leaving once I get back to New York." I knock back the rest of the bourbon in one go, hissing as it burns a trail down to my stomach.

Clay studies me, before he looks out over the ocean.

"You'd rather she stays?"

"I'd rather she was my wife."

His brows shoot up.

"Hallie's…" I run a hand around my jaw. "She's everything I lost faith in."

There's a peal of laughter from inside the house and Clay looks back toward the door with a grin.

"You're a lucky man. Beautiful family… grandkids," I muse as I listen to the sounds of life coming from inside.

"Molly will have company one day. Give Sullivan and Sinclair some time."

"Perhaps."

I run my thumb around the rim of my empty glass. Molly's my only grandchild. A shining little ball of sunshine. Her mother's long gone. How anyone could leave a little girl like that I'll never understand. She's pure innocence and love. Molly and her little baby dolls she takes everywhere.

The memory of Hallie talking so animatedly with her as she pretended to feed Molly's doll grabs me around the heart and squeezes. It's the moment I knew, *really knew*, that I never wanted Hallie to leave. Ever. That if I could have slid a ring on her finger there and then, I would have. And if I could have put our own baby in her belly that night in my office, then I would have done so without hesitation.

I could keep getting her pregnant as my wife and fill the world with tiny little versions of her. Fill it so damn full of her magic.

The Matchmaker

The thought grabs hold of my heart and pierces it like a dagger.

I'm fifty and dreaming of a life I can't have.

Those things are for Hallie. The beautiful woman who monopolizes my thoughts night and day. She's thirty. She has her whole life ahead of her. It would be selfish to tether her to me. No matter how much I want her. No matter how deep this connection to her is.

No matter that she's my *magic*. That thing everyone talks about, that I'd stopped believing in.

But she had a choice, and she's made it.

As soon as I return to Manhattan, she'll be leaving.

Clay and I stay out on the deck until well after midnight, catching up. The following morning, I'm coloring in a giant red dinosaur with the two boys who slept over too. They're laughing at the Beaufort Diamond earring I give the T-Rex as I soak up every minute I have with them before Denver arrives.

Sullivan's name lights up the screen on my phone.

"Son?" I smile, adding an Indiana Jones style hat to the dinosaur. I wink at them, and they erupt into more giggles.

"Dad?"

His grim tone makes me put the crayon down.

"What's wrong?"

"I'm on my way to the hospital. Halliday was taken in. There was an issue with the paparazzi when she was out with Sinclair."

My blood turns to ice. "What?"

"Sinclair said they're both fine. But I'm heading there now to meet them."

"Jesus… Okay." I scrub a hand around my jaw. "Denver's on his way to Clay's now. We'll be back as soon as we can. Call me when you get to the hospital and tell me what's going on."

"I will."

"And, Son? Take care of the girls."

"I will. See you when you get back."

I hang up and check my watch. It'll be at least five hours until we make it back.

I dial Denver immediately, but the sound of a vehicle screeching to a halt outside drowns out the ringing.

Seconds later, there's hammering on the front door, and I rush to open it.

"Boss. Sinclair—"

I meet Denver's dark expression. "I know."

He grabs my packed bag that's on the hallway floor.

"I'll wait in the car."

I say goodbye to Adaline and Clay, giving the boys a hard squeeze before I stride out the door and to the waiting vehicle.

Denver speeds off before my door even closes.

17

HALLIDAY

Sullivan steps into the hospital room, his jaw set as he looks from Sinclair to me and back again.

"The doctor said she'll be back to speak to you. But because the CAT scan was clear, it looks like you'll be able to leave soon."

My shoulders sag in relief where I'm sitting on the hospital bed with Sinclair. We've been here for hours.

"About time. I fainted, that's all."

Sinclair squeezes my hand. "We needed to get you checked, though. You were out cold. It was super freaky."

I smile at her gratefully. She hasn't left my side since I woke up, laid out on the sidewalk, surrounded by a sea of cameras clicking.

"I'm fine."

I reach up to touch the bandage wrapped around my head, covering the cut and lump. My head aches, but it's not too bad. I know the medical staff are doing their job, but I just want to get out of here now.

"Thank you for coming to get Monty," Sinclair says to

Sullivan as he stands at the foot of the bed, his dark brows flat over his eyes as he watches us both.

"It's fine. Molly was pushing him around the apartment in her stroller when I left."

"I'm sorry we ruined your day," I add.

He huffs. "Talking business with Mal all day while he flaps, or dealing with head injuries? Tough choice."

"Who knew shopping for baby gifts would cause so much drama?" I say.

Sinclair snorts. "We didn't even make it to half the places I wanted to show you. Don't worry, there'll be plenty more days we can go." She gives me a reassuring smile that makes my stomach knot.

We were having such a nice day shopping for gifts for Sophie before a hoard of photographers swarmed the front of a boutique when we were exiting. All the jostling and shoving as they tried to get Sinclair's attention, mixed with the fact I skipped breakfast, made me crumple like a tower of cards.

I was planning on telling Sinclair I was leaving today. That I can't fulfill our contract due to unforeseen circumstances. I want to be honest with her and tell her the real reasons. But I need to talk to Sterling first, ask him how he wants to broach the subject. *If* he does.

Maybe he'd rather keep it quiet and forget everything that's happened once I leave.

Sinclair's face lights up. "Ooh, I know exactly where we need to go next time—"

The door flings open and a blur of suited silver storms in.

"Dad!"

His jacket flies out behind him as he crosses the room in long, determined strides. Sinclair throws her arms around him in a hug. His blazing eyes meet mine over her shoulder, and my stomach erupts into flutters.

He pulls back to look at her. "Sweetheart, are you okay?"

She nods. "I am. It's Halliday who got hurt."

Sterling tips his chin at Sullivan, then his eyes are back on mine. He steps around Sinclair and leans over the bed and cups my face.

"Hallie? I got here as fast as I could."

I'm surrounded by his rich, intoxicating scent as he looks so deeply into my eyes that my cheeks heat.

"Thank you, but honestly, I'm fine," I force out as he scans over me before zeroing in on the bandage around my skull.

"Jesus," he utters. "You're hurt, Baby girl."

His thumbs track over my cheeks before the stubble on his jaw brushes my forehead and he kisses me there.

"Sterling," I murmur, stiffening.

My eyes dart behind him to where Sullivan's face is devoid of any reaction. Denver's come into the room and has placed himself one step behind Sinclair.

She gasps and reaches out, grabbing his bicep to steady herself.

"Baby girl?" she splutters.

I swallow and look back at Sterling in panic. I swear everything we've done together is written all over my face.

"Dad? You can't be serious? You and Halliday?" she shrieks, her eyes bouncing between the two of us.

Sterling straightens, but the lingering look he gives me tells her everything.

"Did you know about this?" She glares at Sullivan.

"I suspected."

"Oh my god." Her eyes widen, and she looks at Denver. "What about you? Did you know?"

Denver's jaw tightens, and she yanks her hand away as if she's only just realized she was touching it.

"Seriously? Even *he* knew before me?"

Denver's steely gaze remains straight ahead as Sinclair scowls at him.

"How long has this been going on?" she snaps.

"Not long," I say at the same time Sterling rasps, "I knew the moment I met her."

He looks at me and reaches out to link his fingers with mine.

"I'm the one who pursued Hallie," he tells Sinclair. "Not the other way around. Neither of us expected this. But it's happened. And I'm not about to apologize for it. I don't regret it for a second."

Sinclair studies him, her expression shifting from shock into something else.

"Do you love my father?" Her attention zones in on me, and she folds her arms. "Or is this just sex? Because he needs more than that. He deserves more than that. You can't come here and then—"

"Sinclair!" Sterling growls.

"No, Dad!" she counters. "You know I'm talking sense. I hired her to find you love. Not to play out some daddy fantasy she might have."

"Enough!"

His voice cuts through the air, leaving a silence so thick I'm surprised any of us can breathe.

"Enough, Sinclair," he says in a soft voice. "Hallie and I are both adults. We can do what we like."

"But—"

"But nothing." He gives her a look that makes her clamp her lips together. "Sweetheart, you wanted me to be happier. Well, I am. And regardless of what happens next, that happiness will always be because of what you did for me."

"Because of Halliday," she says, her eyes meeting mine.

"Yes. Your gift," he rasps.

She watches me with pursed lips for a minute. "I can't

believe it took baby gear shopping for me to find this out. If those paparazzi hadn't showed up, we wouldn't be here, and then you two wouldn't have just..." She waves a hand at me and Sterling.

"We'd have told you," Sterling says in a deep voice. "I don't want secrets in our family."

Sinclair looks from him to Sullivan and her eyes take on glassy quality. "Agreed. Secrets in families suck," she whispers.

I know she's thinking about her mother's affair.

I meet Sterling's eyes, praying for someone to say something.

Anything.

Sinclair's phone chimes, and she huffs as she looks at it. "Really? This is ridiculous! The press is already announcing I'm pregnant."

Denver stiffens beside her but keeps his eyes ahead as she scrolls her phone with a scowl.

"We were shopping for Halliday's friend, not me. Someone must have tipped them off. There's no way they'd have gone wild like that unless they thought there was a story." She snorts.

"I'm going to get you protection," Sterling says.

"No! We've talked about this before. It's bad enough that Denver has to pick me up when I go out at night. I don't want a clone of him following me around during the day as well."

She stares at the side of Denver's face, but he keeps his gaze ahead.

"See? Monty has better social skills. Please, Dad. I promise I'll get my head around..." She gestures to me and Sterling again. "...Just do not subject me to being babysat. *Please.*"

Sterling looks at Sullivan, who inclines his head with a small shrug.

He sighs, rubbing a hand around his brow. "Fine. But if I even think there's a chance you need it—"

"I won't," Sinclair replies.

The door opens, and the doctor enters.

"Miss Burton?" She looks up from her clipboard. "I can see you'll have no problem getting a ride home. Who can I hand over your care to for the next twenty-four hours?"

"Me," Sterling replies in his deep baritone. "I'll take care of her."

The doctor looks at me. "Great. So, no alcohol or exerting yourself. Get plenty of rest, and any worsening headaches, come back in."

"I'll bring her straight back if there is, Doctor," Sterling says.

The impulse to argue that I don't need babysitting fires inside me. But the authoritative command in his voice as he fixes his eyes on me makes the flames die out.

"You'll let me look after you, won't you, Hallie?" he rasps.

I nod reluctantly, but he lifts his brows.

"Yes." I sigh.

He lowers his voice so only I can hear. "Good girl."

Then he turns to the doctor.

"Can I take her home now?"

18

HALLIDAY

"It's ready," Sterling calls as he walks out of the bathroom, a billow of lavender scented steam following him.

I look up from where I'm perched on the end of his bed.

"You can make yourself at home," he says, frowning at the unpacked bag by my feet.

He sent Denver over to collect some of my things for me that Sinclair kindly packed.

"Get in the bath, it'll help with the aches." Sterling stops in front of me.

I let my lower lip go from where I'm biting it. "Thank you." My gaze tracks around the bedroom. "Isn't there a guest bathroom I should be using?"

"Mine has the deepest tub." He takes my hand and helps me to my feet. "And my room is the only one that has a bed and a couch."

I look past him at the giant velvet couch against the wall.

"You're not sleeping in another room, Hallie. I need to know you're okay."

"I'm fine." I sigh. "But you're going to watch me like a hawk for the next twenty-four hours anyway, aren't you?

"You're a fast learner." He winks at me before leading me to the bathroom, stopping at the door to let me enter first.

The tub is filled with bubbles, and the room is bathed in a soft light from multiple lit candles placed on every available surface.

"Take your time." His warm breath flows over the back of my neck, making me shiver before he closes the door with a soft click and leaves me alone.

I stare around the room, taking in the floor-to-ceiling windows with views over the city.

Something tightens in my chest, and I push it as far down as I can as I strip off my clothes and sink into the heavenly water. It comes up to my neck and every tightly coiled muscle in my body slowly starts to unravel as I soak.

This feels so normal. Like I belong here. With Sterling. In his apartment. In his bed. But there's too much at stake if I let myself dream like that.

I lose track of time, finally stepping from the tub once the water has cooled. I reach for a towel on the rack to dry myself, but stall as I spot the familiar fabric of my pajamas hanging amongst the white fluffy towels. Sterling must have placed them here when he was getting the bath ready, making sure they'd be warm for me to put on.

After dressing, I walk to the twin basins, assessing the bandage on my head in the mirror. It looks a lot worse than it is. The doctor said I could take the dressing off tomorrow. I reach up and unwind it. What's a few hours? Like I keep telling everyone, I'm fine.

Running my fingers through my hair, I inspect the lump. It's smaller than when we left the hospital, even though my head is still tender.

I try to keep my attention away from Sterling's things. But

my gaze keeps tracking back to his electric toothbrush and the bottle of aftershave and other grooming products on the marble counter.

I pick up the aftershave and take the lid off. The scent has my core clenching immediately. That familiar warm, woody spice that's totally him. I shove the lid on and place the bottle down. What am I doing? In a couple more days I'll be leaving. I'm not helping anyone by losing my head to my emotions.

I blow out the candles and head into the bedroom, spotting a sweater on the bed. I run my fingers over the soft fabric with a Statue of Liberty print on the front of it.

"I figured you might want something comfortable."

I turn.

Sterling's leaning against the doorframe watching me. He's wearing suit pants and a light blue shirt with a couple of buttons undone at the neck. The only time I've seen him without a suit and tie is when I walked in on his exercise session with Sullivan and Mal.

The day I saw the corded muscles rippling in his broad back.

"Thank you." I lift the sweater off the bed.

We hold each other's eyes for a beat before he straightens up. "You need to eat."

I pull the sweater on, trying not to notice that it smells like him even though it's brand-new. It's probably because it's been amongst his things and lying on his bed. The bed I have to sleep in tonight.

I head into the kitchen, and Sterling sets a bowl of soup and a plate of warm bread in front of me as I climb up onto a stool at the giant granite island.

"Where did you get this? It smells amazing." I breathe in the comforting scent of chicken soup, like Jenny and I would have as kids when we were sick.

"I made it." He sits next to me where there's another place

set, looking at me pointedly when I don't move. "I'll feed it you myself if you don't start eating."

"Sorry." I pull my eyes away from his soft smile and pick up my spoon.

It's delicious, and soon, I've finished the entire bowl.

"You're tired. You need rest." Sterling studies my face, looking at the lump on my head that's no longer covered by the bandage.

"I'm fine."

"You don't have to pretend with me, Hallie."

I hold back my wince at the dull ache that's been building in my head since I got out of the bath.

"Maybe I'll go and lie down," I murmur.

He abandons the bowls and follows me to his bedroom like he's concerned that taking his eyes off me for a second could have catastrophic consequences.

He pulls back the thick throw on his bed and watches me as I take off the sweater and climb in.

"I'll get you some water."

"Thank you."

The covers have barely been laid over me before my eyelids grow heavy and his retreating footsteps are just echoes.

◆

I wake into near darkness, and it takes a minute for my eyes to adjust. The only light is from the glow of the city through a gap in the blackout shades.

Sterling's sleeping on the sofa, both hands resting on his stomach as he takes soft, rhythmic breaths. I can make out the hoodie and sweatpants he's wearing. The thin blanket that was covering him has slipped to the floor.

Pushing the covers back, I slide out of bed and look around for the Statue of Liberty sweatshirt, but don't see it. If I put another layer on, Sterling can have the throw from the bed. It's not fair that he gets cold and has to sleep fully clothed because I've stolen his bed.

I tiptoe to the other side of the room and rummage through the bag Sinclair packed for me, looking for something I can put on over my pajamas. My hand brushes something hard and I grab my phone from the nightstand, using the light on it to see as I take the object out.

Jenny's giant smile radiates through the glass, and my throat thickens. I glance over at Sterling, sleeping. Sinclair's never noticed this photo before. Why would she? It's always facing out of my window.

I swallow, recalling the hushed tone Sterling used to speak to Denver while he was waiting for Sinclair at my apartment.

This man...

I clutch the frame to my chest and screw my stinging eyes shut. He deserves more, just like Sinclair said. He deserves it all.

"And you really think I'm the one to give it to him, don't you?" I whisper, partly to Jenny, partly to the universe.

I walk to the window, setting the frame down, facing it toward the city. My steps are gentle as I return to the bed and lift the thick comforter off. I carry it to the wide couch and drape it over Sterling.

Then I lift one side and slide underneath it, beside him.

"Hallie?" The gentle rasp of his sleepy voice has me inching closer, and he lifts his arm, welcoming me into his side like it's the most natural thing in the world. "Is your head hurting, Baby girl?"

"No." I place my head over his chest and listen to the steady thump of his heart as I sink into his warm embrace.

"Good," he murmurs, his lips dusting my forehead in a tender kiss.

I squeeze my eyes shut and wrap myself around him, relishing every inch of where our bodies melt into one another.

I can't tell him it's my heart that hurts. Not my head.

The heart that wishes and prays that I didn't have to leave.

I thought I was coming here to help him. That he was the one who had to learn how to open himself up. What if it was actually me who needed his help? Only in accepting it, I've made everything more complicated.

And those complications mean one thing.

Someone will get hurt.

19

STERLING

I KISS HALLIE'S FOREHEAD.

I should get up. But I allow myself a few precious moments watching her as the early morning sun seeps in through the shades.

She's an angel. A beautiful, magical angel. I brush a lock of ice-blonde hair from her face and hold my breath as she sighs, then settles again. I haven't slept well in over two years. But with her in my arms last night, I came the closest to feeling peace that I ever have.

A vibrating breaks my gaze from her face, and I slide my arm out from beneath her slowly, careful not to wake her. I climb off the couch, heading straight for the source before it disturbs her. Her phone is on the nightstand, lit up with an incoming call from an unknown number. I pick it up and hit answer as I walk out of the bedroom and close the door behind me.

"Halliday? I'm calling from work so this needs to be quick. But I need you to transfer me thirty—"

"Sorry, Miss Burton isn't available right now. Who is this?"

I walk into the kitchen and flick on the coffee machine.

The guy on the other end stalls.

"Who's this?"

"I asked first," I reply, fetching two mugs.

"It's Rory. Can you get her to call me back ASAP?"

"Rory?" I murmur, recognizing the name. "You're a friend of Hallie's from England?"

"Uh-huh," the guy replies. "You could say that I'm a close friend."

The way he says *close* makes me place the mug down harder than intended on the counter.

"I see. I'll tell her you called to check on how she's doing."

"How she's doing?"

I rest back against the counter. Rory can't be as 'close' to Hallie as he likes to think he is if he doesn't know she spent the day in hospital. She called her mum and dad and Sophie in the car.

She didn't call Rory.

"Is she okay? Did something happen?" Genuine concern fills his tone, and I run a hand around my jaw.

"She hit her head. But she's in good hands. Nothing for you to worry about. I'll tell her you called when she wakes up."

"When she wakes up? What...? Who did you say you are?"

"I didn't. Goodbye, Rory."

I hang up, abandoning the coffee and heading into my office. I pick up the desk phone. I don't want to risk disturbing Hallie by going back into the bedroom to retrieve my cell.

Denver picks up in one ring.

"Boss?"

"Morning." I check my watch—6 a.m. I'm sure this guy never sleeps.

"Just wanted to check if Sinclair was okay last night when you took her home?"

"She didn't say a lot. We went to Sullivan's to get Monty on the way. She seemed happier after that," he replies gruffly.

"She loves that dog," I murmur. "God help us if anything ever happens to it."

Denver remains silent on the other end as I walk to the window and look out at the city's skyline. "Listen, I'm going to be out of the office today. Maybe tomorrow as well."

"That's what I planned for. I've set up some training to do with the BD team. They've got thirteen minutes to get here before they get their asses handed to them."

I chuckle. Denver takes leading both the Beaufort Diamond team, and Jenson and Killian seriously. He takes everything seriously.

"How are the boys doing?" I ask, my chest tightening with the familiar burn it gets every time I think of that marina in Cape Town. Jenson and Killian headed back over there before Denver and I left for LA, still hunting for any new information we can get.

"They've got the marina's CCTV footage for the days surrounding the fire now. They're working through it.

"What about the day itself?"

"The staff there still claim they can't find it," Denver grunts. "But the boys have some extra persuasion they can use if they don't locate it soon. We'll have it in the next couple of days."

"Fine." I pinch the bridge of my nose. "Let me know if you need anything."

Someone there must know something. It's only since the old manager there died that we've started to get somewhere.

Someone knows what happened to my wife and son that day.

And I won't stop until I find out the truth.

"Will do, Boss."

I hesitate before I end the call.

"Denver? I also want you to run a check on someone."

"Sure. What's the name?"

"Rory," I reply, running my thumb over the screen of Hallie's cell in my other hand. "The guy's name is Rory."

20

HALLIDAY

"I can't believe this." I grip Sterling's thigh, giving it an excited squeeze as the helicopter does another loop and Lady Liberty comes into view again.

"I wanted a date." He rests his hand on top of mine, and I grin.

After two full days of house arrest, during which Sterling wouldn't let me do anything except be pampered by him, we're finally here. *Having our date.* It started with breakfast in one of The Songbird hotel's stunning restaurants. Then he took me to his friend's art gallery where I gazed in wonder at a private early showing of Zoey's fiancé's work. Then we had a picnic in Central Park, followed by a ride in a rowboat. Then he took me to see the Broadway showing of Aladdin, before taking me for dinner, then finally taking us up in a helicopter to fly over the harbor at sunset.

The only thing tainting it is that I haven't heard from Sinclair since the hospital, and she won't return my calls, but Sterling's said she just needs time and she'll come around.

"You've given me at least seven dates all rolled into one," I say as I admire the view.

No matter how much I look at her crown, all lit up against the night sky, the glow it brings to my chest never dims. I picture Jenny's beaming smile as I watch the light flood out from it.

My fingers tingle and a warm buzz blankets my chest as it sparkles like a heavenly glow through the helicopter window. It's like the universe is constantly pushing me to accept what I've known to be true all along.

Sterling Beaufort is meant for me, as I am for him.

"It's amazing. Thank you," I breathe, turning to look at him.

Heat smolders in his gaze and his eyes drop to my mouth. "You're welcome."

I turn back to the window and fight the desire to pull him to me and get lost in one of his kisses.

We loop Liberty Island twice more and then our pilot takes us back to Sterling's penthouse building, landing on the roof. Once it's safe to get off, Sterling exits first, then holds his hand out to me, like getting a ride home by helicopter is completely normal.

I slide my palm into his. He's a billionaire; riding home in one is probably normal to him.

"It belongs to a friend," he says, his warm blue eyes twinkling like he's reading my thoughts. "But if you like it, I'll get you your own."

"I'd prefer a jet. Longer range." I laugh off his joke. Because that's what it is. It isn't real. I'm supposed to be leaving.

"Are you tired?" Sterling asks as we step inside his penthouse. He undoes an extra button at the neck of his shirt as we walk into the open living area.

"I'm okay." I rest one hand on a table so I can take my shoes off.

I've quickly become very at home here. And I shouldn't

be. But every time I've done something that shows I'm at ease, the resulting light it brings to Sterling's eyes has only encouraged me more.

I can't get enough of the way he looks at me. Like he's trying to decide whether to kiss me slowly, rip my clothes off in a rush, or both.

We slept on the couch together again last night with me curled into his side like I was made to fit there. His kisses haven't strayed away from my forehead, and he's been a perfect gentleman since I came out of hospital. But memories of him slamming me against his front door and making me cry out his name have replayed over and over in my head. If they weren't, then I might think I'd imagined it.

"It's been a long day and you're still healing." Concern fills his gaze as he walks over and stops in front of me.

"I'm fine," I breathe, tracing the smile lines at the edges of his eyes.

I trail my fingertips over his jaw, loving the way those lines deepen as he leans closer and murmurs my name.

"Hallie."

Warm tingles dance over my skin.

"I still haven't booked my flight," I confess in a whisper.

"You haven't?" He searches my eyes, and the deep rumble of his voice makes me lick my lips.

"Every time I've picked up my phone to do it, I've put it off. It's like I *can't* do it."

"You don't have to do it." His eyes darken with an intensity that makes my breath catch in my throat.

Every vibration I've felt, every bolt of energy in his presence all hit me at once; swirling around inside my gut like glitter in a snow globe as I admire the beautiful warmth in his blue eyes.

"I don't want to do it," I admit, finally speaking my truth. Not that it will make everything easy. But at least for the first time since coming to New York, I'm finally being honest with myself.

I don't want to leave Sterling. I want to grab onto the happiness, the belonging, the *fate* that I feel when I'm with him.

I want it all. I just don't know if having it all is possible.

"If there was a way I could stay here and not hurt Mum and Dad, not risk my business, not—"

My words cease in my throat as he cups my face and presses his thumb against my lips.

"What if I told you we'll find a way together, no matter what it takes?"

"Then I'd want to believe you. I'd really want to believe you."

"Then believe me. Because I swear, I won't give up searching for it as long as there's life in my body."

I look at the complete and utter determination in his eyes. He's always had faith in something bigger than us. In there being a way that this all works out.

Jenny would be so disappointed in me for not grabbing what's right in front of me.

I used to be that person, filled with hopes, dreams and faith. When did I lose her? Is it enough just to choose to be her again? To start now? Making new choices. Listening to my instincts. Not allowing happiness to be something only for other people, but for myself as well?

I place my hands on top of Sterling's, where he's cupped my cheeks.

"I want to go to bed."

"Does your head hurt again?" Concern knits over his brow.

"No. I want *you* to take me to bed." I hold his eyes, driving my point home.

"You're sure?" he asks, his voice like velvet being dragged over rough gravel.

"Have you changed your mind?"

His lips curl into a sexy smile tinted with tenderness. "Baby girl, I will *never* change my mind about that."

"Then show me—"

Before I even finish speaking, he grabs me, hoisting me up into his arms and crashing his lips to mine.

His kiss is urgent and burning with passion, consuming every doubt I have and letting them fly away like dandelion seeds on a summer breeze. *Gone.*

A wave of bright sparkling energy ignites heat in my veins, traveling through me at lightning speed.

And I soak it in.

I let go of every doubt and fear that I've been controlled by since I met him. And I welcome the magic that I fought so hard to re-direct. Our magic. This indescribable, soul-altering connection that's always been there between us.

"Sterling," I whimper.

I wrap my legs around his waist, trying to get as close as possible. Our breath tangles, and he gifts me with another kiss that sets my head spinning.

"Hurry," I urge, trailing desperate kisses over his jaw and down his throat, making him groan as he walks us into his bedroom.

He holds me with one hand beneath my ass and angles my face to his, kissing me and smiling against my mouth.

"I've been waiting to worship every goddamn inch of you. Maybe I'll take my time."

I huff in aroused frustration as he lowers us to the bed and cages me between his arms.

"Ever since that day I met you, and you sat in my apartment like you belonged here, I was dreaming of this moment."

He looks into my eyes with a searing heat before swooping

on my neck. His kisses trail down, along my collarbone as he grips a handful of my thigh, wrapping my leg around his hip.

His cock pushes against the desperate heat between my legs.

"You sat there looking so damn beautiful. *So damn right*," he growls.

I writhe, but he's got me pinned by his hips as he kisses his way down my chest to the neckline of my dress.

"Sterling," I pant as he tugs my dress to one side, yanking my bra out of the way.

His hot mouth engulfs my nipple and sucks.

I arch into him with a whimper, and he cants his hips, pushing his cock harder against me in response. He looks at me from beneath his brows and flicks his tongue over me.

"I bet every inch of you tastes this sweet, doesn't it?"

He sits on his heels, bringing me with him.

Our kisses turn more frantic as we rip my dress off over my head, crashing our lips back together immediately. He reaches around to unclip my bra, and I fight to undo the buttons on his shirt.

I tilt my head back with a moan as he dips his head to my breasts, sucking, kissing, and biting them. He kneads them, thumbing my nipples before cursing and repeating the move.

My nipples are pulled so tight that they're throbbing by the time I manage to coordinate myself enough to get my hands back to his shirt buttons again.

"Help me," I plead.

Sterling sucks my nipple again, grazing his teeth over it before he lifts his head.

His eyes take on a new intensity as he straightens up. He takes over what my eager fingers were struggling with and slowly unfastens the buttons one by one.

Inches of his skin begin to show, and I part my lips with anticipation.

Once he reaches the last button, he slowly slides the shirt down his arms, freeing them of the fabric.

I let out an involuntary gasp.

"It's okay, Baby girl," he soothes.

My eyes flick up to his and then back to his torso.

Scars run up one side of it. The skin is uneven and red, angry-looking raised lines lance across the surface. Some areas are shinier than others, like the skin has healed too tightly and been stretched too far.

"Does it hurt?" I whisper.

"Not anymore."

His nostrils flare as I reach out toward him hesitantly. My hand hovers halfway between us, and he nods.

I move closer until the pads of my fingers make the lightest contact beneath his ribcage.

He sucks in a sharp breath that I feel all the way to my toes.

His eyes never leave me as I stroke him slowly, tracing each crease and mark that's been made where he's healed. I follow them up and up. Over his torso, all the way to underneath the base of his neck, and then down his left arm to his wrist.

"You were burned." I force air into my lungs, past the bowling ball-sized lump that has formed in my throat.

"I tried to save them."

A sob bubbles in my throat. "My god..."

"Ssh," he coos, cupping one side of my face. He lowers his forehead and rests it against mine. "Don't get upset."

"I'm sorry. Just knowing what you went through. Everything that you've..."

I kiss beneath his collarbone where the scars begin. He sucks in a ragged breath, his chest expanding beneath my lips.

"Is this okay?"

"It's okay, Hallie," he rasps in a thick voice.

I take my time kissing down his torso. When I get to the

area below his ribs where the scarred skin ends, I move to his wrist and kiss my way up his arm, back to where I started.

"Baby girl." His hand tangles in my hair and he pulls me to him, screwing his face up and kissing me in desperation.

I cling to him, our kisses growing deeper and deeper until his hands fall to my hips and he pulls me against him with growing urgency.

"Sterling," I moan.

My mouth doesn't leave his as I reach for his belt and slowly undo it.

His grip on my hair tightens as I drag his zipper down, the hard length of him pressing against the back of my fingers.

"Take them off," I whisper.

He kisses me again before rising from the bed. His eyes fix on mine as he pushes his pants and underwear to the floor and steps out of them.

My mouth goes dry.

Each defined muscle in his lower abdomen and legs scream with strength as he stands with his legs apart. His cock juts out, solid and thick, the slit at the end glistening with beads of pre-cum.

He takes a step back toward the bed and his balls swing heavily behind his dick. I can't help but stare. It's as though they're taunting me, knowing they're about to pound against my skin.

And that I'm going to love every second.

"You okay?"

I gaze at his face, speechless.

He grazes his lower lip with his teeth before rolling his tongue over it. "Take off your panties, Hallie."

Arousal swims in my core at the way his eyes heat. I hook my thumbs into the sides of my panties and slide them off.

"Jesus Christ, you're beautiful," he chokes out hoarsely.

I shuffle on my knees to the edge of the mattress. His skin

is hot where I run my palms down his shoulders and over his chest. When I reach his hips, his cock jumps against my skin, smearing me in hot liquid.

"So are you." I press a kiss to his chest.

He hooks two fingers underneath my chin and lifts my face to his, capturing my mouth in a kiss that has me moaning around his tongue.

"Sit for me," I whisper breathlessly, pulling my tingling lips from his.

He moves up the bed to the headboard and turns, sitting back against it. The blue of his eyes glints, and he grabs hold of my hips as I slide one leg over his hips to straddle him.

"I want to feel every part of you," I whisper.

He nods in understanding. "Me too. It's safe. I'd never put you at risk."

"I knew when I met you… the way I felt… this energy that ran through me the first time I looked into your eyes." I stroke his jaw, my gaze softening. "I was so scared of what accepting it meant that I blocked it out. I ignored everything my intuition was trying to tell me."

"Hallie," he murmurs, stroking my hip bones with his thumbs.

I press my lips to his.

"I'm so sorry it took me this long." I position the head of his cock against me. "So sorry," I repeat as I circle over it, allowing the fat tip to stretch me as I take the first inch of him inside me.

The groan that leaves his throat sends an army of butterflies raging in my core.

"Thank you for being so patient."

I sink down another inch, and his eyes flare with desire.

"Thank you for never giving up when you knew all along it was always meant to be us."

I circle my hips and try to push down further, but my body struggles to accept his size.

A hiss leaves him as I circle and stretch around the first couple of inches I've managed to take. His look of awe sends a rush of warmth from my core, and I try to sink down again.

"That's it, Baby girl. Just a bit more," he groans.

The sexy husk in his voice acts like a key, allowing me to sink down until our bodies are fully flush.

"Jesus," he chokes, tipping his head back.

Every muscle in his upper body goes taut as I flutter around his long, thick length.

His grip tightens on my hips, his eyes dropping to where he's buried inside me.

"I'd have waited an eternity for you."

He lifts me by the hips, staring at the wetness coating his cock before he pulls me down and buries himself inside me again with a rough groan.

"You're everything I gave up hoping for a long time ago."

I run my hands down over his straining chest as he digs his fingers into my hips like he's trying to hold back. His eyes stay locked on my face as I curl my fingers through the short hair on his chest. It's thicker on the side without the scars.

He squeezes my hips, lifting me again, and encouraging me to start riding him slowly.

"Hallie," he utters.

I hold on to his shoulders as I work with him, moving in deep, slow strokes, our breath mixing in the tiny gap between us.

"You've never felt like someone's first choice, have you?" I whisper.

My heart cracks as something shifts behind his eyes before he blinks it away.

A muscle in his neck twitches, and he groans, as I clench around him.

"You're not only my first choice." I lift up and sink down onto him again. "You're the *only* choice I will ever make. It could never have been anyone else."

"Jesus," he utters, tightening his grip on my hips.

I increase my speed, spurred on by Sterling's deep moans of pleasure as he guides me up and down his length.

"That's it, Baby girl. Ride my cock. It's yours. Ride the hell out of it."

His eyes glint, and his pupils dilate as I cry out and clench around him.

Our speed increases, and he works his hips, thrusting into me mercilessly.

"That's my girl."

I whimper.

"Damn, you know just how to make me crazy. That's it. Bring that perfect pussy back down."

He grabs my ass, squeezing hard, his eyes glued to my face.

I moan as he bottoms out inside me again.

"Yeah, like that. Exactly like that," he rasps.

We fuck harder, desperate, and greedy. All gentleness is gone as we buck and thrust together, sweat slicking our skin where our chests press together.

Every minute since I arrived in New York has led to this moment. It was inevitable, no matter how much I tried to fight it. *We* were inevitable.

I grab on to his shoulders, digging my nails in as he fucks up into me so deeply that I cry out his name like I'm begging.

"You like that, my beautiful girl?"

"Yes!"

"So goddamn perfect, aren't you?"

His eyes are glued to mine, like two blue flames. I hand over all control, letting him set our pace. He spreads his thighs, forcing my legs wider around his hips. When he drives inside me again, my eyes roll in my head, and I gasp.

"Good girl, give yourself over to it. Come on my cock. All over it."

I clench in response to his filthy growl.

"Jesus," he hisses, spanking my ass with a sharp flick of his wrist. "Show me, Baby girl. Show me what you look like when you come with me buried inside you."

He slams me back down onto him, circling my hips inside his powerful grip, so that his body drags over my clit. I fight to think straight.

"Sterling," I whine.

He kisses the column of my throat, his voice vibrating against it. "Let it go."

My eyes roll as the pressure mounts inside me. Sterling slides a hand into my hair and grips it tight, holding me in place so he can watch.

"Let it go," he urges.

My mouth falls open and my vision blurs.

I come so hard that all I can do is cry out and trust that he won't let me go.

Wave after wave crashes through me. My body ripples around him, and he swells inside me, stretching me even more.

I choke out a sob as my body spasms, wringing out his pleasure with it.

The way he curses my name as he comes inside me, filling me with surge after surge of blazing heat, is a sound I'll never forget. It imprints itself, burning into my memory as he thrusts hard.

He comes so deep inside me that the sensation of him burying himself, mixed with his guttural growl, makes my orgasm stretch on and on until I screw my eyes shut, unsure how much more I can handle.

"God!" I shriek.

"Hallie."

His voice anchors me to him as my chest begins to shake

uncontrollably. The warmth of his mouth meets my quivering throat, and I suck in trembling breaths. He slows down his movements until he's still, nestled inside me, my body pulsing in aftershocks around him.

"I-I feel funny."

Emotion bubbles in my chest. But I can't control it. I feel happy and sad and vulnerable all at once.

Strong hands cradle my face, and I manage to open my eyes. His understanding gaze blurs as I realize my eyes are full of tears.

"S-Sterling."

"It's okay, Baby girl." He thumbs away my rapidly falling tears. "You're coming down, that's all. Don't be scared, I've got you."

My breath splinters, and I sink into his arms, sobbing.

I cry, soaking up every reassuring sound he makes, every gentle way he touches me.

All bringing me back to myself with tenderness and care.

Bringing me back to him.

I stay like that, safe and protected in his arms, letting him take care of me until my tears stop and my heart rate slows.

He's waiting for me when I'm fully present, his eyes latching on to mine as I lift my head from the crook of his neck and refocus on him.

He takes one of my hands and places it over his chest, over his scars.

"You're okay, Hallie," he breathes.

My heart feels like it could burst inside my chest. I lunge forward and crush my mouth to his in a desperate kiss.

"I love you."

His breath leaves him in a rush like he's waited his whole life to hear someone say that and really mean it.

He takes my face between his palms and holds it still.

"I love you too, Hallie. I love you in a way I never thought

I'd ever be able to say. In a way I gave up believing in. You've brought magic into my life when I started to think it didn't exist."

I sob and press my lips to his again, losing myself in him, soaking up every spark of magic as they fire through my body.

And they keep firing over and over as he kisses me, holding me in his arms, taking care of me.

And I let him.

For the first time in my life, I hand over all responsibility to someone else.

This time, I'm not scared.

I *welcome* it.

Because it's him.

And he's exactly where I'm supposed to be.

21

STERLING

I'M GETTING EGGS OUT OF THE REFRIGERATOR TO make Hallie breakfast when the intercom buzzes.

"Mr. Beaufort?" the building's concierge greets after I answer it. "There's a guest here to see you."

I study the image on the screen.

"Okay. Send them up, please."

"Certainly, Sir."

I walk back into the living area as Hallie appears from my bedroom, rubbing the back of her tousled hair. She yawns and gives me a shy smile.

"Is this okay?" She gestures up and down her body with a finger.

I take in her long slender legs and her mid-thigh, where the edge of my shirt is hanging.

"Is it okay?" I chuckle and walk to her, wrapping her in my arms and pressing a kiss to the top of her head. "It's more than okay. All of my shirts now belong to you. They look much better like this."

She slides her arms around my waist, placing her cheek to

my chest. "I just saw it and wanted to wear it. I should go and shower, though."

My eyes slide across the room toward the hallway that leads to the front door.

"No. Stay as you are."

She hums contentedly as I stroke her back before there's a knock at the door.

"Just a minute."

The man on the other side of the door when I open it is at least three inches shorter than I expected.

"Is Halliday here?"

I lean against the doorframe in no rush. "Depends on who's asking."

His upper lip curls in an unimpressed sneer. "Tell her Rory's here to see her."

I hold my hand out, giving him a smooth smile. "Sterling Beaufort. Why don't you come in and tell her yourself?"

He looks at my hand before placing his in it and squeezing like he's trying to crush my fingers. I bite back a smile. Molly could teach him a thing or two. She has a better grip on her baby dolls if you try and extract one from her arms to get her in her car seat.

His nostrils flare before he lets go.

"Please." I stand back, opening the door wide to allow him entry.

He strides in, not bothering to wipe his feet, his gaze fixed forward but his eyes darting side to side to scrutinize the artwork I acquired at a generous price at auction.

I follow him into the living area and stand to one side. His gaze falls on Hallie with her back to us, making herself a coffee at the counter.

His cocky footsteps grind to a halt as he registers what she's wearing.

He turns and glares at me.

"Who was at the door?" she asks without turning.

She places the mug down, and I see it's mine. My girl's making me a coffee before she does her own. I hold back from knocking this idiot out of the way so I can go over there and pull her into my arms.

"Hi, Halliday."

She turns, her eyes widening when she sees him.

I walk over and slide my arm around her waist.

"Your friend came to visit," I say, looking at Rory, and curling my hand around her hip. "A surprise visit," I add, hitching my brows at him.

His eyes drop to my fingers stroking her hip bone.

"Friend, huh?"

He lifts his eyes to mine, something flashing in his that makes the hairs on the back of my neck spring to alert.

"Oh, Halliday," he tuts in a mocking voice. "You didn't tell him?"

Hallie stiffens as his eyes slide to her, then back to mine with a glinting arrogance.

"Maybe I should introduce myself again?"

"Stop," Hallie urges in a pained whisper.

But he's already stepping forward with a smarmy grin.

"Nice to meet you, Mr. Beaufort." He sneers. "I'm Rory. Halliday's husband."

22

HALLIDAY

"What the hell? What are you doing here?" I gape at Rory standing with an arrogant smirk on his face.

"I was worried. I heard you had an accident. I thought you'd be at your apartment. I didn't expect to find you here." Rory's gaze roams around the room, and he frowns as he looks out of the windows at the multi-million-dollar view. "Looks like you've settled in just fine."

I whip my gaze beside me. "Sterling, I—"

His arm has already detached itself from me before the deep rumble of his voice makes my heart squeeze. "Sounds like you two have some talking to do."

"It's not—"

"Hallie," he says, his eyes pinned on Rory. "Why don't you go and get dressed. I'll keep your *husband* company until you come back."

I turn and rush from the room.

I go into Sterling's dressing room and pull a knitted dress from a hanger. I take off his shirt, unable to look at it as I place it carefully down onto the large stool in the center of the room. I pull on some underwear and the dress, then drag on a pair of long boots and grab my coat.

I rake my fingers through my hair as I race back into the living area.

The two men are facing one another in silence. Sterling's leaning back against the counter drinking his coffee, seemingly relaxed, while Rory has his hands on his hips, glaring at him.

At least there isn't blood.

"Sterling—"

"Why don't you go to that place two blocks over that does good coffee? I'm afraid I've run out."

His eyes meet mine for a brief moment, and I swallow, my voice stolen from me at how business-like he's being.

How devoid of emotion.

I nod mutely, looking at the floor.

"Hallie?"

I snap my eyes back to his, hope burning in my throat.

"It's okay, we'll speak later."

His eyes darken, then his gaze leaves mine, taking the air in my lungs with it. He's dismissing me. He won't even hear me out. Won't let me explain.

I stare at him while he sips his coffee, his eyes back on Rory. What was last night about? He said he loved me. I told him I had fallen head over heels in love with him. I *cried* while he was inside me because everything between us had felt so intense.

How can he switch off from that in the blink of an eye? All from one word?

Husband.

I know it's a big word, but if he'd listen to me... If he'd let me speak...

Bile rises in my throat as he leans back against the counter, one ankle crossed over the over.

A picture of calm.
I knock past Rory and head straight for the door.
I need air.

"You look great." Rory scans the top half of my body as I sit opposite him at a window table for two.

He reaches across the table for my hand, but I slide it away and wrap it around the mug of my untouched Americano instead. I keep my other hand beneath the table, a small piece of black onyx wrapped inside my palm. It's a crystal that aids in strength and moving beyond bad relationships. I always keep a pouch of mixed crystals in my purse. You never know when time might call for one to assist you.

And I need all the help I can get for this conversation.

"Why are you here?"

He leans back with a smirk. "Is that any way to greet your husband?"

"You've never been my husband!" I snap. "That was a mistake, and you know it. I don't even remember any of it."

"Shame. I remember it all. Especially how eager you were to say, 'I do'."

I roll my eyes. I doubt that was the case, but the fact I was so drunk I can't remember means I keep my mouth firmly shut. Rory can say whatever he likes about that night in Vegas and our so-called 'marriage'. None of our friends who were out that night can fill me in, either. Apparently, Rory and I disappeared, and the next morning was the first they heard about our little visit to the walk-in chapel. I'm just glad I woke alone, with Rory on the couch of the hotel room and not in the bed with me. He confirmed we hadn't... *consummated* it. I called Sophie immediately in a wild panic, and she was already on our annulment before I'd dragged my aching, hungover body out of bed.

"Calm down, I'm only teasing," Rory says, throwing his hands up in mock surrender when I glare at him.

"Yeah? Just teasing when you called yourself my husband in front of Sterling too, huh? You had no right."

"Hey, I didn't know you haven't been honest with the old guy." He leans across the table, resting on his forearms. "You're not... You're not actually *fucking* him, are you?"

"That's none of your business!" I hiss. But my gut twists. He's right. I should have been honest with Sterling sooner.

"Never had you down as a grave robber."

"Will you shut up and tell me what you're doing here?"

"Your mum and dad's new TV is great."

The blood in my veins boils as he lifts his coffee to his lips, taking a leisurely sip. I want to knock it out of his hand and slap him.

"Your dad needed some help setting it up. I ended up staying for lunch. They're so proud of you. They didn't stop telling me the whole time I was there."

"Don't."

"Don't what?"

He smiles at me like we're old friends catching up without a care in the world. He might think we were friends once. I even did. But he would never have kept Vegas hanging over me like an axe all these years if he was truly my friend.

"Don't bring my parents into this. I won't let you do that anymore."

He whistles. "Coming to New York gave you some extra sass. I like it on you."

I swallow the bile in my throat as his eyes drop to my cleavage.

"I'm not doing this again."

I stiffen at the negative energy surrounding him. He's a liar. He said he'd stop. But here he is. Again.

"It's only thirty grand, Halliday. That's pocket change to you. Definitely pocket change to—"

"Keep Sterling out of this."

His eyes glint before he shrugs. "Sure, whatever. I just need it to tide me over while I wait for some things to get sorted. It'll be the last time."

I snuff out the spark of hope that ignites in my gut at his words before it can gather momentum. It's not worth it. I stopped believing a word that came out of Rory's mouth a long time ago.

I exhale wearily and my gaze wanders over the row of parked cars on the street.

"No."

"No?" he scoffs.

"No," I repeat with more force.

"You don't mean that." Desperation creeps into his tone. He's never heard that word from me before.

I turn back to him. "I've had enough of you turning up in my life like this. It has to stop."

"It will. This is the last time, I promise." His eyes bore into mine, and a tiny part of me feels sorry for him.

"You say that every time."

"I mean it."

I shake my head. "Rory—"

"Don't say no. *Please.* Just... think it through first. One more time, that's it."

His gaze is pleading, and I grip the crystal in my palm so hard that my fingers ache.

What will he do if I really do put a stop to it all? He's more riled today than I've seen him before. He's a man on edge, and that's dangerous. He could finally do what he's been hinting at all this time.

He could destroy everything.

But if I let this go on when will it end? He might never stop. And now he knows I'm with Sterling, he could try and use that. Sterling's got a lot more money than me. Rory doing this to me is bad enough. But I can't allow him to drag Sterling into any of my mess. I can't.

"Go home, Rory," I say as I stand, fighting to keep my voice from betraying how terrified I am at what he might do.

What he might ruin.

"Halliday?"

"Enough is enough." I look at him with a mix of pity and disgust.

Before my strength deserts me, I walk out.

Glancing back through the window as I rush down the sidewalk, I spot Rory.

He's sitting with his head in his hands.

Like a man who's lost everything.

◆

"Don't tell me he won't see me!" I glare at the doorman outside Seasons.

Walking from the coffee place to Sterling's office has allowed me more time to think. More time to get angry. So much of that anger is at Rory. And so much is at myself too.

But all of the energy bubbling beneath the surface, ready to fly out now, is for Sterling.

The doorman listens to something in his earpiece, his eyes on mine.

"Mr. Beaufort was on a call. I'm checking it's finished."

"And has it?"

He inclines his head, opening the door for me. "Go ahead, Miss Burton."

"Thank you!" I snap, storming down the corridor.

Rory dropping in all those little things about my parents—he really enjoyed telling me those parts—and flying over here to use me again has started a storm inside me.

Bastard. Bastard. Bastard.

But at least my disdain for him is distracting me from the pain seeping through my veins at the way Sterling let me go with Rory. The way he didn't let me explain.

The way he did *nothing*.

His office door hits the wall as I throw it open and rush inside without knocking.

"Is that it? This is how you're going to be? You're not going to listen to what I have to say? You're going to let a guy like Rory turn up and ruin it all?"

"Hello, Hallie." His blue eyes flick up from the paperwork he has in his hand momentarily. Then he takes his time signing it, before putting the lid on his pen and placing it down.

He sits back in his seat and runs a hand around his jaw, his eyes scanning over me and making my cheeks heat.

"How was your coffee?"

I stomp to his desk, ripping my coat off on the way and chucking it onto the sofa as I pass it.

"How was my coffee?" I splutter, screwing my face up.

He holds my eyes, looking completely unruffled, while I worry I might pop a vein at any minute.

"It's good there. The beans are brought in fresh daily. That's why I recommend it's where you two go."

"I have no idea how my stupid coffee tasted. You know why? Because I couldn't drink a drop after the way things were left between us at your place.

"The way things were left?" His eyes pinch a fraction.

"Why are you so calm?" I shriek. "A man just appeared claiming to be my husband, and you aren't even bothered. If that were me, I'd be spitting feathers. I'd be..."

I slam my palm down onto the desk, sucking in air like I'm in danger of passing out.

"I'd be—"

"You'd be all fired up like you are now," Sterling muses, studying me. "All that energy when I first met you. All that grit. You've been worrying so much that it's been doused recently. Not anymore." A small smile curls his lips. "Welcome back."

I falter, taking a step back from his desk. Is he messing with me? Is this all a big game to him?

He holds my eyes but makes no attempt to stand or come to me. No attempt to stop me from spinning on my heels and stalking out of his office again.

"He isn't my husband."

"Come here."

My brows shoot up at his demand.

"Come here, Hallie." He pushes his chair away from his desk, making a gap big enough for me to slide in front of him.

Something in his low tone makes me comply. I have to know what he's thinking. Why he'd cut me off like this without letting me explain.

Even if I'm about to get my heart handed back to me, ripped to shreds, I have to know what he's going to say.

And after everything that's happened, I need to look into his eyes as he says it.

I slip into the small gap and lean back against his desk, my arms crossed tightly over my chest like they'll offer protection.

His eyes burn into mine and he reaches up to loosen his tie.

"Sit," he commands.

I don't move.

He uncurls my arms gently, placing them down by my sides. Then he grips my waist, lifting me onto the desk.

My ass lands on top of the paperwork he was signing, creasing it, but he doesn't seem to care.

"Lean back."

I stare at him, my chest heaving with angry, confused breaths. He takes his time rolling one shirt sleeve up, followed by the other with meticulous care.

My eyes drop to the scars running up his left forearm. He was so tender last night. So loving. I desperately want to hold on to those memories if they're all I'll have left of him after today.

He plants a hand over my chest. "Lean back," he repeats, easing me down until I'm resting on my elbows.

"What? Why?"

He slides his hands down my thighs slowly.

Then he shoves my dress up around my waist like his patience has snapped.

"What are you doing? Sterling?"

"Removing obstacles."

He holds my eyes and hooks a finger into my lace panties, ripping them. Cool air whips against my clit and I shudder, trying to clench my thighs together.

He brackets his hands around my flesh, the veins in his arms popping as he forces my legs apart.

"You won't even remember his name when I'm done with you, Hallie. Husband or not."

His gaze drops between my thighs and each warm breath he takes skates over my skin leaving goosebumps behind.

"I don't understand. Don't you have questions? Aren't you mad?"

"I'm livid. But I've also waited a long time to do this."

There's a shimmer glossing over the rage. It passes through

those dreamy eyes the way it does when he does something charming. When he acts like a gentleman.

His attention returns between my legs where he's spreading my pussy lips wide with two fingers.

He pulls his chair closer.

And spits directly on my clit.

"Mine," he growls.

I jolt off the smooth wood surface as he engulfs my clit with his mouth and sucks.

"No, you don't, Baby girl. You aren't going anywhere." He slides both hands under my ass and grabs it, slamming me down on the desk, sinking back into me with a groan like he's in ecstasy. "So damn beautiful."

My breath comes in pants as arousal thrums through my body, all at his command. It doesn't matter that my head's spinning with confusion, my body reacts to him like a crazed fan meeting their hero; eager and desperate to relish every second.

He gives my ass a firm squeeze before freeing one hand and spearing me with two fingers. He curses at the way I whimper from the intrusion and gets straight into eating me out fiercely.

"Jesus, you're soaking." He pumps his fingers in and out of me, and my body makes obscene wet sounds.

"Sterling," I whimper. "What—?"

"You learn so much more by listening and not talking, Hallie." He sucks my clit hard again, making my back bow as another wave of wetness runs down his fingers. "So why don't you talk? And I'll listen."

He pushes his face into me, eating me out like a man possessed. His darkened gaze bores into mine.

Last night was amazing. Hot, but tender too.

This is... this is pure carnal desire.

"Start talking while I enjoy your pretty cunt, Baby girl," he growls.

Yep, dirty, filthy, carnal desire.

"H-he's not my husband," I moan as Sterling adds a third finger and my body accepts it greedily.

I pause and his fingers halt in their movements, his tongue leaving my clit. I want to squeal at the loss.

"B-but he was for a few hours," I confess.

He curls his fingers and strokes my G-spot, sucking my clit between his lips again.

"God, Sterling, please."

"Keep going, Hallie."

He swirls his tongue in circles over my swollen clit, rewarding me for every word I speak. I'm desperate for him to keep going. Not just for the mind-blowing pleasure that's taking over my body, but because I want to tell him.

I need to tell him.

"It happened in Vegas at a friend's birthday," I say in a rush. "I had too much to drink. It's why I don't drink anymore. We didn't... Nothing happened... I've never liked him that way. I don't even remember going to the chapel."

"What else?"

I reach down and grab a handful of Sterling's hair, throwing my head back with a moan as he pushes his tongue inside me.

"Sophie's a lawyer. She annulled it for me the minute I found out what had happened."

His growl vibrates against me and my body sends wetness flooding his tongue. He inches back, swallowing with a curse.

"So damn sweet."

He pushes his fingers inside me and fucks me roughly with them as his mouth returns to my clit. His stubble rubs against my inner thighs, and I tighten them around his head.

"I'm going to come if you keep doing that," I whimper as he tongues my clit with precise skill.

He holds my eyes and confusion swells in my chest.

"I don't understand. Are we over?" I choke, teetering on the edge of coming, yet fighting against it.

I don't want to be his angry fuck. The one he has before he breaks my heart and pushes me away.

"I wish it had never happened. I never wanted it. I've regretted it every second since." I twist my hand in his hair as a roll of pleasure curls its way around my throat and squeezes. "I love you. Does that mean nothing now?"

His eyes darken. "It means everything, Baby girl. You damn well know it does."

He speeds up his lashing on my clit, massaging my G-spot again with thick fingers.

"Sterling—"

"I believe you. I know you would have told me yourself when you were ready," he says against me, like he doesn't want his mouth to leave my skin for a moment. "I told you it was okay. Right before you left. I told you it was okay."

"But—"

"Come on my face. I've spent all morning missing you."

His tongue flattens, working over my clit with the perfect amount of pressure. My core coils tighter and tighter. But I still can't let go. My head is stuffed full of doubt.

"I love you, Hallie," Sterling soothes. "And I'll still love you after the last breath leaves my body. Now come back to me, Baby girl, and show me you're mine."

He circles my clit over and over, watching as I toe the line between giving up control or desperately clinging to it. "That's it, let it go."

Every muscle in my body draws in tight, and my thighs quiver around his head.

"Let it go, my beautiful girl," he purrs.

"Fuck!" I come hard and a gush of wetness squirts out of me and sprays over his cheeks and chin.

"Jesus Christ, yes." He sinks into me, lapping up every drop he can. "Damn, Baby girl, drown me with it, come on."

I shudder and shake against his relentless sucks, licks, and kisses as more seeps from me, running down his chin.

I've never done that before.

Our eyes lock. The blaze in his has me mesmerized. It's hypnotic.

I ride out the last clenches in my body, then sag back onto my elbows, my grip falling from his hair.

He takes his time pressing gentle kisses over my sensitive flesh, and my pussy clenches when his stubble grazes my clit.

I can't talk. I can barely breathe.

All I can do is stare at him in shock.

His silver stubble glistens with wetness. He runs his tongue over his lower lip like he's savoring the taste of me. Then he lifts the length of his tie and mops up the drops from his chin.

The silk is stained, ruined.

"I might damn well frame it," he rasps, arching a brow at the way I'm staring at him.

He leans back in his chair, eyes swimming with tenderness again, just like they were last night.

Before Rory showed up.

"I don't... I thought you were mad. You told me to leave. You—"

"I said you two needed to talk. I never told you to leave. I would *never* tell you to leave."

He tugs me into his lap so I'm sitting sideways with my legs draped over his.

"I—"

"I've been wanting to taste you on my desk since that first night we kissed."

His lips travel to my neck, and he kisses beneath my ear, murmuring about how good I smell.

"I... thought you were angry."

"I am." He looks me dead in the eye. "I'm angry at myself for not preventing the look on your face when you saw him." He cups my jaw, tilting my face toward his. "You looked so worried."

Shame and guilt attach themselves to me like a million tiny parasites, the way they do whenever I think about Vegas.

"My parents don't know. I planned to tell them, but it was the first anniversary of losing Jenny, and Rory talked me out of it. He said they'd be ashamed, and I'd break their hearts. He said I'd completely wrecked everything she believed in. And he was right. I was so drunk I married someone I don't even like."

A sob bursts out of me, and I press a hand to my mouth.

"Jenny believed in love and soulmates. She's the one who gave me my faith in it too. And yet, I did *that*."

Sterling holds me as I break into ugly hiccups and sobs.

"You were grieving, Hallie. We do stupid things when we feel like we've lost everything."

He looks at me with such love and understanding that my chest splinters into ragged breaths and more tears fall.

"I don't even remember it. I didn't think I'd had that much to drink. Rory said I was the one who... the one w-who suggested we do it." I cover my face with both hands. "I'm a f-fraud. I vow to find people true love. And I married on a drunken whim like it was n-nothing."

Light filters through my eyelids as Sterling eases my hands from my face.

"Rory told you all of that?"

His eyes are narrowed, pinned on me as I peel my lids apart. If I thought there was rage in them before, then it's nothing compared to the murderous intent that's there now.

I wipe beneath my eyes. "He's right. I will never forgive myself."

"No. He's a cockroach who's been manipulating your grief. How long has he been calling you every day?"

I falter. "It can be weeks. Months, even, without a word from him. But it always starts again when he wants something."

I feel so pathetic admitting it. I run my own successful business, but I can't get a guy like Rory to leave me alone.

My gaze drops to Sterling's hand on my thigh, and I gently dust my fingers along his forearm, over his scars.

"When he wants something?"

I grimace.

"What's he threatening you with?"

I fight back the growing lump in my throat.

"Hallie?" Sterling growls.

My fingers tremble against his skin. "He said he'll tell my parents. I'm worried they'll never forgive me for lying all this time. And he said my clients might be interested to know that I divorced my husb—"

"Annulled! He was never your husband," Sterling thunders, his grip tightening on my thigh.

I trace over his scars with shaking fingertips, desperate to cling on to something that grounds me in the way the touch of his skin against mine does.

He exhales slowly, stroking my thigh gently as though my touch is calming him too.

"What else?"

I glance up.

"What else?" he presses. "I can see it in your eyes."

What I'm about to say next pains me more than knowing I married Rory in the first place. At least that was one isolated mistake. Just one.

"He helped my family... with money. My parents used

their savings for Jenny's school. I thought he was being a good friend and was so grateful. When my business began doing well, I repaid him. But then he asked me for a loan.

"I gave it to him. I was scared he'd tell my parents, jeopardize my business. He said he'd pay me back, but I haven't seen any of it. All that money I've loaned him is gone. I might as well have stolen it from Jenny's charity myself."

Even Sophie doesn't know how much I've lent Rory over the years. I'm too embarrassed to admit it. I thought he'd stop asking. He always says it's the last time, just like he did today. I hoped I'd earn enough from my matches that I could give more to Jenny's charity than Rory has cost me.

"Every time I think it's over, I start to hope. But he always shows up again sooner or later. I told him to never come back today. I'll tell my parents. I'll deal with whatever happens to my business. I can't let him keep doing this. I'm not a woman who deserves your love if I don't stand up to him."

"Let me take care of it. I'll make sure you never have to see him again," Sterling says with a finality that makes me suck in a breath.

I didn't think Sterling would ever be capable of hurting another person. This is the man who has held me when I've cried, who donates millions to charity, who has spent his entire life feeling like he was never anyone's choice.

A man with so much love in every cell of his body.

But one look into his eyes now and I see that, for those he loves, there isn't any limit to how far he'll go.

I shake my head. "No. This is my fault. I need to fix it. Enough is enough. And I can't risk him pulling you into it. You don't deserve that."

He presses the softest of kisses to my forehead.

"I'm so proud of the woman you are. It's one of the reasons I fell in love with you. You care for others more than yourself. He's abused the purest part of you. But you don't need to do things alone anymore. I'm here. And I will be here for you no matter what."

I sink my face into his neck, drawing strength from his trust and faith in me.

From his love.

He strokes my back, his touch strong and reassuring.

"You've got me now, Hallie. You don't need to worry about anything. I love you. I love you so damn much."

It takes everything in me to focus on his words and hope that he's right.

23

STERLING

"Give me an update."

I stare out of the car window at the Upper East side buildings as we drive, my cell pressed to my ear.

"He went to the deli on the corner. Got a pastrami sub, then went back to his hotel room," Denver replies.

I grind my teeth as I picture Rory, relaxed enough to eat when it took me half an hour to calm Hallie down after what she told me.

I knew that bastard was up to something the second I answered her phone and he demanded she send him 'thirty' something. Now I know he meant thirty grand. He's a prick that's never going to get the chance to look at her again if I get my way. No more coffees with her while Denver sits outside, keeping an eye on him.

Rory's lost all chances for me to be civil.

"What else did you find?" I run my pointer finger over my lips.

Mal clears his throat from the seat next to me and arches a brow. I've already filled him in on Rory's surprise arrival.

"Denver, I'm putting you on speaker. Mal's here with me."

"Mal," Denver clips as I hold my phone out so we can both hear. "So I checked his finances. Seems Rory is in debt to the grand total of four hundred and eighty thousand. A mix of bad investments and horse racing bets."

"Idiot." Mal snorts.

I clench and unclench my free hand, easing out the tension in my fingers.

"He fell behind on his mortgage and the bank repossessed his house two months ago. He's been couch-surfing since," Denver says.

"The parents?" I ask.

"They don't appear to be aware. He's still holding on to his job as an accountant. But that's about all he has left right now."

"Thanks, Denver. Stay where you are, keep an eye on him, and keep digging. I want to know everything there is to know about this guy. Especially what you can find out about what happened in Vegas. I'm going to pay him a visit myself, but I need to do something first."

"Yes, Boss," he replies.

"How are Killian and Jenson getting on?" Mal asks.

Rory's so in debt he'll be coming after Hallie for months if he thinks he can. I don't believe he'll tell her parents like he's threatened to, at least not yet. He needs the money too badly.

Mal knocks my arm with the back of his hand and gestures to my phone to make sure I'm listening. But I know Denver's got nothing new to report. If the boys had made a huge breakthrough in Cape Town, then he'd have already told me.

"They're still going through the CCTV footage, trying to identify the people present at the marina that week. Some are staff or regular visitors, so have been straightforward. But there are a lot of tourists, not all with good facial shots. And none of the cameras show the yacht, only the end of the jetty leading to it."

"Along with the other sixty vessels that were there at the same time," I mutter.

"So they're no closer to figuring out if there's even anything to follow up." Mal sighs and sinks back into his seat. The deep lines caused by grief and too many sleepless nights that have appeared over his face since losing his sister and nephew look like they're worked their way even deeper into his skin.

None of us came out of it without scars of some kind. Physical, mental, they're all there just the same.

"They're working hard," Denver says. "If there's something to find, they'll find it."

"They are," I agree, looking out of the window and seeing we're only a few blocks from where I need to be. "I'll send them something extra for their time later. You too," I add to Denver.

"Thanks, Boss," he replies.

"And thank you for taking care of Sinclair while her car was getting fixed. I know she doesn't go easy on you when you have to drive her around."

"She was relieved to have her own vehicle back," Denver replies gruffly, making me chuckle. I'm sure he's the one who is more relieved.

We hang up, and I press the intercom button for my driver.

"Pull over on the next block, please? I need to make a stop."

"Certainly, Mr. Beaufort."

"What are you planning? You have that look in your eye," Mal asks.

"Do I?"

He snorts through a quiet laugh. "Whatever it is, I hope the bastard doesn't cause Halliday any more problems. She's been good for you. I haven't seen you like this for…"

I side-eye him, waiting for him to finish his sentence, but he shrugs. He doesn't need to say it. I know what he's thinking. What everyone's thinking.

He's never seen me like this. No one has. Because I've never been in true, can't-get-enough-of-each-other love before.

Not like I am with Hallie.

And my whole family sees it.

"My flight's at eight tomorrow morning," he says, running a hand back through his sandy, slicked-back hair.

He colors his. He'd be more silver than me if he let it grow out. But Mal's never been one to accept ageing for what it is—a privilege denied many. He'll still be fighting to hold on to a part of the past until his deathbed calls.

"Give Ade and Sammy my regards."

"I will." Mal purses his lips like he wants to say something else. "You know, Ade will be trying to up his commission for the exports again."

I bite back my smile. There it is. The same thing he brought up weeks ago.

"Yeah. And you'll be reminding him of what a generous contract he already has. Just like Sullivan pointed out."

"You assholes." He chuckles.

I know he's messing. He's friendly with Ade, the guy who handles our mined imports from Africa, that's all. He'd love to offer him a bigger cut to enjoy with his wife, Sammy. But this is business. We own and run our own mines, employing the team in Africa that Mal heads up. They get a good deal. We look after our staff. And for as long as Ade remembers and appreciates that, then we'll look after him too.

But everyone gets greedy sometimes.

And some overstep, like bastards named Rory.

My driver pulls over, and I open the rear door.

"Circle the block a few times. I won't be long."

Mal peers at the building behind me and nods in understanding. "We'll be waiting."

24

HALLIDAY

"Interesting setup," Sullivan comments as he studies the circle of crystals I've laid out on the living room rug.

Sterling went into Seasons early this morning, and I'm planning on calling some potential new clients before meeting him for lunch later. Sullivan hasn't visited before unless Sterling's been here, so it's a nice surprise, despite catching me off guard.

"I was meditating. You can join me if you like?" I offer.

His brows rise sharply like I've suggested a stroll through Times Square stark bollock naked.

"It's good to take time out for ourselves. Life can get really busy sometimes," I add.

"How else would we want it to be?"

"Not a fast-track ride to burnout?" I smile weakly as he pins me with an unimpressed look.

Sterling didn't need to tell me that Sullivan's a workaholic, it's obvious. He'd benefit from some breathing and visualization techniques. but it might take a while before I persuade him to try some.

"Would you like a drink? Matcha latte?"

"No, I'm not staying. I only came to give you this." He holds a brown envelope out.

"What is it?"

"Open it."

I take it hesitantly, my eyes dropping over him. He's dressed in one of his usual suits—dark and impeccable. Just like him. I've never seen him flustered. Never actually seen him smile, unless it's for his daughter, Molly.

His gaze shifts from the envelope to my face as I pull the paperwork out and he waits for my reaction. The cool blue of his irises penetrate me like a shot of icy water as I glance at him. No wonder he's a formidable force in business. I've heard grown men have left his boardroom in tears. Now I understand how.

"Read it, Halliday."

"Umm, sure..." My heart rate picks up with each new sentence I scan over. "Are you serious?" I scoff, unable to stop myself.

Sullivan's eyes pinch a fraction at the corners. "Deadly."

Ouch.

I straighten, pulling my shoulders back as I read the document more thoroughly.

"Let's make this quick, I don't have all day."

"You want me to sign a non-disclosure agreement?" The words swim in and out of focus as the finality of them slams into me like a lead weight.

He doesn't answer. Instead, he pulls a pen from the inner pocket of his suit jacket and presses the lid with an ominous click.

Miss Burton agrees not to talk to the press about her relationship with Mr. Beaufort. Miss Burton will decline, if asked, to acknowledge, confirm, or deny, that a relationship occurred between herself and Mr. Beaufort.

It's not just an NDA. It's a gagging order. One that prevents me from talking to anyone about Sterling, not even my family. It erases our relationship if we were to ever break up. All traces. Gone.

"This is... very specific."

"The same courtesy has been extended to you. My father will sign it as well." Sullivan sounds bored as if he wishes I'd hurry up and stop taking up his time.

"Does he know I'm signing this?"

"*Are* you signing it? Or are you going to drag this out far longer than necessary?" He holds my gaze. "Beauforts stick together, Halliday. You know that from the *little* time you've spent with my father so far. Or were you not paying attention? Too busy thinking about your husband."

"Ex-husband! Not even that," I bite, irritation bursting up my spine that he's bringing up Rory. I glare at him before snatching the pen from his hand.

"That might be so. But I don't know you. And I don't like not knowing a person's... *motivations*. Besides, if you love my father, then why wouldn't you sign? This is only in the event you... part ways."

I get it. I do. I'm twenty years younger than his father. And Sterling is eye wateringly rich. But it's the way he says it, insinuating that there's something underhand to this. When our love is one of the purest, most magical things I've ever been blessed with.

"Okay." I take a deep breath, centering myself, and turning my attention back to the contract.

Flipping the pages, I find the parts I'm looking for and score through them with determined slashes of black ink.

"What are you doing?" Sullivan snaps.

"Making some adjustments," I retort, scoring through another paragraph of text.

I check I've not missed any parts I want to remove, then sign on the line and date it.

"There." I slide it across the counter toward Sullivan and place the pen on top.

"Adjustments?" One dark brow hitches in curiosity. "Enlighten me," he drawls like a cat toying with a mouse.

I soften my voice. "No one should ever have to go through what your family has. Sterling's been through enough. And I'll do whatever it takes to protect him like he's always protected me since we met."

I'll give it to him; his poker face is impenetrable. But I see the way his pupils flare in reaction to my admission. He flicks through the paperwork, looking at the sections I've crossed out.

"You sure about this?" he clips.

"Couldn't be surer." I smile but am met with eyes that still hold suspicion. Beauforts really do stick together. And it's painfully obvious Sullivan considers me to be outside of that circle. I can only hope that time will prove to him that I genuinely love his father and don't have any hidden motives.

"You crossed through all the parts that prevent my father talking about you," he states.

"That's right. I won't talk about him or your family. But I'm not subjecting him to the same silencing. He's had people make decisions for him before. He's had his choice taken away. If things ended between us..." Pain sears through my heart, the thought is crushing even though my soul tells me it will never happen. "If things ended, then I want to give him freedom to say what he wants about me and talk to whoever he wants. Because I will *never* take away his choice."

We fall into silence, until I ask. "How's Sinclair?"

"Still mad at you."

"Oh," I murmur.

It's been so long, and I miss her friendship. The thought

of her never coming around to the idea of me and Sterling together hurts me more than Sullivan asking me to sign an NDA. I'm happy to sign it and move on. But nothing I've said in texts or voicemails has made a difference to Sinclair. What if she never accepts our relationship?

I turn away to return to my meditating, needing the calm more than anything.

"Wait!" Sullivan barks. He slides the paperwork back into the envelope and buttons his suit jacket.

"Do you need me to sign something else?"

"That won't be necessary." His jaw clenches.

"Okay then." I turn away and his low-spoken words sink into my back.

"I've spent three years answering questions from people about how my father is. And 'fine' is not a word I want in my vocabulary when I have to answer them. Do you know what I told someone who asked yesterday?"

"What?" I frown, turning around.

"I told them he's the happiest I've seen him since that day. That he's in *love*." He grimaces at the word. "Now... you're the divine power facilitator, as you call yourself, so garner that power and facilitate whatever the hell it takes to make sure I can always tell people that."

"I will, I promise."

He nods curtly but says nothing.

I stare after him as he strides away, the sound of the front door closing echoing through the penthouse.

25

STERLING

"Are you serious?" Rory's eyes bug out in his head at the open briefcase filled with neatly wrapped bills.

"Deadly."

He looks at me before his gaze drops to the money on the bed in his hotel room. I'd have liked to have gotten here sooner—every second he's in New York near Hallie is a second too long—but it took the bank awhile to get half a million in cash ready on the spot.

"It's all in sterling," I say, taking no pleasure in the fact I'm paying him off in currency of my own name. I'd pay him off in any damn currency he wants if it means the prick will leave Hallie alone for good.

"I can see that." His lips twitch, and he lifts up a thick wedge and tears open the wrapper to sniff it.

My lip curls in disgust. "You don't ever call her again. You don't ever look her up online to see how much she's thriving without you leeching off her. You. Don't. Come. Back." I step closer, and he takes a step back, even though his chin juts up in defiance. My nose grazes his as I lean in. "From now on, you don't damn well *exist*."

He clears his throat, readjusting his collar, and inches back, eyeing the money again.

"Must be nice for Halliday, having a billionaire who wants to look after her." His eyes drop over my suit. "How old did you say you were? Sixty?"

I slam the briefcase lid closed, narrowly missing cutting his fingers off with it. I lift it by the handle and shove it into his chest.

"I performed the courtesy of booking your flight home. Your cab will be here for you within the hour."

He takes the briefcase, and my blood finally cools a degree for the first time since I hammered on his door. I could do a whole lot worse than send him on his way with enough money to solve his problems. But I'm giving him a chance to do the wise thing, the mature thing.

For Hallie.

If he cares for her at all, then he'll see this as an opportunity to do what's best for her.

Disappear.

I'm halfway to the door when his words hit my back.

"I bet you were born with a silver spoon in your mouth, huh? Living your life and having all this money, never getting your hands dirty. Bet you never did a real day's work in your life."

I don't turn around, but I swivel my head over my shoulder just enough that he can't miss my glare.

"It's best you don't think about what my hands get to do every day, Boy."

His face pales before he scoffs. "No! Last night will have been a one-off for her. A mistake. She won't chain herself to an old man who needs a pill to get it up."

I chuckle, and he stares at me as if I've gone mad.

I don't care what he thinks. I've got the love of a beautiful woman who burns as fiercely for me as I do for her. I'm not getting pulled into a dick measuring contest with a kid who looks like his mom still buys his shirts.

"Start packing. You don't want to miss your cab."

Hallie jumps up from the large sectional sofa as I walk into the living area.

"Are you okay?" She rushes to me and loops her arms around my neck, pulling me to her for a kiss.

"I am now," I murmur, kissing her back and lifting her into my arms. She wraps her legs around my waist, and I carry her to the kitchen counter, resting her on top of it.

"I thought you might have gone to see Rory."

"I did."

"Sterling..." She exhales in a rush. "You don't know what he's like. He's this bad smell that comes back worse the more you try to get rid of him. We're better off avoiding him until I've had a chance to see my parents. I have to tell them face-to-face."

I gently extract her lower lip from where she's biting it and study her face. I can still see the worry in her eyes. Rory turning up has rattled her.

"If he's smart, then he'll not be bothering you again."

Hope blooms in her eyes, and I hate that it even needs to be there in the first place. She's strong and capable. But Rory has been playing on those strengths—her love and devotion to those she loves, her pure heart—and he's used them to blackmail her. He's taken her fears about not being able to fulfill Jenny's legacy by spreading love and about letting down the charity. And he's used them for his selfish gain.

I should have killed him in that hotel room.

"You're so tense."

I kiss her, wanting to shed the events of the day.

"I'm fine. I'm more than fine."

I hold her around her waist and stroke my thumbs side to side across the base of her ribs. Being with her, touching her, is enough to clear my mind of anything and everything, except how damn lucky I am that she's mine.

She parts her thighs wider, balling my shirt between her hands as she pulls me closer and opens her mouth, inviting me in deeper. My straining dick weeps in my pants at the taste of her.

"You don't have your tie on," she murmurs between kisses.

I drop to kiss her neck. "Told you; I want to frame it."

I smile at the sound of her giggle.

"Did you say Sullivan has a thing on tonight? An early viewing of the new designs?"

I suck and kiss my way to her collarbone, peppering more kisses along one until I reach the little dip between. I inhale the scent of her before I lick her there, making her tip her head back with a moan.

"He does," I rumble, considering where to kiss her next. I move downward, kissing the swell of her breasts as they rise and fall with each quickened breath she takes.

"Are you going?"

I gently cup her breast in my palm. She watches me, a soft whimper escaping her lips—a sound that sends a jolt straight through me—as I gently nip her nipple through her clothes.

"No. We're going."

"You want me to come?"

"Hallie..."

"Okay." Her lips curl into a small smile. "So we're kind of official now?"

"Good girl, you're catching on." I bite her nipple again. "My family knows about us now, and we can tell the rest of the world whenever you're ready. I don't want to spend any more time apart from you than absolutely necessary. Besides, it won't be for long. It's just a small group of people going. We can come straight back here afterward."

"Uh-huh."

I chuckle again as she struggles to concentrate on what I'm saying. Her eyes are glued to my hand rubbing her breast.

"What do you want, Baby girl?"

She blinks through dark lashes.

"You."

"Me?"

"I want you inside me." She wiggles her ass against the countertop and pulls me up for a kiss. "I want to still feel you when we go out later." She brushes her lips side to side over mine. "I want you to come so deep inside me that it runs down my thighs tonight and makes me think of you."

"Jesus Christ."

I rip her dress over her head, followed by her bra. I unzip my pants and let them drop around my ankles. Within seconds, I yank her panties to one side and thrust inside her.

"Baby girl, talk like that and I'll be coming before I even get inside you next time."

I draw back and slam deep, burying my head into her neck.

"Sterling," she whimpers as I suck on her silky skin.

Her wet, needy body hugs me so tight it's like she's trying to suffocate my throbbing dick. I drive deep again, unable to get enough of the way she cries my name and sinks her nails into my shoulders as I fuck her.

"I want skin on skin," she pants, pulling at my shirt buttons.

I grab either side and rip the thing open, throwing it behind me onto the floor.

Her eyes don't widen when she looks at my scars this time,

no. They remain filled with molten desire as she strokes my torso, one hand gliding over it before gripping my shoulders for leverage, her nails biting into my flesh.

I groan and slam deep. Her wetness coats my cock. Her body clenches around me, and a new wave of arousal lets me pump deeper.

"Yes, like that. Fuck me hard," she mewls.

My ass cheeks tighten like steel as I let her have it.

I don't need asking twice.

26

HALLIDAY

"What do you think?" Sinclair asks, cradling a champagne flute as she appears beside me.

I school my expression as my heart pounds from the shock of her not only approaching me, but actually speaking to me after so long.

"I think you look stunning."

I gaze up at the giant image of her, dripping in various pieces of diamond jewelry, which hangs on one wall of the flagship Beaufort Diamonds store where Sullivan is showcasing an early viewing of the new designs.

She frowns, following my gaze.

"Ugh, not that. I hate that one. Sullivan chose it. I mean, Zoey and Ashton. They're so cute together, aren't they?" She bumps my shoulder, inclining her head in their direction.

"They are."

I smile over at where Zoey is wrapped around Ashton like a baby monkey, happily showing off her custom-made Beaufort ring to everyone they talk to. They look perfect together. He hangs on to her every word, looking at her like she's the most exquisite creature he's ever seen. And every time he murmurs something in her ear, she giggles and then kisses him.

"I want to be an artist's muse." Sinclair sighs and sips her champagne.

"I sense you'll be inspiring someone soon."

Her eyes drop to the glass in my hand in question.

"It's just orange juice. I haven't been drinking. I just have a feeling."

"Oh. You have a feeling?" Her brows shoot up. "Well, excuse me, but the last time you had a feeling, you had sex with my dad."

My eyes bug out and she snorts into her glass. Her eyes are bright as she catches mine. I let go, joining her in a laugh that starts deep in my stomach.

After a moment, she sighs. "I'm sorry for giving you the silent treatment. It just took me a little time to get my head around you and Dad."

"What made you... okay with it?"

"Something Sullivan said."

"Really?" The last time I really saw Sullivan, he was asking me to sign that NDA.

Sinclair shrugs. "Yeah. And Zoey reminded me that I hired you to make Dad happy. And he is. So I guess I shouldn't concern myself over how it happened, only that it did. I need to be more open to things happening in ways I'm not expecting. I just don't like surprises so much since everything that's happened."

"I understand that. And for what it's worth, thank you."

Sinclair returns my grateful smile and Sterling looks at us from the other side of the store, his eyes crinkling at the corners before he turns back to his friends.

"He's happy." Sinclair sighs. "It's what we wanted, me and Sullivan. And Uncle Mal. The whole family. He needed you."

"No, I was the one who needed him."

He says something that has the men with him nodding along in interest. One is Lawson, the art gallery owner. Another is Frankie. I'm sure Sterling said he worked in real estate when I met them both at the charity gala. And there's a third man with them tonight, a lawyer, who Sterling introduced as Roman.

They look like a real-life commercial for sexy men's suits, all standing together like that.

Sinclair gives me a coy look like she can read my mind.

"I've always thought Roman was pretty hot, as far as older guys go," she says, her eyes tracking to the tall dark-haired man.

I follow her gaze but my attention fixes on Denver by accident instead. He's standing against one wall, in his usual black suit, close to where the group of men are talking.

"Do you think Denver misses giving you rides now that you have your car back?"

Sinclair laughs, her eyes rolling. "You're funny. That sparkling personality of a man has barely spoken to me in the last five years. I figure he was born like it. Must have been at the back of the line when God handed out conversation skills."

I look back over at Denver, his eyes are on Sinclair, but he looks away the moment he sees me looking at him.

"Do you want another drink?" Sinclair asks.

"I'm good."

"Okay. I'll be back."

I smile at her before she makes her way to one of the long glass display cabinets that is serving as a bar area for tonight.

I sip my juice, soaking up the ambiance. Sterling said it was a small 'intimate' affair. But there must be around eighty people moving around the store, not including the staff who are carrying around the velvet display stands, showcasing the new designs. I've seen many of the guests try pieces on and marvel at how beautiful they are. I knew Beaufort Diamonds was a world-famous brand. But seeing it like this is still spectacular.

The store area itself is double height and has a huge, intricate crystal chandelier. All of the lighting makes the jewelry in the display cabinets glimmer so brightly it's almost blinding. Sterling gave me a tour when we arrived while Sullivan barked out meticulous orders to his staff. The rear office areas and private viewing rooms are dripping in luxury. Marble floors, velvet seating, silk cushions. Fish tanks with jewelry displayed inside them in large ornamental shells. The whole building smells of something expensive, like they pump out fragrance from the walls.

It's an experience just setting foot through the doorman operated entrance.

Sterling showed me the safe too. All of the millions of dollars' worth of jewels they haven't made into pieces to sell yet. I was too nervous to touch anything.

Sinclair looks at me from over at the bar where she's been pulled into a conversation with a couple who are admiring one of the new pieces—a bracelet—that she's wearing. I smile back to let her know I'm all right by myself before heading to the restrooms to freshen up.

My face glows in the ornate mirrors that are inside. Maybe it's all the orgasms. For every one of Sterling's, I have at least three. I'm so sexually attracted to him, it's insane. Now I'm finally letting it all in, my body literally hums with this aroused energy for him constantly. It's almost unbearable at times. I want his skin against mine all the time.

I bite my lower lip at the warm dampness in my panties, the evidence I asked him to leave for me so I could still feel him this evening while we're apart.

I exit the restroom and slow my steps as I recognize two deep voices coming from around the corner at the end of the corridor.

"I've got some in my office. I'll get them for you. You need to wrap it up, Dad. Unless you want to get Halliday pregnant."

I clap a hand over my mouth, creeping closer. I'm not sure whether to laugh or be mortified that Sullivan is talking to Sterling about us in this way.

"I don't need a biology lesson, Son. I know how these things work." Sterling chuckles.

I don't know what I expected him to say. But the way he's so calm about it, not panicking, makes something glow inside my chest.

"Fine. Don't say I didn't warn you if you end up getting called Daddy again," Sullivan grumbles.

"Being called Daddy, huh?" Sterling muses in his deep gravelly tone.

Sullivan scoffs out a disgruntled huff. "I don't want to know."

Footsteps echo in my direction but I don't move fast enough. Sullivan strides around the corner, his jaw set as he pulls his cell from his tuxedo jacket pocket. He almost collides with me, his eyes glued to the screen.

"Halliday," he greets, his blue eyes—so much like Sterling's—narrowing with curiosity as he looks at me.

"I chart," I blurt. "And we haven't had sex on any of my fertile days, so we're good. In fact, we could probably have nonstop sex for the next three days without issue. Then, we'll avoid Sterling finishing insid—"

Sullivan looks at me in horror.

"—Lovely party." I smile, internally wincing.

Sterling walks up behind him, chuckling.

"It is. A lovely party."

He pats Sullivan on the shoulder. Sullivan shakes his head and looks at the two of us like we're a couple of teenagers caught playing hooky, before he stalks off.

"I don't know why I told him that." I meet Sterling's twinkling eyes.

"He's a big boy, he can handle it."

He holds his hand out and links his fingers with mine.

"We should talk about it, though. Like he said. I don't want you to worry. I know the days we can do it safely. I should have brought it up sooner," I say.

"Hallie, it's fine." Sterling uses his other hand to lift my chin, tracing his thumb softly over my skin. "I knew we were taking risks, and I was going to talk to you about it. But if you're happy with this charting and it's a reliable method...?"

"It is."

"Okay." His eyes soften. "In that case, send me your chart so I can put it in my calendar."

"Send it to you?"

"I need to know which days I can't come inside you."

"Oh." Just him saying those words has my core pulsing with arousal.

"We'll find other ways to enjoy each other." He gives me a soft kiss.

"Mm-hm, we will," I agree, taking my time to kiss him back and wondering if anyone would catch us if I were to enjoy him again right now.

He pulls away with a groan. "Now I need to wait a few minutes before we walk out there."

My eyes drop to his impressive dick tenting his tuxedo pants. Maybe I could drop to my knees and help him with it.

He chuckles. "Later, Baby girl. We've got all night."

I thrum with light, bouncy energy as he leads me out into

the store a few moments later, his hand resting on my lower back.

"Did you try any of the new pieces on?" he asks, his deep voice husky in my ear.

"No. I'm too scared, they're all so beautiful."

"They're almost as beautiful as the person wearing them," he recites the company slogan, winking at me as he waves one of the staff over who's holding a large velvet display cushion in white-gloved hands.

He stops in front of us, and I stare at the collection of rings.

"Sterling," I murmur, my eyes darting around to see if anyone's watching.

"It's okay." He takes my left hand and holds it in his. "Which one?"

"Which one?" I balk.

He can't be serious. I look at the giant, glinting diamonds, then back at him.

He arches a brow in amusement.

"Which one?" he repeats.

I purse my lips, heat blooming across the back of my neck as I fluster.

"I mean, I guess I like that one best out of all of them." I point to a ring that has a row of diamonds. The one in the center is the largest, and either side taper down in size. "It reminds me of the beams of a sunrise."

"Hmm." Sterling takes the ring from the display and studies it. Then he slides it onto my wedding finger. "Looks good on you."

My breath snags in my throat, and I follow his burning gaze to my hand. He's stroking my knuckle above the huge ring. I can't deny it, it does look good, all twinkly and pretty. But it's the way his thumb moves over my skin without breaking contact to prevent me from taking if off that sets my heart racing.

"Looks really damn good," he rasps.

My cheeks heat as we stare at one another, just like we have so many times now, with something magical swirling between us. He's told me multiple times, and I've told him, that we're in this together. Yet, seeing a ring on my finger and noting the way his eyes are full of an intense, sinful possession, entwined with all that love and adoration, makes my head light and fuzzy.

"Nice," Sinclair says, nodding her approval as she appears next to me. "This is my favorite." She points to a solitaire princess cut diamond the size of a dime.

"They're all gorgeous."

I slip my hand out of Sterling's and remove the ring, placing it back onto the display cushion. His eyes are fixed on my face, a darkened heat smoldering in them. His hands might have kept to respectable places tonight, but the way he's looking at me is enough to let the world know there's something between us.

I shake my head, indicating to cool it down. He clears his throat, looking away and biting back a grin.

"This one looks like Trudy's." Sinclair points to an emerald cut diamond flanked by other smaller stones, making it look like a flower, oblivious to the come-fuck-me eyes her father was just giving me. "Uncle Mal chose the diamond himself from one of our mines. It's a shame she couldn't make it; she'd have liked to have seen these."

"Where is she?" I ask, concentrating on Sinclair so my cheeks will cool.

"Some college reunion with girlfriends."

I glance at where Mal is talking to an older couple, the woman pointing at a display of necklaces.

"He's flying to Botswana in the morning for a week to visit

the mines. I'm so jealous," Sinclair groans theatrically. "I haven't been out of the city in weeks. All my jobs have been here."

"Do you have any location shoots coming up?" I ask, a familiar head of blonde hair across the room catching my attention.

"Yes, next week, thank god. A swimwear shoot in Bermuda."

"That sounds great," I say as Lavinia makes her way to us.

Sterling steps closer to me and slides his hand onto my lower back as she reaches us. She gives me and Sinclair a small smile and says hello, but her eyes quickly dart to Sterling.

"Quite the turnout." She moves closer, then retreats like she's about to kiss him hello but thinks better of it.

"It is. Sullivan's done a great job. You look well," Sterling says, oozing his usual polite charm.

Lavinia's eyes brighten. "So do you. I was hoping we could talk. I accompanied William here"—she waves in the direction of man wearing glasses—"but we can't stay for long."

"Nice to see you, Lavinia," Sinclair chirps as she's drawn away by another guest.

Sterling clears his throat. "Lavinia—"

"I want to apologize." She looks at me and I feel bad for her. She must be embarrassed after what happened at his penthouse. She has no idea I was there and heard everything.

Or any idea what Sterling and I did against the door after she left.

I shift a little on my feet, ready to excuse myself, but Sterling slides his hand from my back and around to my hip, clasping it so I don't move.

"I'm sorry," she continues. "We've been friends a long time. I'd like it to remain that way."

The man she gestured to appears by her side and holds his hand out.

"Sterling, good to see you."

"William," Sterling greets as the two men shake hands.

William's eyes move to me, and Sterling's grip tightens on my hip.

"Hallie, this is William Fulton. He's a very talented chef with three restaurants in the city. William, this is Halliday Burton. She's a very talented businesswoman who works magic."

I smile as William takes my hand. "Pleased to meet you, Halliday."

"And you," I reply.

"So, magic?"

I smile. "I bring people together. Find them love."

"Ah, so you're a matchmaker?" His eyes move from me to Sterling. "And you're working together? How long ago did Elaina—?"

"Two years," Sterling clips, stiffening beside me.

William's brows shoot up. "Two? And you're ready for...? That's... Well, good luck. I don't expect dating at our age is easy." He chuckles uneasily, his eyes roving around the room as if he's looking for an escape.

"William," Lavinia chimes in, "two years is plenty of time. And Elaina was no saint. If you knew what she'd been up to, you'd be applauding Sterling for waiting this long."

William pales, his throat bobbing. "Of course, I didn't mean anything by it."

"No harm done," Sterling replies smoothly.

I look at him, but his eyes are fixed on Lavinia. A muscle in his cheek clenches.

"It was nice to meet you, Halliday," William says quickly before looking at Lavinia. "My car's outside. We should..."

"Of course." Her gaze drops to Sterling's hand on my hip before she paints a bright smile on her face. "Halliday, I hope you're successful in your search. And Sterling, it was good to see you." She squeezes his forearm, then leaves with William.

"You said no one knew about the affair."

"I didn't think they did," he murmurs.

"They were friends. Elaina must have told her."

"Perhaps. Lavinia's never mentioned it, though, and she didn't see Elaina much those last few months. She was overseas on a charity mission."

"Oh. That's.... a little weird, then," I say.

Sterling's brow is furrowed as he watches Lavinia and William exit through the main door on the far side of the room.

We stay until all of the guests have left and only staff and family remain.

Sterling pulls me into his arms and presses a kiss straight to my mouth with a groan. "Do you realize how hard it's been not to do that all evening? Especially knowing you aren't wearing a bra underneath this dress?"

I smile into his kiss, ignoring the staff around us, packing up all of the jewelry to take to the safe.

He slides his hand down over the silver satin until his fingertips graze the top of my ass. He doesn't move any further, maintaining some gentlemanly manners. But the heated glint in his eyes conveys all the filthy things he's planning for me when we get back to his place.

"Let's go," he murmurs, kissing me again.

"Don't you want to wait for the others?" I look over to where Sullivan is giving out instructions to his staff. Sinclair folds her arms as she says something to him.

"No, they're fine." Sterling holds my small wrap out, slipping it around my shoulders.

"Boss?" Denver clears his throat as he walks over. "Sullivan's suggested I take Sinclair home instead of him. He says he still has things to finish up here."

"Good. As long as she's safe."

"I always make sure she's inside and the door is bolted before I leave," Denver says, his expression serious.

"Thanks, Denver. See you in the morning." Sterling pats his shoulder, and Denver strides in the direction of Sinclair, who looks like she's complaining to Sullivan, shaking her head as she talks.

As we exit, the cold night air hits me, and I lean gratefully against Sterling's warm, solid side as he wraps his arm around me and holds me close.

"Safe flight," Sterling calls to Mal as he heads to his waiting car.

"See you in a week," Mal replies as he opens the rear door.

Sterling reaches out and opens our car door for me. His warm lips catch my cheek in a kiss. "In you get, it's cold."

I turn to smile at him but freeze as a man pushes off from the wall a little further up the street and moves toward us.

"Hell no," I mutter, watching Rory get closer. I knew it was too good to be true hoping he'd actually listen to me and keep away.

Sterling tenses and whips his head around, causing Rory to freeze in his tracks.

"Get in the car, Hallie," he says calmly.

I glare at Rory, my fingers tingling with the urge to run at him and bite and scratch. Why can't he leave me alone?

"You look... That's a nice dress," Rory says, his eyes dropping over my body.

I pull my wrap around me tighter, but it does little to hide my nipples, puckering against the fabric from the cold. Rory doesn't even try to hide the way he's zeroed in on them. Maybe he's been drinking. He looks kind of glassy-eyed.

Sterling positions himself in front of me. "You either believe you're brave, or you're just plain dumb."

"Better than being old and delusional," Rory says, tipping his chin as he tries to look down at Sterling. But Sterling's at least four inches taller, so the move is pointless.

"Please get in the car, Hallie," Sterling says again in a deep, confident gravel.

I lay a hand on his bicep and look out from behind him at Rory. "He's not worth it," I say as his muscles harden beneath my grip.

"Sterling? Everything all right?" Mal calls from the sidewalk where he hasn't gotten into his car yet.

Rory looks at Mal, then back at Sterling and snorts. "What's the matter, old man? Scared your hip will give out if you fight me? You going to get your ancient buddy there to help you?"

"We're fine," Sterling calls back to Mal.

"Can we go?" I ask, my hand still curled around his solid arm.

"It's okay, Hallie. I'm a gentleman and I'll settle this like one," Sterling replies, his hardened eyes pinned on Rory like a hunter lining up their shot.

"How's that?" I whisper.

A muscle in his neck tenses, his vein pulsing steadily next to it. "In private."

He helps me into the car before sliding into the rear seat beside me. He shuts the door, ignoring the slow clap coming from Rory on the sidewalk.

"Think you can buy me off, old man?" he says, tapping on the window with a leery grin. "Well, bravo, nice try. But I'm not going anywhere."

"Oh my god." I press my fingers against my temples.

Sterling's right. He's plain dumb.

The car pulls away, leaving Rory behind us.

Sterling takes my hand, interlinking our fingers. "You okay?"

"You tried to pay him to leave me alone?"

"I did. I'll always take care of you, whatever it takes," he answers without hesitation.

Three hundred thousand dollars at the charity fundraiser, plus whatever amount he gave Rory.

"You'll do it no matter what I say, won't you?"

Despite the tension over his face, his lips quirk. "You're catching on."

I can't be mad at him for trying. I'd do exactly the same for him if he needed it, and I thought it would work.

"I don't know why Rory wouldn't just take it and go. He sounded so desperate for the money."

"Some things make men more reckless than money."

I frown in confusion.

"He didn't want that annulment, did he?"

I stare at him, realization coiling around me and squeezing until I think I might be sick.

"No," I whisper. "He suggested we give the marriage a go the next morning. I thought he was joking. Oh god!" I screw my eyes shut and rub my forehead. "He's never going to leave me alone. The sooner I get back and see my parents, the better. I can't stop him from trying to ruin my business, but I can at least make sure they hear it from me first."

"I'll get us a flight organized."

"Really?"

"You need to see your parents, Hallie." He lifts our joined hands to his lips and kisses my fingers. "So we'll go and see them. I'd like to meet them."

"Thank you." I exhale, my shoulders loosening.

"Now, lose all thoughts of him because I have plans for us when we get back."

Despite the sour turn of the evening, my core thrums to life, and I press my thighs together.

"You do?"

Sterling chuckles.

I'll never get enough of him looking at me like this, happiness making the blue of his eyes shimmer like tropical waves.

Even Rory can't ruin that.

27

STERLING

"You're so deep," Hallie gasps as I thrust inside her.

My grip tightens on her trembling hips as I retreat, pulling all the way out. I marvel at how damn beautiful the shine of our mixed cum is as it coats my rock-hard dick.

"You look so good from this angle," I groan.

My abs clench and I pull her ass back to meet my balls and slam inside her again. We've been fucking for hours. I haven't been able to let her go since we walked into my penthouse this evening.

After we saw Rory.

That bastard.

I thrust again, and she clenches around me and arches her back, making her filled pussy lift as if on display for me. I might be a grown man, but I haven't been able to quell the insatiable need to fuck her over and over and claim her as mine.

Because she is *mine*. And I'm hers. He needs to get it through his thick skull that he will never have a chance with Hallie.

"Baby girl, you're going to have me everywhere soon."

"Please," she whimpers.

I bend so my chest is flush with her back, and I can whisper in her ear. "Where do you think will have taken the most of my cum tonight? Your mouth or your cunt?"

"God, Sterling," she moans as I reach forward and force two fingers inside her mouth. She sucks on them greedily, swirling her tongue over them the way she did to my cock the minute we got through the door.

We're damn well feral for one another.

"Those days on your chart?" I groan as I straighten up again, curling my hands back around her hips.

"The ones where you can't come inside me?"

"Yeah, those." I suck in a sharp breath as her thighs begin to shake. She's about to come again. Jesus Christ, she's perfect. And mine.

I deepen my thrusts, loving the way she mewls for more and pushes back onto my dick, taking it so eagerly.

"Maybe you'll have to…" She pushes her ass up and whimpers.

"That's it, Baby girl, come again for me."

She obliges, screaming out my name as her pussy falls into rhythmic spasms around my dick. I fuck her through them, smiling to myself as I manage to squeeze a second orgasm from her before the first has even had time to finish.

"Maybe you'll have to come somewhere else inside me instead," she pants, riding the waves out over my cock.

"Somewhere else?"

"In my ass."

"Jesus!" The mental image steals my control, and I come hard without warning.

I place my thumbs on her ass cheeks, prizing them open further so I can see her perfect tight hole as my balls unload with each harsh drive of my hips.

"You're so damn perfect."

I pull my firing cock out of her pussy and press the swollen head against her asshole, watching the white spurts shoot from it all over her.

"So damn perfect," I growl as I push the tip against her skin, rubbing it up and down.

"Sterling," she whimpers, rolling her hips and pleading with her eyes as she looks back over her shoulder at me.

I take her invitation and ease just the head of my dick inside her ass.

"God, yes. I want to take all of you there soon."

Looking at her beautiful face is the final straw, and my balls give their all, pumping a fresh wave of cum up my shaft and spilling it inside her.

Her eyes widen at the sensation, and I hold her gaze, squeezing her hips, circling the swollen head of my cock inside her as the final drops pass from me to her.

"Did I tell you how much I love you?"

"I think you showed me." She smiles.

Sweat beads on my chest as I take in a deep drag of much-needed air.

Yeah, I think I damn well did.

My fingers trail up and down the silky skin on Hallie's naked back as she lies on her front next to me, her icy blonde hair splayed out over the pillow. Her cute little snores make me smile as I watch her sleep.

She looks like an angel. Some days I think she is one, sent to rescue me from living my whole life without experiencing the kind of love that makes you crazy. Because I'm damn crazy about her. And I wouldn't change a thing.

I lean over and press a kiss to her shoulder. She's exhausted. I kept her going until she could barely keep her eyes open. I lost count of how many times we fucked before everything slowed down and we made love gently, staring into each other's eyes as I held her beneath me. No matter how much of her I get, it's never enough. I always want more.

My cell vibrates on the nightstand, and I reach for it, answering Denver's call as my gaze returns to Hallie.

"Denver?"

I keep my voice low, so I don't disturb her. I called him when Hallie fell asleep and told him Rory didn't get on his flight. He's been trailing him since, keeping an eye on his movements.

"Boss," he greets. "I've followed him to your apartment building. He hasn't tried to get inside, but he's pacing up and down the sidewalk."

I slip out of bed and walk to the windows even though it's too high up to make much out at street level below.

"Keep an eye on him. I'll come down."

"There's more." Denver's tone is grim. "It's about Vegas."

"Go on."

I grit my teeth knowing that whatever he's about to tell me isn't going to be good. Rory ought to run while he can.

◆

"I heard your club in LA got burned down. Shame." Rory smirks, eyeing me as I walk up to him on the sidewalk.

He looks disheveled. His light brown hair is messy, sticking up in places, like he's been raking his hands through it. And his eyes are dull and tired, the whites holding a yellow sheen. He could have been back in England with all of his debts paid off. Yet here he is, looking for a fight that he doesn't have a chance in hell of winning.

"It's just a building." I shrug. "I'll remodel it and make it better."

"Yeah, an old rich guy like you can afford to see it like that." He snorts.

"You're right. I am rich."

Rory eyes me with disgust, his top lip curling.

"I'm the richest man in the world. You know why? Because I've got the love of that incredible woman who's upstairs sleeping in my bed right now."

"You keep your hands off her!"

He dives at me, but his punch is poorly executed, and his eyes widen as I catch his fist in my palm.

And squeeze.

"Argh!" He yanks it back, his face contorting in pain.

I stand calmly, waiting for him to—

"You dirty old bastard!" He comes at me again, but I move at the last moment, leaving him stumbling around.

"I tried to give you an out. You should have taken it."

"Fuck you! I'm going to kill you!"

Sighing, I check my watch. I don't want to leave Hallie any longer than is necessary.

"If this is how you want this to go, can I suggest we step around the corner?"

"Fine," he spits.

I follow him around the corner of a building and into a darkened alleyway. I signal back at the dark SUV parked curbside for Denver to stay put.

Rory's all mine.

He stomps down the alleyway, then spins to glare at me. "You're too old for her."

"I love her."

His eyes bug at my calm admission.

"You can't love her!" He jabs a finger into his temple. "You're going senile if you think she wants you."

I take my time removing my jacket and finding the cleanest looking part of a dumpster lid to place it down onto.

"I know what you did in Vegas, Rory," I say calmly.

"You mean when she asked me to marry her?" He laughs, waiting for me to react.

I fold one sleeve up to my elbow meticulously, keeping the cotton neat.

"I mean when you spiked her drinks."

"I never drugged her," he spits. "I don't drug women."

"I said spiked, not drugged." I sigh at having to explain this to someone not worth my breath. "Putting extra shots into a person's drink is spiking. You got her drunk so she wouldn't know what she was doing. So she'd go along with your suggestions. *You took away her choice.*"

Choice. Something we should always have. Yet, I've lived much of my life having mine dictated by other people. My parents, Elaina's parents.

Hallie will never have her choice taken away from her again. I'll die before I let that happen.

"There's evidence. You're looking at a potential jail sentence should those videos come out," I tell him.

Someone won big in Caesars that night. It's the only reason Denver's buddy was able to get copies of the CCTV for us. We were lucky they kept them.

Rory won't be so lucky.

His eyes widen before he shrugs. "Halliday would love that. Going to court, the whole world knowing we were married."

"Say her name again and I'll cut out your tongue," I say simply.

I fold up my other sleeve with the same care as the first.

Rory's gaze drops to my forearm, and he recoils. "Are you deformed?"

"What I am, is done acting like a gentleman toward a man who doesn't know how to treat a lady. This will be the last time you ever hurt her."

He stares at me for a beat, then strides forward, drawing back his fist.

"Hope you're ready for your nursing home, old man."

I grab the collar of his shirt, pulling him to me. Then I rear back my head and slam it into his face, headbutting him.

The sound of crunching bone echoes off the high concrete walls around us.

"Fuck!" He grabs his nose and staggers back, folding over at the waist. "You broke my fucking nose!"

I dust down my shirt and wait for him to stand.

He spits a mouthful of blood out on the ground.

"You're just a charity case to her. She feels sorry for you after your wife and son died. I read all about it. How they were burned to a crisp."

I take a deep breath so I don't snap his neck here in this dank, stinking alleyway and throw him in the trash where he belongs.

"She told me you were a piece of work. Now I see, you're just a piece of shit. Go back to England."

He straightens and lunges for me again.

One undercut to his gut and he's wheezing for air.

"I can do this all night, Boy," I tut as he comes at me again.

This time, my fist connects with his jaw and sends him hurtling backward.

When he comes at me again, I deliver one quick open-handed jab to his windpipe.

He collapses to the floor, clutching his throat, struggling to breathe.

I roll each of my sleeves down, adjusting my cufflinks, then pick my jacket up. He's writhing around on the ground as I walk over to him.

"We could have discussed this like adults."

"Fuck you," he chokes out. "Hall—"

I press my shoe against the side of his face, pinning his head to the ground. The leather hand-stitched sole applies just the right amount of pressure that his lips pucker and he winces.

"I warned you what would happen if you said my girl's name again. So maybe you'll want to re-think how you finish that sentence."

I remove my foot, and he glares at me with pure hatred darkening his eyes.

"You're an old man."

I crouch and pat him on the cheek.

"The only thing past it here is you. Now be a good boy and get yourself on a flight to London while you can still walk yourself onto the plane."

I stand and stare at him as he scrabbles up to a sitting position. He stares at me, nose pouring with blood. A few seconds pass between us in silence before I turn and stroll away, leaving him sitting alone on the cold piss-stained floor.

I head to the tinted window of the SUV and tap on the glass, waiting for it to roll down.

"Make sure he goes and packs."

Denver's eyes track up the alleyway behind me. "You don't want me to dispose of—?"

"No." I frown, looking in Rory's direction.

As tempting as it is, Hallie deserves a man who can look her in the eye and promise her Rory didn't meet a painful end. Because I know someone with a heart as pure as hers would blame herself if he did.

Even if he does deserve it.

Giving him a beating him tonight would already be pushing boundaries in her eyes.

"Just make sure he gets on the damn flight," I say, patting the roof of Denver's car.

"Will do, Boss."

Nodding, I head back inside.

I strip off my suit, depositing it all in the laundry before I go into the bathroom and wash my hands. The water has a pink tinge. I went easy on Rory. The temptation to do a hell of a lot worse to make sure he can never come near Hallie again was overwhelming.

"What are you doing up?"

Warm soft fingers dust over my abs as arms encircle me from behind and a soft kiss is pressed between my shoulder blades.

"Hallie," I rasp, grabbing a towel to dry my hands. I throw it to one side and turn to wrap her in my arms.

"Come back to bed." She pouts at me sleepily, and I reach up to brush the hair away from her face. "What?" she asks, studying me.

I shake my head softly. "I love you so much, that's all." I stroke her cheeks, overcome with emotion at the trust in her eyes.

She leans into one of my hands, a soft smile on her face. "I love you too. Now come back to bed."

"You know I have to take care of the people I love, don't you?"

Her brows flatten and she studies me. "I know that. And you do. You always do. Is this about Rory?" She places her hands over mine, curling her fingers around them and stroking the back of them with her thumbs.

"I'll do anything to keep you safe, Hallie," I confess. "Things that you might not like. Things that mean I'm not always the man I should be for you."

"I know who you are, Sterling. And I love you no matter what. You are always going to be the only man for me, no matter which part of you is the one on show, you hear me?"

"Hall—"

She places her fingers over my mouth. "I won't hear you say a bad word about yourself, okay?" Her eyes shine with tears. "You are everything and more to me."

I take her wrist, keeping her hand to my lips as I kiss her fingertips.

"You don't need to worry about Rory. Because no matter what he does, I'm not going anywhere. You won't lose me. And I won't allow him to ruin things. I've been scared for far too long. And that's not who I am. I didn't start my business to let him take it from me without a fight. I did it for Jenny. And I'll do whatever it takes to keep her legacy alive."

"You're amazing," I breathe.

"No. You are. You've given me my strength back. I didn't even realize how much of it I'd lost."

"Hallie," I rasp, resting my forehead against hers. "You've given me everything back. A life I'm happy to wake up to again each day. Without you, I don't know where I'd be."

She slides her fingers to my jaw, running them through my stubble.

"Come back to bed," she whispers.

I let her lead me back by the hand, pulling me down onto the cool sheets. I lie on my back and gaze at her as she straddles me, her lips parting with a soft moan as she takes me inside her and starts to ride me slowly.

She holds my eyes, the city lights twinkling behind her.

"I love you," she whispers.

"I love you. I *need* you, Hallie."

I urge her to increase her pace, gripping her hips.

"I need you, Baby girl," I groan as I work her up and down my cock with mounting desperation.

The desperate need to have her.

To keep her.

To protect her.

To love her.

It's only when she grabs my hands and places them on her breasts moments before her first orgasm hits that I see the blood I've missed, shining like a beacon on the base of one thumb nail.

I stare at it for far too long, only ripping my gaze away as she moans my name and comes a second time, her body gripping mine inside it like it can't stand the thought of ever letting go.

Her eyes hold mine as she works herself up and down me, inching me closer and closer until I spill inside her with a choked growl.

I pull myself up while I'm still emptying inside her, and crush my body to hers, my mouth taking hers in a fierce kiss as I wrap her in my arms.

I failed to save and protect my family once. I cannot let that happen with Hallie.

No matter what, I can't ever let anyone hurt her.

But I also have to be the man she deserves.

I can't lose her.

I wouldn't survive it.

28

HALLIDAY

"What are we doing here?" I look out of the car window at the aircraft hangar we've driven into.

"I've got something to show you." Sterling's eyes glitter as we come to a stop.

He steps out of the car and then leans back inside it, holding his hand out to me.

"What is it?"

He chuckles. "Come and see."

I grin and take his hand to climb out.

I've been worried about him. He hasn't been himself since I found him out of bed the night we saw Rory. He looked like he had the weight of the world on his shoulders. And the way he said he has to protect those he loves almost had me in tears. He's been through so much. And that fact that he thinks he has to explain his need to protect people, that he has to apologize for it, breaks my heart. I will never feel anything other than blessed that he deems me worthy enough to fight for. That he's chosen to love me with all of his strength, whatever that looks like.

Seeing him smiling again today, the soft lines at the edges

of his warm blue eyes back again, makes my heart lift. I don't care what he's brought me to see. I've already got the sight I've been wishing for.

I gaze around the giant space. There are three small jets lined up with their front steps lowered.

"I still don't know what we're doing here," I say as I look at their perfect sleek white fuselages glinting in the morning sun, like three graceful swans sitting on the calm surface of a lake.

"I wasn't sure which one you'd like most, so I bought all three."

I start to laugh, but the serious look on Sterling's face stops me.

"Wait. What?"

"Choose which one you want to keep, or keep them all, either is fine with me."

"Um..."

He takes a step closer, tilting my chin toward him with his finger and thumb.

"I'll try to buy you the whole damn world, you know that. And I know I've caused you concern. Think of it as a thank you for not giving up on me."

"I'd never."

I look into his eyes, understanding the tinge of pain there. He was worried Rory was going to cause problems. From now on, Rory holds no power over me. If anything, I despise him more for seeing how his presence has affected Sterling. It's like the threat against me has brought all his grief back to the surface. He's told me how he couldn't save them. And he's scared that he can't save me. But he doesn't have to. I'm going to save both of us.

There's nothing Rory can do now that I won't be prepared for.

I press a kiss to Sterling's lips, one that's gentle and conveys a million *I love yous* all at once.

He smiles against me. "Now go and choose which one we're taking to visit your parents in."

"You bought these so I could go and see my parents?"

"I know you miss them. And I'm sure they miss you. Anything that I can do to help with that, I will."

"I don't believe this. You're mad." I smile up at him, loving the way his eyes fill with easy happiness.

"No. I'm just in love. Now go pick one."

I bite my lower lip before pulling him to me for another kiss. He sinks into me, sliding his tongue inside my mouth and making me forget where we are. I reach down and wrap my fingers around his dick.

"Careful, Baby girl, we have company." He chuckles.

I break our kiss, looking from his driver to a staff member standing at the rear of the first jet's steps. Both have politely averted their gazes from us.

I keep my hand curled around him, squeezing the hard length.

"You mean I have to wait until we get back to your place before I can have you in my mouth again?"

His deep groan makes me giggle, and I remove my hand as he gives me a warning look that's full of desire.

"Baby girl, you're going to be sitting on my face the moment we get back to *our* place."

"Our place?" I question at the way he emphasizes the word.

"That's the next thing I want to talk to you about. But first, go and choose your damn plane," he growls, making me giggle.

I love this Sterling. The playful, sexy version with a glimmer of teasing lighting up his warm blue eyes.

The sex has been more intense since Rory showed up. Sterling's seemed driven to make my body bend and sway to his every whim. It's like he's needed to have that constant connection with me. And I've never felt so desired and wanted in my life.

He's not been to work. Instead, he's spent more time inside me than not. The only time he's let me up for air has been when he's taken calls from his family or from Denver. And even after those, he's rushed back to me and insisted on making me come for him all over again. Insisted on sinking inside me and telling me over and over how much he loves me.

But the hidden pain in his eyes has torn at my heart.

He's worried all this happiness will be taken from him.

"Come on then. Help me." I grin, linking my fingers with his and pulling him toward the first jet. "I've got to say, as far as presents go, they beat chocolates."

He laughs, following me. I've been desperately seeking every smile and laugh from him that I can, hoping the more I can create, the less worried he'll feel.

"Wow."

I clasp my hand to my mouth as I climb the steps of the first jet and gaze around at the plush beige interior.

"This is like a luxury apartment," I gush as my eyes ping-pong from the thick carpet to the walnut trimmed furniture and giant vase of lilies set up next to a champagne bucket.

Sterling's gaze brings a warm glow to my core. He's watching me with pure happiness. He loves this. Spoiling me. Taking care of me. And he's the first person I've ever felt comfortable enough to let do it. He's right, I've spent my whole life looking out for others. Having someone in my corner now feels right. Because that person is him.

"If they're all like this, I don't know how I'll choose."

"Keep them all, then." He shrugs like it's no big deal.

I roll my eyes and pat him on the chest. "I'm only just starting to get used to you spoiling me. Don't push it."

He chuckles as we head to the next jet.

The moment we step onboard, I turn to him. "This one."

His brows hitch as he looks at me in amusement. "You sure?"

"What color are the seats?"

He opens his mouth, but I press a finger over his lips.

"You matched them to my dress, didn't you?"

"Which dress?" His eyes are full of mischief as his voice comes out muffled beneath my finger.

"You know which one. The *sterling* silver one."

"I thought that was light gray."

His eyes heat as I remove my finger from his lips and arch a brow.

"Ah, yes. I know which one you mean. The one that your nipples look edible in." He smiles and pulls me into his arms. "Yes, okay? I got them to match the color to that dress. Because damn, it's my favorite color to see you in."

I slide my arms up around his neck. "It is, huh?"

He nods, dusting his lips up and down over mine. "Sure is."

"I love you," I whisper.

"Hallie, love isn't a strong enough word for what I feel for you."

We stand staring at one another, soaking in the magic that swirls around us in moments like this.

"So now I've picked," I stroke my fingers along his jaw, "what was the other thing you wanted to talk about?"

"This is it, Miss Burton? You travel light," Harry says with a smile as he wheels the luggage trolley out of the elevator and across the foyer.

"Thank you, Harry."

He takes it toward the main door where Sterling is waiting on the sidewalk with the trunk of the car open. He won't let his driver put my things in, he's been insisting on doing it himself.

I bite my lip as I watch him in his midnight blue suit, pressing a wad of bills into Harry's hand before he takes the large jade Buddha ornament off the trolley. He smiles as he lifts the giant crystal and places it carefully into the trunk.

I would never have been able to fly that back home. Maybe my subconscious knew when I bought it that I wouldn't have to. Because Harry's right. Apart from the large crystal sculpture, I do travel light. But now I'm moving in with Sterling, I might have some more packing to do.

Back in London.

My stomach knots with a mix of excitement and dread at telling my parents I want to live in New York.

Permanently.

Sterling straightens up, muscular arms bulging in his jacket as my suitcase follows the Buddha into the trunk. I'm going to be living with him. I smile as I watch him.

"Stop drooling for a minute so I can tell you how much I'm going to miss you," Zoey says as she pulls me into a hug.

I hug her back. "You don't even live here anymore. It's your—"

"Don't call it a sex pad." She laughs in my ear as she squeezes me.

"I wasn't going to. I was going to say your sentimental place. The one you can't say goodbye to."

"You're right." She lets me go with a grin. "But it's also our sex pad. Ash likes to…" Her brows rise. "… reminisce."

She's told me snippets of how the two of them met. How

she was his life model, but he never saw her face because she always wore these beautiful masquerade masks. But that he fell for her anyway due to the way they spoke about everything. He'd seen every inch of her body and her soul before he finally got to look into the face of the woman he fell in love with.

No wonder Sinclair believes in love so much and hired me. Her best friend is a living example of what happens when magic intervenes.

"You're going to see me all the time," I tell her. "We're having dinner with Sinclair as soon as we get back from visiting my parents."

"I know." She shrugs. "But you're going to be living with a guy now. It's going to be different."

"You live with a guy!" I laugh at the way she wrinkles up her nose.

"I know, what are we letting ourselves in for?" She catches my eye and grins. "Seriously, I'm happy for you. Both of you. And Sinclair's loving it. You know she's buzzing about you two finally coming out to the world."

"I know."

I smile at the thought of Sinclair. Once she got her head around me and Sterling she went full steam ahead, calling up Harry and making sure he was ready to help me move out. Sterling told her he was going to ask me to move in before I knew a thing about it. And I love the way he wants his family's approval. That he cares about them being happy too.

I can only pray to have a reaction as understanding from my parents.

"Your man's waiting," Zoey says, gesturing toward Sterling as he strides toward us.

I can't help the giant grin on my face as he gets closer, his eyes sparkling as they fix onto mine.

"Oh my god, you two are so cute." She laughs. "Enjoy christening your new home," she whispers.

29

STERLING

"Warm enough?" I pull the blanket higher over Hallie's legs as she snuggles into her seat beside me, my arm looped around her shoulders.

"Uh-huh." She lets out a small yawn, covering her mouth with the cuff of her sweater.

I bought her a bigger size when I got the Statue of Liberty sweater. I wanted her to be cozy. And if I'm honest, I also like the way it's big on her. She looks cute. So damn beautiful and cute.

And mine.

I press a kiss to her forehead. "Why don't you get some sleep in the bedroom? We've got a few hours until we land."

"Are you going to work, or are you going to join me?"

I chuckle. "How am I supposed to resist that invitation?"

"You're supposed to tell me you have too much work to do." She teases, looking at my laptop on the seat opposite, and the stack of paperwork I brought to catch up on.

"I do have too much work to do. But it can wait." I lift her chin so I can kiss her pouty lips. "How about I come and tuck you in and then I'll leave you to rest?"

Her eyes sparkle. "You'll come straight out here?" She lifts a brow.

"Yes."

"Promise?"

I chuckle.

"Is it going to be like when you said I needed new luggage for this trip and I insisted I didn't, and you said you wouldn't get me any when I asked you not to waste your money?"

"You did need new luggage. Your suitcase was scratched."

"It was barely noticeable." She rolls her eyes.

"I never promised anything," I say, smiling as she pokes me in my side.

"I do like it, though. It's really pretty."

Her eyes track to the matching carry-on on the floor beside her seat. It's dark blue with a sterling silver 'HB' embossed on it.

"Thank you." She presses a kiss to my jaw.

I groan and unfasten my seatbelt. "Come on, Miss Burton. It's time you went to bed."

The flight attendant just took the pilots a coffee, so no one sees me as I lift her into my arms bridal style, causing her to giggle as I stride off to the rear of the aircraft where there's a private bedroom.

I open the door and maneuver us inside.

"Lock the door," I instruct.

Hallie blinks at me and then reaches out and slides the lock over, keeping her eyes on mine.

"Are you going to put me to bed now? Make me rest?"

"That's exactly what I'm going to do."

I walk to the bed and place her on it. A small huff of disappointment passes her lips and I smile internally. She's been up for everything since I moved her into my place yesterday. She wanted to have sex in every room before we left for London. She said I should think of it as a cleansing ritual.

I live in a one hundred and seventy-five-million-dollar penthouse on 57th Street, aptly named 'Billionaire's Row'.

With two floors and seventeen rooms.

If she didn't bring me to life with her energy, then I'd feel every day of my fifty years today. Seventeen times in less than twenty-four hours and she's still reaching for my belt as she bites her lower lip and gives me *that* look.

"Baby girl," I murmur.

"I'll rest after," she breathes. "Besides, you want it, don't you?" She squeezes my already rock-hard dick as if to prove a point.

I inhale slowly and let out a slow groan as she unfastens my belt and slides my zipper down. She bends to press a kiss to the head of my dick through my underwear.

"We can be quick," she says, pulling the waistband of my boxers down and freeing my cock. She swipes up the bead of precum leaking from my slit with her tongue and moans as she swallows it down.

"Jesus Christ."

All decorum leaves me as I'm overtaken by red-hot desire. I rip my pants out of the way, kicking them off my feet, then grab a handful of her hair and hold her face in front of my crotch. She looks at me, eyes glittering.

"You want your mouth fucked, Baby girl? Is that it?"

"Mm-hm." She bites her lower lip as I rub my thumb over it.

"Say it," I urge.

"I want you to fuck my mouth," she whispers, pressing a kiss to the head of my weeping dick. "Even harder than the last time."

Her next breath is turned into a gurgling sound as I ram my cock so far down her throat that she gags.

She loves this. I love this.

We've been together so many times in so many ways now

that I know without a doubt she trusts me to do whatever I want to her. She knows I'll only bring her pleasure and that I'd never hurt her. And that trust makes everything between us electric. More powerful than anything else I've ever experienced.

My ass clenches tight as I fuck her mouth with deep strokes. She swallows every inch of me happily, moaning as she gazes up at me.

"Baby girl," I utter, stroking the side of her face. "I love you so damn much."

She smiles around my dick, one hand stroking my balls and tugging them gently.

"You ready?"

She nods, her eyes lighting up as my abs tense, and I let out a rough curse.

"Here it comes then."

She whimpers, hollowing her cheeks and sucking hard, as I shoot pulse after pulse of hot cum down her throat.

She swallows some before I tut.

"You know what I want to see, Baby girl. Get that pretty mouth open."

I pull her off my cock and hold the base of it, aiming the thick spurts onto her outstretched tongue.

"God, yes," I groan, coating her tongue and spilling over her lips and chin.

I squeeze up the length of my dick, jerking the end of it to empty out every drop.

"Baby girl," I groan, smearing the final glistening bead over her lower lip.

She blinks at me, her mouth full of un-swallowed cum.

"You're so goddamn perfect. Sitting there and begging to be given my cum like this."

She rises and grabs the back of my neck, bringing my face to hers.

"Give it to me," I husk.

Her eyes spark and she parts her lips as I tilt my head back, opening my mouth so she can let my cum drip into my mouth.

Then she swallows and kisses me, swirling her tongue over mine. I growl, tasting myself on her and deepen our kiss.

"Let me make you feel good." I slide my hand to the apex of her thighs in her yoga pants.

She holds my wrist, stilling my hand. "I do feel good. I wanted to taste you, and I did. Now I need to rest."

A rumbled huff vibrates from my throat, and she smiles against my mouth. "Sometimes all I want is to take care of you. And you need to let me."

She presses a gentle kiss to my lips and runs her fingertips along my jaw.

"Go and get some work done. I know it's been on your mind. I'll stop distracting you and stay here for a bit."

"Knowing you're back here, in this bed, *will* be a distraction."

She presses another kiss to my lips and pats my chest lightly with her palm. "Go."

Pulling my clothes off the floor and getting dressed, I arch a brow at her with a grumble.

"I'd rather be making love to you than working."

She bites her lip with a smile, and I grab her face between my hands, pressing a lingering kiss to her mouth.

"I love you, Hallie."

"I love you too," she hums happily. "Now go do some work, and if you're done before we land..." She kisses me again.

"If I'm done?" I counter.

"If you're done," she murmurs, "then wake me up any way you like."

If that isn't an incentive to get my work done as fast as I can, then I don't know what is.

"You know my favorite way to wake you up is with my head between these gorgeous thighs?" I say, sliding my hand up one and squeezing a handful of soft flesh.

"I know," she teases, nipping my lower lip. "So go get your work done."

"And you get yourself to sleep, Baby girl. And leave your panties off for me."

Her eyes light up, and I chuckle as I tear myself away.

Hallie's palm twitches inside mine as we stand on the doorstep of her parents' house. The front garden is immaculate. It's a quiet area. We've only seen a couple of dog walkers and a mom pushing a stroller since we arrived. I imagine Hallie here growing up, coming in and out through the front door that's got a stained-glass window of a sunrise on it.

"They love this house," she says. "They're always saying how many memories are here."

"I'm sure." I give her a reassuring smile as she chews on her lower lip.

"Don't be concerned about meeting them. They're lovely, and they'll like you, I know they will. Just... don't be surprised if they are bothered by the age thing to start with. They're ten years older than you, and they're bound to ask your age. I know them. And my dad, he says what he's thinking. It's if he gets quiet that you need to worry."

"Okay."

She reaches for the doorbell, then stops.

"I'll tell them about us first. Then Vegas. Otherwise they'll be wondering why you're here with me. They still think you're my client."

She lifts her hand toward the doorbell again.

And stops.

"Now I know that Rory was responsible, I..." She shakes her head. "It doesn't make this easier. They'll be more upset that I didn't tell them than how it happened."

She looks at me with worried eyes and my chest tightens. When I told her that Denver found footage from that night and that Rory had been spiking her drinks, she sat on the couch with her head in her hands for the longest time. I held her as relief flowed through her body. She's finally starting to see that it wasn't her fault. She didn't let Jenny down. And she doesn't need to carry around the guilt with her anymore.

But the tension is back in her stiff shoulders now.

"They're your parents, Hallie. They'll forgive you."

She nods, then takes a deep breath and lifts her hand to the doorbell again.

And pauses. Again.

"And maybe let me—"

I pull her into my arms and kiss her.

"It'll be okay," I soothe, holding her face in my hands.

"It'll be okay," she repeats. Her eyes soften. "I love you so much."

"I love y—"

She cuts me off, kissing me again just as the front door opens.

"Halliday?" The man's eyes widen behind his glasses as Hallie shoots back from me.

"Dad!" She pulls him into a hug before he can react. He sinks into it, patting her back.

"I thought I heard someone at the door. Your flight got in early?"

"We had a tailwind," she replies just as a woman with short silvery-blonde hair joins her father at the door.

"Sweetheart!"

The woman pulls Hallie into an embrace, and I hang back, watching as they fuss over her and tell her how much they've missed her.

"Mum, Dad, I want you to meet Sterling." She moves back to my side and wraps her hands around my bicep. "Sterling, this is my mum and dad, Julie and Garth."

"It's a pleasure to meet you Mr. and Mrs. Burton." I extend a hand which they both shake as they look between the two of us, their eyes full of questions.

"You're her client from New York?"

"He was, Mum," Hallie answers. "I've got a lot to tell you."

Her father stares at me in silence as her mother masks her shock more effectively.

"Of course you do. And we can't wait to hear it all, right, Garth?"

Her father says nothing.

"Now, come in." Her mother opens the door wide.

I nod politely at her father. But his gaze is firmly planted on Hallie's hand that she's wrapped inside mine, tugging me over the threshold.

"Garth!" her mother snaps.

He finally moves, shutting the door behind us with a deep thud.

Fifteen minutes later, we're sitting in the front room with a tray of tea and biscuits on a small coffee table in front of us. Garth gave me a tour of the garden, showing me his new chainsaw that he said can cut through bone like it's butter, while Hallie helped her mom get the tea ready.

Everyone has been too polite to talk about why we're really here.

"So, you live in New York?" Garth asks me, his eyes narrowed in suspicion.

"I do. It's where I was born. My family's from there."

He nods and takes in my suit.

"What do you do?"

"My family runs a jewelry firm. We're known for our diamonds. I've taken a step back from the day-to-day running now though. I own a chain of piano lounges."

"They're amazing," Hallie gushes. "People go there to relax. It's like another world stepping inside."

I smile as her face glows. She understands Seasons and why it's so important to me. Hearing her talk about it with such passion only makes me love her more.

"And you hired our daughter to find you a partner?" Garth asks.

"No, Sterling's daughter, Sinclair, hired me," Hallie tells him.

"And now you're here." His eyes move from Hallie and back to me. "And you're kissing my daughter on my front doorstep."

"Dad!" Hallie scoffs, pressing a hand to her forehead. "You weren't meant to see that until I'd had a chance to talk to you."

"Well, I did see," he grumbles.

Garth's eyes remain fixed on me as Hallie speaks. As much as I'm ready to jump in and aid her, she doesn't need me to. She wanted to be the one to tell them. I'm only here to support her.

"Yes, Sterling was my client. And neither of us expected this. But it happened and here we are."

"Here we are," Julie says, her brow furrowing. "Forgive me, but, how old are you?"

"I'm fifty, Mrs. Burton."

Garth snorts, and Julie jabs her elbow into his thigh.

"How well does your business do?" he asks, setting a penetrating look on me like a spotlight in an interrogation room.

"It does well."

"My daughter is a very successful woman. She was employed by a royal family only last year."

His gaze drops over my suit again, and he narrows his eyes at my Italian handmade shoes.

"I'm aware. She's an incredible businesswoman, and I can see you're very proud of her."

"Dad," Hallie interjects. "Sterling has his own money. He's not interested in mine."

"That true?" Garth hitches a brow, his gaze suspicious.

"It is," I reply simply.

"What are we talking?"

"Dad!" Hallie says, exasperated, as Julie knocks his thigh again.

"My businesses do well, Mr. Burton. My interest in your daughter is not for financial gain, I can assure you."

Her father snorts. "Your idea of well and mine might differ."

"Dad, please." Hallie sighs. "I appreciate your concern, but—"

"I'm your father, I have to protect—"

"Sterling ranks twenty-first on Forbes's rich list. He's a billionaire. We flew here on a private jet," Hallie announces.

I wince internally at how pompous that makes me sound, but I keep my eyes on her father's. He's looking out for his daughter, and I commend him for it. I'd do the exact same thing with Sinclair if she were to meet someone.

Garth nods. "Number twenty-one, huh?"

"I got pushed out of the top twenty by the family who owns Walmart."

"More people need affordable food than they do diamond jewelry," Garth clips.

"I agree. The carats we sell don't really bake so well."

A tiny hint of a chuckle graces Garth's throat before he clears it and rearranges his expression back to a serious one.

"And you have a daughter?" Julie asks.

"I do. Sinclair's twenty-three. And I also have a son, Sullivan. He's twenty-nine. I had another son, but we lost him two years ago."

Julie sucks in a breath and grips Garth's thigh. "I'm so sorry to hear that."

"Thank you. And you have my sincerest condolences over Jenny. Hallie talks of her often."

Julie's eyes slide to the mantelpiece above the woodburning stove. It's lined with various framed photographs of their family. Jenny is in each one, her radiant smile shining.

"Hallie?" Garth frowns as he looks away from me for the first time and pins his eyes on his daughter.

"I know, Dad," her voice wavers.

He looks at me with shining eyes. "You call her Hallie?"

"I do."

"I asked him to," Hallie says softly.

Garth nods before lifting his tea and taking a sip like he needs something to do.

"I'm a parent too, Mr. Burton. Our children's happiness comes before all else. And I promise you that Hallie's comes before my own as well. I know I'm older than her, but I don't see a number when we're together. I just see her. And I will only ever do what will make her happy. She will always have a choice. For as long as I am her choice, then I'll look after her. And even if I no longer am, then I'll do whatever I can to ensure she's okay. That, I promise you."

Her parents stare at me until Garth puts his mug back down and exhales heavily.

"The mother of your children?" he asks.

"She also passed away two years ago."

Julie presses her fingers to her lips. "I'm so sorry."

Hallie slides her hand onto my thigh and squeezes softly.

"My daughter can't replace her if that's what this is."

"Dad," Hallie murmurs. "It's not like that."

"No, she can't. And I would never want her to. Your daughter is unique and passionate. And everything about her has enchanted me since the moment I met her. I could never compare her to anyone because there is no one like her. I've never felt like this before in my life about anyone. But if for a moment I didn't think I could make Hallie happy, then I would walk away. I swear on my life. But I believe I can make her happy. She's brought light into my life, and I'll do everything in my power to show her how grateful I am for her every day."

"Sterling," Hallie whispers, emotion brimming in her eyes as she grabs my hand and interlocks our fingers.

"He lives in New York," Julie says, her eyes on Hallie.

"I know, Mum."

Understanding fills her mother's eyes, and she presses her lips together and looks away.

"There's something else I need to tell you." Hallie exhales, and I stroke her knuckles with my thumb.

"There's more?" her father chokes, shaking his head and looking to the ceiling. "Bloody hell."

"Something happened a few years ago and I kept it a secret because I was scared of hurting you. And because I was ashamed. And I've regretted it every day since. It's concerning Rory."

"I saw his mother yesterday. She said he had a fall down the stairs. Black and blue, he is," Julie says.

Hallie stiffens and her eyes dart to me. I clench my jaw as I hold her gaze, conveying all she needs to know.

"I'm sure he wasn't being careful," she says carefully, turning back to her parents. "But this is… this is hard for me to say, so I'm just going to come out with it."

"You're pregnant?" Julie gasps.

Garth's eyes snap to mine in accusation.

"No!" Hallie says. "It's… Rory and I did something stupid when I went to Vegas that time. We got drunk and ended up getting married in one of those walk-in chapels. I didn't even know what had happened until the next day. We had it annulled immediately."

Her shoulders drop instantly, and she breathes out a sigh of relief. It's like the secret has finally shed the weight it's been putting on her.

"You did what?" Garth splutters.

"It wasn't Hallie's fault. He got her drunk and took advantage of her. And he's been blackmailing her ever since."

I fix her father with a stern look. I might be in his house sitting next to his daughter, but if he blames her for this, if he upsets her…

"I've never trusted that boy," Julie says. "He used to shoot at the neighborhood cats with that little potato gun. Do you remember?" She looks at Hallie's father who's still staring at Hallie in shock.

"Garth!" Julie nudges him and he focuses.

"Yes, he did. Odd kid. And no better as an adult. Always showing off his latest car or bragging about something."

"I thought you both liked him?" Hallie shuffles to the edge of the couch as she gapes at her parents. "You'd invite him and his parents around all the time."

"We thought you two were friends. And his parents are good neighbors. Rory isn't like either of them. I think he gets it from his grandfather. He was a nasty old bastard," Garth mutters.

"He's been blackmailing you?" Julie's face crumples with concern. "With what? I don't understand."

"He's said he'll ruin my business. That people won't trust me if they know I got married when I was drunk. But I'm not going to let him do it anymore. I was scared losing my clients would mean losing the ability to donate to Jenny's charity. But I'll find another way. I'll get past it. I'm not letting Rory take another thing from me," Hallie says, sounding determined.

I turn and rake over her profile with admiration. I'm so damn proud of her. She was so worried about coming here and telling her parents. But this strong, vibrant woman reminds me of the first day I met her.

My girl is back in fighting form.

"You've been donating to the charity?"

Hallie nods at her mother as her father clears his throat.

"How much, Love?" he asks.

Her grip on my hand tightens, and I squeeze her fingers in reassurance.

"Almost everything I make," she confesses in a quiet voice.

The room falls silent for a long time until Julie straightens.

"We... this is a lot..." She presses her hands to her cheeks. "We need to talk. Will you both be staying? I've made up the guest room, and I can make up the couch, or?" She looks at me in uncertainty.

"Yes, please." Hallie nods. "Our flight back isn't until tomorrow."

I clear my throat. "Actually, I've booked myself a room at The Kingsbridge hotel."

Hallie blinks at me, her forehead furrowing.

"The tea's cold. I'll make a fresh pot," her mom announces, standing.

"You need some time with your parents," I tell Hallie quietly. "And I'm not about to invite myself to stay in their house when they've only just met me."

She swallows, giving my hand a squeeze before she slides hers free and stands.

"I'll help Mum."

The bar of The Kingsbridge hotel is quiet. Only a few people, who look like business travelers are dotted around its intimate seating area. I've been nursing the same cognac for an hour, hoping that Hallie's okay.

She was reluctant to let me leave. But she needs time with her parents. Me being there might hold them back from saying what they really think. And I need her to have their honesty. They're her parents and she needs them. If I have to step back and give them time to discuss the past together and decide how they heal and move forward, then that's what I'll do.

And if after speaking with them she decides she can't come home with me, then I'll accept it. It'll obliterate me, but I'll accept it if it's what she truly wants. I told her we'd find a way together. But that's only if she wants it too. It has to be her choice.

I take a sip of my drink and tip my head back with a long sigh. I haven't been able to concentrate on anything since I checked into my hotel suite. It feels too empty without her. I wear her absence like a bullet through my heart. Even hearing Sinclair's voice and chatting to Molly on video call didn't ease the aching in my chest.

"*Courvoisier?*"

I drop my head and look straight into a set of weary eyes behind thin-framed glasses. He indicates to the seat opposite mine at the small table.

I nod and hold out a hand in invitation.

"*Louis XIII.*"

Hallie's father inclines his chin in approval, so I signal the bartender. "Two more please."

Neither of us speaks until the drinks are brought.

Garth inhales before he takes a sip, letting out an appreciative sigh. "Good stuff."

"It is."

I sit back in my chair and wait for him to lead. He's come all this way to speak to me. It's only right that I listen, regardless of whether I'll like what he's going to say.

He has the power to destroy me should he choose. I can see how much Hallie cares about her parents and not hurting them. If they beg her to come home to England, then she will. I'll make sure she does. Because if she stayed in New York with me, I know the guilt would eat away at her. And I can't see her in pain. Even if it means losing her.

"We came for dinner here when Jenny turned eighteen," Garth says finally, looking at the deep amber liquid in his glass as he rolls it between his fingers.

"I wasn't aware."

"The restaurant here makes the best chocolate fudge cake in the whole entire world. Jenny's words." He smiles sadly before looking me in the eye. "We've already lost one daughter, Mr. Beaufort. I can't see my wife go through that again."

The breath leaves my lungs, burning on its way out. I fight to maintain composure, pushing my thumb and finger into my eye sockets as I swallow around the steel ball that's wedged itself in my throat.

I nod, unable to speak.

If they've asked Hallie to stay, I can't let her choose me. Her relationship with her parents will be severed. And it will be my fault. I would never do that to her. She won't be happy.

"Do you know what they were doing when I left?"

I drag my hand down my face and look at him through bleary eyes.

"Tell me."

I ask, because as much as it'll pain me to hear, when it comes to Hallie I want to know everything. For as long as I still get to have a part of her, I need to hear every tiny detail.

"They were watching a romance film." He shakes his head, smiling. "Something Julie's wanted to watch since it came out."

"Hm." I smile at the image of Hallie watching a romance with her Mom. A romance just like she's told me Jenny loved.

"It's going to take them hours to watch it. They keep pausing it to talk."

I blink away the grit that's stinging my eyes.

"They keep talking about you."

I lift my gaze to his.

"She hasn't stopped talking about you since you left. I think I know every bloody thing there is to know." He huffs out a small grunt. "Do you know what else I learned?"

"No," I answer, taking every ounce of my strength to form that one syllable.

He smiles, but it's bittersweet.

"I learned what my daughter sounds like when she's happy. It's been a long time since I saw that look in her eyes. And even longer since I heard it in her voice. She's in love with you."

I rub a hand over my jaw to distract myself from the deep drag of despair pulling at my gut.

"And I'm in love with her."

He leans back in his chair, swirling the brandy in his glass.

"So now I have to do what a parent has to do."

He meets my eyes, the same glassiness in his that I'm sure is reflected in mine.

"I have to let my little girl live her life. Because seeing her today I realize how lost she's been. Jenny died. But Halliday..." His face screws up with emotion. "Halliday... she stopped *living*. We didn't just lose one daughter that day. We lost them both."

I give up trying to hold back the tears that are misting my eyes. Instead, I swipe one away as it breaks free. Hallie said she thinks she was really the one who needed me all along. Hearing the same from her father is almost too much to handle. Because I know she's changed my life since she came into it.

And he's telling me I've changed hers too. For the better.

The universe knew each of us needed the other.

"She loved Jenny. She's been the driving force that's motivated her to create what she has," I say. "They're both an incredible testament to you and Julie."

"No." Garth shakes his head. "They're an incredible testament to themselves. Both of them. When you have kids, all you can do is prepare them the best you can. But after that you have to—"

"Let them go," I say.

Garth sighs. "Precisely."

I can barely breathe. My chest is on fire. My heart is on fire. My soul is on damn fire. The sound of it all raging inside, tearing through me fills my ears.

He's leaving the choice with Hallie.

He's letting her choose.

She has their support. Not receiving it was what she feared the most. It's what *I* feared most. Not Rory. Not what could happen to her business.

It's what her parents would say about us.

Because they held the key to whether she would find it impossible to live in another country, away from them. They could have made the decision for her, made it impossible for her to choose any other way. I know Hallie. She wouldn't have been happy without their blessing. The pressure it would have put on their relationship would have broken her eventually. She wouldn't have been happy, no matter how hard I loved her every day.

I signal the bartender. "Can you bring the bottle, please."

I take another mouthful of cognac as I look her father dead in the eye and level with him.

"I'll give her everything. I'll love her with all I have every second of every day, I promise you."

The bartender places the bottle down onto the table and Garth pours himself a generous serving.

"But this is her choice. It will always be her choice," I add.

"I know."

He sips his drink, his face weary. He looks like a man who knows that he's about to sacrifice a part of his own happiness for the love of his family.

He looks like a father.

And in this moment, the respect I have for him couldn't be greater.

"There's something else you should know."

"Go on," he sighs, like he's already processing exactly what his self-sacrifice will cost him.

"If Hallie chooses to come back to New York with me, I want to ask her to marry me. I want her to be my wife. And I'm asking for your permission to give her that choice too."

Garth looks at me until the back of my neck heats. But I never break his gaze, and when he finally blinks, I know that he understands.

I will do absolutely anything to ensure her happiness.

He nods at the half empty bottle. "We're going to need another. I've got a long list of things my daughter deserves. And you're going to sit and listen to every single one."

I hold his eyes. "Damn right I will."

30

HALLIDAY

"Aren't you going to tell me what you two talked about?"

"No." Sterling purses his lips as I lean over from my seat on the jet and place my palm over his chest.

"You can't spend all evening with my father, who is not a talkative man, by the way, and expect me not to want to know what you both talked about."

"I don't expect that. I knew you'd want to know. But I'm still not telling you."

He lifts my hand to his mouth and kisses my fingertips, his brow furrowing as he reads the document he's opened on his laptop.

"I know you're only pretending to work so you don't have to endure my questions."

His eyes crinkle at the corners and he closes his laptop, placing it on the floor.

"There. You have my full, undivided attention. But I'm still not telling you."

"I'll find a way," I purr, trailing my fingers up his chest.

He chuckles as he pulls me to him for a kiss. "I'll enjoy you trying, Baby girl."

I huff as our lips break apart.

"What's that look for?" He traces a thumb over my frown.

"I feel guilty about Lavinia. She has strong feelings for you, and I feel like we've been lying to her."

"We didn't know what was going to happen. We haven't lied to anyone. And now your parents know, we can be honest about it. If you're ready?"

"I am. I've been drafting a statement to send out to my clients. I want them to hear it from me."

Unease bubbles in my stomach, making it cramp like it has been doing every time I've thought about what might happen when Sterling and I go public.

"Everything I've been afraid of might actually happen," I breathe. "But at least I don't need to be scared anymore."

Sterling's gaze softens. "It'll be okay, Hallie. We'll deal with it together."

"Will you read it and give me your opinion?"

"Of course. Show me."

He opens his arms, and I slide onto his lap, curling my legs up as he wraps his arms around me. I bring up the document on my phone and hand it to him.

He strokes gentle circles over my ribs with his thumb as he reads. I watch him, holding my breath.

"It's great," he says finally.

"Really?"

"Hallie, it's great," he repeats, smiling.

"Okay. We're really doing this."

He chuckles before pressing a kiss to my forehead. "We sure are."

"What's going on?" Sterling clips as we slide into the backseat of the car that's come to collect us from the aircraft hangar. Denver's behind the wheel and Killian is sitting in the front passenger seat with a grim expression.

"We have a situation," Denver says, his eyes meeting Sterling's in the rearview mirror. "As of forty-five minutes ago, the press knows about your relationship. And they know about Vegas, too."

"Oh, god," I murmur.

I glance at Sterling's taut profile as he threads his fingers through mine. We spent the last hour of the flight in the onboard bedroom together, coming out just in time for landing. Neither of us have had time to check our phones.

"Someone tipped them off," Sterling hisses, running a hand over his jaw. "How bad is it?"

"Jenson's waiting at your place. He said there're around twenty journalists there."

"Twenty?" I echo.

My stomach drops. This is what I feared. The whole world is going to know. My clients will see it in some gossipy headline instead of hearing it from me.

"It's okay, Hallie," Sterling soothes. But his brow is pinched as he keeps his eyes forward, deep in thought.

I pull out my phone and bring up a New York news site. It's not the top story, so there's that at least. But my breath catches at the photograph of the two of us getting into the car to catch the flight to London. Sterling's hand is low on my back and I'm beaming at him like a woman who's head over heels in love. In his other hand is the personalized carry-on luggage he bought for me. There's a smaller, zoomed in picture of the 'HB'.

Halliday Burton or Halliday Beaufort? Do we hear wedding bells for widower, Sterling Beaufort, with his thirty-year-old dating coach?

I squeeze Sterling's hand and show him my phone. His nostrils flare.

I've dragged him into this. It's what I never wanted to happen.

"I'm sorry," I whisper.

He runs his thumb over my knuckles. "It's not your fault. We'll deal with it. It'll all be fine."

I sit and stare out of the window as he talks with Denver and Killian about tracing who leaked it to the press. But it doesn't matter, it's done now. And we have to deal with it, like he says. I wish I could believe him that it will all be fine. But as we pull up outside his building and raised voices call to us from the sidewalk, my faith falters.

"I've got you. Let's go," Sterling says.

He holds my hand firm in his as Denver gets out and opens the rear door for us. Then he and Killian walk either side of us like a shield, blocking long-angled lenses and microphones that are shoved in our direction. I put a hand in front of my face and keep my gaze down.

"Mr. Beaufort, what does your family think about you dating your daughter's friend?"

"Was it your baby Miss Burton was shopping with Sinclair for? Is that why she fainted? Did you get a woman twenty years your junior pregnant?"

"Miss Burton, is it true you've been divorced once already?"

Jenson's waiting by the entrance and he opens the door for us as we approach, ushering us inside.

"Oh my god, this is so much worse than I thought it could be." I've still got my face covered as Sterling sweeps me into the foyer.

The door falls closed behind us, drowning out some of the rabble from the sea of reporters outside.

"See what you can do to get rid of them," Sterling says to Denver.

I peek out from behind my hand, then let it drop.

"On it, Boss." Denver turns and goes to talk to Jenson and Killian.

"Do you think Rory did it?" I look at Sterling's set jawline as he marches us toward the elevators.

"I don't know, but I'll damn well find out." His lips twist as he presses the thumb scanner for the private elevator that serves the penthouses on the top levels.

"It's too late. There's nothing we can do. I just wish I'd had the opportunity to tell my clients myself. I wanted them to hear it from me."

"They can still hear it from you." Sterling scrubs a hand around his jaw as he leads me into the elevator, and we ride it up. "You can tell them in your own words exactly what you wanted to, just as you planned."

"An email seems kind of... it's not enough. Not now."

I chew my lower lip, unease skating up my spine, climbing higher just like the numbers on the elevator display.

"Record a video. Send them that. Be yourself and be honest. Your clients come to you for *you*, Hallie. Remind them who you are."

I blow out a shaky breath. "You're right." I lean into his side, snaking my arm around his bicep. "You always know just what to say to stop me freaking out. Thank you."

He dips his head to press a kiss to my hair. "I love you. It'll be okay."

We step out into a private hallway, and he unlocks the front door.

I'm hit by the scent of fresh flowers. A bouquet the size of a small country is on display on the circular table in the center of the entry space.

"Sinclair?" he asks as I pluck out the card.

"Yep. She's so sweet," I murmur, reading her message welcoming us home and saying how excited she is to see us. She must have put these here before the news broke.

"I should call her again," Sterling says as he takes his wallet and keys from his pocket and places them down on the table.

He pulls his cell out from his jacket pocket and puts it to his ear as he walks up behind me, sliding a hand around my stomach and dropping a kiss to my shoulder.

"Sweetheart? Yes, we're home now."

Home. I turn and look at him as he holds me.

"Mm-hm." His eyes narrow in question, and I signal I'm going to go into the other room.

I step out of my heels and pad into the living room, sinking down onto the sofa.

This is it. The day I've been dreading. The day everyone finds out I'm a fraud. My clients will know I was married once, and that I took New York's most eligible bachelor for myself.

I could lose my business.

I wait for the fear to take over and twist its way around my torso.

I wait.

"It'll be okay, Hallie. We'll deal with it together."

I clasp my hands in my lap as Sterling's voice plays inside my head.

A tremor of cold slithers through me. But it's like an underwater river, not having broken the surface. Maybe... maybe there's a way through this. A couple of weeks ago the thought of this day terrified me. But so did the thought of telling my parents about Vegas.

And I survived that.

They survived as well. They were shocked and hurt that I'd kept it from them. But Sterling was right, they're my parents and they forgave me. I could see in their eyes that what worried them the most wasn't what I told them I'd done in the past, but what I wanted to do in the future. That I want to stay in New York with Sterling. But when they hugged me goodbye they told me how seeing me happy is all they care about, and that they're proud of me. I cried as Dad shook Sterling's hand and told him to 'take care of my daughter'.

That one gesture told me all I need to know.

They'll miss me, but they know I belong in New York.

Sterling's already asked when they can come and visit. He thinks it will help them to see where I'm living and that I'm settled. And I'll be flying back all the time to see them. And to visit Sophie. I managed a very brief lunch full of hugs and baby bump strokes before she had to go back into court, and Sterling and I needed to fly back.

But we all survived.

Maybe my business won't. If it doesn't then I'll build it again, the same way I have done once already. We'll make it work, just like Sterling promised.

This isn't over.

"She's going to come by later. I think she missed you," Sterling says as he walks into the room, his gaze tracking over me, searching for signs of a meltdown. "Hallie?"

I give him a reassuring nod. "I'm okay."

"You're okay?" He raises one brow, and I hold my hand out to him, trying my best to smile.

"I will be. After I've recorded that video you suggested, and you've taken me to bed."

"In that order?" His lips curl a fraction.

"Unless you want to record both?" I bite my lip, loving the way his eyes glitter.

He walks over slowly, sliding his hand into my outstretched one. He doesn't comment on the slight tremble in my fingers. He knows me. He knows that the adrenaline of pushing through the hoard of press downstairs is wearing off and I'm starting to process all of this.

But I'm not scared anymore. I'm so nervous that the knots in my stomach won't stop twisting. But I'm not scared.

"Let's go and take care of your clients." He pulls me to my feet and presses a lingering kiss to my lips. "Then I'll take care of you."

I run a finger along his jaw as I draw in a calming breath. "Let's do this."

It doesn't take long for me to freshen up. And then I'm sitting, staring down the camera lens on Sterling's laptop as he sits behind it, one hand cupping his jaw as he leans forward over his thighs and nods at me.

"Ready when you are. Deep breath."

I do as he says, pausing for a moment before I begin.

"I'm making this video to explain the news you might have seen today. I can only apologize if you didn't hear it from me first. That was never my intention. You've put your faith and trust in me, and I am so grateful."

I take another breath, and Sterling nods at me.

"There are two things I need to share with you. So I'll start with the one that happened first. And that was five years ago when I lost my sister. She's the reason I started Cosmic Connections. No one believed in the magic of true love and the power of the universe more than Jenny. Bringing people together has always been my way of keeping her magic alive. But around the anniversary of her passing, I made a mistake."

I swallow hard and glance at Sterling.

It's okay, he mouths.

"I went to a chapel in Vegas, and I got married. And I don't remember a single second of it. I didn't marry a man I loved. None of our friends or family were there. It was the farthest thing from magic. It wasn't who I am or what I believe in. It was just... wrong. It was annulled immediately. And that's when I opened up my journal and started writing. I wrote a letter to Jenny and told her how much I missed her... And I asked her to help me."

I reach up to swipe some tears away. Sterling listens intently, his eyes full of love and support. I haven't told him this before, but the way he's looking at me makes me want to run into his arms and never let go.

"I asked her not to be angry at me, not that she ever would. She was the sweetest person you'd ever meet. When I went to bed that night I dreamed of her. She told me not to lose faith. And then she passed me a handful of purple skittles." I laugh and shake my head. "The next morning I started making plans for ways I could spread love around the world like she did. It began with a neighbor in my apartment building, and a man two floors below who always held the elevator whenever he saw her coming. And then..." I slump my shoulders as I smile. "... it grew."

I take a moment to compose myself.

"Then I came to New York." I look into Sterling's eyes. "And I was tasked with my most difficult client to date. A man who's sitting on the other side of the camera right now, looking at me in a way that's making my entire body tingle all over." I sigh tenderly as he smiles at me. "And I fell head over heels in love with him, despite fighting that feeling every chance I got."

"You sure did fight it." Sterling chuckles and I know the camera will have picked him up.

"He's my client and I fell in love with him myself. And for a long time I was scared about what that meant for my business. For my reputation. But then I realized, how could I ever help another person find love if I'd turned my back on it myself? Nothing would make me a bigger fraud. Nothing would go against the whole reason I began Cosmic Connections in the first place."

I open the hand that's remained clasped in my lap the entire time and look at the small rose quartz heart. I saw it in Sterling's luggage as he opened it to get his laptop to record this video for me. The fact that he took it traveling with him fills my heart with a sense of amazement.

"So there it is. I'm Halliday Burton. I run Cosmic Connections. And I can help you find love. And if you're worried about the fact that I fell in love with one of my clients myself, then I guess all I can say is..." I turn the crystal over in my palm. "It will never happen again because he's it for me. He's my choice. The only one I'll ever make."

My tears fall faster. "You can stop recording now," I whisper.

"Hallie."

He's there in seconds, wrapping me in his arms, holding me to him, anchoring me. Being everything I need him to be.

"I'm okay." I sniff. "I'm okay."

I lift my head and allow myself to be captured by warm blue. The way he looks at me makes me feel warmth all the way to my toes.

It will all be okay.

"I kind of need you to get me naked, though. Like right now." I take his hand and place the crystal heart in his palm.

"Right now?" He smiles as he looks at it, before meeting my eyes again.

"I need you to make love to me. I'm feeling kind of needy."

He sucks a breath in through his nose. "Baby girl, do you

need me to worship every inch of your body until those tears stop?"

"I do," I whisper. "If you can manage it?" I tease.

"If I can manage it?" He fixes me with a look that I feel deep in my core.

I squeal as he scoops me into his arms and strides toward the bedroom.

"I can manage it. In fact, I'll manage it three times just to prove to you how well I can manage it."

I sink my face into his shirt, the fabric drying my wet cheeks as I laugh. His matching chuckle rumbles in his chest as I grip on to him.

No longer afraid.

31

HALLIDAY

"Rory must have really had a thing for you to go all crazy like that," Sinclair muses, sliding the diamond pendant up and down the chain around her neck with one hand while holding Monty's leash in the other.

"He's crazy, all right. I just hope he leaves us alone now," I reply as we walk along Fifth Avenue.

I've spent a couple of days lying low, but I'm finally venturing out. Sinclair talked me into shopping and lunch. She insisted I need to treat myself to some new business outfits. Because ever since I sent that video out to my clients, my enquiries have tripled. *Tripled!*

No publicity is bad publicity it seems, just like Sullivan grunted when he came to see Sterling this morning. The two are working on something at Sullivan's office today, but I have no idea what. Sterling seemed unusually coy about it.

"He's out of ammo. He's outed you to the world. It didn't ruin your business. And Dad's been labeled as some new face for the 'fit, fifty, and finding love' gang," Sinclair says.

I smile for the first time in days, and it feels amazing.

"Yeah, he kind of has, hasn't he?"

Sterling's had his share of negative press as well. Some stories focused on how Elaina only passed two years ago, and he's already moved on with a younger woman; printing pictures of their wedding day where both just looked shell-shocked more than in love. But there were more who sympathized with him and ran stories on other widows and widowers who found happiness again after their darkest times.

What I thought would ruin everything has actually put us all in a better place.

"Ooh, we should totally go in here."

Sinclair stops in front of a store that has beautiful cream and gold lettering swooping over the glass window in front of a display of stunning lingerie.

"I have a shoot coming up with them. I want to see what their current season line is like."

She lifts her nose in the air and inclines her chin over her shoulder. "You think you can wait out here?"

Denver looks at her with his usual set expression from behind us. "Your father asked that I accompany Halliday."

She snorts. "Like the press will be hiding amongst the G-strings in there."

Denver's brows pull low, making his eyes darken as he looks past us inside the store like he's running a risk assessment in his head.

I give him a sympathetic smile. I'm sure he'd rather be doing something else than keeping an eye on me. But Sterling insisted that Denver come with me for a few days when I leave the penthouse. Just until the press gets bored. Although so far today we've only seen one person trying to snap a picture of me. This is the city that never sleeps. A million and one more interesting things have happened over the past forty-eight hours. Sterling and I are old news already.

"We'll be okay," I assure Denver.

His clean-shaven jaw cuts a perfect line over his muscular neck as he nods once. "I'll wait here."

He widens his stance and stands with his hands clasped in front of him over his black suit.

"Seriously?" Sinclair rolls her eyes. "This isn't men in black. No one is going to try anything when we're in there trying on those." She points at the tiny strip of champagne-colored silk on the store mannequin.

Denver's eyes slide to it before he looks away.

Sinclair's eyes soften with longing. "That's so pretty. I'm going to see if they have it in black too. But I won't be able to wear it to the club tonight; the dress I'm wearing is too tight for panties."

Denver clears his throat as she crouches and kisses Monty on the head.

"I'm sorry you have to stay with Mr. Boring. Mommy won't be long." She stands and thrusts Monty's leash into Denver's hand. "I'm trusting you with him. Don't let me down."

"I'll guard him with my life," Denver replies seriously as Sinclair links her arm with mine.

"Come on. Let's go inside."

Fifteen minutes later we walk out armed with a bag each. Sinclair talked me into buying a sexy silver lace set. She really has taken mine and Sterling's relationship well. She wasn't the slightest bit affected when I paid for it and the sales assistant commented on how lucky my partner would feel when they saw me in it. She was even giggling as we walked out of the store, and she shoved her shopping into Denver's hand for him to carry as she took Monty's leash back.

"You and Dad are coming to dinner with everyone tomorrow night, aren't you?" she asks as we walk. "Uncle Mal returns in the morning."

"We are. It's worked out better that it was rescheduled to

tomorrow. I don't think I'm ready for dining somewhere busy today." I look warily across the street at a guy with a camera slung around his neck. I glance back at Denver, but his eyes are already on the man.

"The Verenelli is always busy. They have the best steak in the city. But yeah, it's better that it's not tonight. It means Zoey and I can hit that club. You sure you don't want to come?"

"No, thanks."

The man with the camera crosses at the intersection ahead of us bringing him onto our side of the street.

"I guess Uncle Mal must have been visiting friends and that's why he was late."

"Yeah," I murmur. Sterling said Mal had stopped in London and that's why his trip was extended by a day.

"Halliday!" Denver clips in warning from where he's moved next to me.

The guy moves fast, getting his camera straight up and thrust in our direction. Denver steps in front of us, blocking his view with his broad body.

"Sinclair? Can I have a quote about the Celestia swimwear line you've just modeled for? I've got a great shot of you in that little red two piece to go with it."

Denver's body seems to expand in size as he makes a noise that sounds like a cross between a grunt and a growl. Whatever it is, the camera man falters, taking a step back.

"Miss Beaufort only gives pre-planned interviews. You want a quote, contact her agent."

The man pulls back his shoulders, deciding Denver isn't going to stop him getting his scoop. He snaps another couple of images.

"Come on, Sinclair. Tell me, which was your favorite? Was it the red one? You've already made that one sell out. Or was it the one with the thong panties? That was my favorite."

He snaps another image before Denver covers the lens of his camera with his hand and shoves it away. "Fuck off."

The guy throws his hands up, smiling as he backs away. "Thanks, Sinclair. Looking beautiful as always."

"Thank you," Sinclair calls sweetly as he walks off.

She spins to Denver. "Will you relax? God, I'm so glad you're not usually with me. He just wanted a picture."

Denver grunts, his eyes burning into the guy's retreating back.

A car pulls up alongside us and the rear window rolls down.

"Halliday?"

I turn. Lavinia's looking out of the window, her face pinched with worry.

"Is everything okay? Was that man bothering you?"

"We're fine, thank you. He wanted a quote from Sinclair."

"Hi, Lavinia." Sinclair gives her a little wave.

"Hello." Lavinia smiles and looks at me. "I was hoping I could talk with you?"

"Oh, um..."

"Go ahead." Sinclair holds Monty's leash up. "I want to take Monty for a walk in the park to get some pictures for his Instagram."

She blows me a kiss and then plucks the lingerie bag from Denver's hand.

"See you later." She crinkles her nose up with a cute little smirk knowing she's about to ditch him.

"I'll give Halliday a ride," Lavinia says to them both. "You don't need to concern yourself. I'll drop her home or wherever she needs to go."

Denver looks at me and pulls his phone out.

"Boss?" he clips, and my stomach does a little dance knowing he's talking to Sterling. "Lavinia Weston just offered Halliday a ride. Sinclair's taking Monty into the park, but she's just been harassed by a pap. I think I should stay with her."

Sinclair grumbles something under her breath as Denver nods.

"Understood."

He hangs up then steps forward to open Lavinia's car door for me.

I throw Sinclair an apologetic smile and she sighs but doesn't look angry.

I climb into the backseat beside Lavinia. Sinclair's already strutted off up the street and he strides to catch up with her. She turns and says something to him before flicking her hair and marching on ahead. He's fallen into pace one step behind her and Monty as we pull out into the traffic and drive past them.

"I'm glad I ran into you," Lavinia says, tucking a piece of hair behind her ear. Her diamond earring sparkles. It's one of the new designs from Sullivan's showcase last week. He told Sterling he'd taken a lot of orders that evening from the invited guests. Lavinia must have spent a lot of money on their pieces over the years.

"It's lovely to see you too," I reply.

"I wanted to congratulate you both on your relationship." Her eyes fix on mine as she smiles. "I'll need to come and see Sterling too, of course. But I'm happy that I've been able to tell you first."

"Thank you."

She looks and sounds sincere, and the familiar guilt returns to my gut. She's in love with him. It's obvious from the way her eyes soften each time she says his name. And all those looks I saw her give him. All that energy flowing out of her whenever I saw them together.

"I know he values your friendship," I say.

She looks away and purses her lips.

"We've been friends a long time. In a way, I've grown closer to him than I ever was to Elaina. He's a good man. And I could see the way he looked at you. Even before last week when he had his arm around you like he did, I knew. A part of me always knew the day would come when he met someone."

My mouth dries as I wonder what to say. Apologizing for the fact he loves me and not her would be wrong. And I'm not sorry. I'm sorry she's hurting. But I'm not sorry for me loving him and him loving me. I never could be.

"You knew about the affair?" I ask instead, because it's been bothering me since she defended Sterling that night. He seemed surprised that she knew.

"Yes, I knew." An empty laugh tinkles out of her perfectly lined lips. "He didn't deserve that. Elaina was so selfish. That's not a nice thing to say about a friend, especially one that's gone. But it's true."

"You're one of the few people who know."

She sighs. "Sterling's a gentleman. Elaina was a very loving mother. That's how he'd want people to remember her. He didn't keep it a secret out of embarrassment or a desire to hide it. He kept it secret because it's no one else's business. His family is the most important thing in the world to him."

"They are," I agree.

"And lucky you, you're part of that now."

I return her smile, hoping it doesn't portray the unease swirling in my stomach. I assumed it was Rory who tipped the press off about our relationship. He's the one who kept threatening to do it. But something about the way Lavinia's smile seems forced and doesn't meet her eyes sets off alarm bells.

It doesn't make sense, though. Lavinia has no reason to do it unless she aimed to cause us unnecessary stress, perhaps even force us apart. And like she said, they've been friends for years. She wouldn't do that to him.

"Yes, you're so lucky," she repeats, giving me another brittle smile.

32

STERLING

"How am I supposed to sit through the rest of this dinner with you next to me in that dress?"

"What do you mean?" Hallie teases.

We've come out with Sinclair, Sullivan, Trudy, and Mal for dinner. I gave Denver and the boys the night off. Press interest is dying down, and I'm not going to let Hallie out of my sight, so I figured it was time they got to blow off some steam. They've been working hard for months.

I lean closer and inhale oranges and honey, which I now know is from the brand of shampoo she uses. The shampoo that's now sitting on a shelf in my shower.

In our shower. In our home.

"You know exactly what I mean. You look incredible. The most beautiful sight in here."

She smiles and darts her eyes around the room.

The restaurant is famous for being amongst the best in the city to dine. And its buzzing atmosphere and rooftop bar with views over the harbor make it a place my family has enjoyed many times. But tonight I don't notice any of that. The only time my eyes have left Hallie for any length of time is when she wanted to take a walk onto the roof terrace to look at the Statue of Liberty all lit up.

She places her cheek against mine, so her lips brush my ear. "How about we cut dinner short by not ordering dessert? You can have it when we get home."

"Baby girl," I rumble, heat firing in my groin instantly. "You know it's a chart day."

"You actually put it in your diary?" She pulls back, her eyes bright with surprise.

"Of course."

"Oh." She blinks up at me from beneath dark flirty lashes as she positions herself back in her seat. "Well, then maybe it's time we tried something new."

I clear my throat and adjust my tie before sliding my hand onto her thigh beneath the table. She slides hers on top, interlinking our fingers.

Mal continues telling the table about his trip and how he went out with Ade at sunrise, and they saw a pride of lions. I inhale through my nose and lean toward her, keeping my voice hushed.

"What exactly are you suggesting?"

Her soft lips graze my ear. "I'm suggesting you put it in my—"

I push my chair back, and it scrapes loudly on the polished marble floor.

"I'm sorry, everyone. Please excuse us for a moment."

I pull Hallie to her feet and take her out of the main dining area toward the hallway that leads to the restrooms.

I pin her to the wall the second we're alone and claim her lips with a groan, kissing her like it would cause me physical pain to stop.

"Baby girl, what are you doing?"

"What do you mean?" She slides her hands to the nape of my neck and strokes my hair with her fingertips.

"You know exactly what I mean. You've got me acting like a frat boy," I moan against her mouth, swallowing down her whimper as my erection presses into her. "I'm a fifty-year-old man, and I'm sat at dinner with this in my pants because my beautiful girlfriend just told me she wants to have anal sex when we get home."

She gasps out a giggle. "That's the most ungentlemanly thing I've ever heard you say."

I chuckle against her mouth and hold her chin between my thumb and forefinger, slowing our kisses down to tender ones.

"It's hard to maintain any kind of composure around you most of the time."

She sighs happily. "I love you."

"I love you too. Just wait until I get you home," I groan, stealing another kiss.

We return to the table and finish dinner. Sullivan announces he needs to get home to Molly, who's being watched by Arabella, and I take it as an opportunity to say Hallie and I need to be leaving as well. We say our goodbyes and I take Hallie's hand in mine as we ride the elevator down and head out onto the street.

"Your car's that way," Hallie says as I lead her in the opposite direction.

"I thought we'd take a walk first."

Her eyes narrow in question, but a smile plays on her lips. "Sure, okay."

I wrap my arm around her as we stroll in the direction of Battery Park.

"I love this city. I bet you can't imagine living anywhere else, having been here your whole life."

"True. It's where my family is from, it's where I grew up. But I haven't spent a huge amount of time here over the past couple of years. I was out on my yacht as much as possible.

The new one. The old one was completely unsalvageable. Not that I think I could have stepped foot on it again."

Hallie leans into my side, her voice full of love. "Sterling."

I press a kiss into her hair. "Don't get upset. I just want you to know that you've made being here easier. It feels like home again. I spent so many months on the water after losing them both. Not just in Cape Town. I went all over. Being on the water made me feel better. Like I was closer to my son. I feel like that's where he is. Even though we brought him home, I…"

Hallie tightens her arm around me.

"I still need to know what happened that day," I murmur.

"You couldn't have done anything."

I exhale heavily, my chest tightening. "I know that. It was too late before I ran onboard to help. They'd already gone. I don't know what started the fire. I don't know how it spread so fast to the fuel tanks. I don't know why neither of them got off in time. There are so many questions that I want answers to. And I need to accept I might never get them."

I bring us to a stop on the path, the harbor to our left. The Statue of Liberty shines in the distance, lit up by floodlights. I move us so Hallie can stand in front of the railings and look.

I wrap an arm around either side of her and hold her from behind.

"I can't live in the past anymore. We've both lost people we love. But we're still here. And we've found each other. That's a damn miracle to me, Hallie. You're my miracle."

I dip my head and kiss her neck beneath her ear.

"And you're mine," she breathes. "I don't know where I'd be without you."

"You'd be sprinkling magic, just like you are now."

"God, I hope so." Her eyes stay fixed in the distance.

"Your business is going to keep growing. You'll keep Jenny's memory alive. I'm never going to stop you from working. I'll support you. If you have to travel, spend time away, we'll make it work."

"I know you will. And that means more to me than you'll ever know." She turns inside my arms and smiles at me. "I'm going to apply for an extension to my working visa to start with. I've had some inquiries from clients in New York, so I won't need to travel anywhere for a while."

"Okay."

"Which is a shame." She walks her fingers up my tie, her eyes alight with teasing. "Because it means I won't be able to use my beautiful new Halliday Burton luggage you got for me."

"Beaufort."

"What?" Her brow scrunches up.

I reach up and stroke the backs of my fingers across her cheek.

"I bought you that luggage and asked them to put Halliday Beaufort's initials on it for me."

She laughs and then stops and searches my eyes. "You're serious?"

"I am."

"I don't... What?" She looks more confused before she clamps her hand over her mouth.

I look up at her from where I've dropped to one knee at her feet.

"I asked your father's permission when we were in England. And I've waited three long, excruciating days since we got back for this to be ready."

I take out the signature blue velvet box with gold Beaufort Diamonds logo on it from my inner jacket pocket.

"Sterling." Hallie's eyes are round as she looks at me in shock.

I take her left hand and kiss the backs of her fingers.

"You came into my life and told me my kissing needed work."

She breaks out into a smile and her eyes mist.

"I did do that," she whispers.

"And then you gave me the one thing I've never had. You gave me you. All of you. You chose us over everything."

"I chose *you*," she breathes.

"You chose me," I say, looking up at her.

"I hope there's a ring in that box and not some earrings, because now I'm crying thinking you're about to ask me something." She laughs, wiping at her eyes with her free hand.

"I am going to ask you something." I smile up at her as her breath catches and she stares back in silence.

"Hallie, will you marry me?"

She's nodding before I even flip open the ring box.

"I need to hear you say—"

"Yes." She nods over and over, her voice breaking. "Yes."

Her finger trembles as I take the ring out and slide it on.

"Sterling?" her voice wavers as tears track down her cheeks.

"Hallie," I counter, gazing up at her.

"I need you to hold me up before I fall."

I'm on my feet, pulling her into my arms a split second later as she crushes her lips to mine.

"Yes, I'll marry you." She kisses me over and over, her fingers dusting over my jaw before she pulls back enough to take a proper look at her ring.

"You had this designed and made in the last three days?"

"No. I had it designed weeks ago, hoping I'd be able to have it made in the last three days."

She laughs and stares at the three rows of emerald cut diamonds banded together around her finger, all framing one central pink diamond. They're so big it almost reaches her knuckle. But I couldn't leave a single one out.

"There are twenty-five around that middle one. I chose pink because it reminds me of—"

"The rose quartz heart I gave you."

"The heart you gave me, Hallie. Yours. The most precious thing in the world."

Her eyes widen as she looks from the ring, up at me, and back down again. "You said twenty-five?"

"I did."

My heart swells in my chest as she whips her head in the direction of the harbor, staring out across the water. "The number of windows in her crown."

"The number of windows in her crown," I breathe as she looks at the ring again.

"You're amazing." She sniffs before looking back up at me with sparkling eyes. "I love you."

"I love you too. I knew the moment I met you that I wanted this. But I didn't dare dream it. I never thought for one second it was possible."

"I can't believe it. I'm going to be Halliday Beaufort," she whispers. "It sounds—"

"Perfect. It sounds damn perfect," I say, lifting her lips to mine.

"Oh wow, that looks..."

Hallie bites her lip as she wraps her hand around my hard as steel cock and pumps it up and down slowly. The giant ring on her finger catches the light and sparkles as she reaches the head and runs her thumb over the weeping slit.

"Looks pretty damn good. It'll look even better when your

wedding ring is next to it." I groan as I stand next to the bed and look at her kneeling on it as she jerks me off.

"There won't be room. It's huge."

"We'll make it fit, Baby girl."

She laughs. "Uh-huh. I guess you're good at giving me big things to take care of."

I tip my head back with a groan as she swallows my dick, moaning and sucking it until it pops free of her lips.

"I want to taste you. But I also want to ride you... and I want to..." She lets out a disgruntled huff that makes me chuckle as she pulls me onto the bed with her and kisses me.

I move up, positioning myself against the headboard like our first time together.

"We've got all night. We can do it all."

I hold her eyes as she straddles me.

"We've got the rest of our lives, fiancé." Her eyes glitter.

I grasp her hips and relish the way her lips part on a moan as I pull her down onto me, burying myself inch by inch until I'm deep inside her, filling her completely.

"We do." I press a soft kiss to her neck as I squeeze her hips, flexing my throbbing cock inside her, taking a moment to rein in the desire to work her up and down my dick fast and hard until I come inside her. "But I still want all those things tonight."

She moans as she starts to ride me slowly. "Me too."

Her hands wander from my shoulders to my chest, her eyes following the trail of her fingers as she traces them over the scars covering the skin above my heart.

"You're the most beautiful man I've ever met," she says softly, stroking me with such tenderness that my throat dries up. "All of you. Heart, body, and soul."

"Hallie."

"Sterling," she muses, her eyes creasing at the corners as she smiles.

She sinks up and down me slowly, tilting her head back with a moan as the head of my dick rubs over the special spot inside her.

"Baby girl." I tighten my grip on her hips, trying to stop her from moving.

She places one hand on top of mine on her hip, putting her other hand on my shoulder and using it as leverage to ride me harder and faster.

Her breathy moans are like a shot of adrenaline to my dick, and it pulses and thickens inside her.

"Hallie," I groan as the head of my cock throbs inside her. "It's a chart day." I curse as she clenches around me and a wave of pre-cum flows out inside her.

"I know. It just feels so good," she hums, sinking down on me again and making me drop my head back with a moan.

Her lips slide over my throat, and she kisses my windpipe as I drag in a deep breath.

"Hallie," I utter.

She licks my neck all the way up to my ear.

"What is it, fiancé?" she whispers, her breath warm against my skin.

"You know what."

My groan is choked as she circles herself back down onto my dick and her perfectly puckered nipples brush over my skin.

The base of my cock heats and I know more hot drops are seeping out of me inside her.

"You'll be walking down that aisle pregnant if you keep this up." I squeeze her hips as she brings her mouth to mine and kisses me.

"You feel so good inside me, though."

She fucks me harder, and I grab a handful of her hair and deepen our kiss.

"I'm going to come inside you if you don't stop," I pant.

"Just one more minute," she breathes against my lips.

I grit my teeth and use every ounce of my strength to keep my balls under control as they tighten. Each time her slap-able ass bounces down onto them I fight not to unload inside her.

"Hallie," I plead.

"I'm..." she pants against my mouth, and I slide a hand up to hold her neck.

"Damn it, Baby girl. You're about to come on my cock, aren't you?"

She whimpers.

"And you expect me not to explode inside you as you do?"

"If you hold it, then I know where you can put it." She bites her lower lip, her lids hooded as she looks at me.

I can't help my growl coming out sounding angry. "Jesus Christ, you're going to be the death of me."

"Just one more second..."

She slams herself up and down my cock twice more and then drops her head back, her throat pressing into my palm as she cries out my name and her pussy falls into pulsing waves around me.

I groan like I'm in pain as I watch her.

"I can feel every squeeze of your cunt as you're coming," I scold. "Every damn twitch, and you expect me not to come inside you?"

I hold her throat tighter as she whimpers and shakes above me, using my body to make her feel good.

Coming all over my goddamn painful cock.

"You better be damn ready," I hiss, screwing my eyes shut, sweat beading on my chest as I fight the heavy draw in my balls that's threatening to detonate.

"Okay," she pants. "Okay."

I lift her off me and flip her over onto all fours.

"Naughty girl," I say as I grab my cock and squeeze it hard to stop my impending orgasm in its tracks.

I want to come inside her. I don't want to waste a drop by shooting my load before I even get there.

I sink my face in between her legs from behind and lick her.

She cries out as I spear her with two fingers. My dick is still rock-hard, pre-cum dripping out of it onto the bed sheets. But the urge to come has eased off.

"You think you can fuck me like that, coming all over me, and expect me not to blow inside you?"

"Sterling," she cries out, jerking forward as I slap one ass cheek, loving the way the skin turns pink before I flatten my palm over it and rub in circles.

"No, you don't. Come back here."

I wrap one arm around her waist, pulling her back onto my hand as I fuck her with my fingers.

"You can give me another before I put my cock in your ass, just like I know you've been wanting me to."

I smile against her back, kissing her skin as she comes instantly, rippling around my fingers with a strained mewl.

"You like it when I forget to be a gentleman, huh?"

"Sterling." She shudders, a gush of wetness running out into my palm as I pull my fingers free.

"Now rub that clit for me, Baby girl."

She murmurs an incoherent cross between a moan and a gasp as I straighten up, kneeling behind her.

I press the head of my cock against her asshole.

"You sure you want this?" I ask, my voice softening as I stroke her hip.

"Yes," she moans, rolling them so her body rubs against my crown.

I reach to the bedside drawer, pulling out a tube of lube.

"I'll take it slow," I say, squeezing some onto my dick and letting some drip down between her ass cheeks.

She flinches as the cold liquid hits her, then moans and

pushes back toward me as I rub it into her skin with my fingers, sliding the tip of one inside her.

"Are you rubbing your clit?"

"Yes," she murmurs.

I look forward. Her left hand is on the bed, scrunching up the bedsheets, her engagement ring twinkling between the fabric.

"Good girl."

I pump my dick a couple of times, coating it in the lube. Then I press the head against her asshole.

The moan she makes almost makes me come on the spot as her body opens up for me, letting me ease inside a little.

"Jesus."

My jaw clenches and I pause, then slide in a couple of inches. I circle gently and ease another inch forward.

"So goddamn tight." I suck in a breath, stroking up and down her spine tenderly with one hand. "You're so beautiful. I love you."

"I love you too," she moans, pushing back. "Keep going."

My eyes drop to where she's taking me and I push forward slowly, giving her body time to stretch for me.

"Yes, like that. That feels good," she whimpers.

Her hand is moving frantically, buried between her thighs.

"You want to come, Baby girl?"

"Not yet," she pants.

"You want more?" I stroke up her spine again, my fingers dusting the dip of her waist on the way down.

"Yes, please."

Her breathy moans spur me on, and I keep the pressure up, easing deeper and watching inch after inch disappear inside her.

"Damn, that's good," I rasp.

Stilling my hand on the base of her spine, I push forward,

closing the final gap until my hips meet her skin. I look at how we fit together. She's quivering, like she's holding back.

"You okay?"

"I feel so full."

My cock flexes inside her and she whimpers my name, which only makes it swell more.

"You are full, Baby girl." I run my thumb around the base of my dick, admiring the way her skin is stretched around it, clutching onto it so damn tight.

"Sterling," she whimpers again. "Move... fuck me."

It's barely a whisper, but it's enough to almost tip me over the edge. I withdraw a couple of inches before sliding back in with a groan.

"Oh my god, that feels good," she moans.

I watch her take me as I repeat the move. She told me she's never been with anyone like this before. She said she's never wanted to. Yet she's been asking me to do this with her for a while. And as much as I wanted to, I've never been with anyone in this way, either. And I was afraid of hurting her.

I could never hurt her.

"That still feel good, Baby girl?" I ask as I set a slow, steady pace, going a little deeper each time.

"Yes. Do it faster."

My hips pump quicker, and I lose all coherent thought as my body is spun out with pleasure.

"Damn." I drop my head back, clenching my teeth. "You're so perfect."

She moans over and over, getting louder as I increase my pace. Her ass cheeks ripple each time I bottom out inside her, my hip bones hitting them.

"You like it like that? Nice and deep?"

"Yes," she whimpers.

"I wish I could see your face."

She drops her hand from her clit so she can steady herself on both hands and looks at me over her shoulder. Her eyes are darkened with lust, her cheeks flushed.

"That's better. You're so goddamn beautiful."

"Sterling," she moans, her eyes dropping to where my hips are driving my slicked-up dick inside her.

"You can't see what I can. But let me tell you, it looks and feels incredible."

Her mouth makes an 'O' shape as I speed up, the muscles in my torso all rippling with the force of holding back. I've been ready to come since I first pushed inside her.

"I'm close," I grit, digging my fingertips into her hips.

She turns back around, scrabbling to get her hand back to her clit.

"I'm going to come again," she pants.

"You want to do it together?"

"You first," she moans.

"Where do you want it?"

"You know where."

I grunt as my knuckles turn white against her hips and I thrust faster, my ass cheeks clenching.

I'm the luckiest man on earth.

"You want me to come inside your ass, Baby girl? Is that what you're saying? You want me to fill your perfect little asshole with all this cum you've made me hold onto?"

"Oh god, Sterling. *Please.*"

The way her voice breaks as she begs is my undoing.

"Hallie!" I growl as I come hard.

I keep thrusting, my eyes rolling in my head as my dick swells and liquid heat fires from it in breath-stealing pulses.

"Damn, Baby girl."

I watch my cock pumping in and out of her knowing that I'm coming deep inside her right now. I groan, my balls slapping against her ass as another wave builds up inside me, crashing out in searing shots as I pump out more heat inside her.

"God, Sterling, I'm coming," she cries. The sound of her crying out my name is enough to make my dick swell and my balls pull tight all over again.

"Come for me. That's it," I growl, flexing my hands against her hips so I don't leave bruises. They're damp where even my palms are sweating against her shaking body.

Her whimpers and moans increase.

"You've got your fingers inside yourself, haven't you?"

"Yes," she moans, swirling them around so I feel them press along the underside of my dick.

"Jesus Christ," I hiss as the extra fullness makes her body's grip on my dick even tighter. I thought I was coming down, but my balls throb again and heat races up my shaft.

"I've got more for you," I choke.

I spill inside her with a curse. All the breath leaves my lungs and my vision blurs. Every coiled muscle in my body tightens as my dick squeezes out its final drops inside her.

She rides out her orgasm, my name falling like a prayer from her lips.

I keep pumping into her, slowing my movements gradually. My heart pounds in my chest as I fight to take a deep enough breath.

"You okay?"

She shifts her weight onto one hand and reaches back with the other.

"I'm okay," she breathes.

She sounds like she's smiling, and a grin breaks out onto my face as I exhale with a groan.

"That was amazing, Hallie."

I take her hand inside mine, twisting my fingers around

hers, and around the giant twenty-six diamonds gracing her ring finger.

She's mine.

I'm her first choice.

And I'm going to make damn sure she never regrets that decision.

33

STERLING

"He's been using client's money to keep the loan sharks off his back."

I run a hand over my jaw as I look at the paperwork that Denver's managed to get ahold of. It's all here in black and white. I could ruin Rory if I choose to.

"No one will know if he pays it back in time. But if he doesn't, he'll lose his job, his license to practice, he could face jail."

"Stupid boy. He could have sorted all this with what I gave him. What's he done with half a million?"

Denver looks at me from beneath his dark brows. "My guy in London has been keeping some tabs on him. He's already gambled a lot of it."

I shake my head as I drop the papers onto my desk.

"And he spent a night in a hotel with two hookers," he adds.

I snort out a disgusted grunt. This is the man who thought he was worthy of Hallie. Who actually believed he stood a chance with her.

"You want me to tell my guy to keep an eye on him?"

I sit back in my chair, steepling my hands in front of my face. Hallie has been so happy since we came back from England. She knows Rory didn't get those bruises her mom mentioned from a clumsy fall. She's also told me she understands that Beauforts do anything for family.

And she's one of us now.

I'll dispose of every Rory on this earth that so much as breathes in her direction if I have to.

But she's also asked me to leave it in the past. She wants to move forward, and she doesn't want Rory's parents to hear what he's been up to from someone else. Just like she didn't want hers to hear about Vegas from someone else. She's always seeing the good in other people. She wants to believe that he'll tell them himself and deal with his problems like a man.

I can guarantee he'll be a coward and not come clean to them.

But Hallie's asked me to leave it behind us.

"No. Tell him he can stop. If Rory has the balls to come back here, I'll deal with him."

"Boss." Denver nods as he rises from his seat.

"Denver?" I say as he reaches the door of my office.

He turns back.

"Keep Killian and Jenson here from now on. They've spent long enough chasing thin air in Cape Town."

He nods, his eyes holding mine. "We still have some people to identify on the CCTV."

"Finish it. And after that..."

He doesn't need to say anything. I know from the look in his eyes that he understands. It's been two years and we've gotten nowhere. Nothing is going to bring them back. Living in the past suited me until now. It gave me a purpose, chasing an answer that I thought had to exist. But now I have a real reason to keep going.

Denver closes the door behind him as he leaves, and I pick up my phone.

"I just wanted to hear your voice," I say the moment Hallie answers.

I close my eyes as we chat, relaxing in my chair and just listening to her excitement flowing from her as she tells me about another new client who has reached out to her today.

When we finally hang up I'm smiling.

This is living in the present. This is what I need. No matter how many times I tell her what she's done for me, I don't think she'll ever truly know just how much I love her.

She's given me a future.

The intercom on my desk phone flashes and I reach out to answer it.

"Yes?"

"Boss?" It's the security guard from the main door. "Ms. Weston is here for you. Shall I bring her through?"

I exhale, my shoulders dropping. "Yes, show her through."

I stand and walk around my desk, hands going into my pant pockets. A few minutes later the door opens and Lavinia steps through. My security guy closes it behind her.

"Lavinia. This is a surprise."

She walks to me, sweeping me into a double-cheeked kiss.

"I was in the neighborhood and thought I'd drop in."

She walks to the two sofas facing one another and places her handbag down on the floor in front of one as she takes a seat.

"Would you care for a drink?" I walk to the cabinet where I keep everything and reach for the fridge to get out some water or juice.

"Some of that will do."

I turn and follow her line of sight to the crystal decanter on top of the cabinet.

"It's after lunch." She laughs nervously.

"I didn't say a word." I offer her a small smile as I fix two glasses.

I turn and hand her the glass of brandy. She shifts as though she's making room for me on the couch next to her, but I move around the coffee table and take a seat on the couch opposite her instead.

She takes a large gulp from her glass.

"I came to congratulate you on your engagement."

"Thank you."

She fiddles with a diamond tennis bracelet on her wrist, a Beaufort design from last year, before taking another large gulp of brandy.

"I understand why I had to hear it from someone else. We aren't... we're not as close as we once were. I'm not the one you confide in anymore."

I bite back my retort that she has never been the one I confide in. That one night we had. That *mistake* has completely skewed her interpretation of our friendship. If I could erase that night I would. She was there when I felt alone. But I've never confided in her. Not once. I never told her about Elaina's affair, or about how my entire life felt like a lie some days. How I was never in love with my wife in the way the world believed.

"I would have told you myself," I say. "Just like I would have told you that Hallie and I were dating. But we both agreed to tell our families first, and I haven't seen you since Sullivan's viewing evening."

Her lips lift into a small smile. "I figured out there was something between you both that night." She brushes some invisible lint off her skirt. "You've chosen well. Halliday is a lovely young lady. I hope she will make you happy."

I take another drink, my grip on the glass tightening at the way Lavinia slides the word 'young' in.

"She already does. I'm happier than I've ever been."

Lavinia's brows shoot up before she recovers herself. "Good, that's wonderful."

I allow a few seconds of silence to stretch between us. She's on edge. Her eyes keep darting around the room and she's fidgeting, her fingertips drumming against the side of her almost empty glass.

"Was there something else on your mind?"

I know Lavinia well enough to know she won't mention the evening she came to my place and suggested we spend another night together. Especially now she knows I'm engaged. If she had wanted to discuss it, we'd have done so already. I haven't pushed it because that seemed like the gentlemanly thing to do.

But looking at her now, I wonder if it was a mistake not to clear the air sooner.

"I just wanted to see you to..." She sighs. "To make sure you know what you're doing."

I clear my throat to stop myself from speaking too harshly.

"I appreciate your concern. But I know exactly what I'm doing."

She nods, her lips twisting like she's chewing on the inside of her cheek.

"Hallie is—"

"Halliday," I correct. No one calls her Hallie since she lost Jenny. No one except me. Not even her own parents.

Lavinia's eyes snap to mine, and she purses her lips. "Halliday is twenty years younger than you."

"I know how old she is." I take another sip of my brandy, wishing I'd poured a larger glass.

"As your friend, I want to make sure you've thought about this. She might want children."

"I understand that. She'll be an incredible mom."

Lavinia's brows shoot up her forehead for the second time since she walked into my office.

"You... That's something you want to do again?"

"That's something Hallie and I will decide together." I place my now empty glass down onto the low table between us.

"I see. I suppose I never saw you getting married again. Not after the way your marriage to Elaina started. I thought you were put off for life." She presses her lips together like she's said too much.

"Lavinia." I lean forward over my knees, holding my hands out. "I know you were Elaina's friend all those years. And I know you were there when it all started. But you were also there all those years we were married, and when we had our children. Maybe neither of us chose the other. Our parents made that choice for us. But I wouldn't change it. I have Sullivan and Sinclair. And for as long as he was here, I also had—"

"She cheated on you," she hisses, her eyes flashing with an uncharacteristic hate that I've never seen in her before.

"She did."

"She never gave up on the man who broke her all those years ago. She had you. She got to marry *you*. And yet she still talked about him. Wondering what he was doing. Whether he'd met someone else. Even after I lost Jared." She presses a hand to her lips and blinks rapidly at the mention of her late husband. "Even after I lost him, she still couldn't appreciate what she had. Couldn't see from my loss just how lucky she was."

"It's all in the past."

She shakes her head, ignoring me. "Such a selfish woman. She never deserved you. I had to listen to her pine after him like a puppy," she spits.

I wait for the betrayal to hit me like it used to, carving itself into my gut like this deep, ugly cancer. But nothing comes. No matter what happened, it's all done now. I refuse to take any lingering resentments forward into my life with Hallie. Yes, I felt betrayed at what Elaina did. But I wasn't heartbroken. Because she never had all of my heart, just like I never had hers.

"She made her choices, Lavinia."

She sniffs and looks at me with glassy eyes.

"She did. She could easily have said no if she'd wanted to. But I knew for certain that she didn't deserve you the minute she told me she'd replied to his letter."

I sigh. "Elaina wrote to him first."

I damn well remember that much. How when I found the box of letters that Elaina had hidden, the earliest dated one was from him, Neil, thanking her for reaching out and tracking him down online. That's what hurt the most when I found them. That she'd been the one to initiate contact.

"No, she didn't." Lavinia picks up her glass and drains what little is left inside it. "I was so fed up listening to her that I found him online and messaged him, pretending to be her. I thought if he replied that it would be a wakeup call and make her come to her senses. That she would do the right thing. That she might finally look at you the way you deserved."

My heart thuds in my chest as I stare at her.

"You did what?"

Lavinia looks at me, her eyes brightening like I'm actually about to thank her. Tell her she was so smart, and I'm grateful.

She's damn well deluded.

"I gave her an opportunity. One to prove that she deserved you. And she failed. She wrote back to him and started up their filthy little affair behind your back. I told her she had to tell you, and she promised she would. I volunteered for a charity mission overseas because I couldn't bear to watch as she made a fool of you every day."

"You were the one who started it all?" I all but growl.

She falters.

"I didn't make her reply to him. I didn't invite him back to your old apartment and have sex with him in your bed the very first day I saw him again."

I fly to my feet. "You need to leave."

She looks at me, her mouth dropping open.

"You don't mean that. I did you a favor. I was going to tell you myself when I came back if she hadn't. But then the accident happened and... I did it for you, Sterling. You deserve better."

She stands and faces me, her eyes burning into mine.

"You're a gentleman, like my Jared. You and I could have been together after what she did to you. I would never have treated you like that. I would have loved you the way you needed."

"You've been lying to me for years!"

She flinches as my voice rises.

"You put my wife back in touch with a man she wasn't strong enough to say no to. A man who walked all over her years ago and left her alone. What kind of a friend does that?"

"She was fucking him for months before she died. She had to get tested when he gave her something. Did you see that in those letters? How he gave her some disgusting infection? Maybe you need to talk to Halliday."

"Leave," I growl.

She swipes up her purse from the floor, her façade cracking as she looks into my eyes.

"Sterling, I—"

"Now!"

She swallows, her lower lip trembling like she's about to cry.

"I'm sorry. I never meant to cause you pain. I just wanted her to either realize what she had, or move out of the way so I could..." She sucks in a shaky breath and then turns and walks to the door.

I glare at her back, saying nothing as she pauses and looks back at me.

"I'm sorry, Sterling. I did it because I love you. One day I hope you'll see that."

"This *friendship* is over, Lavinia," I say calmly.

She straightens her shoulders and gives me a pitying look.

"I guess it's true what they say about middle-aged men losing their mind over sex with a younger woman."

"Get. The. Hell. Out," I hiss.

Her lips part before she clamps them together tightly and attempts to disguise the sob from her throat. She spins and marches through the door, and I fight the overwhelming urge to put my fist through the wall. Instead, I pick up my crystal tumbler and refill it. I lift it to my nose and inhale the warm hit of alcohol curling up my nostrils.

I tip my head back and drain it in one, slamming the glass back down.

"Jesus Christ."

34

HALLIDAY

"You're back early?" I call absentmindedly from the couch as I twirl the manila envelope between my fingertips.

Sterling walks into the living room behind me, and the scent of his aftershave fills the air as he tosses his jacket onto the back of the chair to my left. I turn to look at him, noticing that his usually warm blue eyes are dark and troubled.

"Sterling?"

He swoops in, claiming my lips in a searing kiss that sets my pulse racing.

"What is it?" I whisper as he cups my face and kisses me again, the taste of brandy on his tongue.

"Lavinia came to see me," he says, his lips traveling to my neck and delivering lingering kisses. "God, I missed you." He inhales deeply like he needs the scent of me to ground him.

"Was she coming to..." I swallow, not wanting to think about that night. "Was she coming in the hope something would happen between you both?"

He rests his forehead against mine.

"No. She came to ask me if I knew what I was doing,

getting married again to a woman twenty years younger than me."

I search his eyes, waiting for the punchline.

But it's not a joke.

"What?" I scoff. "But she was the one who defended you to that guy she was with at Sullivan's party."

"I know." He runs his thumbs over my cheeks softly and looks into my eyes. "I don't think she has a problem with me moving on. But she wanted it to be with her."

I place my hands over his wrists, cupping them and keeping his palms wrapped around my face, needing his touch as much as he needs mine.

"I knew she had feelings for you, but... she actually said that? She threw our age difference in your face?"

He sighs. "That's not all. She admitted to searching out Neil online."

"What?"

"She said she did it to test Elaina. Hoping she'd either get scared and stop thinking about him, or that we'd break up, and that she could... that we might..." His eyes pinch as tension flows off him in waves.

"She thought she could love you better than Elaina did," I finish for him.

He exhales heavily and I press my lips to his in a soft kiss.

"She had just lost her husband. I'm not excusing her behavior, not for one second. But you said it yourself, we do some stupid things when we're grieving."

"You're amazing." He tries to smile but it doesn't reach his eyes. There's a weariness in them that makes my heart sink. "You always try to see the best in people, Hallie. It's one of the infinite things I love about you."

"Her world had just collapsed. Do you think she regretted it, but it was already too late once she told Elaina where to find him?" I ask, wishing that's the case. Sterling's been betrayed enough already.

"No," he says softly. "She knew exactly what she was doing. She's the one who made first contact. She sent him a message, posing as Elaina."

"No," I gasp.

"Yes."

I look back at him, pain lancing through my chest at how after everything, he's still getting hit with more hurt. More betrayal.

"I don't understand. Why would she even...? And she thought you and her could have a future together after that?"

"I doubt she ever planned to tell me. I think hearing about our engagement is what brought it out. The way she was when I saw her earlier was nothing like the person I thought she was. She was vicious and spiteful, trying to make me doubt what you and I have. I told her to get the hell out."

Unease curls up my spine.

"What exactly did she say?"

"That I've lost my head over sex with a younger woman."

"Wow."

My shoulders sag. Lavinia might be proving that she was never a good friend to Sterling. But now she's another person in his life that he's lost. And I hate that he's going through this.

"She really feels that way?" I ask, stroking his wrist.

He presses a kiss to my lips and sighs as he moves back and sinks into the couch.

"She does."

"I thought she seemed off when she gave me a ride. But I never thought she was so bitter about you being happy."

"Neither did I. She actually looked like she enjoyed telling me about the fact Elaina fucked Neil in our old apartment the first time they met up."

"Sterling," I soothe.

"I already knew, Hallie. Every sordid detail was in those letters between them both. Elaina and I hadn't…"

"You can say it." I place my hand on his thigh and squeeze reassuringly.

"We hadn't had sex in months. I'm just glad she wasn't screwing us both at the same time. I still got tested the moment I found the letters, and I've always used condoms since—"

"I know. You don't need to explain."

He pushes a hand around his jaw. "I'm sorry."

"Why are you apologizing?"

His eyes meet mine and my heart goes out to him. He looks shook. Like the past has all been stirred up, and it's burning him all over again.

"We've just got engaged. We should be celebrating and enjoying every minute. Not dealing with stuff like this."

My eyes fall to the manila envelope on the floor that I dropped when he came in.

"Would it make you feel better if I added some shitty stuff in as well? So you're not the only one bringing it home?"

His expression morphs into concern instantly. "What is it? Are you okay? I didn't hurt you the other night, did I?"

I take his hands in mine. "No! You didn't hurt me. I've told you that already. We're definitely doing that again." I smile at him, but it falters as I slide my hands free and pick up the envelope, handing it to him.

"I mean, this."

He takes the envelope, pulling the card out that I've spent the past half an hour staring at.

"What the hell is this?" His brows lower, and he grits his teeth.

"I hoped maybe, just an innocent gesture?" I shrug.

The Matchmaker

"This isn't a damn gesture, Hallie. It's a great big, 'screw you'."

He throws the 'Congratulations on your engagement' card down on the couch and scrubs a hand around his jaw with a muttered curse.

"Rory was sending a message when he sent that." He points at the card, glaring up from the cushion like a taunt.

"So what if he was? He doesn't matter anymore. He can't hurt us. My clients know about us. My parents know about Vegas. He has nothing." I curl my fingers beneath Sterling's jaw and turn his head, so his eyes meet mine. "He has nothing," I repeat. "He's just doing what Rory does best—being a prick."

"If he won't leave you alone, I'm going to have to make him. You understand that, don't you?"

I look into his darkened eyes, my stomach clenching. Sterling is a gentleman, like everyone says he is. But he's no saint. I know he had a fight with Rory. He told me how Rory came to the apartment after he tried to pay him off. And I know Rory took the first swing, but that Sterling ended it.

I also know Sterling has the strength to kill him with his bare hands if he'd wanted to.

But he didn't.

"I don't want you to do anything that could get you in trouble. I know Rory. He's just trying to stir things. But that's all he's got. We need to ignore him."

Sterling sucks in a breath, his nostrils flaring and his hands flexing against his thighs. I reach out and take one in mine, feeling it soften instantly before he entwines his fingers with mine.

We sit in silence for a few minutes as I stroke the back of his hand with my thumb, watching the tension slowly ease from his body.

"Do you want to hear what else I did today that I think will make you feel better?" I ask in a sweet voice.

His eyes soften a fraction. "Of course, I do. Tell me what you got up to, Baby girl."

"So after I spoke with some potential new clients, I met up with Sinclair and Zoey, and we had a video call with Sophie. They want to plan my bachelorette party."

Sterling smiles for the first time since he came home, and the sight makes my heart swell.

"Whatever you want to do, just let me know how much you need."

"You can't pay—"

"Hallie." He arches a brow. "We've had this conversation before. I want to take care of you. You're going to be my wife. I'm paying for it."

I hold back my huff as I look into his unwavering gaze. I want to argue it out with him but now's not the time. He's only just starting to relax.

"The same as the wedding," he adds. "Your mom and dad want to buy your dress, but I asked if I could take care of the rest."

"And my dad agreed?" I shake my head with an incredulous laugh. "Gosh, he must really like you to let you talk him into that. He can be so stubborn."

"That's where you get it from, then?"

His eyes twinkle as I bat him on the chest.

"How about you? What are you going to do? I know Mal has some ideas, and Sullivan said he'll take care of all the planning."

Sterling brings our joined hands to his lips.

"I don't need one." He turns my hand so he can press a kiss to the inside of my wrist.

"Yes you do."

"You know what I do need?"

"What?"

He pulls me into his lap so that I'm straddling him and looks up at me as he slides his hands down my sides and curls them around my hips.

"Right now, I need to make love to my fiancée while I have the chance. Because if you think I'm waiting a long time to make you my wife, then you're wrong."

I settle happily in his arms, rolling my hips and smiling at the aroused groan that rolls out from the back of his throat.

"We need time to plan it."

"One month," he rasps, pressing a kiss to my windpipe as he uses his hands on my hips to grind me on the erection in his pants.

"What? That's impossible. I need at least nine."

His lips travel down my neck, peppering kisses over my collarbone, and he slides one hand up to cup my breast.

"Two," he groans, circling my hard nipple through my dress with his thumb.

"Six," I counter.

He yanks the neckline of my dress down, freeing one breast. His hot mouth engulfs it, and he sucks.

"Sterling," I whimper.

"Four," he murmurs, flicking his tongue over it as his other hand continues to circle me down over his dick.

"Four?" I gasp as he slides one hand up my thigh beneath my dress.

"Four," he repeats.

He slips his thumb underneath the edge of my wet panties and presses it to my clit. He rubs in circles, and I sink my hands into his hair as he sucks and kisses my breast.

"Deal," I gasp as he slides two fingers inside me.

"Good girl," he rumbles, lifting his head.

His blue eyes capture mine and we stare at one another as he fucks me slowly with his fingers. My breathing quickens and I pull his lips to mine, kissing him as I dig my knees into the couch cushions so I can ride his hand.

He gives me a sexy smile as I work myself up and down it, my fingernails scraping his scalp with how good it feels.

"Just so you know," I pant, shuddering as he curls his fingers and rubs my G-spot. "I'd have done it in one if you'd insisted."

His eyes glitter with amusement. "And just so you know, if I'd had to, I'd have waited nine."

He dips his head to suck my nipple again, making me cry out.

"Sterling," I moan as my wetness covers his hand.

"Hallie," he mumbles as he sucks.

"That feels so good."

"*You* feel so damn perfect," he groans, bringing his lips back to mine and kissing me hungrily. "If you really need to take nine months to plan it, then I'll wait. I'll be a man on the edge, counting down every single day, but if it'll make you happy—"

"Four," I whisper into his kiss. "I don't want to wait, either."

"I'll give you everything," he promises, his voice deep and hoarse as my thighs tremble.

"You already have."

A lust-filled gasp hitches my breath as my body clenches around his fingers. I run my fingers through the hair at the back of his head before trailing one along his jaw.

"And I'm going to give you the most incredible wedding you've ever seen. In four months' time," I whisper against his lips as my core pulls tight. "Okay?"

"Okay," he replies, holding my eyes. "Four months."

I cry as my orgasm hits, sending my body hurtling into waves of pleasure around his fingers, each one gripping him tighter than the last.

His eyes blaze into mine as he maintains his pace in and out of my body, wringing out every spark of delicious release from me like they all belong to him.

He tears his zipper down and repositions me, replacing his fingers with the fat head of his cock.

"I'm going to fuck you fast and hard. But it's only a warmup, just so you know," he groans, holding me above the tip of him. "I said I wanted to make love to my fiancée, and that requires you being naked so I can kiss every inch of you."

I smile against his mouth. "Again... Deal."

He chuckles and kisses me back, his hands going to my hips and gripping hard.

"Hold on, Baby girl."

He thrusts up inside me, making my eyes roll.

His eyes are glued to my face as I look at him through hooded lids as he works me up and down him like his own fuck toy.

His lips curl into a sinful smile, the tendons in his neck popping with the force that he's driving up into me.

"Deal," he growls.

35

STERLING

I FLICK THE LIGHTER, WATCHING THE BRIGHT FLAME burst from it like a golden flare. I let it dance in the air for a few seconds before flicking it closed.

I flick it back open again and stare again.

"What's that?"

I look up at Mal as he enters my office and walks straight up to my desk.

"Fire."

He grimaces. "I mean that." He jerks his chin toward the manila envelope in my other hand.

"An engagement card from Rory," I say.

I hold it between my thumb and forefinger and pass the lighter underneath the corner of it. It catches alight instantly. Heat moves closer to my skin, until a familiar flash, like that of a sudden pinching wind hitting at full force, makes me curse.

I drop it onto an empty metal tray on my desk. The edges lift as smoke curls up toward the ceiling.

"Rory? That little shit needs putting in his place."

"I thought he was in it," I reply, my stomach twisting as the paper turns to black ash on the tray.

Burned to a crisp.

Mal sinks into the seat on the other side of my desk, resting one ankle over his knee, and stares at the remnants of the envelope. His grim expression matches how I feel.

Rory's still hurting Hallie. She said she's not bothered by this little display he's put on with the card. But I can tell she's playing it down for me. She says he can't do anything to her now everything is out in the open. But she should be free to enjoy working with the new clients she's taken on, and free to plan our wedding, without Rory tainting it with his disgusting touch.

"I'll apply more pressure. Let him know we're aware he's stealing money from his clients. All that evidence Denver found should shut him up once and for all," I tell Mal as I lean back in my seat.

"All right." Mal rolls his lips. "And if that's not enough, you can tell him you'll share these."

He throws an envelope down on the desk that he's been holding.

"What's this?"

"Call it an engagement present." He gives me a sly smile as I scoop the envelope up and pull out the contents.

"When was this?" I ask as I study the photograph on the top of the stack.

"When I went to Africa. It's why the trip took an extra day." He raises his brows at me.

"Is this—?"

"Bella." He rolls the name of his tongue with a smirk. "Frankie recommended her, and her friend, who acted as photographer. They even slipped Rory some extra drinks to get him in the spirit. A little touch in Halliday's honor."

I rub my hand around my jaw as I look at the image of Rory snorting up white powder off a pair of tits. I sift through the photographs. They get worse. Rory burning a fifty-pound note with a wasted grin on his face as she gives him head. Rory behind her as she's on all fours, his face screwed up.

"Could almost feel sorry for the poor fucker. I wonder if he knows that's how he looks when he comes. Bet Bella was glad she was facing away." Mal snorts out a chuckle.

I flick past the photograph in disgust, looking at the final one in the pile.

"Saved the best until last," Mal says.

I grimace at the image of Rory, laid out completely naked on the bed, his unimpressive erect dick jutting up from his body.

"Even the camera struggled to pick it up." Mal smirks. "I gave Bella and her friend an extra tip for only getting that to work with. No wonder the prick tries to act big. He's got a dick the size of my pinky."

"Denver said Rory spent the night with a prostitute. I didn't think I'd have to hear about it *and* see it," I mutter.

"You're welcome." Mal holds out his arms with a grin. "I've met enough Rorys to know that that asshole will care more about people seeing his tiny cock than he will about getting investigated for theft and losing his job. It's all jacked up pride with guys like him."

I slide the photographs back into the envelope.

"Don't thank me. He had it coming," Mal says before I can speak. "I'm not going to sit back while some little fucker messes with you." He looks at me and exhales, his voice dropping and losing its heat. "You're happy. You deserve to be. And we're family."

"We are," I agree.

"So put those in your safe." He points to the built-in one set into the wall behind my desk. "They're the only copies."

I nod. "Thanks, Mal."

"The only copies except..." He checks his watch, sucking his teeth. "Except the ones that should be arriving by courier at Rory's office right about now."

"You sent him these?" I bark, my fingers tightening on the envelope.

"What good's a threat if they don't know they're being threatened?"

"Jesus Christ." I pinch the bridge of my nose. "Hallie—"

"Halliday doesn't want you to be the bad guy, I get it. So I did it for you. Now you can look her in the eye when you tell her it wasn't you." He shrugs. "It's not like I sent them to his parents or posted them online where they'd exist forever. Not yet anyway."

"Mal," I warn.

"Sterling."

He arches a brow as I fix him with a leveling look, but he holds my eyes without backing down. He's known me for years. And he's right. We are family.

I shake my head. "Damn it. You mean I have to put the prick in my safe?"

"I'm sure you can find a tiny little corner for it," he replies.

My lips curl up, matching his.

"Thanks, Mal."

He stands and does the top button of his jacket up with one hand. "You thanked me already. Now get your ass home to that fiancée of yours. You've got a wedding to prepare for." He winks at me before he leaves.

I pick up the envelope of photographs and take it to the safe, placing it inside.

I do have a wedding to prepare for.

And a fiancée who I haven't kissed since I left for work this morning.

I grab my jacket from the back of my chair and pull out my phone to call her.

"I'm on my way home," I rasp as soon as she answers. "You want to take off whatever you're wearing and wait for me in our bedroom?"

I chuckle at her reply.

"Okay, Baby girl. Wait for me in the shower. But don't start without me."

36

HALLIDAY

THREE WEEKS LATER

"I COULD EASILY SPEND ALL DAY HERE." I sigh happily, resting my head against Sterling's chest.

"You stay in this bed a minute longer, and I'll do what I just did all over again and make you late for your yoga class."

He presses a kiss to my hair, and I smile.

"You can wake me up like that every day on our honeymoon. In fact, I should put in our pre-nup. Wife requires awakening by use of hot husband's very skilled tongue."

He chuckles, caressing my hand in his.

"Baby girl, I'll wake you up every day of our marriage like that, not just our honeymoon. But you're not putting it in a pre-nup."

"You think the lawyers might get offended?" I incline my head and grin at him.

"They can't get offended about something that won't exist."

I look at him in confusion. "But when I mentioned it before you never said anything? You're a billionaire, I expected to sign something."

"I never said anything because I thought you were kidding.

We're not having a contract, Hallie. If I ever do anything in our marriage that causes you enough hurt that you leave me, then you can take what you need. I won't fight you over it."

"If you do anything?" I frown. "What about if I screw up? What if you don't—"

"Would you ever stop loving me?"

I search his eyes, my heart sinking. After everything, that still haunts him. The thought of losing love. He's lost too much already. A part of him still believes he doesn't deserve this happiness we've created together. It tears at my soul seeing it hiding in the depths of his eyes.

I intend on spending every day loving him with everything I have until that part shrinks away to nothing.

"Never," I whisper.

He tightens his arm around me and brings his other palm up to cup my cheek.

"Then it'll all be okay, no matter what."

"It will," I agree, shuffling up the bed and pressing my lips to his in a tender kiss.

He threads his fingers through my hair as he kisses me back.

"You need to go if you want to get those sun salutations in," he says against my lips.

"I do."

I kiss him one more time, then slide out of bed.

I look back at him, watching me. The silk sheets pool low on his hip bone, showing the top of the defined 'V' of muscles and the scattering of 'happy trail' hair leading down.

"I need to go," I say, talking to his abs.

"You do."

"I really do." My gaze inches up, dipping into every ridge and valley of his defined torso until I meet his amused gaze.

"I love you. Now go, before I pull you back in here with me."

I bite my lower lip with a groan as I spin on my heels, heading into our dressing room.

"I'll come by Seasons on my way back and bring breakfast," I call, pulling on my workout gear.

"I'll look forward to it," he calls back in a deep velvety voice.

I grab my bag, giving him a last lingering eye-fuck and little wave as I head out of the bedroom. Then I stop and spin straight back around, poking my head around the door.

His eyes connect with mine instantly, and a smirk tugs at his lips. The sheet has moved lower, and his gorgeous dick is there in its full glory.

"You forget something?"

"Just to tell you that I love you." My eyes linger on his dick before moving back up to his glittering gaze.

"Go, Hallie," he growls softly. "Before I get out of this bed and drag you back into it and underneath me."

I flash him one final smile. "I'm going to picture you like this for the rest of the day."

His expression turns tender and his eyes drift over my face like he's committing it to memory. I shiver from the intensity of it.

"And I'm going to picture you smiling like that and telling me you love me for the rest of my life. Now go."

My stomach bursts into flutters and my cheeks heat as I give him one last parting look.

"The rest of our lives... *together*, Fiancé," I call, tearing myself away.

There's a bounce in my step as I exit Central Park and pass the iconic Songbird hotel.

I smile at the beautiful building. Maybe I should add it to the list of places to consider for the wedding. So far I've been unable to decide whether we should get married in London or New York. Sterling says whatever makes me happy will make him happy. But he's lived in New York his whole life and his family are here. And I'm going to be living here now. It makes sense it should be in New York. I only have Mum, Dad, and Sophie, who I really want there. I don't need some huge elaborate affair filled with people I hardly know.

Hesitation slices through me.

That would be exactly like Sterling said his wedding to Elaina was—arranged by their parents as more of a business deal than anything else. He didn't know eighty percent of the guests. They were all colleagues or associates of their parents'.

And they were married here in the city.

Maybe we shouldn't get married in New York, or London. I could look for somewhere overseas. Somewhere we can have something small and intimate. Meaningful.

I pull my phone from my purse to check the time, 7:30 a.m. Sterling will be on his way to his office soon, if he's not there already.

I snap a selfie, blowing a kiss at the camera and send it to him.

> Me: I'm on my way to give my fiancé breakfast, served with a kiss. I love you.

His reply comes instantly, and I smile. He always replies straight away.

> Sterling: Serve yourself to me on my desk, Baby girl, and I'll die a happy man.

I giggle and drop my phone back into my purse, heading

into a deli to grab something. I'm thinking banana nut muffins, hot coffee, and a side of melon. He loves nuts and I know he's only just getting back into eating them again. Elaina had an allergy.

Fifteen minutes later, I prepare to open the front door to Seasons, using the key Sterling gave me, but the door's ajar. One of the security team must already be here.

I walk inside and head down the dim hallway. It's all mood lighting from here to the main bar area.

I head through the door at the end that leads toward Sterling's office, flicking on the light with one hand and balancing the tray of coffees and brown paper bag of breakfast things in the other. I use the key Sterling gave me to open his office door. It's definitely one of Denver's team who are in. If Sterling was here then his office would already be unlocked.

I step inside and turn on the light.

I don't know how he spends so much time in here without natural light. His office doesn't have any windows. Probably a good thing considering that time he went down on me on his desk. My eyes rake over the dark mahogany wood on the far side of the large room, the memory making my thighs clench.

Maybe I should lay myself out on it like he suggested? I'm sure I'd like his reaction if I do.

I smile to myself as I place our drinks and food onto the desk, then put my purse down on one of the sofas and shrug out of my coat. He'll be here any minute. Maybe I should send him a text of me sitting on his desk to make him to hurry up.

I pull my phone out of my purse and curse at the dead screen.

"Ugh. Again."

The battery has been draining ridiculously fast for a couple of days now. I've been meaning to get a replacement, but I've been busy talking with new clients and haven't done it yet.

I pull my charger from my bag and plug it into the socket beneath Sterling's desk, leaving my phone next to our coffees to charge. The pink rose quartz heart I gave him catches my eye and I pick it up, turning its smooth surface over and over inside my palm.

"Unconditional love and healing emotional wounds," I muse, placing it back beside the desk phone.

I lift up the receiver and am halfway through punching in Sterling's cell number to see how close he is, when a bang that sounds like the door to the main bar area stops me.

I grin. It's probably him. He always checks the main bar area on his way in each morning to make sure the team from the night before cleaned up properly.

Another bang catches me off guard and I drop the handset on the desk.

"You're so loud!" I call with a giggle as I walk out into the hallway.

I head to the door at the end of the hallway, serving the bar area and main entrance, and reach for the handle.

My phone rings in his office.

It could be the newest client I've taken onto my books. A widower from San Francisco. I think Sterling inspired him that it's never too late to choose to live again.

I falter for a moment. I can call him back.

I grab the door handle in an excited rush. It's only been a couple of hours, yet I'm giddy to see Sterling again.

I'm ridiculous. *Ridiculously, sickeningly in love.*

I yank the door open. The hallway seems darker than when I arrived.

I squint, my eyes starting to water. Maybe the light went out. There's a smell of... I take in a breath and immediately choke out a cough.

The Matchmaker

The air is thick, cloying.

Unbreathable.

Thick black smoke billows up the walls, circling around the ceiling in a cloud.

Something's on fire.

The sound of shattering glass pierces the air from inside the bar area as smoke pours from the open doorway.

I rush to the fire extinguisher on the wall, but the metal is hot and sends a sudden lancing pain up my arm. I recoil, cradling my hand against my body as the thickening smoke makes it harder to see.

Fire reaches out through the open bar doorway, and the sheer heat of it steals my breath.

My exit is blocked.

Shit. Shit. Shit.

I turn back toward Sterling's office. If I can get inside and close the door I can call for help. It must be a fire door. It'll buy me time.

It's impossible to see more than a few feet in front of me, and even harder to breathe. I drop to my hands and knees and crawl like you're supposed to. Keep low, away from the smoke.

I make it back through the inner hallway door and reach out, feeling along the wall. What takes seconds on foot feels like long, excruciating minutes on all fours. The throbbing in my hand is overtaken by a scratching in my lungs, and I fight not to breathe in the smoke. But no matter how hard I try; some claws its way into my lungs making them burn.

The wheezing in my ears is almost as loud as the roaring coming from the fire behind me.

I hit blank space and wave my arm around, knocking it against the doorframe. I struggle to focus, my head's heavy and my eyes feel like acid's dissolving them. I drag myself through the opening, pushing the door closed behind me.

Sterling's warm blue gaze rushes into my head as I stagger to my feet and toward his desk, scrabbling to get to the phone.

"Get it together," I scold myself with a sob, struggling to see the buttons on the handset.

It's fine. I'm behind a fire door. It'll keep the flames back. It has to.

I fall into Sterling's desk chair and punch in one number after the other.

9-1-1

Another bang from inside the building makes me almost jump out of my skin.

My hand shakes as I hold the receiver to my ear.

Sterling's face is all I see.

And as the room spins, one voice filters through the haze, calling to me.

I answer it. And I beg.

Help me, Jenny.

37

STERLING

Denver strides in the second I open the door, his face set in his usual taut seriousness.

"Good morning," I say as Jenson, and Killian storm inside behind him.

"You need to see this, Boss," he clips.

All pleasantries leave me as I look between the three men's tight expressions and then lead them into the living area. We were scheduled to have a meeting later this morning after my breakfast with Hallie. Whatever it is obviously couldn't wait.

"Show me."

Denver places his laptop on the coffee table and opens it up.

I take a seat beside him. Killian and Jenson stand to one side in silence.

"We found something on the CCTV from the marina." Denver clicks into a folder and selects a file to play.

I look at the shot on the screen. It's from a distance but...

"Son of a bitch," I hiss.

"You recognize him?" Denver asks.

"I do." I run a hand around my tense jaw, my teeth clenching so hard they could crack.

Denver nods. "He had history with Elaina?"

I roll my lips. "That's one way of putting it."

I've never told Denver outright that Elaina had an affair. He didn't need to know that in order to do his job. But he's an intelligent guy who has worked for my family for years and misses nothing.

I look at the image of Neil on the screen. "When was this taken?"

"Half an hour before the fire broke out," Denver says.

"Jesus Christ. You think he had something to do with it?"

The thought tightens my chest and makes taking another breath a challenge.

Two years.

That's how long I've relived that day over and over in my mind, wondering what happened. If I could have done something differently.

If I could have saved them.

"No. The timing's off. Plus, we've tracked him over the cameras. He didn't step onboard the yacht once."

I nod, my eyes fixed on the image of the man Elaina loved. The one she was willing to risk everything for.

"But I don't believe in coincidences. We'll keep digging," Denver grunts. "Whatever this guy has been up to since… wherever he's been… we'll know every movement he's made soon. He won't be able to take a dump without us knowing about it."

"Do it. You have unlimited resources. Whatever you need. I want to know why that asshole was there that day," I snarl.

"Already on it, Boss." Denver nods.

A combined chime cuts into the air as all four of our phones ring and vibrate at the same time.

Killian's fastest, pulling his from his pants pocket.

The Matchmaker

"It's Seasons, Boss. The fire alarm's been activated."

"Not LA again?" I clip, as I stand. The re-furb the judge paid for has only just been finished.

"No. Here," Denver states, his eyes on his own phone.

Dread fills my veins.

Hallie.

"Damn it!" I slam my fist against the dashboard as her cell rings out. I immediately dial the landline for my office, but it won't connect.

"Drive faster!" I bark at Denver.

He screeches round a corner and straight through a red light earning us a blast of several horns.

"Boss, NYFD are on scene," Killian says, his phone up to his ear, listening to one of our other guys who got there ready to start work shortly after the alarm was activated.

"Do they have her?" I snap, turning in my seat to glare at him.

One swift shake of his head has me balling one hand into a fist and pressing it to my lips with a choked groan.

"Jesus Christ, she's inside."

I suck in a breath through my nose, my head about to explode with the amount of pressure inside it.

"Maybe she didn't get there yet," Jenson says.

"She's in there. The security alarm was deactivated," Killian says to him.

I stare out of the window as we cut through the traffic leaving blaring horns in our wake.

She can't die in there.

I can't lose her.

We turn another corner and Denver hits the brakes. The entire street is gridlocked with flashing lights up ahead.

Seasons.

I throw my door open and race through the unmoving traffic. There are two fire trucks, an ambulance, and three cop cars outside. A cordon is being set up to keep everyone except emergency personnel away.

"Did anyone come out?" I shout as I run straight up to a guy in an NYFD uniform. "I'm the owner. My fiancée is in there."

His eyes meet mine. "My team's preparing for full entry. The fire is out in the entrance, but—"

I don't wait to hear whatever he's about to say.

She's still in there.

I knock past another NYFD uniform as I run into the building, keeping to one side of the massive water hose that's snaked along the ground. The smoke is thick, flooding the hallway in big noxious clouds. I lift my arm, burying the lower half of my face in the crook of my elbow.

Two firefighters in full protective gear are inside the hallway, tackling a blaze that's spilling from the main bar.

I pin myself against the wall. A billion tiny needles all pierce my skin at once. The left side of my torso. My arm. Memories brought to the surface by the sheer heat being forced from that room like the inside of a volcano.

She wouldn't be in the main bar area. Please God, don't let her be in there. It's a raging inferno.

I cough, forcing myself to keep moving. The door at the end of the hallway is open and I speed up as I turn into it. The smoke is still thick here, but there aren't any flames.

I move as fast as I can, straining to see properly. I place one hand to the wall, running the back of it along, feeling for the door.

Even the wall is blistering, hotter than the sidewalk during a freak heatwave.

The second I reach my office adrenaline storms my veins. I pull my sleeve over my hand and try the handle, but the door doesn't budge. It's warped with the heat.

"Damn it!"

I roar and use every ounce of strength I have to ram my shoulder against it.

It flies open, taking me with it, and I stagger a couple of steps to balance myself, my chest heaving.

There's smoke in the room, making it hazy and out of focus.

But then I see her.

Slumped over my desk.

"Hallie!"

I run over and push her hair back from her face.

Her eyes are shut. She doesn't respond.

Something rolls out of her left hand as I pull her body up from the desk.

The pink heart stares at me from where it comes to rest on the wood.

"Jesus Christ."

I wheel back the chair and lift her into my arms. She's heavier than she's ever felt. A dead weight, falling limp against my body. Her head lolls back.

"Hold on. I've got you. Just hold on. *Please, Hallie.*"

I stride from the room and back down the hallway, ignoring the stinging in my eyes from the smoke. I incline my body, using it as a shield over her as I pass the main bar doorway where heat is still radiating out like a furnace. More firefighters are inside, and one comes to aid me, clearing a path to the main entrance.

Flashing lights and sounds punch into my senses as I step

outside. Arms slide around my back, supporting me, guiding me.

Someone calls for help.

Then hands are trying to take Hallie from me.

"Don't touch her!" I cry.

A stretcher is wheeled in front of me.

"Put her down. Let us help," someone says.

A strong hand lands on my arm, and I turn.

Denver nods at me, a graveness tightening his eyes. "Let them do their job."

I place Hallie on the stretcher and she's immediately swarmed. Lights shining on her. Hands reaching for her. Voices talking to her. Asking her questions she can't answer.

"Sir, let's get you looked at."

I shake my head roughly at the medic. "I stay with her."

Denver's hand lands between my shoulder blades and he says something to the medic, then follows me as I stay as close to Hallie as I can.

She's still not waking up. They're shining a torch into her eyes, and she's got an oxygen mask over her face.

But she's not moving.

"Pulse is getting weaker," someone shouts.

I drag in air to keep standing, but my lungs immediately crumple, sending me into retching coughs that feel like someone is slicing open my chest with a blade.

A medic comes at me again, but all I can see is Hallie being worked on.

"Sir—"

"She comes first!" I yell.

"My colleagues have her. Let's get you checked so you can be with her, okay?"

A garbled sob bubbles in my throat.

Denver grabs my upper arms and forces me to meet his eyes.

"Listen to them. You're no good to her when you can hardly stand."

I stare into his green eyes and nod once.

He tips his chin at the medic.

An oxygen mask is placed over my face and Denver steps back and says, "I'll handle things here, Boss. Stay with her. She needs you."

My eyes track back to Hallie. To her limp body. And her unresponsive eyes.

Please, goddamn it. Please don't let her die.

38

HALLIDAY

My body feels like it's gone ten rounds with a heavyweight boxer as my senses start to swim into focus. There's a gentle murmur of voices around me. My throat's thick and dry, and my head's foggy. I remember people helping me—hands, voices, Sterling by my side—before exhaustion won over.

"Sterling?" I croak.

Warmth against my hand intensifies and my fingers tingle, the life easing back into them.

"I'm here, Hallie. You're safe."

I peel my eyes open and blink. Everything is bright and blurry. I seek out his voice and my vision clears slowly. Warm blue is waiting to find me.

We look at one another for a few seconds and I note the bloodshot whites of his eyes, and the deepened lines etched into their corners. It's the worst I've ever seen him, yet he still looks handsome to me.

I reach up and clumsily feel at my face.

"It's an oxygen tube," he explains as I touch the object beneath my nose. "You're in the hospital, remember?"

Lowering my hand, I stare at the back of my palm. It's dirty but looks like someone's tried to clean it.

"There was a fire... I was in your office." My voice comes out hoarse and I force a swallow, wincing at the scratchiness there.

"Not what I meant when I said to wait on my desk for me." Sterling's eyes soften.

"What happened?"

"Dad saved your life. Strode in there thinking he's invincible and carried you out himself."

I look into Sullivan's hardened gaze where he's standing near the end of the bed. His expression melts as he looks from me and then to Sterling and lets out a deep sigh, pinching the bridge of his nose.

"Thank God you're both okay."

"The cops say it was arson," Denver says from his position next to the door.

"Arson? But..." I try to take in a breath, but it turns into a wheezy cough.

"You need to rest, Hallie. Don't try and talk. We'll find out who did this."

Sterling's tone changes to one that's icy as his eyes track to Denver and the two exchange a knowing look.

"You think it was Rory, don't you?" I ask.

"Don't think about it now." Sterling sighs, taking my other hand in his.

I allow my gaze to rake over him. His suit is ruined and covered in soot and dirt, and his shirt is open at the top with buttons missing. A dusting of silver chest hair peeks out, made dull by the smoke residue coating it.

His scars are just visible on his left side beneath the ruined fabric.

"The building was on fire, and you came in anyway," I whisper.

The Matchmaker

"You were inside," he replies simply.

I look into his pained eyes as the hospital room door bursts open.

"Oh my god!" Sinclair rushes over and the mattress dips next to me as she sinks into it and leans down, hugging me. There are tears in her eyes as she pulls back and then grabs Sterling in a hug across me.

"We're all right, Sweetheart," Sterling soothes her.

"I got here as quick as I could." Her lower lip is trembling as her eyes volley between the two of us like she's assessing us for damage. She blinks hard and then turns to Sullivan.

"Where's Molly?"

"Gone with Killian and Jenson to find the coffee machine."

"Uncle Mal and Trudy?"

"On their way," Sullivan replies.

She nods and smooths her hair back over her shoulder, taking a slow breath. "I can't believe it. *A fire,*" she says the last words like a haunted whisper.

I look at her, dressed in a sparkling silk bodycon dress. Even in a crisis, she looks incredible.

"I was out last night and ended up staying with a friend," she explains as she sees me looking at her outfit.

"Who?" The single barked syllable flies across the room like a bullet.

Sinclair turns, acknowledging Denver for the first time.

"Mind your own business."

"Your family is my business. Give me their name and I'll run a check," Denver growls.

"I'm not giving you his name!" She snorts.

Denver's chest expands and his eyes flick to Sterling's. "It's protocol," he grits.

"Whatever." Sinclair turns away from him.

"Give Denver the guy's name, Sinclair. He's just doing his job," Sullivan says.

Sterling nods. "Do it please, Sweetheart."

Sinclair purses her lips. "Fine. But I don't know his full name. I only know where he lives."

Sullivan mutters something with a huff, and Denver's expression darkens like he's about to lose it any second.

"I think there are more important things happening right now than who I was with," she snaps at Sullivan before bringing her worried eyes back to me. Her voice drops low and soft. "Are you okay?"

"I'm okay." I give her a small, reassuring smile, and her shoulders loosen.

"Dad?"

"I'm fine. Hallie's the one who took in the most smoke," Sterling says, a heaviness in his voice that makes my heart crack.

"I'm okay. Because of you," I add, looking at him.

His eyes hold mine, but they're still brimming with concern.

"What did the doctor say?" Sinclair asks.

"That rest is needed. Time to let the lungs recover." Sterling strokes the back of my hand, his eyes trained on my face.

"That goes for you too," I say.

"They're waiting on extra tests. But all being clear, we should be out of here soon," Sullivan says, pushing his hands into his pant pockets.

"I'll stay with them both today. I'll head home and change and fetch Monty from Zoey's place." Sinclair's attention flicks to Denver in question.

"I'll drive you," he clips.

She nods, then looks back at Sullivan.

"I'll take care of everything at the club with Mal when he

arrives. And I'll head over tonight and switch with you," he says.

A fuzzy warmth fills my chest as I watch them plan out our care package.

"We'll be fine," Sterling says.

"Don't argue, Dad. You two are getting us whether you like it or not."

"Fine." His lips curl a little at Sinclair's scolding tone, and the twinkle in his bloodshot eyes makes my heart soar.

This is what family does. They take care of one another no matter what.

The door to the room opens and a doctor comes in holding a chart.

"Miss Burton, good, you're awake. We need to discuss some things, but then I'm happy to discharge you."

"Thank you." I smile gratefully at the him as he walks to the side of my bed and stops.

I just want to get out of here and go home.

Have a bath and lie in Sterling's arms.

And try to block out the heat, the smell, the fear, the—

"I'm going to put you in touch with someone you can talk to," the doctor says kindly, studying my expression.

I nod and squeeze Sterling's hand. It's a good idea. Maybe Sterling will go too. Or come with me. My eyes dart to his face, but he's looking at the doctor, listening intently.

"Your tests came back normal..." The doctor pauses, taking in Sinclair, Sullivan, and Denver.

"Go on," Sterling urges, a muscle in his neck tensing like he's preparing himself for bad news.

The doctor looks at him, then me.

I nod. "They're family. You can say whatever it is in front of them."

My stomach rolls with nausea at the way his brows furrow.

I feel fine, but maybe the smoke inhalation has caused complications, or maybe—

"Miss Burton, were you aware you're pregnant?"

No one speaks. I'm not sure any of us even breathe.

The entire room is silent.

Maybe my hearing was damaged in the fire. I can't have heard him correctly.

"Your HCG levels indicate you're a few weeks along. We'll have a better idea once we perform an ultrasound," the doctor continues.

"Pregnant? Are you sure?" I try to swallow but my tongue is too big for my mouth, and my throat has joined my ears and stopped working properly.

"Yes. It showed up in your blood test."

I whip my gaze to Sterling's. "I-I had no idea."

His brow creases. "Hall—"

"She inhaled a lot of smoke. Could it...?"

Sinclair's words hang in the air.

The doctor gives me a reassuring smile. "I'd like to take you to for a scan and not delay."

I turn to Sterling, fear dripping into my veins and replacing my blood with ice. "What if—?"

Haunted blue stares back at me before warm hands cup my cheeks.

My breath catches as I stare at him. "I didn't know. We didn't... How did..?"

Tears course down my cheeks, over his thumbs as he places his forehead to mine.

"I love you," he whispers.

"I love you too," I mumble. "But all the smoke... What if?"

He kisses my forehead. "It'll be okay," he soothes.

I recognize his voice. It's the one he uses when I'm anxious. Like before we saw my parents. And when we landed back in New York to that sea of reporters.

But those times there wasn't a sliver of doubt tainting it.

Not like there is now.

I fist his shirt, needing something to cling on to.

Because as much as I want to cling on to his voice, this time, I'm not sure I believe him.

39

STERLING

A HEARTBEAT PULSES ON THE SCREEN.

Strong and steady.

"My god," I choke, running one hand around my jaw.

"Baby looks to be developing normally at this stage," the sonographer says as she takes some measurements of the small blob. "But we'll have you back in a couple of days to check again. You said your last period was five or six weeks ago?"

"About that," Hallie replies, glancing at me.

"Seems about right." The sonographer finishes up and then hands a wad of tissue to Hallie. "I'll go get the images printed for you while you clean up."

The sonographer closes the door, and Hallie wipes up and pulls the hospital gown down, sitting up on the bed.

Her eyes search mine. The relief in them the moment she heard that heartbeat has vanished has been replaced by doubt.

"I didn't know, I swear. I didn't even realize I was late. Our engagement, planning the wedding... I lost track."

"Hallie," I breathe. "You think I'm angry?"

"We didn't plan this. We didn't—"

I crush my lips to hers in a desperate kiss, ignoring what I must look like, all filthy and messed up.

"You're carrying our baby. *Ours.* I'm damn ecstatic. I'm surprised I haven't flown off this chair with how light I feel."

"You mean that?"

"I do."

I kiss her again, swallowing down her whimpered sob as she reaches for my ruined shirt and curls her fingers around the fabric above my heart.

"I know we've talked about the possibility of us having children. But Sinclair and Sullivan are adults. Do you really want to do this again?"

"With you? Of course I do. Children are a blessing, Hallie, however they come. Planned, surprise, age twenty, age fifty."

She lets out a small puff of air, her face lighting up. "We're really doing this?"

"We are."

Her beautiful eyes are wide and uncertain as she searches mine. I need to work on showing her what this means to me. I meant it when I said I could float off this damn chair.

A baby. Our baby.

"It must have been around the time we got back from London. I was so emotional I wasn't thinking straight. They were chart days. You finished *inside* me the night we got back," she whispers.

I dust her cheek with the pad of my thumb, following the curve of her skin as I let out a slow breath.

"I did. Many times." I smile.

Her brows hitch. "You're not mad that I forgot?"

"Hallie. It takes two. I forgot too. Or maybe my subconscious made me forget on purpose."

She frowns. "You think the universe wanted this?"

"*I* want this." I search her eyes, my heart hammering against my ribs. "Are you okay? Talk to me. What do you—"

"I want this too." She blinks rapidly, her eyes shining. "I want it all with you. I want everything." Her breath leaves her in a shaky sob which turns into a cough. "I'm sorry," she wheezes and covers her mouth.

I rub her back. "You need to rest. Jesus, Hallie. I need to get you home so I can take care of you. *Both* of you."

"You need taking care of too."

"I'm fine." I move my hand down her body and rest it on her stomach. "I'm better than fine. I don't want you worrying about me." I drop my gaze to where my fingers are splayed over the hospital gown. "We're having a baby," I whisper in awe.

Her eyes fill with unshed tears, pooling along her lower lids.

"We are." She nods as the first of many slips free and coats her cheeks.

I crush my lips to hers.

"I love you so damn much. I thought I'd lost you today," I choke, pressure building in my chest. I've held it together since I saw her collapsed on my desk. But my resolve is now as thin as a strand of fine silk and about to break.

"I thought I'd lost you."

"I'm here." She places her hand over the top of mine on her stomach.

"I can't wait to marry you." I kiss her again. "And I can't wait to meet you," I say, dropping my head to kiss her stomach.

Her hands thread through my hair and she strokes my scalp as I nuzzle into her.

"I love you, Hallie," I rasp. "Today was almost the worst day of my life all over again."

"Sterling," she sobs, her fingers gathering up strands of my hair like she's trying to hold the cascading pieces of me together.

"I couldn't carry on if I lost you too. Not you. I walked into that fire, and I saw you." My body shakes, and I lose all control.

I wrap my arms around her and grip on tight, giving in to the tears that are making my throat burn.

"I'm so sorry," she cries.

"I didn't lose you," I choke out. "You've given me everything to live for, Hallie. There have been days where—"

"It's okay," she says softly, stroking my hair.

I press kiss after kiss to her stomach before moving up to cup her face. "I love you."

She gives me the most beautiful smile that bathes my soul with light.

"I love you too."

"I'll go and find Sinclair. She called Mal and Trudy and asked them to pick some things up from our place on their way. We'll get you changed and then I'm taking you home."

"Okay."

"Okay," I repeat softly, pressing another kiss to her lips.

I step from the room and stride up the corridor toward where we left everyone to go for the scan. They're all waiting to see if everything's okay. If the...

Jesus Christ, I'm going to be a father again.

My steps slow momentarily and I scrub a hand around my jaw.

She's having our baby.

Hallie's having *our* baby.

Emotion clogs my throat, and I force myself to keep walking. She's given me everything and more. I gave up on the idea of ever having a love like ours. And now not only has she given me that, but she's giving me the chance to be a father again.

My chest tightens. I love her more than I'll ever be able to show her. But I'll spend every day of my life trying anyway.

I round the corner, a disbelieving smile lifting my lips.

"Sterling?"

It's slapped off with the efficiency of sniper fire.

"Lavinia?" I snap. "What are you doing here?"

She's clutching a purse, holding it in front of her body like a shield.

"My goodness, look at you!" Her eyes widen as she takes in my wrecked clothing. "I heard it on the news, I... I came to see if you were okay. Why do you look like that? You weren't inside, were you?"

"I wasn't. Hallie was."

She gasps and presses a hand over her lips, the color draining from her face. "Is she...?"

"She'll be okay."

"Thank goodness." Her shoulders sag and she drops her trembling hand back to her purse, fiddling with the clasp. "I'm so sorry, Sterling."

I stare at her. I might have considered her a friend once. But after what she did to Hallie, tipping off the press like I suspect she did, and the things she said about the two of us being together, I can barely stomach looking at her.

"I have to go."

I step past her, but she reaches for my arm. "Wait—"

"Boss?" Denver calls, striding down the corridor toward us.

"What is it?"

Something about the low pull of his brows and set of his jaw has every muscle in my body tensing. He walks right up to us, ignoring Lavinia as he holds my eyes.

"They made an arrest. He's been brought to the hospital to get checked over."

"Rory?" I growl.

Denver gives me a stiff nod. "He said you had it coming after the incident with the two hook..." His eyes flick to Lavinia. "He wanted to destroy any evidence you had of it."

"Where is he?" I spit.

Denver's eyes darken.

"You better damn well tell me. Rory's going to wish he stayed inside my club and burned his way to hell when I get my hands on him."

I step toe to toe with Denver, but he doesn't flinch. He knows my anger isn't aimed at him.

"He's got two cops with him." He inclines his head toward a corridor leading off from where we are.

I storm past him with one thing on my mind.

Killing that son of a bitch.

The second I round the corner, he's there, being escorted by two uniformed officers.

"You piece of shit!"

I land one punch straight on his nose, knocking him flat out on the floor.

His hands fly to his face, and he howls like a coward.

"Get the hell up!" I growl, stepping forward and grabbing him around the neck, squeezing his windpipe.

"Boss." Denver appears next to me, his voice lowering as he leans in close. "They let you have that one punch. But I won't let you get yourself arrested if you kill him. He'll get what's coming to him."

I grit my teeth and look at both cops. Neither are helping Rory, who's desperately clawing at my hand in silence because I'm cutting off his air. Instead, they're looking between Denver and I like they're questioning their decision.

My grip tightens on Rory's neck, and I look into his panicked eyes and savor the feel of his miserable life being leached from his body beneath my palm.

"You piece of shit," I snarl, before throwing him back against the floor, making his head bounce off it.

He coughs and splutters as the two cops grab him under each arm and haul him to his feet.

"He tried to kill me," he gasps. "You need to arrest him."

"You slipped," one cop says.

"Yeah. Fell right on your face. That's gotta hurt," the other adds.

"Get this asshole out of here," Denver grunts.

"Good to see you, Denver," one says as they lead Rory away.

"You're a dirty old man!" Rory twists his head, blood dripping from his nose, his eyes unnaturally wide. "She's young enough to be your daughter!"

I stare after him.

"That the best you can do? Maybe you'll think of something better on those lonely nights in your cell. Only I won't give a damn because I'll be too busy taking care of my wife and our baby."

His face pales, confusion contorting it.

"Baby?"

I give him a small, menacing smile as the cops drag him further down the corridor. Lavinia is standing at the end of it, and he stares at her, straining to keep his eyes on her shocked expression as they lead him past.

The hairs on the back of my neck stand up.

"Give us a minute," I clip to Denver.

"Boss." He nods, his eyes narrowed on Lavinia.

She rushes up the corridor, her heels clicking on the floor. "Was that him? The man who started the fire?" Her words tumble out like she can't control them.

"Don't you recognize him? Because he seemed to know you."

"I..." she splutters.

"What the hell did you do, Lavinia?" I spit.

She flinches. "I saw him outside Sullivan's party, waiting for Halliday and... he said he's her *husband*."

"He's not."

Her eyes widen, her lower lip trembling.

"He swore it. He was heartbroken, saying you'd taken her from him. That she still loved him, and he just needed a chance to remind her. I thought he was telling the truth and just needed a chance to—"

"You mean you needed a chance? Another way to ruin what Hallie and I have."

"I didn't know what he was going to do! He said he wanted to talk to you man-to-man but that when he tried, you'd cut him off. He thought if he waited inside for you that you'd have to listen. I told him I didn't know what the code was, but that he should try S—"

"Don't you dare say my son's name!" I yell, pointing a finger in her face. "Don't you dare."

How could I be so stupid? She's right. The code was my son's birthday. A date I will never forget.

"He could have killed her! How damn naïve can you be?"

"I swear, Sterling I..." She drops her purse to the floor and reaches out, desperately clinging to the lapels of my jacket. "I thought he loved her and just wanted her back."

"I love her!" I knock her hands off me, making her suck in a gasp. "And she loves me. You reunited my first wife with her ex. And you thought you'd have the same luck interfering with my life again."

"No... I thought. You and I, we could have been..."

I lean close, pinning my eyes to hers as I lower my voice.

"You and I are nothing. You disgust me, Lavinia."

She reels back, looking like she's about to pass out, throw up, or both.

"Th-this isn't you. You've always been gentle. She's turned you like this."

"You don't know me at all." I hold her eyes as she stares at me in shock. "Hallie is going to be my wife. She's carrying my child. She's a Beaufort now. And I will destroy anyone who threatens a member of my family."

"You..." She splutters, frowning. "That's not—"

"Who I am? Yes, it is. And if you don't believe me, then come near Hallie again. Talk to her. Look in her direction. But you'd better be ready for me to come for you. Because mark my words, Lavinia. I will kill you myself." I turn my face to whisper in her ear, my voice the epitome of calm. "And I'll feel nothing as I do it."

I move back as her breath leaves her in a silent sob.

"Now please excuse me," I say, straightening my jacket. "My fiancée is waiting for me."

"I'm sorry," she whispers, her voice small and weak, like her. "I'm so sorry for everything."

"It's too late. The best thing you can do now is disappear."

Her face crumples and she bursts into sobs.

I walk away without looking back. Lavinia might be interfering and selfish, but she's not stupid.

Not like Rory.

She'll heed my warning and stay away.

40

HALLIDAY

The door to the hospital room opens and I look up, expecting Sterling or the sonographer.

Instead, icy blue eyes meet mine as Sullivan steps inside and closes the door. He frowns as his gaze roams around the room, taking in the medical equipment.

"Oh, Sterling just came looking for you all to give you an update," I tell him, standing from the edge of the bed.

"The baby?" he asks.

"Is okay."

He places his hands onto his hips and exhales, his shoulders softening. "*Thank god*," he murmurs quietly. "And you? How are you feeling?"

His gaze comes back to me, and I struggle to keep my surprise at the genuine concern in his voice from showing.

"I'm... yeah, I'm okay. Happy and relieved."

He nods, before reaching into the inside pocket of his suit jacket. "I was on my way to see you today, before I got the call about the fire. I was coming to give you this." He pulls a brown envelope out and hands it to me.

My heart sinks as I recognize it—the non-disclosure agreement. Maybe he's made adjustments to it since Sterling and I got engaged. Added that I should return the ring or something.

"Okay. Let me look over the changes, and—"

He tears the envelope in two.

I frown. "Did Sterling ask you to—"

"My father doesn't know it existed," Sullivan clips. "I fully intended to take it to him to sign before registering it with our family's lawyers, but..."

"But you didn't?"

His terse expression softens a fraction. "No, I didn't."

"Why?"

He looks away, shaking his head to himself. "I asked myself that many times, but then my father would talk about you and his eyes would light up and... I didn't want to be the asshole who ruined that."

"Because you believe in love," I breathe.

He brings his eyes to mine. "I believe in my father deserving to be happy."

I hold his gaze, and I can tell he's holding back, trying to keep his barriers firmly in place. The ones that stop him from dating anyone seriously, and that only allow room for the constant casual encounters Sinclair gets so annoyed with him for having.

"I believe in him being happy too. And I'll do everything I can to make him happy every day. I love your father, Sullivan."

"I believe you. Your *amendments* to the contract demonstrated such. You sacrificed any protection you had for yourself by removing them."

"I didn't care about me as long as Sterling would have been okay."

"Hm," he grunts, holding up the remnants of the envelope, "This is something I'd prefer you allow me to tell him about myself, once things have settled down and you've both had time to recover."

"Absolutely." I offer him a smile.

I was expecting him to want to keep the entire thing quiet to prevent any tension between himself and Sterling. But this makes sense. Sinclair always talks about how secrets can ruin families. Sullivan must share that belief.

He nods at me. "Right, well then—"

"I can matchmake for you," I blurt, internally wincing as his brows shoot up.

The words came out before I could stop them, and I know I've overstepped, but seeing him tear that contract up—he can claim it's nothing more than him wanting Sterling to be happy, but I know he couldn't have done that if there wasn't a teeny tiny part of him that didn't believe in love.

I wait for his reaction—a scathing look, or remark.

"Why don't you concentrate your energy on continuing to make my father happy? And looking after the new addition? Molly will be thrilled to have a baby in the family."

One corner of his mouth lifts into the ghost of a smile.

I straighten a little in shock. "I can do that."

"Good, see that you do," he rasps, walking to the door. He looks back before he exits. "And Halliday?"

"Yes?"

"Congratulations."

I rest my hand over my stomach, warm tears building along my lower lids. "Thank you."

41

HALLIDAY

"Let's wait until Mum and Dad arrive tonight before we do another," I say to Sterling as he walks barefoot around our kitchen, fixing me breakfast, the same way he's been doing every day since we came home from hospital a few days ago.

Sullivan, Sinclair, and Mal have all been around nonstop and this is the first day we've had to ourselves.

"Good idea." He lifts his warm blue eyes to mine, and they crinkle at the corners.

"What?" I twist my lips into a smile as he gives me a knowing look.

"You sure you can wait?" He arches a brow.

"Um, I think it's you who can never wait."

He chuckles and tips his head to one side. "You got me."

The toaster pops and he takes the bread out and butters it. I love watching him in the kitchen like this. He seems happy and relaxed when he's doing things for me. I still make his coffee every morning for him, but he's been insistent on making me breakfast.

"I know they're excited to see." I grin at him as he puts the toast onto a plate and then spoons two perfectly poached eggs on top.

"I'm sure they are." He places the plate in front of me on the breakfast counter and watches as I pick up my cutlery.

"They thought I was joking when I said you'd bought an in-home ultrasound machine."

"I want to see our baby every day," he replies seriously, his eyes on me to make sure I'm starting to eat.

He's become obsessed with making sure I eat properly, saying the baby needs it. He's actually become obsessed with everything baby related, and my heart melts more each time he places his hand over my stomach and talks to it or presses kisses to it when we're lying in bed.

And then there's the ultrasound machine that arrived the day we came home from hospital. He's been insistent on checking on the baby frequently even though it still resembles a blob.

A blob with a heartbeat.

I smile at him as he watches me eat.

"I'll come with you to the airport to meet them," he says.

"Don't you have a meeting about the repair work at Seasons?"

Sterling pulls the stool next to mine out and sinks into it, his body facing me.

"I rescheduled it."

He wraps an arm around my waist and dips his head to kiss my shoulder.

"You sent your private jet to pick them up from England. I'm sure they won't expect you to miss work to collect them too."

"I sent *your* private jet, Hallie."

"Oh yeah. How could I forget? *My* jet that you bought three of so I could choose my favorite."

He chuckles and presses another kiss to my shoulder as I shake my head at him with a smile.

"I like to give. You'd better get used to it, because it's not long until you vow to agree to a whole lifetime of it in front of our family and friends."

"We need to decide where to have it first, otherwise there won't be a wedding."

His eyes take on the intensity that they get when he's about to say something important.

"What is it? Do you have an idea where we could have it?" My voice lifts in hope. I've been looking for places, but nothing has stood out as special enough.

"I do," he murmurs. "But I'm not sure how you'll feel about it."

"Tell me." I place my cutlery down and turn, giving him my full attention.

His eyes search mine as he exhales slowly.

"Cape Town."

"Cape Town?"

He falters, his brow creasing as apprehension passes through his eyes.

"It's where the worst day of my life happened. And call me strange, but I want it to be where the best day happens as well. I feel like my son will be there with us."

"Sterling." My voice breaks as I jump up from my stool and fling my arms around his neck. "You're not strange. I think it's perfect."

"You do?"

I pull back to look into his eyes. "I do." I nod, dusting my fingers along his jaw, hoping to ease the tension in it.

He rests his hands on my hips as I position myself closer, standing between his spread thighs.

"How does it make you feel when you imagine us all there?"

He drops his eyes to my stomach and rests his hand on it.

"It feels right, Hallie. It feels so damn right."

"Then we do it in Cape Town." I press a kiss to his forehead.

"We do it in Cape Town," he echoes.

We look at each other for a few moments, the air sparing between us before Sterling breaks my gaze and looks at my half-eaten breakfast.

"I haven't finished yet, I promise," I say, biting my lower lip.

"No, you haven't." He kisses me on the lips before guiding me back into my seat. "You're still healing. And our baby needs Mommy to eat."

A goofy smile spreads on my face. "Mommy sounds weird."

"Mommy sounds damn perfect to me." His eyes twinkle as he stands from his seat and starts tidying up.

My eyes fix on his butt in his suit pants as he turns his back to me.

"Eat, Hallie. Or I'll feed you myself," he says with a deep rumble.

"How do you know I'm looking at you?"

He chuckles. "It's my job to know everything when it comes to you."

I push a forkful of toast and eggs into my mouth and chew, my appreciative gaze still glued to his ass.

"Okay, then, Mr. Know-it-all. What color theme are we going with for the wedding?"

He hums as he wipes down the counter in the same spot for a third time. He knows I'm still checking out his ass, and I swear he gets off on me eye-fucking him as much as I do.

"That's easy."

"Oh yeah?" I muse, happy that we're joking and everything is starting to feel good again.

Rory was arrested for starting the fire at the club. He wanted revenge, and a chance to destroy the photographs Mal took, which Sterling told me about. But the safe is fire-proof, so Rory's plan didn't achieve anything. He's unlikely to be given bail before his trial. And Sophie said from a legal standpoint she doesn't think he has a hope in getting off.

He's going to jail.

Lavinia, on the other hand, will get off lighter if her involvement is investigated which I'm sure it will be soon. Rory will be slinging around accusations like sprinkles in a cake factory if he thinks telling the cops she gave him the security code will help deflect attention away from him. But as of two days ago she set off overseas on a charity mission and stepped down as board member for all the charities she was involved in in New York.

She isn't planning on coming back unless she's made to.

"Go on, then, if it's so easy," I say to Sterling.

He turns to face me, his lips flat and serious.

"Silver."

"Silver?" I arch a brow.

"The shade of that dress of yours I love you in so much."

"Oh? You mean the *sterling* silver one?"

He shakes his head and strolls around the counter, stopping next to my seat.

"No. I mean the one that showcases your nipples like a damn work of art."

I drop my mouth open in mock outrage. "You said you were a gentleman."

He chuckles. "I am. But I also know my girl loves it when I lose all decorum around her."

"Oh, she does." I stand and wrap my arms around his neck.

"That she does," he rasps, dropping his hands to my hips.

"I can't wait to marry you," I whisper, rising on my toes

and press a lingering kiss to his lips. My stomach flips at the way his grip tightens on my hips as his breath melts into mine.

"I'm so blessed to have met you, Hallie."

I bite my lower lip. "You want to spend the day showing me how blessed you feel before we leave for the airport?"

"Baby Girl," he groans as I drop one hand to palm his growing erection.

"Yes?" I say sweetly.

"Are you still sore from last night?"

I shake my head. He fucked me so deep from behind last night, stopping each time I got close, that the volume at which I cried his name when he finally let me come even surprised me. I'm pretty sure it's why Sullivan vacated the guest room at the crack of dawn this morning and announced he didn't think we needed help with our recovery anymore, and he was off to collect Molly from her sleepover at Mal and Trudy's.

"In that case, hold on tight." Sterling chuckles.

I squeal as he lifts me into his arms and strides toward our bedroom.

The bell at the front door halts him mid-step.

"Ignore it," he says.

I shove him in the chest playfully. "We can't. It could be important."

I press a kiss to his jaw. "It'll only take a minute. We can continue this after."

He sighs, lowering his mouth to catch my lips in a kiss.

"It better be important."

42

STERLING

"Oh, you both look better," Sinclair comments the moment I open the door. "Sullivan said you both seemed fighting fit when he left earlier. But I wanted to drop by and check anyway, and bring some things you might need."

She holds a bag out toward me as she cradles Monty in her other arm.

"That's thoughtful of you, Sweetheart," I say, taking it from her.

She places Monty down onto the floor and he runs straight to Hallie, his tail wagging.

"Hi Boy," Hallie coos, bending to fuss him.

"There are some bridal magazines in that bag, too. I thought we could have a look?" Sinclair's eyes light up.

Hallie smiles at her. "Sure, that would be amazing. Come on through, we just ate, but did you want some breakfast?"

"No, thanks." Sinclair waves a hand. "I won't stay long. Just an hour."

I catch Hallie's gaze as my daughter heads off into the apartment, Monty trailing behind her.

"You can't wait an hour to continue what we started?" She arches a brow.

"Of course I can. Doesn't mean I want to, though."

She giggles and I follow her into the kitchen. I head straight for the coffee machine, fixing one for Sinclair as the two women sit side-by-side at the counter and start talking about flowers. I can't help the smile on my face as I listen to them. For a long time I prayed to hear excitement in my daughter's voice again. And finally it's back.

Put there by Hallie.

"I wonder how big your bump will be on the day?" Sinclair assesses Hallie's flat stomach beneath her sweater.

"I don't know. I guess it'll show. It's going to be a few months until we get married."

"True," Sinclair hums. "Thanks, Dad," she says as I slide her coffee mug toward her.

The bell at the door goes again.

"Jesus Christ, we're popular this morning," I say, heading off to answer it, the women's happy chatter echoing behind me.

At this rate, Hallie and I won't get any time alone before her parents' flight arrives. And I really wanted to see if I could make her scream my name louder than she did last night. That was quite something.

I stiffen at the sight of Sullivan, Mal, and Denver standing fully suited with matching sour faces on the other side of the door.

"What's happened now?"

"Let's talk inside," Sullivan clips, striding past me.

"You look good," Mal says, clasping me on the shoulder as he slides past.

"Boss," Denver greets, following the men inside.

I walk after them, into the kitchen. They all choose

different areas to stand in rather than taking any of the numerous seats at the counter, or on the giant couch.

"You look much better. You must have had a good sleep last night," Mal says to Hallie.

"Thank you. I feel much better." She blushes, her eyes darting to Sullivan who's picked up Sinclair's coffee and is drinking it.

"I need it more than you, Sis, believe me," he grunts.

Sinclair studies the three of them, her lips pursed. "We were talking weddings before you all interrupted. What are you all doing here with faces like that?"

"We need to talk to your father about business," Denver says.

Sinclair rolls her eyes. "Ugh. And it couldn't wait? He's supposed to be recovering."

"He's recovered just fine, haven't you, Dad?" Sullivan says, taking another large mouthful of Sinclair's coffee before placing the cup back down on the counter.

Hallie looks at me and bites back an embarrassed smile. I walk over and place a hand on the back of her neck, rubbing it with my thumb.

"What is it?" I ask.

"It's about what we were talking about with Killian and Jenson," Denver says.

"Go on," I urge.

Mal's eyes flick from Sinclair to Hallie in question, but Denver knows if I'm asking that I'm happy for him to say whatever it is in front of them. I don't want any secrets in this family. They can destroy everything and everyone if you aren't careful.

"He's in New York," Denver says. "Killian tracked him in on a flight yesterday. We looked back over the past two years. He hasn't been back here until now."

"I know some people who could make him disappear,"

Mal says, his jaw hardening before he looks between Sinclair and Hallie like he doesn't want to admit to that in front of them.

"We keep an eye on him," Sullivan says. "Don't go acting dumb before we know if he even wants anything."

"Who?" Sinclair pipes up. "Stop being so cryptic. They made an arrest over the club fire, so who the hell are you talking about?"

I exhale slowly. "Neil."

Sinclair's eyes widen. "Why are you keeping tabs on the man Mom had an affair with?"

Hallie's neck tenses beneath my thumb and she looks up at me. "Sterling?"

"He was there the day we lost them," I say, taking my hand from Hallie to scrub it around my jaw. I grit my teeth. "He couldn't have started the fire. But he was still damn well there. And until we know why, I want you all to be on extra alert."

"No staying at friend's houses overnight without telling anyone," Sullivan says to Sinclair. "We need to be vigilant. He's stayed away from New York all this time. We can't assume his return is purely an innocent visit."

"And until we know why he's here, everyone needs to check in with me daily. I'll install trackers in all your phones so I can see your location at all times," Denver instructs.

Sinclair snorts. "Like hell you will."

"Sinclair," I warn. "We're all going to be doing this. And for the time being, I'd prefer you call one of us if you need any rides at night. I don't want you driving alone after dark."

She tenses, her eyes sliding away from mine guiltily.

"Seriously? You damaged your car again?" Sullivan says, recognizing her sudden silence that comes each time she's scraped tens of thousands of dollars' worth of crystals off that damn car.

"No!" She shakes her head, her eyes glittering in defiance. "God, you always want to blame me."

"Because it's always you who hits something. What was it this time? Another parking meter?" Sullivan clips.

"Forget it." Sinclair sniffs and pretends to leaf through one of the bridal magazines.

"Sinclair?" I coax.

She stops, her shoulders drooping with a sigh as she looks up at me. "It wasn't my fault. I thought I'd parked in a safe spot."

"What are you talking about?" Sullivan asks.

"It..." She rolls her eyes. "It's not that much damage. The workshop said they'll fix it."

Sullivan scowls at her and she huffs in annoyance.

"It was vandalized, okay? Someone scraped it and wrote 'Beaufort Bitch' across the windscreen."

"Oh my god, are you okay?" Hallie asks.

"I'm fine, thanks. It's nothing," she says.

"That's not nothing," Sullivan barks. "Jesus, why didn't you tell us?"

"Because you always overreact, like you are now," she snaps.

"No one's ever done anything like that before, Sinclair," Mal adds. "We're just looking out for you."

Sinclair folds her arms, her lips clamped together.

"It's not the first time, is it?" I ask, unease bubbling inside my chest from her tense posture.

She shifts in the seat. "They've never damaged my car before. Usually they just leave a note under the wiper."

"Fucking hell," Sullivan snaps, pushing his hands into his pant pockets and turning away.

My throat dries up at the fear radiating from him. It might look like anger to everyone else, but I know my son. He's been scared of something else happening to our family ever since he saw his mother and brother die in front of him.

"What kind of notes?" Mal asks.

Sinclair shrugs. "Just ones saying I should watch my back. Or that I'm not as special as everyone thinks I am. Stuff like that. I get nice ones too." She brightens. "Someone left me a flower and told me I nailed the runway last week."

"Jesus Christ," I husk out.

Sullivan turns and meets my eyes. A darkness swirls in his, a flash of the pain I know he fights so hard to conceal so he looks like the strong one. The oldest of the three. A role he's always taken seriously, even before we lost them both.

"It's fine, Dad. It's—"

"It's not fine." I cut Sinclair off and turn my attention to Denver whose face is like thunder as he stares at her.

"Denver?"

His jaw clenches and he takes his eyes from Sinclair and meets mine.

"From now on, until we work out who's been sending Sinclair these threats and find out what Neil is doing here, you're with Sinclair."

"Yes, Boss." He nods.

"What?" Sinclair gasps. "What does *with me* mean?"

"It means he's your personal bodyguard as of now." I point my finger at the floor to make my point. "You don't go anywhere without him."

"No!" She stands from her seat and glares at me.

"Yes."

Her mouth flaps and she looks around the room for support. Sullivan nods and Mal wisely keeps quiet. Hallie offers her a sympathetic smile.

"Dad," she begs, "not him. Please. I'll take Killian or Jenson... but not him."

"Denver's the best we have."

She doesn't bother to hide the disgust in her voice. "It'll be like being babysat by a gorilla. He barely talks, just grunts. At least Killian's interesting, and Jenson's fun."

"You've got Denver."

"My life is over," she mutters.

"Don't be so dramatic." Sullivan sighs, the earlier fear I saw in him lessening as he looks at Denver and gives him a curt nod.

Denver returns it. "I'll take good care of her."

Sinclair snorts and scoops Monty up from the floor, whispering in his ear, "I'm so sorry. I know this means you're stuck with him too."

"Monty too," Denver says to Sinclair. "No one will touch a single one of the few hairs he does have while you're both under my protection."

She shifts slightly, lifting her chin and flicking her eyes to him as she strokes Monty. "You'll protect him as much as you will me?"

"Yes," Denver replies instantly.

She stares at him a few seconds before looking back at me. "Fine," she huffs.

I meet Denver's eyes, and he holds mine without faltering. He is the best we have, like I just said.

And right now, Sinclair needs him the most.

"I trust you with my life," I tell him.

"Boss."

I narrow my eyes at him, praying I'm making the right choice.

"And, Denver?"

He holds my eyes.

"Now, I'm trusting you with my daughter."

43

HALLIDAY

I toy with the short strands of hair at the base of Sterling's skull as he carries me to bed.

"You look worried," I breathe.

He's had this deep line between his brows since everyone left.

"I'm fine."

"You don't have to pretend with me."

He sighs and traces his nose up my temple before kissing it.

"Last time Neil was near my family, two of them died. And even though he couldn't have started the fire, until we know more, I don't want to take any chances. Sinclair will get over having Denver with her. But I'm not going to lie, I'm angry at her for not telling us about the threats she's been receiving."

"She probably thought they were harmless notes until they wrecked her car."

I slide my hand up over his shirt, bringing it to rest above his heart. It's beating out a steady rhythm in his chest.

"I hate seeing you so worried. What can I do?" I press slow kisses up over his throat and along his jaw.

He groans as my lips travel to beneath his ear and I plant more soft kisses there.

"You can help me stop thinking for a while."

"Stop thinking? You just want to feel, huh?" I toy with the buttons of his shirt as I unfasten them one by one.

"Something like that."

He places me onto the bed, and I kneel, pulling him in for a kiss. His tongue entwines with mine, one hand sinking into my hair and holding me in place so he can kiss me deeper and groan into my mouth.

"You're so damn perfect."

"I need you inside me," I plead, palming his dick impatiently through his pants.

I slide the zipper down and push my hand inside, curling it around his length in his boxer shorts and squeezing.

"Hallie," he tsks as I lose patience and free his rock-hard dick through the open zipper. "You feeling eager, Baby girl?"

"Always for you." I bite my lower lip and glide my hand up and down his shaft, my body buzzing with energy at the moan it creates from deep in his chest.

"You want me to fill you up?" His eyes glitter as my hand reaches the tip of him.

"Or maybe you can fill my throat." I dip my head and spit on his throbbing erection, rubbing my saliva into his already glistening slit with my thumb.

He tips his head back as I wrap my lips around him and take as much of him as I can in my mouth.

"Jesus Christ." His large hand cups the back of my head, holding me down. I blink up at him, my throat filled with him. "You're my perfect girl, aren't you? Look at you, sucking on my cock with those innocent eyes."

I bat my lashes and his grip on my head softens, allowing

me to suck all the way back up. I sink back onto him for a few more delicious sucks before letting his dick pop free of my mouth.

I press a kiss to the smooth, shiny head of his cock and he curses as it jumps against my lips.

"Lie down, Baby girl," he growls.

I pull my Statue of Liberty sweater off over my head, and peel my yoga pants down my thighs, loving the way his eyes darken when he notes my lack of panties.

I lie back on my elbows, looking up at him.

"Like this?" I pout, letting my thighs drop open in invitation.

He swoops on me, and I cry out as his tongue crashes against my clit. I sink my hands into his hair and tug at the roots as he wastes no time in eating me out like the expert he is. My orgasm winds up inside me. But I know he won't let me come. He wants the first one the same way I do.

Together.

"Sterling," I gasp. "Please."

He groans in response, sliding his tongue around my clit, then lower, dipping it inside me. I arch against the bed, my hands holding his head deep between my thighs.

"You're so good at that," I whimper as he slides his tongue free and moves it further back, teasing my asshole.

"I practice every morning." He chuckles.

"I want you inside me," I moan.

He holds my eyes and kisses my clit tenderly, and I'm so close to coming from that one single, sexy move that my thighs shake against his ears.

"Hurry," I beg.

He stands, never breaking eye contact as he slides each sleeve of his shirt off and drops it to the floor. My eyes roam over his torso and I press my thighs together to ease the ache of needing him there. I don't even see his scars as scars anymore.

They're just a part of him. A part I kiss and stroke every chance I get.

"Hurry," I urge again in a breathy plea, rising to my knees so I can watch him properly.

His lips twitch and he takes his time unfastening the waistband of his suit pants. His dick is still poking through the open zipper, deep pink and glistening on the end. I lick my lips in anticipation.

He slides the rest of his clothes off and sits at the head of the bed, resting against the headboard. His lips curl into an amused smile and he takes his cock in one hand and fists it slowly.

"You want to get on it, Baby girl?"

I scrabble to do as he says, straddling his thighs.

His hands take up their favorite position on my hips, his fingers pressing into my skin as he grips me. I slide a hand around his jaw, and he twists to kiss my inner wrist.

"I love you," I say, grasping him and lining up his cock where I need it.

"I love you too."

His eyes hold mine and he kisses my wrist again. His fingers flex against my hips as I rotate his dick in a circle, sliding it through my wetness until he's coated in it.

I grip his left shoulder, my palm flattening over the scarred skin in my usual place I like to get leverage when I ride him.

Then I sink down.

His lips part with a hiss so laced in arousal that it makes wetness pool between my thighs, and I stretch all the way around him easily, taking inch after inch of his length until our hot skin presses tightly together.

"God, Sterling," I mewl shamelessly as my body flutters around him.

"Baby girl," he utters, his chest muscles tensing like he's fighting not to come just from the feel of entering me.

I love that I do this to him. He's all strong and composed usually. But the second I ride him like this, the same as our first time, it takes everything in him to maintain control.

"You like it like this, huh?" I rise up and sink back down slowly, smiling as his head falls back and his throat thickens with a tortured groan.

He looks at me beneath hooded lids.

"You know I do, Baby girl. Now ride me. Make it damn torture for me not to fill you up before you come on my cock."

I lean forward and kiss him, nipping his lower lip between my teeth.

"You feel so good inside me," I purr.

I lift my hips, setting a steady pace, working myself up and down his dick while my mouth hovers against his, delivering kisses in-between my lust-filled moans of his name.

His grip on my hips tightens and I lick the corner of his mouth.

"You love testing me, don't you?" He groans out a chuckle, his cock thickening inside me and making me gasp as he pulls me up and down over it with more force.

"I love that I'm going to be marrying you soon," I whimper.

He lifts his hips, thrusting up inside me and fucking me from beneath. I kiss him again, allowing my lips to brush side to side over his.

"And I love that we were doing it like this the day you got me pregnant."

His heavy lust-filled lids lift in question, and I nod slowly.

"I worked it out on my chart. I think it was the day we came back to New York. Remember it?"

"Hallie," he utters. "You needed taking care of that day."

"I know."

I keep my hand on his shoulder and use the other to take

one of his from my hips and place it over my stomach. I hold mine over the top as we continue to move.

"You did take care of me," I breathe, kissing him again. "You took care of me just like this. In your arms. Kissing me. Loving me. Just like you always do."

"Jesus," he murmurs, his thumb rubbing over my lower stomach as I increase our pace.

"You loved me so hard you created something magic."

I ride him and he urges me on with a firm grip on one hip.

"You are my magic, Hallie." His upper torso tenses and he looks down at our hands on my stomach, the giant engagement ring glittering against my skin. "The moment I met you, you changed my life."

I wait until he brings his blue eyes up to meet mine and then I increase my pace, my breath growing ragged.

"You changed mine too. You are my first and only choice. I chose *you*. I'll always choose you."

His pupils blow wide, and I hold his eyes, shuddering and crying out as my orgasm crashes through me.

"Always you," I pant, coming hard.

Sterling tightens his grip on my hip as I clench around his cock in rippling waves, my orgasm stretching on into another that bursts like a warm shower of sunlight through my body.

"That's it. Milk me, Baby girl. God, yes. Just like that. You're going to make me come."

I clench around him, and he comes deep inside me with a choked groan, his head dropping back.

But not enough that his eyes leave mine.

"You're so damn perfect. Squeeze me harder."

I clench again and he hisses, his cock jerking inside me as he keeps coming.

"Baby girl. Damn, that's it."

"More?" I pant.

"More," he confirms, his jaw tightening.

Another wave of cum floods me inside and the sensation makes me come again.

"Sterling," I whimper.

I keep working myself over him long after our orgasms have subsided, and our combined wetness has started running out over his thighs.

"You okay?" I ask, kissing him on the lips.

He smiles. "I'm perfect. Damn perfect."

I allow my gaze to trace over his face, along his silver-flecked jaw that I love to stroke so much, over the smile lines that crease the corners of his warm blue eyes. Eyes I've spent hours looking into and falling deeper and deeper in love.

Energy dances through me, buzzing over me like a million kisses of stardust against my skin as he brings his lips to mine and kisses me softly.

"I don't think your kissing needs work anymore," I breathe.

"No?"

"But you know that expression, use it or lose it?"

He chuckles and I return his kiss with a gentle one of my own.

"In that case, I'll choose to use it every day with my beautiful soon-to-be wife."

"That's a good choice." I beam at him.

"My only one," he breathes.

His eyes twinkle as I gaze into them.

"Your only one," I repeat. "Just like you were always meant to be my only one too."

I trail my fingers along his jaw, catching his next kiss against their tips.

"My only choice," I whisper. "The best one I'll ever make."

44

HALLIDAY

THE WEDDING - SIX MONTHS LATER

"Time to get your dress on," Sophie calls from inside the bedroom.

A soft smile lifts my lips as I stand on the balcony looking over the ocean.

"I can feel them. That sounds silly, but I can. I can feel both him and Jenny here with us."

"It's not silly." Sophie stands next to me, and we're shoulder to shoulder in silence for a couple of minutes, watching the hot Cape Town sun shining onto the water and making it glimmer like a jewel.

Sterling says he still feels his son when he's by the water. But here, in Sterling's beach house, that he hasn't wanted to stay in since that fateful trip where he lost them, I can feel his son, despite being on land. He's an energy. One that's been pushing closer and closer since we arrived two days ago. Like the incoming tide, moving toward you until your toes finally feel it's warmth around them.

It was the right choice getting married here. I don't know how I know that this was exactly what fate had planned for us all, but I do. We're all supposed to be here today. It took a little longer to plan everything, but we're finally here.

"It's beautiful." Sophie wraps an arm around me as we look at the deck below, and the long white wooden table and chairs that has been set up for dinner after the ceremony.

The table is overflowing with mounds of white flowers and candles, ready to be lit at sunset. The only pop of color are little bowls filled with purple that weren't there when I woke up in Sterling's bed without him. He stayed in another room last night, keeping the tradition of not seeing the bride until the ceremony.

"What are they?" Sophie asks as I dab at my eyes with my fingertips.

"Skittles." My voice cracks, and I smile.

"Skittles," Sophie repeats softly, understanding their significance.

Jenny might not be here in person, but she's here in spirit. Sterling's made sure of it.

"He really loves you, Halliday."

"I know. I love him too. More than words could ever describe."

The door opens to the bedroom behind us and my mum walks in, flustered.

"Sweetheart? You're not dressed? All the guests are being seated."

"It's fine, Mum."

Her face breaks into a watery smile as she looks at me. "Oh, my darling girl." She walks over and stops in front of me, her eyes taking in my hair and makeup. "You look radiant. He doesn't know how lucky he is."

I let out a soft breath. "He does. But I'm the lucky one. Did you see—?"

"I did." Her eyes mist over. "Purple."

"Purple," I echo, blinking back tears as she pulls me into an embrace and just holds me for a few beats.

"Right," Mum breezes, straightening up and shifting her smile from a bittersweet one to an excited one as she looks between Sophie and I. "Let's get this gown on. You have a groom waiting patiently for you."

The air takes on a magical quality as I take off my Statue of Liberty sweatshirt and my best friend and Mum help me into my bridal gown. It's a sheer silver silk overlaid with a crystal-embellished mermaid train. Sinclair called in a favor with a designer she knows to get it for me without having to join the two-year waitlist; and to have it altered to allow for my bump.

My hand rests over my abdomen as Mum pins the long, barely there veil into the back of my hair. I know Sterling will be missing seeing our baby while we're here in Cape Town. We left the ultrasound machine at home, something he still likes to use religiously every night when the baby is most active. I swear I fall more and more in love with him each night when his warm blue eyes soften with love and adoration like he's seeing our baby for the first time.

My parents came round to the idea very quickly once we told them. They ended up extending their visit to New York for an extra week after I came out of hospital because they were having such a wonderful time with us. Dad and Sterling found a mutual appreciation of art to talk about, and a shared guilty pleasure of Reese's peanut butter cups after I brought some home and they all disappeared within the day. Sinclair can't stop shopping for baby things, and even Sullivan was talking to me about the safest car seats a few days ago.

Baby Beaufort will be so swarmed with love from everyone.

I take in a deep breath and look at myself in the full-length mirror, the warm, hazy breeze flowing in from the open balcony doors next to me.

"I'm ready," I tell Mum and Sophie. "I don't want to make Sterling wait a second longer. Let's go get married."

STERLING

Sullivan's eyes are narrowed and focused on the start of the white carpeted aisle that's been laid out over boards on the sand.

"I'm turning around, Son."

"As best man, it's my duty to look out for the bride, so you turn at the correct time."

I chuckle, and he grunts his disapproval.

"And as your father who hasn't seen his bride since after we all had dinner together last night, I can tell you that's not happening. I want to see her the second she steps into view."

"Age has made you stubborn," he clips.

"Age has given me everything I ever dreamed of. You, Sinclair, Molly, my family... and now Hallie and the baby."

My son's usual straight mouth curls into a proud smile as his eyes track to where Molly is waiting with Sinclair near the start of the aisle.

"It'll be nice to have another little one for Molly to play with."

"You're a great father to her," I say, clasping him on the shoulder.

"Thanks, Dad. I learned from the best."

I press my lips together, scrubbing my other hand around my jaw, unable to form words. But all I need to say is reflected back at me in his eyes as he nods and lays his hand over mine.

A sparkle of silver catches the light amongst the line of palm trees and the breath is snatched from my body by her standing there, glowing in the sun, her arm linked through her father's.

Hallie.

Perfect.

Mine.

"Take a breath, Dad," Sullivan instructs in a low whisper.

I do as he says, my chest expanding as her smile grows in response to something her father says to her. Her attention is caught briefly by something hidden within the trees and she stops walking, inclining her body toward whatever it is. She stands there for a moment, just looking.

Then she turns.

Our eyes lock and my heart dances its way up into my throat. Her face is glowing like a diamond, polished until its beauty is blinding. Her delicate bouquet is made of crystals—not flowers—each glimmering brightly. But nothing can shine brighter than the smile that takes over her face as she parts her lips and breathes one word to herself.

My name.

It doesn't matter that she's still far away. I know that's what just left her lips because I've committed every time she says it to my memory. Stored them away to keep them safe. To treasure them for eternity.

She chose me.

I am the only choice she ever wanted to make.

Gentle notes of music fill the air as Seasons' pianist, Vincent, plays to one side of the flower-arch serving as an altar. He insisted on flying his own piano over here to play. This one is white, not like the new black Grand we now have in Seasons. The replacement Vincent chose after the fire.

The fire.

My throat tightens as Hallie and her father walk closer. That day I found her unresponsive on my desk I thought... I thought it was over. That this day would never come.

I thought I'd lost her.

Hallie's eyes hold mine. She looks like an angel.

"I'm so damn blessed," I murmur, causing Sullivan to clap me gently between my shoulder blades.

"We want you to be happy, Dad."

"I know, and I love you even more for it, Son."

My family mean everything to me. And that means Hallie too. I can't ever risk losing any of them.

Lavinia is still overseas working on her missions. And Rory was handed a five-year sentence after being convicted of third-degree arson. It could have been longer if he'd known Hallie was inside. As much as I despise him and wish he'd be locked away forever, I believe he was telling the truth when he broke down in court and said he'd never meant any harm to come to her.

It doesn't change the fact that he's been mentally and emotionally hurting her for years, though.

I push the memories away before they can spark into life and singe the edges of our perfect day. But even if I were to let them linger, nothing can ruin this for us. Because where I carry the scars of my pain on my body, visible to those I let see, Hallie doesn't. She conveys the same loving, trusting soul that shone from her in her photograph with Jenny.

The photograph that's sitting on the small table to my left, waiting for us to sign our marriage certificate on.

She breaks my gaze momentarily to watch Molly walk up the aisle ahead of her, scattering petals from a small basket with a tiny, purple-stained hand as Sophie walks with her.

"She found the candy before I stopped her," Sinclair whispers, sliding into the row of seats behind us and standing beside Mal and Trudy.

My chest vibrates with a small chuckle as Molly flings the petals up in the air above her head in delight, nailing her role. She stops momentarily beside Sophie's husband, Drew, who is balancing a baby in each arm, and presents the basket to him. Both babies put their chubby hands in and grab a fistful of petals. There's a collective murmur of awws and laughs as the babies immediately try to eat them and my friend, Lawson, steps forward to help Drew extract them from their mouths.

Sophie smiles at me as her and Molly reach the top of the aisle. Molly walks straight to Sullivan, holding her arms up in the air. "Daddy."

"Good job," he whispers, scooping her up and holding her into his side.

Everyone's eyes return to Hallie and Garth moving up the aisle.

Her eyes are glittering, and she keeps breaking into a wide smile and then pulling it back in to bite her lip and take a breath before it explodes back across her face again.

"So damn perfect," I whisper when she reaches me.

"Sterling," she breathes back, her eyes locked on mine.

For a moment no one else exists except us as we gaze at one another. We've told each other a billion times how we feel about one another. So for this moment, no words are needed.

I see everything I need to in her eyes.

I shake her father's hand before she kisses him on the cheek. Then I hold out both of my hands and she slides hers into them.

"When you're in love, you see the world in her eyes," she whispers.

"And you see her eyes everywhere in the world," I finish, giving her a questioning look as she recites the poetry I read to her so many nights ago now. The night she showed me that I'm not broken. I was just waiting for the right person to ignite me.

Her.

"You're not the only one who remembers things." She bites her lower lip with a cute smile as her eyes dart to one side, landing on Molly in Sullivan's arms, her purple palm resting over his shirt.

"You weren't meant to see those until after the ceremony."

"I'm glad I did, though, they're perfect. Thank you." Her lips part with a quick intake of breath when she notices the table behind me. *"Sterling."*

I follow her gaze to the two photographs, angled so they're watching us.

Jenny.

My son.

A pink crystal heart between them that was found and cleaned up after the fire.

Hallie's eyes fill with tears.

"They're both here with us," I say quietly so only she can hear.

"I know." She looks at the photographs. "I could have sworn I even saw him a moment ago when I was walking over here. He looked like..." Her eyes flit to Sullivan before she blinks and brings them back to mine. "I'm glad we chose here."

"Me too." I stroke her hands in mine. "You ready to be my wife now?"

"You ready to be my husband?" she counters.

"Hallie, I've been ready a long time."

She nods, her eyes twinkling. "Me too."

I lift the champagne flute in my left hand and raise my toast.

"You need to get used to seeing it." Hallie giggles as my eyes fix onto my wedding band again. I didn't have one with Elaina, I don't know why. But I knew I wanted one the second I asked Hallie to marry me. I want the world to know I have a wife who chose me. And one whom I would willingly give up my last breath for.

I wink down at her.

"Family, friends," I say, drawing our intimate gathering's attention to the middle of the long table where we're sitting. "My wife and I—"

"Whoop!" calls out Jenson, setting everyone laughing.

I smile.

"My *wife*, Hallie, and I want to thank you all for being here. And we also want to remember those who couldn't be here today. But we know they are looking out from wherever they are, feeling the love that is here tonight, surrounding us all. We may not all share blood, but you're family to us. Each and every one of you."

I look up and down the table at Sinclair, Sullivan, Molly, Mal and Trudy, my brothers Jagger, and Clay and his family, Hallie's parents and friends, Sophie and Drew, my friends, Lawson, Roman, even Frankie. And finally Denver, Killian, and Jenson. Everyone who is a part of our lives.

"Thank you all for being here to celebrate with us." I place my free hand on the top of Hallie's spine, my thumb tracing circles over the base of her neck. "I'm sure you're all aware now of how we met. But I promised my daughter, Sinclair..." I chuckle as Sinclair gives a little wave from her seat next to Denver, "... that I would give her credit and tell the story again.

So here we are. Please raise a glass while I tell you how one day she changed my life with three words."

Everyone lifts their glasses, and I smile down at Hallie.

I love you, she mouths.

"*Love you too, Baby girl*," I whisper against her lips, bending to kiss her.

Her fingertips trail along my jaw and she kisses me back. A kiss so soft, but full of promise.

A promise to choose each other, always.

I straighten up and lift my glass again.

"Those three words were not 'it requires work', as my beautiful wife said about my kissing technique."

A rumble of laughter passes over the table.

"But they were the words that my daughter said to me the moment I laid eyes on Hallie. And they couldn't have been truer. And those three words…"

I lift Hallie's left hand in mine and kiss the back of it, just above her glittering engagement ring, and the new wedding band sitting beneath it.

"Those three words were…"

My voice grows hoarse, and I look into her eyes. Reflected back is a promise of a lifetime of happiness. A lifetime of love.

A lifetime of being her one and only choice.

"Those three words were…"

I take a deep breath as Hallie beams at me, taking my heart in her hands and treasuring it, like no one ever has before.

"'*She's your gift.*'"

The End.

45

HALLIDAY

BONUS SCENES - THE BACHELORETTE WEEKEND

"I miss you." I twirl the cord of the hotel suite's phone around my finger as I gaze out of the window at London's skyline.

"Baby girl, I've been missing you every damn second since you left."

I grin at the deep rumble in Sterling's voice. He insisted on flying over here with Sinclair, Zoey, and I to drop us off for my bachelorette weekend. I decided to have it in London because it's where I spent most of my days as a single woman. And also Sophie is now quite heavily pregnant, so we felt it was better for her to stay closer to home and to Drew just in case.

"I'll be coming home tomorrow. And then you can show me how much."

He curses softly and I press my thighs together. We've never been apart this long since we met. It's only going to be three days in total, but it feels like an eternity. Sleeping in a bed without him holding me last night felt wrong. I've officially been living in New York for three months now and it already feels like home.

Because of Sterling.

"How's our baby?" he rasps.

"Missing Daddy." I place my hand over my stomach. I'm only a few months and I don't look pregnant yet. I just look like I ate a huge meal.

"I'll come and bring you both home. The minute you're ready, okay?"

"Okay."

"So what's the plan for today?"

"You're asking me?" I roll my eyes with a laugh.

Sinclair, Zoey, and Sophie arranged this entire London trip. And Sterling was privy to their meetings. He knows every surprise they have planned, while I've been blissfully unaware, just left to enjoy them. Yesterday we went on a spa day and my mum joined us. And all I know about today is that I was told to wear something comfortable. Sinclair has taken care of the rest, and she even breezed in here bright and early when I was still in bed to pack the outfits I'll need.

I didn't see what she put in my *HB* luggage that I brought with me.

I already miss looking at the smaller suitcase in the set Sterling bought me.

HB.

"I asked them to personalize it for Halliday Beaufort."

He says he lost faith in magic. But a part of him always held onto hope, otherwise he wouldn't have bought me luggage for Halliday Beaufort. He'd have bought it for Halliday Burton.

My chest swims with warmth. In thirty days I'll be Halliday Beaufort.

There's a knock at the door.

"I think that's the girls," I tell Sterling.

"Go. Have fun."

The Matchmaker

I can hear the smile in his voice.
"I will. I love you."
"I love you too, Hallie. I'll call you later."

STERLING

Hallie looks radiant, a huge smile spread over her face as I walk out into the roof garden bar where the girls are having late afternoon drinks.

I catch Denver's eye where he's sat nearby, nursing his drink as he gives Sinclair space. He's been acting as her personal bodyguard since we found out Neil was in New York, and since she's been receiving anonymous threats. Sinclair likes to remind me it's a huge inconvenience to her having him constantly with her every time she can.

But this is my family, and I won't compromise their safety.

I give Denver a nod which he returns before his eyes track back to my daughter, sitting with her back toward him, her head tipped back as she laughs at something Hallie just said.

I walk up behind Hallie and press my finger to my lips as the three other women spot me.

"Drew will love mine," Sophie says as she expertly averts her eyes from me so as not to give my presence away. "He's got this whole pregnancy fetish, so he'll love that we did it. As long as he doesn't hang them in his office."

Zoey smirks beside her. "Ashton will probably add them to his next gallery show."

The girls laugh as I close the remaining distance and lean close.

Hallie whips her head around, her eyes widening as she spots me.

"I knew it! What are you doing here?"

She jumps from her seat and flings her arms around my neck, pulling me to her. I wrap my arms around her and sink my nose into her hair, inhaling her scent.

"I've missed you so damn much," I groan as I hold her tighter. My fingers slide to her hips, curling around the sequined fabric of her skirt. She's all dressed up and has had her hair and makeup done. "You look beautiful."

"I knew it was you." There's a smile in her voice as she reaches up and dusts her fingers along my jawline, pressing her lips to mine in a soft kiss. "My fingers started tingling ten minutes ago. I knew you were close."

I chuckle. I'll never get tired of Hallie's magic, and her unwavering belief in the power of the universe. I can't say I share her gift for knowing things the way that she seems to. But I can't deny that her coming into my life when she did felt like some type of divine intervention.

"I factored this into our schedule." Sinclair sighs, rolling her eyes. "I knew you wouldn't be able to manage without her this whole time."

I lift my hands in surrender and Hallie giggles and curls herself around my side.

"Guilty, I miss my fiancée. But you factored this in?" I ask Sinclair. "I only decided to come twelve hours ago."

"Yeah, well, I know you well. And I knew you'd be a man on the edge being apart," she teases. Her eyes flick to Denver and away again just as fast.

I look at Hallie and press a kiss to her forehead. "I brought you your sweatshirt. You said you'd forgotten it."

"The one you gave me?" Her eyes light up.

"The Statue of Liberty one," I confirm as she beams at me and kisses me again.

"Yeah, and you told Denver what you were planning." My daughter inclines her head over her shoulder so she can flick her gaze toward Denver sitting nearby. "Having him around had to have some benefits."

Denver's eyes darken as he looks at Sinclair until she breaks eye contact.

"Is Monty okay?" she asks me.

"He's fine. Molly's been taking him to bed with her and staying there. Sullivan's had his bed to himself for a change."

My daughter smiles as her eyes pass between Hallie and I.

"I suppose you want to steal her?" She arches a brow. "You've got two hours until our dinner reservation. Do not bring her back late."

"I wouldn't dream of it, Sweetheart. I know you have a booking."

I don't know what the girls did today. It's the one part of the weekend that Sinclair wouldn't disclose to me. But I asked her to run the details by Denver, and he gave his approval that they should be safe, and I trust his judgment. But I do know that this evening the girls have a dinner booking at a restaurant that's known for its crystal elixir drinks. Hallie will love it, there's no way I'll allow her to miss a moment.

But I also can't wait to have her to myself for two precious hours.

"Go on, then," my daughter huffs, flicking her fingers and shooing us away. But her eyes sparkle as they meet mine. "Have fun."

HALLIDAY

"I can't believe you flew all the way from New York to come and pick me up, whisk me away from the girls, and then get back on a plane again." I laugh as Sterling unfastens his seatbelt the moment we're airborne.

"I missed you." His deep voice sends a shiver racing up my spine.

I unfasten my belt and lean over, whispering in his ear, even though the flight attendant is in the front galley, too far away to hear. "You came over because you were missing us having sex, weren't you?"

"Hallie," he scolds. "I wouldn't come to London when it's your bachelorette and expect that."

"Oh." I move back, my stomach dropping. The truth is, I've been missing it. Sterling likes to wake me up in a certain way, namely with his head between my thighs and his mouth on me doing delicious things, and I've grown used to it.

I'm a spoiled pillow princess.

"I can't admit that I came to see you in London just so I could have your taste that I'm so enraptured with smeared over my face."

I gasp and then laugh at the amusement dancing in his eyes as heat warms my blood.

"So you didn't come for that?"

"Oh, I did." He smiles and stands, holding his hand out to me. I slide mine inside and let him pull me to my feet. "But that's why we're in the air about to circle over the English Channel for the next hour. No one can say I came to devour my fiancée in London."

"Because you'll be doing it over the sea." I bite my lower lip, shaking my head as I follow him toward the bedroom at the rear of the cabin.

"Exactly. It's all in the details, Baby girl."

He grins wolfishly at me as he opens the door and pulls me inside, closing it behind us.

"How do you want me?" I breathe, fluttering my eyelashes at him, my fingers finding the waistband of his suit pants. We don't have much time, and I want to spend as much of it as possible feeling his hands on my skin.

"The mirror," he rasps, arching a brow as he looks over my shoulder at the small full length one attached to the internal paneling.

"Okay." I turn to look at it. "Do you want—?"

"Sit on the bed and open your legs."

My pulse throbs between my thighs at his commanding tone. I follow his order and sit on the edge of the white sheets.

Sterling grips his tie, pulling on it to loosen it. Something about the move is so sexy that I can't help wriggling on the bed, trying to get friction against my clit.

"Sit still. It's my job to do that." His eyes blaze with desire as he drops to his knees and slides my skirt up my thighs, groaning in appreciation as he grabs two handfuls of my ass.

"Sterling," I moan.

"So beautiful," he murmurs as he lowers his head and kisses me through my lace panties.

I lift my hips, desperate to feel him closer. He hooks my panties to one side and then his sinful tongue is on me.

"Please... yes..." I sink my left hand into his hair, my engagement ring glittering out between the strands as I scrunch them between my fingers, spurring him on.

I catch sight of us in the mirror. Now I understand why he wanted me to sit here. I'm flushed, lips parted as he goes down on me like the master of it that he is. And he's fully suited, on his knees for me, groaning my name.

The hottest show for which I have a front row seat.

His tongue flattens against my clit, and I writhe, my fingers tightening in his hair. I'm close. But I'm also impatient to feel him.

"Sterling?"

"Baby girl?" he growls, pushing two fingers inside me.

I moan at the sensation as liquid fire pools in my core.

"It's been too long; I need you inside me."

His captivating blue eyes rise, holding mine as he licks me slowly from ass to clit before gently placing my panties back in place.

I'm vibrating with need as he straightens in front of me.

I crash my lips to his before he can speak. We kiss in a frenzy as he brings us both up to standing and guides me backward. All patience is lost as we reconnect and fill every minute we've spent apart with kisses, nips, sucks, and groans.

"I love you," I pant as I work with him to wriggle out of my soaked panties.

"I worship you," he groans as he rips down his zipper and frees his solid cock.

He spins me, my panties still wrapped around the heel of one of my shoes as he pulls my hips backward, encouraging me to place my palms against the mirror.

My ass is presented at almost the right height for him in my sky-high heels. His eyes drop between my thighs, and he swipes two fingers through my wetness, making me shudder with arousal.

"So damn perfect, aren't you, Baby girl," he murmurs in awe as he dips the two fingers inside me, hissing as my body molds around them, begging for more.

"Sterling, I need you inside me," I plead, my pussy pulsing with need that only him filling me completely will ease.

"Jesus," he utters as he removes his fingers and replaces them with the fat head of his cock.

I lift my head up and watch in the mirror as he thrusts inside me.

"Damn, you're so wet."

He pulls back and thrusts again. Harder and deeper.

I dance on my toes and use my palms against the mirror to push back on to him.

"More," I beg.

He holds my eyes as he sets his pace, fucking me in the way only he can. My body sucks him in greedily, rippling around him every time he drives back inside me. His blue eyes are darkened with lust, and his silver flecked hair shines beneath the aircraft lighting as he pumps into me over and over.

"You're so good at that," I whimper as his grip tightens on my hips.

"This?" His lips curl, and he alters his angle slightly.

His heavy balls slap against me and the rim near the head of his cock rubs against my G-spot each time he thrusts.

"God! Yes, that," I cry as pressure builds in my core.

"You going to come on my cock like this, Baby girl?" he rasps.

I look at him in the mirror. "Yes, please."

"I can't reach your clit at this angle, so you need to come without me touching it."

I nod eagerly. As long as Sterling hits me in the right place inside, then I can come without touching my clit.

And it also means that—

"Sterling!" I moan as the familiar feeling builds.

My fingers stiffen against the cool glass, my inner thighs shaking as a delicious anticipation threads its way through me.

"I'm going to..." I pant.

"Damn, Baby girl. Do it. Soak me."

I can no longer keep my lips together as heavy pant after pant break free from my lips. My eyelids flutter and everything coils tight inside me.

Sterling's blue eyes penetrate mine, and I feel the heat of them right to my toes as I come hard.

"Sterling!" I cry, releasing a gush of fluid that sprays over his cock and drips between my thighs.

"That's what I'm talking about. Good girl," he groans, his cock thickening inside me.

He keeps thrusting, not breaking pace. His jaw clenches as his eyes drop to where he's disappearing inside me.

"Hallie," he grunts.

"Do it deep, I want you to feel you there all night."

"Jesus." He tips his head back, his guttural groan making his broad chest expand beneath his shirt.

"Yes," I moan as he hardens even more inside me.

"Baby girl," he growls, looking at me through heavy lids as he comes with a jerk and empties all he has inside me with a series of deep thrusts.

"I love you," I whimper, my thighs sticky and wet with both of us as he slows.

His grip on my hips loosens, and he inhales, blowing it out slowly.

"I love you too... so damn much."

We gaze into each other's eyes for a couple of minutes, saying nothing, while our heart rates slow. Then he eases out from inside me, placing his hand between my thighs to catch the slickness that's released.

"One of my favorite sights," he murmurs with a smile as he looks at his palm.

I turn and lift his hand, holding his eyes as I slip my tongue past my lips and clean up every drop of us from his palm and fingers.

"Damn, Baby girl, our time is almost up, and you go and do something that makes me need to have you all over again?"

I suck his last finger, the one where the wedding ring we chose together will go in thirty days' time.

"You'll be coming back to collect me tomorrow evening."

"Yes, and tomorrow evening, we'll also have my daughter and Zoey on the flight with us."

I smile. "True."

"I'll just have to wait until we get home to have you all to myself again."

"You will." I kiss him on the lips. "I'll be counting down."

"Can't come soon enough," he rasps.

◆

I return for dinner with wobbly legs and get knowing looks from Zoey and Sophie. I look around, admiring the place the girls chose. It's beautiful inside, but it's the drinks and food menu I'm most excited about. I'm going to go for a rose quartz infused mocktail to start with. The crystal for love.

Sinclair's having a heated discussion with Denver at the restaurant's bar.

"What's going on there?" I ask.

"Some guys wanted to send us drinks over. Denver put a stop to it and Sinclair's pissed at him for interfering," Zoey explains.

"Oh."

Denver's moved closer to Sinclair, his eyes intensely holding hers. His hand skims her lower ribs as he moves her out of the way of an approaching server carrying a full tray of drinks.

Zoey looks at them both, then at me. "Yeah. She'll be back in a minute. What are you going to order?"

"Everything on this amazing menu if I thought I could eat it all." I grin, raking my eyes over all the incredible sounding dishes.

Dinner is amazing and it's only when we're finishing dessert that I excuse myself to the ladies' room and decide to let Sterling in on today's secret activity.

I bring up an image the boudoir photographer took of me wearing a light gray lingerie set.

I click send and smile as his reply comes instantly.

> Sterling: Baby girl, what's this?

> Me: A peek at your wedding present. There's a whole album coming your way. But you'll have to make do with just one for now.

> Sterling: You're stunning. Absolutely breathtaking. And I must be God's favorite to have you in my life.

I laugh. I can picture him, his warm blue eyes full of loving adoration and amusement as he typed that out. He'll be staying nearby tonight seeing as we're all flying home together tomorrow. But I know he thinks he needs to give me my space for the rest of what the girls have planned.

> Me: You know, me and the girls don't have plans between dinner and breakfast.

> Sterling: You suggesting we break some rules, Baby girl?

> Me. You want to meet me in my hotel suite?

> Sterling: I'll be there waiting for you when you get back."

> Me: I love you.

> Sterling: Hallie?

> Me: Yes?

> Sterling: I love you more than all the gems on earth.

I look at my engagement ring. Twenty-six diamonds. Twenty-five to represent the crown that my beautiful sister never got to see for herself.

Sterling thinks I was his gift. But he was mine too. In fact, I was the one who needed him more.

The End.

Thank you so much for reading Halliday and Sterling's story. If you enjoyed it, then please consider leaving a review on Amazon.
Thank you xxx

Ready for Sinclair's story?
Want to see just how much she loves to wind up a certain brooding Head of Security?

Get your copy of 'The Rule Breaker' here:

https://mybook.to/therulebreaker

ALSO BY ELLE NICOLL

The Men Series

Meeting Mr. Anderson – Holly and Jay

Discovering Mr. X – Rachel and Tanner

Drawn to Mr. King – Megan and Jaxon

Captured by Mr. Wild – Daisy and Blake

Pleasing Mr. Parker – Maria and Griffin

Trapped with Mr. Walker – Harley and Reed

Time with Mr. Silver – Rose and Dax

Resisting Mr. Rich – Maddy and Logan

Handling Mr. Harper – Sophie and Drew

Playing with Mr. Grant – Ava and Jet

(Also available, **Forget-me-nots and Fireworks**, Shona and Trent's story, a novella length prequel to The Men Series)

ABOUT THE AUTHOR

Elle Nicoll is an ex long-haul flight attendant and mum of two from the UK.
After fourteen years of having her head in the clouds whilst working at 38,000ft, she is now usually found with her head between the pages of a book reading or furiously typing and making notes on another new idea for a book boyfriend who is sweet-talking her.
Elle finds it funny that she's frequently told she looks too sweet and innocent to write a steamy book, but she never wants to stop. Writing stories about people, passion, and love, what better thing is there?
Because,
Love Always Wins
xxx

Website – https://www.ellenicollauthor.com

Made in United States
Cleveland, OH
21 April 2025